Praise for
Elizabeth Joy Arnold

Pieces of My Sister's Life

"This well-observed story is vibrant and rich with
the subtleties and nuances of family life."
—*Publishers Weekly*

"Poignant and riveting... In prose both elegant
and direct, Arnold delivers a piercingly romantic,
highly readable tale of mystery and loss, longing
and redemption as haunting as the last dusk of
summer."
—*Booklist*

"Poignant, heart-breaking, and at times highly
emotional... The perfect book club read."
—Fresh Fiction

"The perfect summer beach book or engrossing book club discussion novel. Its contemporary characters jump off the page and stay with you even when you've put it down. The plot, while taking surprising twists (like life itself), touches universal nerves, with its emphasis on the strains and joys of family relationships."

—Trenton (NJ) *Times*

"*Pieces of My Sister's Life* is filled with salt air and summer breezes, the dares and secrets of island life, and the mysterious bond that exists between twin sisters. Elizabeth Joy Arnold has written an unforgettable first novel, so beautiful and poignant it will take your breath away."

—LUANNE RICE, *New York Times* bestselling author

"The story pulls you in from the first chapter. . . . Emotional and insightful, this is an engaging family drama that you'll want to read in one sitting. Four stars."

—Romance Junkies

Promise the Moon

"Exceptionally well written and outstanding character choice will make this book a MUST READ for you."

—Coffee Time Romance

"When a book brings out the tears like *Promise the Moon* does, there are really no other words to explain how incredible a read this is. Elizabeth Joy Arnold deserves great praise—and RRT's Perfect 10 award."

—Romance Reviews Today

ALSO BY ELIZABETH JOY ARNOLD

Pieces of My Sister's Life

Promise the Moon

WHEN
WE WERE
FRIENDS

WHEN
WE WERE
FRIENDS

Elizabeth Joy Arnold

❧ a novel ❧

BANTAM BOOKS

NEW YORK

A Bantam Books Trade Paperback Original

Copyright © 2011 by Elizabeth Joy Arnold
Reading group guide copyright © 2011 by Random House, Inc.
Title page photo copyright © iStockphoto

Published in the United States by Bantam Books,
an imprint of The Random House Publishing Group,
a division of Random House, Inc., New York.

BANTAM BOOKS and the rooster colophon are registered trademarks of Random House, Inc.
RANDOM HOUSE READER'S CIRCLE and colophon are trademarks of Random House, Inc.

ISBN 978-1-61129-474-2

Printed in the United States of America

Design by Diane Hobbing

For my beautiful Anna Lily:
This novel was inspired by dreams of you.

In memory of two of the most wonderful women I'll ever know:
Anne Cecilia Zmijewski, gone much too soon,
and my mother, Barbara Ellen Stearns: I miss you every day.

WHEN
WE WERE
FRIENDS

In high school I came up with fifty-eight ways in which Sydney might die. I wrote them in a spiral notebook, numbered them, even illustrated the possibilities that pleased me most.

· Number 18: Stomach penetration by swallowed toothpick.
· Number 24: Curling iron electrocution.
· Number 37: Asphyxiation under sewage.

Etcetera, etcetera, all written in angry black Sharpie. But high school—even when it resembles the seventh circle of hell—is only temporary. Eventually I'd burned the notebook, and in the years after, I'd tried to see Sydney as just an unfortunate chapter in an otherwise not-so-bad life; something I could look back on coolly, thinking only how we'd both had a lot of growing up to do. Tried but apparently had not succeeded, seeing as I was now in the bathtub, digging my fingers into a bar of soap in an attempt to clean the paint embedded under my nails. Not wanting the dung-colored ridges to detract from the gleam of my fake engagement ring. Which, yeah. I know.

But today, for the first time in eighteen years, I was going to see Sydney again.

· · ·

Sydney and I had been best friends since the second grade when she moved from Petaluma to Newport News, Virginia. We were best friends because we both needed glasses to see the board, which when we were seven was enough of a reason. Also because we both sucked at gym, and because neither of us had a father.

I remember her entering our classroom, escorted by Vice Principal Brooks, her reddish-blond hair lit from behind like the haloes in paintings of saints. Her Danskin pants were an inch too short and her T-shirt collar frayed, but still she beamed at us, turning her head loftily right and left as if expecting admiration.

I think the other kids sensed her desperation, because they mostly stayed away. But I felt bad for her and so that afternoon, seeing her standing alone at recess, I approached her. "My name's Lainey," I said. "I'm in your class."

She eyed me warily, didn't speak.

"I like your glasses," I said. "They're cool."

In retrospect they weren't cool, pink cat's eye frames studded with rhinestones. But on Sydney they looked fierce somehow, gave her a tigress edge—a taste of what would, in later years, turn into sexiness.

"Want to try them?" she said, then plucked the plain, oversized tortoiseshell glasses off my nose and replaced them with hers.

I felt a sudden dizzy nausea—Sydney was farsighted and I was horribly nearsighted—followed by a wave of hilarity as I looked over the blurred playground. "I'm blind! I'm blind!"

She slipped on my glasses and snorted. "Your glasses suck."

"Can you walk?" I said. "Pretend this, pretend this. Pretend we're on a tightrope and there's sharks under us, so if we don't walk straight we'll *die*."

So that was how we spent the next half hour, arms splayed, drunkenly wobbling heel to toe across the macadam, howling whenever we stumbled to convey the agony of death-by-shark-attack. And when the bell rang to call us back inside, we exchanged glasses and I turned to her and smiled. "Want to be friends?"

She studied my face a moment, then gave a short nod. "Okay," she said. And the rest, as they say, is history.

It wasn't long before the other kids stopped trying to penetrate the wall we built around our friendship. We did everything together, got A's in language arts and D's in math, grew overbites and whiteheads on our chins. The years went by without anybody especially liking us or hating us, or paying much attention to us at all, which was okay because we had each other, and having one best-best friend is all anyone needs.

But when we were fifteen, Sydney saw an optometrist, an orthodontist, and a dermatologist all in six months, the same six months that I stopped growing and didn't stop eating. That was the beginning of the worst year of my life.

Maybe I should've realized the sort of person Sydney would become; in retrospect the signs were everywhere. But of course I'd only been seven, a reckless, cavalier age, and at the time everything about her had seemed mysterious, from her red hair to her fascination with *Fantasy Island*. That this mysterious creature would want to be my friend was, in itself, mysterious, and I hadn't let myself look any further than my own gratitude.

What would it be like to be seven again? To feel the magic of nightly baths, of plastic cups and propeller boats and the honey-floral smell of Breck shampoo, hair that floated a halo at my shoulders, *Like a mermaid!* Star would say, and I'd picture myself as Esther Williams in her scaly bathing suit.

But I'd lost all sense of that seven-year-old body. Today my head swam in the heat, and even under the water I could feel a furry coat of sweat. You didn't sweat at seven, or if you did you didn't care. You could slide from one end of the tub to the other on your butt until the water drained to a slippery sheen. Seven was good and I should've appreciated it more. I should've learned how to cartwheel and climbed some trees, and chased boys around the playground while that was still socially acceptable. But it was too late now; I couldn't go back again, not even in this little way.

Ironic, then, that my feelings about seeing Sydney today were the same at thirty-six as they had been at sixteen passing her in the hall, her glance like a physical force wringing my insides with nausea, terror and behind it all—pathetically—hope.

She was working in an occult shop of all places, Six of Swords. When I'd called the shop last month to order candles and root powders and amulets for my mother, I'd recognized her voice immediately. After a minute of stunned silence I'd slammed the phone down and never called again. But last week when the owner contacted me to see if I'd consider doing a mural, I'd decided to think of it as fate and . . . a learning experience. "Well what a surprise," I'd say when I saw her. It would have to be spoken with the right mix of nonchalance and sarcasm, and then I'd shrug and turn away like I had better things to do.

I pulled myself from the tub, screwing my face against the groaning in my knees. The reality of baths is always a little disappointing, but you tend to forget the disappointment when you aren't actually in one. I didn't know why I even bothered to take baths anymore, except that they seemed like they should be a good idea, like if I just knew how to do them right they would, in a New-Agey way, bring peace.

I dressed in a black skirt, a little dressy but not too dressy, a little slimming, but not enough. I look better without clothes on. It's an unfortunate fact, since people don't usually see me without clothes. But the way I'm built, muscular and curvy smooth, like something sculpted out of clay that's a little too wet for precise sculpting, the clothes manage to drape themselves in such a way that you'd think my belly starts where my breasts end, and my head looks too small for my shoulders. I've read lots of articles on vertical stripes and A-lines and bias cuts, but the conclusion I've come to is that for my body type, the only way to emphasize the good points would be to strip and show them in all their glory. Not acceptable in most situations, so usually I'll just wear black, which is what the articles recommend for almost everybody anyway.

I combed my hair back into a chignon, decided it was too much and combed it forward again, then took out the ring I'd bought. A gumball-machine sort of ring, gold-painted with a plastic diamond the size of North Dakota, but it'd look real enough for this one day. I smiled into the mirror, showing my teeth. I had good teeth. Excellent teeth. Anyone would be jealous of these teeth.

"Lainey!" Star called.

I tilted my face to the ceiling. "What!"

There was no answer. I started for Star's bedroom. "What?"

She was in bed with her incense dish, her head propped on pillows. She cupped her hand over the burning stick and blew, a patchouli cloud veiling her face and obscuring the smile lines so that with her rounded cheekbones and wide eyes she looked twenty. My mother had been truly beautiful once but now she was sallow, gaunt, as if she'd spent the past decade trapped inside a dark box. Which, in effect, she had. "Mmmm, aren't you pretty today," she said. "Why you all dressed up?"

"I'm not." I pulled up the blinds, waving away the smoke. "You want something?"

"You didn't say good morning."

"You were asleep."

"You're full of crap; I've been up since six. I know when I'm being avoided." She smiled and nodded at the desk. "Bills're done, you can take them out. Oh, and when you get a chance next day or two, I could use a barber." She pulled her hair into her face and wrinkled her nose. "I look like Cousin Itt."

It had been over twenty years that I'd been cutting my mother's hair. I wondered if she even realized women had long ago decided their hair was too precious for barbers. I pulled a brush from her nightstand and sat on her bed, began brushing the hair back from her forehead. "I'll do it tonight. Actually, I'm on my way out to an occult shop if you want anything. They're looking for someone to do their walls, and I was thinking of some kind of Druid theme."

"An occult shop? How fun is that! Which one?"

I hesitated a second. But there was no reason not to tell her; she wouldn't remember it was Sydney's store. "It's called Six of Swords."

Star pulled away. "Six of Swords? You mean Sydney's store?"

My shoulders stiffened. I focused on pulling loose hairs from her brush, holding them to the light to see whether there was any blond left. Seemed like recently it had all gone white. "It's not Sydney's, Ma, she just happens to work there. I'm bringing over my portfolio."

Star nodded slowly. "The Lord works in mysterious ways."

I made a face. "I'm sure the Lord has better things to do. If I'm lucky they'll have me painting at night and Sydney won't even be there."

She kept nodding. "Would you get me my cards?"

"I don't want a reading."

"And I don't want wrinkles or drooping boobs. Don't be difficult. At her best that girl is unpredictable. At her worst, she's dangerous." She said this last in a jovial whisper.

"I'm not sixteen anymore, Ma."

"You are." She thumped her chest as she rose. "In here you're like me, we're both sixteen." She pulled a red velvet cloth from her top dresser drawer, unfolded it and handed the deck forward.

The cards were old and yellowed with age, their edges smudged and worn. I'd bought her three new packs before I finally gave up trying. It was Star's belief that age and use had made the cards more powerful, engrained their connection to the spirit world. Before the pack had been Star's it had belonged to my grandmother, who'd used it in county fairs and then, once she'd established a loyal customer base, in private readings at her parlor in Roanoke. (Rumor had it that my grandmother had done readings for the likes of Lady Bird Johnson and Elvis, but more than likely the stories were just Nana Sterling's imagination at work, because really what would Elvis be doing in Roanoke?)

"Shuffle," Star said. I knew the drill, had known it since childhood, shuffle, cut the deck and stack, shuffle, cut the deck and stack. She'd made a living from her readings back when I was a kid; mostly women, all unsatisfied with marriage, job and children (or lack thereof), who'd confessed their problems while I listened from behind the closed door.

Her clients had dwindled—due, I suspected, to a number of faulty readings—down to seven women who treated the readings like therapy. So with nothing else to take her time, Star had turned all her attention onto me.

With every new year in school, every trip to the doctor, every trek to the swimming pool or sledding hill, anywhere something might possibly go wrong, there was a reading. And as Star grew more afraid of the outside world, the readings became an everyday ordeal. As if laying the future out on the table could protect me from it, in the same way holing herself behind closed doors protected her from what might lie on the other side.

"So this here represents the central issue between you," Star said, laying a card face up. She raised her eyebrows and dealt three more cards on each side: the Relationship Spread. "Well," she said. "Well."

"So what is it?" I tried not to sound indulgent.

Star rolled her eyes meaningfully. "Very strange is all." She traced her fingers over the center card. "Three of Swords represents betrayal, being cheated by someone you trust. And here's the Tower card." She pointed to the crumbling tower, animals leaping from its roof. "Which means a shake-up, unexpected change. This here is Sydney, the Magician, and it's reversed, which means she's a manipulator, intoxicated with her own power." She glanced at me, looking vaguely amused. "Which I guess we already know. And this is you, the Eight of Cups, which means an injury to your heart. Which all sounds bad, but this here is the Ten of Cups which signifies bliss, things unfolding exactly the way they should."

She laid another card on top of the center card, and her face froze. Death. I used to freak myself out with that card when I was a kid, the black-caped man with his scepter, dismembered limbs at his feet. I used to sneak into Star's room and pull it out from the deck, then stare at it, my insides squirming, for as long as I could stand to look. I raised my eyebrows. "So I'm gonna kill her?"

Star gathered the cards, slipping Death to the center of the deck before she looked up into my eyes. "Wouldn't blame you if you did," she said.

. . .

On my way into town I stopped off at Pamela's house, because I needed some affirmation and Pamela is the affirming type. We'd been friends for eight years, ever since we first met at the Newport News Memorial Day Parade. We were sharing a bench, watching little girls in leotards stumble their way through pirouettes, and she was breast-feeding the tiniest baby I'd ever seen. It was while trying to avoid staring at her breast that I noticed she was eating a cheese-less pizza, which is how our conversation started.

Me: Is that a cheeseless pizza?
Pamela (dolefully): Yeah, it kind of sucks. But if I ate the cheese I'd end up spending the rest of the day in the bathroom.
Me: I guess I'd figure, what's the point.
Pamela: Honestly, it's better than not eating pizza at all. Only slightly better, but better.
Me: If I were you I'd eat jelly donuts instead. Which is why I'm fat.
Pamela: You're *so* not fat!

etcetera . . .

And we've been friends ever since, which just goes to show the power of twists of fate and a big mouth.

I knocked on her door, then rang the bell. After a minute I opened the door and called, "You there, Pam? It's me."

"Hey," Pamela called from upstairs. "Just got out of the shower. Come on in."

I walked to the kitchen and started a pot of coffee, then sat at her table and waited. The table was sticky and toast-crumby, as was almost everything in Pamela's home. She took a kind of pride in it, I think, in having three kids and a husband who was too manly to use a sponge. It was a sign of domesticity, being continually blanketed by the presence of mess.

Pamela breezed into the room carrying Matty, who struggled free when he saw me and pulled himself onto my lap. I snuggled him close. How many times had I imagined myself in Pamela's life? All the days I'd spent joking around with Pamela and Craig, an equilateral friendship triangle until he'd do something, squeeze a hand at the back of her neck or hook a finger playfully under her belt, and I'd all at once feel how alone I was. The days I babysat the boys, where after hours of board games and wrestling matches they begged me not to leave. Little Matty crying out whenever I just reached for my purse—seeing it as a sign I was about to go—which made me reach for it again and again at random moments so I could absorb the joy of being so wanted.

Pamela glanced at the gurgling coffeepot. "Bless you," she said.

"Yeah, I'm too good to you."

She smiled and opened a cupboard and I rubbed at Matty's back, ignoring the snot streaming from his nose until it made its way to my blouse. "You have a cold, Matty-kins?"

"Yuh," he said, swiping his nose against my boob.

"Sorry." Pamela handed me a napkin. "It's the day care center, breeds more germs than kids. Hey, you're all dressed up. What's the occasion?"

"Nothing really." I wiped carefully at Matty's nose and then my shirt. "I just have to make an impression today."

Pamela poured coffee and brought it to the table. "For who?"

"It's stupid. Just an old friend I haven't seen in a trillion years."

"Cool. And I guess within the past twenty-four hours you've gotten engaged?"

My face flushed and I twisted my ring to hide the diamond.

"It's okay. When I went to my reunion I got Botox and told people Craig was a neurosurgeon."

"Don't just assume I'm lying. We met last night and we fell in love and tonight we're flying to Vegas. By tomorrow we'll have bought a house and conceived our first kid."

Pamela widened her eyes. "Then congratulations and congratulations! Who's this friend?"

I shrugged. I'd never told Pamela about Sydney; it was embarrassing and there was no reason to contaminate the present with the past. Matty was fingering my gold necklace so I pulled it off and slipped it over his neck. "You're gorgeous," I whispered, then looked back at Pamela. "It's just somebody I used to know. We had a falling-out in high school, she got popular and I didn't, and this is the first time I've seen her since graduation."

"And you have to show how you're popular now, I get it. You don't think she'll eventually realize you're only married to your paint-brush?"

"No, why should she? She lives an hour away so I won't see her anywhere except in the shop where she works, and we don't have any mutual anythings, so I could tell her I have three husbands and she'd never find out the truth."

Pamela hesitated, then said, "Here, take this." She pulled off her wedding band and handed it to me. "Now you're actually married."

This is why I adored Pamela. Talking to her was almost like having an interior monologue, minus the self-judgment. "Thanks," I said, pushing the ring onto my finger. "I'll bring it back tonight." I held out my hand, tried to feel ownership, but with the mammoth diamond the hand felt like a transplant from the type of lady who'd wear knee-high boots with miniskirts. "I'm so stupid," I said.

"I'd pretend to disagree, but you wouldn't believe me." She nodded at my coffee. "Drink up. It's a diuretic and an appetite suppressant, and it'll give you a rosy glow."

I grinned at her and finished the coffee in three quick swigs, then rose with Matty on my hip to pour another cup. Tempted as I was to check my reflection for a rosy glow, I managed to refrain.

Six of Swords was in a Branchbury neighborhood, streets flanked by brick row houses and streetlamps still decorated with last winter's Christmas bows. When I was a kid, Branchbury was the hipster region of an otherwise middle-class county, with its head shops and tattoo parlors and hippie street musicians. A hangout for teens who didn't want to be teens, where one could buy worn alternative rock records, and beer without being carded. Cool until one grew up and realized it was anything but. A few years ago the township had applied for revitalization money, using it in an attempt to become "quaint." But the plastic surgery didn't do much to cure it of its essential nature, just as the dangling cigarettes and tattoos didn't change the kids who still hung out there: neon-loud, dirty round the edges, trying to be something they were not.

Sydney's shop had been refurbished into the "quaint" version of an occult shop—puffy black awning and a trapezoid-shaped purple sign, lettered in the sort of pointy calligraphy one might find on a "magick" scroll. I stood on the sidewalk, portfolio in hand, trying to pretend myself into someone else. It was a trick I'd learned years ago when I'd had my first interviews, that I could be strong and sparkling and self-assured if I imagined myself thin and lovely, made myself into the people I most wanted to be. Often, I actually pretended I was Sydney. Which of course wouldn't work in this particular circumstance. So I closed my eyes and made myself into another favorite choice, regal and slightly petulant, beautiful and saucy, but ultimately good at heart. I was Diana Ross. I smiled and entered the shop.

It was dark inside and smelled strongly of cloves; chimes and stained glass hung from the wood-planked ceiling, and the tables were buried in more odds and ends than you'd ever think could fit on a table. I restrained myself from dodging behind the first available shelf, which was not something Diana Ross would ever do. Instead I lifted my sculpted chin, curled my pouty lips into a smile, and strode to the front counter with the words already formed in my head. And found a baby.

"I'm looking for Ms. Gristler," I told it.

The baby stared back solemnly from its carrier. I flushed and backed away.

And then from behind me, "Can I help you?"

Her voice. I turned. I not just turned, I turned with triumphant superiority, in an eighty-carat-engagement-ring-wearing sort of way. "Why, Sydney Beaumont," I said. And showed my teeth.

"Lainey? Lainey Carson? Wow, gosh. I mean gosh."

The shock was perfect, exactly how anyone would react at the sight of Diana Ross in an occult shop, and I felt my shoulders loosen. "This is such a weird coincidence. What's it been, ten years? Fifteen?"

Sydney nodded, shook her head. "More than that I guess." She smiled widely at me, then pulled me into her arms. And there I was, my chin on her shoulder, my face pressed against the side of her head. I just stood there. I couldn't figure out what else to do.

"Well it's amazing to see you!" she said, pulling away. The happy surprise in her widened eyes had become something fake, like the put-on surprise of the newly anointed Miss America when the first runner-up is called. "You look amazing, Lainey. You haven't changed at all."

"You either," I said. I'd hoped she'd look awful, worn and wrinkled or pocked with adult acne but she looked great, her hair in a strawberry-blond bob, her buttoned shirt tucked neatly into her jeans to emphasize her waist and strain just perfectly around her maybe-silicone chest. Age looked even better on her than youth had, the kind of woman you could picture in an Oil of Olay commercial, *I'm thirty-six . . .*

"You're here browsing?" I said. "Pretty snazzy stuff. I love these earrings!" I lifted a card at random, a pair of pentacles, five-pointed stars, approximately the diameter of my palm.

"I work here, actually. I've been here for about a year, behind the counter and taking orders and inventory, all that."

"Oh! Oh . . ." I made my voice trail off, letting Sydney hear the slight derision in my tone. The tone said loud and clear, *Look at this! Who would've expected you'd end up as a cashier in a dusty shop whose only customers are witches!* "Well I'm here to see Ms. Gristler, if she's around. She said to come by this morning."

"You're here to paint the mural?" At the counter the baby gave a startled-sounding "Ah!" and Sydney glanced quickly at it, then turned back. "You know I read about you a couple years ago, in the *Gazette*. They were talking about actual canvas paintings though, right? Not murals."

The *Gazette* article had been my one brush with fame. They'd photographed samples of my work, and I'd immediately gotten calls from people interested in buying them or seeing what else I'd done. That "fame" had lasted less than a month—which I guess made it only *pseudo*-fame—but in that month I'd imagined that I'd finally be able to stop worrying about the cost of good toilet paper and the timing of shoe sales.

"Murals pay the rent," I said. "Not too many people buy abstract portraits from unknown artists, but I do still get calls sometimes from galleries that want to show my stuff."

"Guess I always knew you'd become an artist; you were so damn talented. A friend of a friend actually has one of your paintings in her living room, these little girls—I think they're girls—at the beach? I recognized your signature."

I remembered that painting, tried to picture it in someone's home. It always gave me a little thrill when I sold a painting or finished a mural, knowing some stranger would see it every day, and looking at it would briefly enter a world that used to reside only in my own head.

"Anyway, Sara told me there was somebody coming to show their work, but she's not here."

The baby's voice rose to a whimper and then a full-fledged wail, and as Sydney turned toward it, waving distractedly at me in apology, I saw it. The scar, a pale white indentation that looked almost like a vein line. I looked down at the scar on my own palm, then made a fist as Sydney walked past me to the counter. She plugged a pacifier into the baby's mouth with the indifference of someone stuffing bread crumbs into a turkey.

The baby was wearing green overalls printed with ducks, had orange hair and a tiny snot-filled nose. I tried to deduce its sex, but came up blank. "It's yours?"

"Her name's Jacqueline and yeah, she's mine."

I gazed at the baby, feeling a pang. Starting a family, having a baby, seemed so straightforward to everybody else. Something they always assumed would happen and so accepted without surprise or gratitude once it did. Me, I would've celebrated every day.

Sydney traced a finger over the baby's shirt cuff and gave a distant smile. "She's mine at least for now. David's trying to say I'm unfit, but that's just because it's the only way he could think of to spite me for leaving him. You remember David? David McGrath?"

I nodded slowly. "He was cute. And rich, right? The McGrath financiers."

"Which made him promising in high school, but now it doesn't mean squat. We started dating after the ten-year reunion and we got married within a few months, which I can tell you is not ever a good idea."

So Sydney was divorced, beautiful Sydney a divorcée with a baby, which really was worse than never having been married. Divorce tainted you, made you moldy around the edges. "Probably not." I smiled brightly. "Although with my husband, I knew I wanted to marry him within a few minutes."

Her lips twitched as she glanced at me. "You got kids yet?"

"Kids? Well no, not yet." I watched the baby suck furiously at the pacifier, her carroty hair mashed crooked against one side of her head, making her look somewhat demented. "But we're trying for them, Keith and me."

Keith was a man I'd dated for six weeks, the longest-term relationship I'd ever had. I'd met him in SoHo, over the couple of months I'd lived away from home. He was—at least aesthetically— perfect: dark-haired, dark-eyed, dark-souled. He'd lived in a studio that used to be a warehouse, complete with cement-block walls and a garage door entrance. And with him I'd become some- one completely different, exactly what I pictured in my head when I said the word "artist": leather-jacket-and-eyeliner-wearing, red- wine-drinking, four-letter-word-using. After our first kiss he'd said he loved me, and I'd been sure I was in love with him too.

But then, two months after I'd left home, Star overdosed on Xanax and called me to say goodbye. I dialed 911 and raced back to Virginia, realizing within minutes after seeing her shrunken form in the hospital bed that I couldn't ever leave again.

Long-distance relationships are impossible for dark-souled artists; they need immediacy, daily dosings of passion. And even as we both cried over the phone about how much we missed each other, I'd known it was the end. But after I'd reverted back to my non-leather-jacket-wearing real self, I'd still thought about him for years, imagining what our life could have been.

"He's an architect," I added, looking down at my rings, hoping Sydney's eyes would follow. Until I noticed a chip in the engagement ring, exposing the white plastic underneath. I tucked my fists under my arms.

The baby began to cry around the pacifier, her lips thin and quivering. Sydney made no move to comfort her, so I found myself setting my portfolio on the counter so I could lift her, delighted at my own audacity, feeling a bright swell of pleasure at her weight against my arm.

"We've been trying for about six months," I said, "since we first got married. We both love kids so much. He's an architect like I said, and he gets me to paint murals if his clients want them, after his houses are built. All kinds of weird things people want, rain forests and manatees, and paintings of their dead cats. And he's built us, Keith did, he built us a pretty little ranch up in the farmland near Norfolk, with a room for the baby once it comes."

The conversation was so weird; not just the lies which were planned out, but the distracted look in Sydney's eyes. I didn't know what I'd expected, but I'd wanted some reaction, *something,* maybe admiration or even a little jealousy considering I had a fake husband and Sydney had nothing. Look who ended up with a happier life, I was trying to say. But instead it all sounded like giddy rambling.

Jacqueline raised one arm, and when I tucked her against my shoulder she swung that arm round to open and close her hand against the back of my neck, like she was trying to soothe me. At the feel of her tiny hand, my eyes unexpectedly started to sting. I pressed my cheek against the top of her head. "It'll be such a sweet room," I said, "murals on every wall, an antique dresser and crib. I can already picture it exactly in my head."

"Sounds nice." Sydney watched the baby as I rocked it foot to foot. "It's great you're so creative. The most I could think to do was paint Jacqueline's room pink, which she probably thinks is such an insult." She flashed a quick smile. "So Sara's not going to be here, like I said. But she's letting me look at your work and make a decision for her. 'Specially because I'm the one who's going to have to be working next to the thing all day, she wanted to make sure I could stand it."

That was the problem, why it seemed so wrong, because Sydney didn't care. Here I was trying to orchestrate every movement, every word, but to Sydney it all meant nothing. No apology, no discomfort at all. Those years we'd been friends were just some old-bad memory she'd left behind.

"Okay," I said. "Go ahead and take a look. First's the toy store." I rubbed at Jacqueline's back, watching Sydney's face as she scanned the photos, looking for at least some sign of admiration. "Cat in the Hat chasing after the Things. And then's the kitchen store and the Sweet Shoppe, and I also put some sketches in back, of ideas for here. I was thinking a Druidic scene on one wall, fairies and smoke and people in dark hoods, and then another wall with a night scene, planets and stars and all that."

"Sounds great," Sydney said, scanning through the portfolio too quick, closing it and handing it forward.

"Thanks." I tried to reach for it and almost dropped the baby. I grappled with her for a moment, feeling the damp on my shoulder, tears or drool, then reluctantly handed her to Sydney. Sydney slung Jacqueline over her arm like she was a wet towel, and Jacqueline stopped crying as if appalled. "So Ms. Gristler will give me a call?"

"Sure," Sydney said nonchalantly, meaning, probably, that I wouldn't get the job. When I always got the job; I was the best around at what I did. Except Sydney must have other reasons for turning me down, which was kind of gratifying in its own way. "She has your number?" she said.

"I think so. It's the same number I had when we were kids, my mother's number. I'm staying there for a while, me and Keith both, because Star's been having a hard time. Keith's so good about it all, though."

"That's great," Sydney said. "Maybe we should get together sometime, drinks or something, reminisce about the good old days. I'll call you."

She had no intention of calling, obviously. I rolled my eyes to the ceiling to show I wasn't stupid. "I'd rather you didn't actually," I said. "I love my life now, it's pretty much everything I ever wanted it to be, so I'd rather not muddy it with the past." And then I strode out the door, nearly tripping on a loose nail. It was only outside that I noticed how wildly my heart was pounding.

I drove home with my portfolio on my lap, trying not to replay every word. I'd always thought the idea of closure was just some psychological bull, but now I could feel the jarring of un-closure, like I was just hanging in midair from a marionette string still tied to those two awful years. I could pretend it wasn't there, but it didn't let me get off that easy. I could create a new life, grow past it, but every once in a while something would happen to tug on that string, a whisper at a party that might or might not be about me, a man who didn't call after a first date, my thighs chafing together when I walked, and that string pulled me right back into adolescence. I had the feeling that if I didn't cut it off, and soon, I'd end up just like Star, locked away because everything outside the window could grab you and pull you back into the things you didn't want to remember. By the time Star was my age she'd been married and widowed and had a kid, but still she couldn't escape that pull of fear.

Back home, I brought the hair scissors into Star's room. "Something pretty this time," I said. "Layers maybe."

Star studied my face intently. "Something happened."

"Nothing happened, absolutely nothing. It was great seeing Sydney; she wants to get together for drinks."

Star raised her eyebrows. "She wants something from you. Get me my cards."

"Christ, Ma, what the hell? You think there's no reason for her to want to spend time with me? You don't think much of me, do you?"

"That's not it, I just don't think much of Sydney." She reached for her deck and handed it forward. "Shuffle."

I took the deck, stuck it into my back pocket. I should've done that a long time ago, crept in here while Star was asleep, jammed the deck in my pocket and sat on it, rubbed my butt hard against the floor. The cards were so old they'd have to crumble eventually. *Well look at that,* I'd say. *How weird.*

"Listen," Star said softly. "God has a plan for you, you know that, right? I made up a chart for you when you were born, and I'd never seen such a thing, your sun signs, your triads. I've never been so excited as when I made up your chart."

"Guess I've been pretty disappointing so far." I made my voice light, but I meant it. She knew I meant it.

She took both my hands. "You haven't fulfilled your destiny yet is all. But I think soon, the universe'll lay it on out for you. You don't have to go out looking for your destiny, it'll find you."

I'd heard this before from her, many times. It used to make me feel special.

I lifted the scissors. "Let's cut your hair, okay?" What I'd do was I'd chop it all off, and not a cute pixie cut either. Choppy, sprigged-out baldness.

I thought again about Sydney's smile, how it hadn't touched her eyes. Maybe she did feel bad after all; maybe that's what it meant. Or—less likely but still possible—maybe after I left she'd burst into sobs of shame that she hadn't wanted to show me. We'd go out for drinks and she'd say, *Look.* She'd say, *Look, I never meant to hurt you, I was just a kid.* And I'd say, *Sure, it wasn't so bad, you didn't hurt me.* I'd say, *It's over now, I hardly even remember.*

But I couldn't stop the scenes from replaying in my head, in the same agonizing slow-mo that they'd played out when I was there. Alone at the cafeteria table watching her whisper behind a cupped hand, the group at her table laughing, staring, bent in whispers that I pretend aren't about me. I am an artist with great talent who will be famous someday, whose work will be sold to rich people at auctions. In private I am funny and cool, have brilliant comebacks that regretfully surface hours too late for actual use, but that crack me up anyway. So I'm destined for greatness, I know it's true. I've felt the heat of destiny ever since I first picked up a crayon, so the person they're whispering about isn't me, just the loser they imagine is under my skin.

Blimp! a boy calls, and I stand to throw away my lunch, pretending not to hear. *The* Hindenburg's *rising!* Sydney shrieks and the girl beside her makes the sound of an explosion and I walk from the room amid a cloud of laughter. Laughter echoing in me for twenty-one years.

We were ten when we decided to found the Cutters Club, a secret society of which we were the only members. Our club activities typically included some or all of the following:

- Signing to each other in class—using a secret sign language with elaborate hand gestures we'd devised for each letter— usually about how much we hated our moms, our teacher, and boys.
- Completing Mad Libs with words relating to sex or bodily functions.
- Writing poetry to go with each of my paintings, the combined brilliance of which we were sure would wow the art world.

These were daring enough activities on their own, but making them club activities seemed to add a whole other dimension of auda- ciousness. And the day we came up with the club's name, that was our bravest day of all.

We were hanging out at Sydney's apartment when she brought up the idea. Her apartment had a rooftop deck overlooking the town, where we lay on towels with Sprites and a kitchen timer to tell us when to flip. We had just about gotten to the unbearably sweaty stage of tanning when she said, "How come you picked Tricia for your gymnastics partner?"

The truth was I'd chosen Tricia instead of Sydney because Tricia never teased me for being too scared to arch into a back bend. But I said, "I feel bad for her. She can't even cartwheel right."

"But I *so* hate her, don't you? I mean she's not just dumb, she's partly retarded. You know she still moves her lips when she reads to herself?"

"Don't use the word 'retarded.'"

"Whatever, I'm just saying you want to be careful. You spend too much time with her, you'll get stuck in her retardo world." She leaned up on her elbows. "Hey, you want to try something? It's called blood sisters."

Blood sisters. It gave me a shiver, both in a bad way and a good way, like picking a scab or touching a snake. "What's that?"

"It means we share blood." She gave me a slim smile, daring me. "We both cut ourselves, and then touch the cuts together so we get each other's blood mixed in our body."

"*Eeew,*" I said, but then I shrugged. "Okay, let's." So we went inside, for a knife.

Sydney's kitchen was even smaller than ours, a galley with avocado-colored Formica counters, and a half-sized fridge holding mostly Budweisers and nonfat yogurts. And also, a block of knives with black handles and sharp, serrated blades. Sydney approached them, widening her eyes at me in mock terror. I gasped exaggeratedly (in alarm that I'm sure sounded quite real), and she grinned back as she chose the knife. Long and skinny and curled at the tip, the kind you'd use to cut roasted chickens.

We sat on the floor of her bedroom facing each other, Sydney's eyes fixed on the knife. "You know what this means, right? We'll be like real sisters, except even more related. Almost like twins."

I gave a shallow nod. "Cool," I said.

And then without hesitating, she squeezed her eyes shut and sliced the knife across her palm.

The slash on her skin was a brilliant red, brighter than I'd remembered blood could be. She started breathing fast and I thought maybe she was going to throw up, and I suddenly loved her more than anybody in the world, that she'd risk puking in order to share blood with me.

She looked down at the oozing slash, her face pale. "After we do this there's no going back," she said. "My blood's going to be inside your veins until you die."

"I know," I said, wondering if parts of me would suddenly change, if I'd start liking Barbies or grow the tiny boob-bumps I'd just today noticed under Sydney's bathing suit. I took the knife and hunched my shoulders and then fast, before I could think of what I was doing, I sliced the knife across my palm.

I sucked in my breath, scared at first I might have cut my hand in two, but when I looked down there was just a large blob of blood, shiny and oval like something that might look nice on a ring.

We watched each other as she reached for my hand, holding it so tight I could feel my cut screaming. I looked into her eyes and both of us were halfway crying because it hurt, it hurt more than anything we'd ever known. But we both knew this was much more important than the pain. We just gritted our teeth, and held on.

I put about as much faith in Star's prophecies of doom as I did in my grandmother's stories about Elvis. I was reasonably sure I'd never see Sydney again, but I couldn't deny that I thought about her every day. Every hour of every day, wondering if she'd call to offer me the painting job. At the end of the conversation she'd pause and say, "Let's have coffee," and I'd shrug. "If you want," I'd say. And she'd want.

But two days passed, then three. And I hated the fact that I cared, hated that I'd let myself give a damn when Sydney obviously didn't. She could at least have called to say they'd found some-one else for the job. She'd think I'd interpret it completely casually, but I'd know what it meant. That she couldn't face what she'd done to me.

But a week went by without a word. I got a call from a natural foods shop that would pay me three thousand dollars for approximately two weeks' boring work, walls painted with wooden barrels of beans and crates of tomatoes. And so I took the job, set out with brown paint and wide brushes, and let the strokes drown any other thoughts.

And then, just when I'd managed to stop obsessing, she called. I was in the back mudroom I used as a studio, working on a still life. The room was cluttered with my canvases, the semi-abstract images I'd been painting over the past few years, of children catching butterflies in nets or blowing dandelion fairies, of young mothers with babies, a man's hand resting on a woman's knee or playing with her hair. But since seeing Sydney, looking at these paintings had started to hurt for a reason I didn't quite understand. I'd turned them all to face the wall, and the only images I'd painted in the past week were a bowl of unrealistically neon fruit and the painting that was in front of me when Sydney called, a perfect vase of flowers on a shiny glass table.

"Listen," she said. "I've thought about calling you probably fifty times since last week. I actually picked up the phone twice but then, I don't know. I guess I got scared."

"Really," I said.

"It was just weird to see you, it brought a lot of stuff back. And it made me compare my life then to now, and what I thought my life would be now, and I hated where that was making my mind go. I don't know, I'm not explaining myself well." She paused, then said, "I was wondering, d'you want to go get coffee or something? Jacqueline's with her dad for the weekend, so I'm all alone and I could use somebody to talk to."

I looked down at the smudges of paint on my hand, spread my fingers, and then nodded for several seconds before I said, "Okay, why not." And smiled.

· · ·

We met at Chelsea's, a café in downtown Hilton Village. Hilton Village was a planned community, set up in the early nineteen hundreds to house shipyard workers during World War I. The homes were mostly English village style, Jacobethan or Dutch Colonial, with steeply sloped gables or hipped roofs. Which made the town quaint from the outside but inside, many of the homes, like ours, were showing their age: walls in desperate need of replastering, small rooms with chipped hardwood floors, narrow staircases and low doors. Downtown was charming though, with its wide brick-paved, tree-lined sidewalks and pavilions, and I walked through it slowly, waving at the shopkeepers and passersby I knew, stopping to chat, stalling.

This was what I'd wanted. Almost exactly, but what would we possibly talk about? I understood for the first time how Star must feel, how terrifying it could be to leave the confines of your home because it was so uncontrolled. Anything could happen.

My last meal with Sydney had been at Custard Queen. I hadn't been out with her for weeks. Star had stopped going outside that year, and I stayed home after school partly to keep her from freaking about the myriad of dangers I might be encountering, and partly because I hadn't had anything better to do.

But that morning Star had done a reading as she'd begun to do nearly every morning. Something important was going to happen today, she said, something that would change my life forever. So I'd invited Sydney out for ice cream so we could try and guess what it might be.

I'd sat with a dish of pistachio, pushing it forward so Sydney could taste, but Sydney wrinkled her nose and pushed it back. "Here's the thing," she said. "You know Mike Garnett? On the swim team? Well we've been dating for a while now, and he's been taking up a lot of my time."

I'd choked in surprise—*they had?*—and a pistachio flew across the table. Sydney flinched, following it with her eyes. And in that one look, with that one stiff-faced recoil, I'd understood what Star had meant. Everything had changed.

Now I turned down an alleyway toward the café, stood behind one of the spindly trees along the sidewalk and checked my watch to ensure that I'd be fashionably late, then steeled my shoulders and entered.

Chelsea's was my favorite café. Partly because the walls were filled with my paintings and I'd sold quite a few of them from here. But mostly because Chelsea was the kind of person you had to love. She treated everyone who came into the shop like her new best friend, and she showed the customers she knew an affection that seemed completely genuine and personal. These things also made Chelsea's the perfect meeting place to attempt to prove the awesomeness of my life.

Sydney was already at a table, so she got to see Chelsea's reaction when I came in. "Lainey!" Her face lit up, and she came from behind the counter to take both my hands into her own. So I gave my attention to her rather than Sydney.

"How's Steve?" I asked.

"Oh you know." She rolled her eyes to the ceiling. "It's baseball season, so I could stride across the room butt-nekkid and he'd tell me to get out of the way." She shrugged. "I'm glad you're here, by the way, it's perfect timing. I just took out a batch of those toffee bars your mom loves. Should I pack you a box?"

"That'd be great, thanks," I said, and raised a hand to Sydney. *See, I am known in this town, and loved.*

"You're the one she's here to meet?" Chelsea smiled at Sydney. "Lainey's one of my favorite people, you know."

"You're full of it," I said.

"No, really! You're one of my top ten favorites. Or, if you count Colin Firth, Nora Roberts, and Tibetan spiritual leaders, at least one of my top twenty. You want the usual?"

I glanced at Sydney's table and saw she was drinking black coffee, nothing else. "I'll have a medium," I said. "Just black."

Chelsea raised her eyebrows. I was a drinker of full fat double-double mochas with extra syrup and foam. But thankfully, she didn't comment.

I sat across from Sydney at the small round table, wishing I had silverware to play with. Instead I rubbed my thumb over the faded polyester rose on the table, like I was testing it to see whether it was real.

I'd planned to play this completely nonchalantly, no anger, no excitement, the same way I'd talk to a potential employer about a job I didn't particularly want. But as soon as I opened my mouth, I failed. "So look," I said. "I don't know why you called. But more than anything I'm thinking, my God, what nerve you have to want to get together after however many years, pretending like nothing happened between us. Wanting to go out for coffee like you're suddenly my best friend."

"I used to be." Sydney smiled at me crookedly. "I mean when you're that close to someone, whatever happens, that never completely goes away. I've been thinking how you share all my same memories, so many things only the two of us know. And I hate how we lost our connection to all that history."

"That sounds lovely," I said. "Actually I've gotta say it's the loveliest bullshit I ever heard."

"Lainey..." She slumped back in her chair. "I just thought, I don't know, maybe it'd be good for both of us if we made amends. I wanted to say something when you came by last week, but I didn't have any idea how to talk about it. What could I do, apologize? Try and explain? You'd probably have hit me."

She seemed suddenly so wavery around the edges, so pained, that I had the ridiculous urge to comfort her. Instead I said, "I'm usually not big on violence but yeah, I might've."

"Lainey, look. Can I show you something?" She unzipped the purse hanging from her chair, reached inside and pulled out an envelope. "I found this in a box of old things when I was moving out of David's house and trying to decide what to bring and what to throw away."

She handed me the envelope. Inside was a handful of photographs, all taken the summer before junior year. She watched me flip through them, then said, "I didn't throw these away."

"Well I'm touched," I said sarcastically, but in truth, I was a little touched.

In the photos we were dressed in clothes somebody should've stopped us from wearing, jeans shorts that were both too tight and too high-waisted, bright-colored tank tops that bunched around our breasts. We were posing for the camera, supermodel poses, our backs arched, chests bared and heads thrown back. Laughing. And studying the photos, the thing that struck me was how very young we were.

A month later would be the Custard Queen talk, and soon after the teasing would start. All those kids I'd been so scared of, had their cheeks and chins been this round? Their smiles this unguarded? How were the actions of children, who'd probably had no idea what they were doing, still echoing so strongly inside me? They probably didn't even remember who I was anymore.

And I didn't know how to process this. Looking at our laughing faces, I found myself wanting to cry.

Instead I shoved the envelope toward her. "It was a long time ago," I said. "If it still hurt after all these years, that'd be my fault more than yours."

"But you're still pissed off."

"I'm not exactly a huge fan of yours, but I'd say I'm over it."

"Yeah." Sydney stared down into her coffee, gripping her cup with both hands. "I know what it must've been like for you. Don't you think I know what I did?"

I pictured the little girl in the photo, her arm around me, smile revealing the flash of her braces. "Do you?" I said. "Do you really?"

"Part of me wants to say how it was just high school, but I know high school is everything. And part of me wants to say how it wasn't just me; I mean there were people who outwardly treated you much worse than I did. But yes, yeah, I guess I can call myself the ringmaster of all the awfulness."

The ringmaster. Apt description. *Ladies and gentlemen, children of all ages, come see the astonishing Lainey Carson! Marvel at the zit on her chin and her inability to dribble a basketball without tripping!*

The Custard Queen trip had been the beginning. Sydney's five-ring stage debut came two weeks later, after she'd invited herself over and then mysteriously left after ten minutes. I found out why the next day, when she got up in front of our English class. In my mind she looked pale and hesitant; she wouldn't meet my eye. But maybe that was just a veneer I'd laid over the memory.

The assignment was to create a character study to read out loud. And Sydney's piece was called *The Diary of L.*

There are things in your life, she read, *that you can play over and over in your head so many times that they just stop feeling real, becoming more like something you've imagined. One of those things happened to me today, when Aaron Walsh smiled at me and I of course did nothing to show I even noticed, because I am a loser.*

She steeled her shoulders, then went on: *Oh I hate myself so much, you know? I wish there was some mating ritual, like peacocks have, or penguins. A series of set steps you follow, he smiles you smile, he nods you nod. We bow our heads together and then . . . make babies I guess. Oh what do I do?*

I sat there paralyzed, listening to her read, each of my words through her mouth like a pointed jab, bleeding me empty. In my head, *Sydney, why, why!* Until her voice trailed to silence.

Were there tears in her eyes? I seem to remember there were tears. But then somebody laughed, and then somebody else, and Sydney lifted her head and beamed at them like she was accepting congratulatory pats on the back.

Everyone of course knew who "L" was, and by the end of the day, word had passed around the entire school. In the halls for the entire year, all the boys made smooching noises when I passed and the girls followed me with their eyes, faces shadowed with amusement. And Aaron Walsh, the object of every one of my fantasies for the past year, started calling me *Bubble-Butt* ("Hey, Bubble-Butt! What'chya doin' Bubble-Butt?") to prove to his friends that I made him sick. Which was what Sydney had been doing in her own way. Proving superiority to avoid association.

And it wasn't even the awfulness of this, or the taunts that would follow me every day after. (Every day through today, for Christ's sake, and who in their thirties still obsessed about high school?) It wasn't the embarrassment of people knowing I had a crush on an unattainable boy, or—from a separate diary entry— that the fart in gym class everyone had blamed on Darren Coe had really been mine. It was that Sydney had done this to me. Sydney who'd danced with me to The Bangles behind my closed door; who'd practiced hickeys on my arm just to see if she could make it work; who'd sat with me poring over *Seventeen* magazine for makeup tips and *Will You Make a Good Girlfriend?* quizzes, then helped me draw mustaches on all the models' faces. Sydney, who I'd loved more than I loved myself, had stolen my diary with the intention of destroying my life.

"You can move past high school," Sydney said now, "which you obviously have, but you can't ever really *get* past it. I haven't gotten past high school either, really."

"Here you go," Chelsea said, setting a pastry box, two plates and a coffee on the table. "And I'm bringing the plates because the bars're still warm, which makes them irresistible to anyone with a nose."

I stood so I wouldn't have to look at Sydney. "Could I actually have one of the cupcakes? Those chocolate ones with white icing?" Without waiting for an answer I brought my plate to the display case, and pulled out the cupcake with the most prodigious icing swirl.

I smiled thanks at Chelsea and walked back slowly, trying to fashion the right response in my head. As I sat back down I said, "It may be disappointing to hear, but I've moved past it *and* gotten past it. Like . . ."—I swept my arm toward the wall—"d'you know all the paintings here are mine? This is what's important in my life now. I don't think about the past; being an artist means living in the present."

Sydney looked around the room, squinting. "Nice," she said slowly. "Very . . . Picasso? Van Gogh? I don't know enough about art to say something intelligent. But I remember the art teacher, what was her name, with that frizzy long braid? She said you could become famous."

"Ms. Douglas. She said I could become renowned if I wanted. That's actually the word she used, *renowned.*" I remembered when she'd said it, how I'd ducked my head, my face burning, repeating the word silently over and over. "And I got a scholarship to Pratt Institute, which is like the most competitive art school in the country."

And then I tried to think of what else to tell her, what else I had to be proud of. All I had was my art, and even that had come up short. I'd never gone to Pratt because I'd had to start working to help support Star. I'd gone to community college part-time, got an AA that had turned out to be a waste of money. And then I'd left home for a total of two months, renting an apartment in SoHo, trying to break into the New York art scene. But then my Nana Sterling passed away, and two weeks later Star attempted suicide. I'd immediately given up the apartment, had my things shipped back to Virginia and never left again.

So what else did I have to use as evidence that I'd gotten past high school? A series of failed relationships? A job painting kidney beans? I took a bite of cupcake.

"Well you've done a hell of a lot more than me," Sydney said. "I got a communications degree, which I realize is for people who can't figure out what to major in, but I was sure I could make it in broadcast journalism. People kept telling me I had the look for it, a kind of attractive authority. But nobody said how impossible it is to break into. I tried for almost a decade interning while I was waiting tables and getting nowhere. And then the one shot I had, filling in for a radio journalist at a local station, I completely froze. I sucked at it."

She traced her finger along the inside of her cup handle. "At the time I didn't let myself regret any of it. I'd gotten married to David and I didn't have to work anymore. But then he left me a few months after Jacqueline was born, and now he's back living with his parents so their lawyers can try and hash out divorce papers and threaten me into signing them. And that's the extent of my accomplishments. Impressive, hunh?"

I watched her face, the pain behind her perfectly blue eyes, and found myself wanting to apologize. An impulse I restrained, of course, but I did push the box of toffee bars toward her. "Want one?"

She glanced at the box, longingly I thought, before saying, "No, thanks."

Of course. One couldn't weigh ninety pounds and still eat toffee bars. And what good had two decades of dieting done her? How could you enjoy life when you were always worrying about the potential for cellulite?

I remembered the food amalgamations we used to create in Star's kitchen: sundae amalgamations, where we'd put everything from Gummy Bears to Goldfish crackers on top of ice cream, as well as cereal amalgamations, frozen waffle amalgamations and grossest of all, Tater Tot amalgamations. Standing on chairs to pull things from the shelves and freezer, tasting each other's concoctions, screwing up our faces in disgust but then finishing them anyway. Had I ever had so much fun since those days? Had she?

"It's like I was saying over the phone," she said. "You have this vision in high school of what your life's going to be, you're sure you know your potential, but then you grow up and realize you hit your peak years ago, and it was more of a grassy knoll than a mountain and you're already on your way down it. Is it like that for everybody? Is there any adult in the world who's not disappointed?"

What had I thought my life would be like? I'd had vague notions that I'd get married someday, but it had all been sort of nebulous, the man's image blurry like a photo where he'd been moving too fast. As for career, well yes I'd been told I could become a real artist, but I'd known the odds and I'd never actually believed I'd be one of the lucky few. So was I disappointed? No, that was the wrong word. Sure, I wished things could've been different, but I knew why they weren't. Mostly I was just unsurprised.

"Remember when we were so sure we'd grow up to be writers?" I said. "We wrote that book—"

"About dogs in space! I forgot about that. We alternated chapters and we wrote about three gazillion pages by hand, which we sent to some publisher in Boston."

"Houghton Mifflin! We were seriously sure we could get published by Houghton Mifflin. We went and sent them our only copy, and then we waited for them to send us the money and a contract."

"And some nice assistant sent the pages back with a little note saying she enjoyed the story and"—Sydney made air quotes—"hoped we'd grow up to be real writers someday. I was crushed."

"Me too. I thought we'd write sequels, have screaming groupies who'd accost us in parking lots and throw us their underwear."

We smiled at each other, and then Sydney shook her head. "I've never had another friend like that, you know? Not even close."

Was she being serious? She sounded like a Lifetime movie. But when I looked into her eyes, I found only wistfulness.

I considered telling her about Pamela, to show how making a best friend in adulthood really was possible. But then I realized that A) I'd mostly be using it as evidence I truly had Gotten Past It, B) it wouldn't be helpful to Sydney at all and C) there was no way I could compare my friendship with Pamela to what we'd had as kids. Yes, I loved Pamela as much, probably even more in some ways than I'd ever loved Sydney, but there were things in Pamela's life that I'd never share. Whereas in my friendship with Sydney, we'd shared everything.

So instead I tried to look just as wistful. "Yeah," I said softly, "I guess I know what you mean."

And so there we were, improbable as it might seem, friendly again. I wouldn't say we were friends, I didn't like her or trust her enough—and wasn't quite adult enough—to take things to that next level, but I could see the possibility of at least wanting to forgive her.

On the day Sydney read my diary aloud I'd filled the hole left in me with a red knot of loathing, and for years I'd let it fester, trying to ignore it. But now that it was dissipating, what would take its place? Not just nostalgia, although nostalgia was the main emotion I'd felt over coffee. Hell, nostalgia wasn't even a real emotion, just the outlines of what I'd lost. I needed something bigger to fill the space, but I had no idea what that something might be.

When we left the café I held out my arm, meaning to shake Sydney's hand, but she tucked herself into it, hugged me for a full minute, both palms pressed at my back. Then pulled away and slid a finger under a lock of my hair, lifted it and rubbed her thumb against it, a gesture that seemed even more intimate than the hug. "We'll do this again soon," she said, and I nodded because I couldn't find a way to tell her that no, we wouldn't.

I hadn't brought up my fake husband that afternoon. But if I saw her again it was sure to come up at some point; she'd ask for details I hadn't yet formulated, wonder why we were still staying with Star. She'd want to meet him. So no, I couldn't do this again. But standing there with her, I guess I can admit that I wanted to.

It was a Saturday, more than a week later, that I returned home for lunch covered head-to-toe in brown streaks, to find a strange car in the driveway. Nobody ever came to the door. Other than Pamela, nobody'd been inside for years, not since I'd let in the Jehovah's Witnesses, a smiling couple whose white hair wafted in startled angles about their faces. They'd showed pictures of children—supported by their ministry—whose legs had been blown off by land mines, and I'd felt so depressed about it that I gave them twenty dollars for a subscription to *Awake!* magazine, and a plastic bag filled with Rice Krispies Treats.

I climbed the porch stairs slowly. Star never let in strangers, never opened the door to them, and certainly never would have left it unlatched. I searched for something heavy, my heart in my throat, and finally settled on the fake topiary by the door. I pushed the door open and peered behind it, then heard the voices from the den.

"Well David's the precise definition of a horse's ass."

It was Sydney. I held the urn against my chest and tried to remember to breathe.

"Excuse my language, but that's exactly what he is. Take the back end of a horse and stick on a pretty face, and voilà. Not thinking about what's right for Jacqueline, not remotely considering how a girl should grow up with her mother, I'm sure you know what I mean."

"I know exactly," Star said. "My Richard grew up without his mom, you know, never learned anything about keeping a home, and I just don't know how he survived before we met. He used to eat spaghetti and oatmeal straight out of the box! And I had to show him there's a lint catcher in the dryer!"

They were sitting on the wide plaid sofa, Jacqueline in Star's lap. Star's face was flushed, either with the excitement of holding a baby or of reliving the past. I felt a bruising in my chest, remembering the weight of Jacqueline in my arms, her hand opening and closing against the back of my neck. "Sydney," I said.

Sydney turned to me and my eyes widened. Her eye was bruised, there was a large welt on her cheek and a cut above her upper lip. I shook my head slowly. "What happened to you?"

She glanced at Star. "It was nothing, just . . . I tripped on the sidewalk. And hit a rock. I'm fine other than the obvious fact that I'm a klutz."

"You need Band-Aids? Or ice?"

"No, seriously, Star already got me ice and this doesn't even hurt anymore." She held up a block of frozen spinach and pressed it to her eye, smiling at me bemusedly. And I realized suddenly how I must look, the streaks of paint, my face still flushed with terror, hugging a plastic plant. "I was just going to water this," I said, and hurried out to the kitchen. I threw the plant into the broom closet, and then rushed back to the den.

"He's a wonderful man," Star was saying. "So caring of her. And you know me with all my problems, but he's always so willing to help."

"How refreshing," Sydney said.

The baby made a grunting noise and Star cooed. "Somebody's gonna need a diaper change soon, won't they? Won't they!" She glanced at me. "We were just talking about Kevin."

"Keith?" Sydney said.

I froze.

"Why yes of course, Keith. I'd swear sometimes that I'm on the edge of senility, doomed to a life of rocking and drooling, but wouldn't you think I'm too young for it?" Star was grinning at me in complicity. I would have been mortified, but there were too many thoughts racing through me to allow me to feel anything other than shock.

"So I meant to call sooner, but I've been . . ." Sydney swiped her hand to one side, as if batting away a fly. "Busy. But listen, let's go out for coffee again, hunh? You want to?"

I held up my hands. "I'm filthy."

"Or we could have coffee here. But I'd love to talk, if that's okay. Things've been happening, and I feel like I'm going crazy."

"I'll just go upstairs," Star said, "leave you girls in private. Do you have a fresh diaper?" She put her nose to the baby's bottom and made a chortling sound.

"Thanks so much," Sydney said, handing her a bag. Star pulled out a diaper and wipes, stood and started for the door, winking at me as she passed.

I stepped backward. "I'll make coffee then."

"No, don't bother. My stomach's too upset for coffee, I just wanted to talk to you alone is all."

"Right, okay." I glanced at the armchair, the one with the puffy cushions that was so hard to get out of, hesitated, but decided to sit anyway. "Let's talk."

"Thanks." She lifted the frozen spinach back to her cheek, eyeing me a minute before she spoke. "First, okay here's the thing. That I realize we haven't been all the way truthful with each other, and it's my fault as much as yours."

I felt a rumbling of fear down my spine. "What're you talking about?"

"I just think we have to come clean with each other; you tell me the truth and then I'll tell you, because I really need to trust you here. I have to know I can trust you."

I watched her warily, and she met my eye. "Keith," she said. "I'm talking about Keith."

My stomach twisted, and it was suddenly hard to breathe. If she'd known, why the hell hadn't she said anything earlier? She must've not wanted to embarrass me; it must be why she hadn't asked questions about him, to spare me from digging myself into a hole. This was like returning home after a date and seeing that I'd been going around all night with nobody telling me my skirt was tucked into my stockings, my underwear on display. *Time to leave!* my body said. *Time to vamoose! Skidaddle! See ya!*

"It's okay." Her voice was heavy with sympathy. "You don't have to say anything."

I gripped the seat of my chair. All I wanted to do was run up to my bedroom, curl up in a corner, disappear. But something stopped me. Partly the compassion in her eyes, but also the sense that she understood. Remembering third grade when we'd told our classmates we had fathers who took us home with them every weekend, confirming each other's story whenever anyone challenged it. She knew exactly what it was like to lie about something unattainable and longed for.

"We can just forget about it, okay?" she said. "Please don't be embarrassed. Plus, look where marriage got me. You've done a hell of a lot better in your life than I have. I respect you, Lainey, you're one of the few people in the world that I respect because I know how *real* you are. And I completely understand what it's like wanting to impress people; I've been doing it my whole life. Like when we met at Six of Swords? There you were, this professional artist, when all I'm doing is working a cash register, and I felt so inferior I was seriously considering telling you I was working on a law degree."

I bit the inside of my cheek, watching her, then said, "It was stupid. I'm sorry."

"Don't be, okay? I'm kind of flattered that you'd think I'm worth lying to." She lifted a glass candy dish from the end table beside her and studied it from all angles like she was considering whether to buy it. "So I'm glad we got that out of the way. I feel better, don't you?" She smiled. "And it's so great being here; the house hasn't changed at all, has it. I mean same furniture, same decorations . . ."

It was true, nothing had changed since my childhood: the green walls and rag rug, the same porcelain angels on doilies, and pillar candles that were never burned for fear of explosion. I wondered if I should feel insulted, if she was disparaging our lack of taste.

"It reminds me of all those afternoons we spent here, just hanging out. This was probably more of a home than my own home was." She put down the candy dish, folded her hands between her knees and suddenly, startlingly, her eyes glazed with tears. Were they tears-tears? They seemed so out of character that they might just be allergies or a stray eyelash. "You okay?" I said.

"Oh hell, Lainey." She took a deep breath. "It's just there's all these things going on. Some of them I can tell you about and some of them I can't, but the gist of it is that my life's starting to fall apart, and I'm running out of options for putting it back together."

Upstairs there was a high-pitched baby squeal, and then Star's voice. "Is that a poopy diaper? Is that a poopy-poop?"

I made a face. Put a baby in front of Star and her brain shriveled like a slug in the sun.

"So I was sitting at home this morning and thinking what the hell I could possibly do, and all I could think was how maybe running into you was providence, that maybe you could help."

I felt a sudden flush of anger. "After eighteen years you show up and ask me to help you?"

"You have no idea, Lainey, I'm desperate." She inhaled a quick breath, as if she was about to sneeze or break out in song. "Okay. Here's the thing. I have to get away from David, get Jacqueline away from him, but he's going to win custody is the thing. The courts are going to think he's got this perfect life, he doesn't have to work, Mommy and Daddy will support him so he can be home with the baby. But he's not good for her."

"I'm sure you could at least get joint custody, unless he can prove you're unfit. And with joint custody you'd have more time to yourself, right? Be able to maybe find a new job if that's what you want, figure out what to do with the rest of your life."

"Jesus, Lainey." She leaned back on the sofa cushions and squeezed her eyes shut. "The thing is, the thing is, I didn't actually fall on a rock."

I watched her for a minute before speaking. "What do you mean?"

"I mean the bruises, my face, it was him. He hits me, Lainey."

I stared at her, then realized my mouth had dropped open so I snapped it shut.

"Yesterday we had a mediation session which . . . mediation is such a crock. It's sitting there and letting him harass me and lie about me while the lawyers nod sympathetically and waste two-fifty an hour." Her voice was shaking. I reached to touch her hand but she pulled away. "And then this morning he shows up at my door to get back at me for 'slandering' him. This was his retribution."

I shook my head. "Sydney, Jesus . . . Does anybody else know?"

"I can't tell anybody. You're the only one I trust at this point since you don't know David or his friends. If he found out I went to you I don't know what he'd do, kill me probably, but I need help. I'm so scared, and I don't have any idea what to do next except that I have to get Jacqueline away."

There was another squeal from upstairs and Sydney's head turned to the doorway, her eyes filling again. "Because this isn't even the worst of it, Lainey. I can deal with being hit, I lived with it for years, but the thing is . . ." She pressed her fingers against her eyelids, held them there. "The thing is, I think he abuses her. There've been marks on her body."

My mouth dropped back open.

"Burn marks," she said, "cigarette burns, I think. Little red spots on her back."

I thought of Jacqueline's sweet round face, clammy fingers clutching my stomach. "Sydney. You have to tell somebody, call the cops. Or Child Protective Services, get a restraining order."

"You'd think that might work, wouldn't you. That's what I thought after he broke my arm, that I could go to the cops."

"He broke your arm?"

"But the McGraths have friends in all the right places. His parents saw us fight, what it used to turn into, but they still managed to twist it around and blame it all on me, and I know that's what would happen here too." She looked up at me, her eyes pleading. "If I'd noticed the burns the day I picked her up from David, I could've gone straight to the cops. But I was too busy to give her a bath that night, and by the time I saw them I realized how it was going to look. I'd gone a full night without telling anybody? Who'd believe I wasn't the one who hurt her? Cigarettes when I'm the only one of us who ever smoked, it's brilliant."

"This is crazy." My voice was an awed whisper, not an appropriate tone but it was all I could muster.

Her face went suddenly pink. "Look, maybe I shouldn't have come to you. I couldn't stand being alone with it anymore and I thought maybe you could help me figure out what to do, but you're probably looking at this as some kind of twisted payback."

"Of course I'm not! I'm just in shock I guess. I'll help you, I want to help, just tell me what you're thinking."

"I'm not thinking anything, it's impossible to think, I'm all adrenaline and the only thing I want to do is run. But run where? And what if I get caught? If I'm arrested, who's going to believe my reasons for running? They'd give the baby back to him."

With her red eyes, cheeks bruised and damp from the sweating spinach block, Sydney's face looked raw and diseased. I listened to Jacqueline's squeals from upstairs and Star's lilting voice, then said, "When're you supposed to leave her with David again?"

"He gets her every weekend, so I have to drop her off this afternoon."

I remembered the weight of the baby against my shoulder, the crinkle of her fatly-diapered bottom and the sweet and eggy scent of her head, and I suddenly felt like crying. I glanced at Sydney, met her eyes for a brief, bewildered second, then raised my chin. In that one second I had made up my mind, and the next words I heard, words that seemed to be coming from my own mouth, were, "What if you left her with me instead?"

Sydney widened her eyes, sat perfectly still a moment and then said, "What would I tell David?"

"Tell him you know what he did to Jacqueline, and that you're not leaving her alone with him again."

"No, no Lainey, he'd kill me if I accuse him of anything! Why do you think I haven't already?"

"Okay, then don't outright accuse him. Tell him you don't want her exposed to all the fighting, and that she's staying with a friend till the custody battle's over. But you can say it in such a way that he knows what you're really talking about."

Her eyes filled again and I reached for her hand. "And don't actually go inside his house, okay? Talk to him outside, just in case. And if you think you're in any kind of danger then come here, you can stay with us."

Her shoulders stiffened and she pulled her hand away from mine. Refusing, I thought, but then she said, "But what would happen after? How long would you take her?"

"I'll keep her until we figure out what to do next. We have to find some way to prove he's abused you both so he'll never get unsupervised custody. We'll figure it out, but the important thing right now is to keep her away from him."

She shook her head slightly. "You'd do this for me?"

"I'm doing it for Jacqueline," I said. "And, I guess, for you too."

"I'm so scared, Lainey." Sydney made a strange hiccuping sound, then suddenly rose and bent over me, perfume like a halo around us both, wrapping me into a tight, bony hug.

I looked out at the room over Sydney's shoulder, feeling numb. It seemed strange, broken into parts like a collage, furniture pinned on a flat background and two girl-women taped haphazardly on top. Women with no history, their simple needs just as two-dimensional as the room around them. Impossible to believe that the stronger, surer one was me.

⁕{ 3 }⁕

"You told her what?" Star asked.

I glanced at the baby. She was sitting on the floor by our feet, sucking contemplatively on a quartz crystal from Star's altar. Jacqueline was an awful name for a baby; it put too much pressure on her. Babies should be named Kimmy or Meggie or Molly. "How d'you like the name Molly?" I said. "Just as a nickname."

"Come on, Lainey, you can't be serious."

"Come here, Molly! Sweetie Molly. Do you spell it with an i-e or a y?"

"You're going to hide the baby away from her own father? Isn't that criminal?"

I glanced at her, then reached for the baby. "Sydney said he abuses her, Ma. She says he's burned her."

Star stared at me, her eyes round, then looked down at the baby as if waiting for it to give her some confirmation.

"The bruises on Sydney's face today? David did that to her. He's been abusing her and now he's turned to Jacqueline, so Sydney has to keep her away, okay? It makes sense to leave her with me because I'm the last person anyone might expect to do Sydney any favors."

"I don't know, I don't know, Lainey, there's going to be trouble around this. My intuition's saying she's not telling you something, and you know how good my intuition is. There's something not right about this."

"Screw your intuition, I'm trying to keep a baby safe from her abusive father! You could be a little more compassionate here. I was thinking you might be able to watch her while I'm working, you'd like that, and then I could take over. Sydney'll come by every night after work, and it's only for a few days until we figure out how to prove David's abused her. It's the right thing to do, Ma, at least for now."

"Let me do a reading."

"Not on this. I don't care what the cards tell you." I pulled the baby up onto my lap, and tickled my lips against her hair.

Star watched me carefully. "She's not your child, Lainey."

"Don't you think I know that?"

"Intellectually maybe you know it." Star walked to her drawer. "I'm doing a reading."

"Do it on yourself," I said, striding to the hall, realizing how childish I sounded but not caring.

I walked downstairs with Jacqueline . . . with *Molly* and sat with her on the sofa, lifting the spinach block Sydney had left behind. Other than taking care of Star, what good had I ever done in the world? But now I felt like a different person than I'd been just hours ago, sturdier, so much more purposeful.

Molly made a pleading sound and I studied her face, trying to interpret it. Was she hungry? I looked in the diaper bag Sydney had left. There was a bottle half-filled with apple juice, a pacifier and four diapers. Would that be enough till tomorrow when Sydney came by with more? No, probably not, and depending on how bad things got with David she might not even want to risk coming here right away. I'd have to buy little things, a change of clothes and more diapers, baby food, maybe plastic plates with cartoon characters. In the store, ladies would look at me and smile like they did at pregnant women, that inclusive smile like I was carrying on their tradition. I gave Molly her bottle and tickled under her chin. "Let's go for a ride," I said.

As we approached the car, I realized with a jolt that Sydney hadn't given me a car seat. I should really leave Molly at home, I knew that, but it wouldn't be the same without her. I wanted to look down at her face as we shopped, see her look back up with her questioning blue eyes. So I put the carrier into the backseat and strapped it in as best I could. As I started the engine I glanced into the rearview, saw her sitting there goggle-eyed, amazed. Since Sydney left she hadn't cried, not once. It must be a sign.

I parked in front of Babies "R" Us. I'd been in the store twice: first with Pamela and then again a day later, to surreptitiously study everything that had entranced me. Lifting a tiny baseball cap and jacket, sneakers that fit in my palm; I'd avoided the eyes of the women who roamed the aisles, but now I smiled at them, comparing their babies to mine. My completely unbiased opinion was that mine was better.

"You're the Heidi Klum of babies," I told her. A woman ahead of me turned, smiled hesitantly and I smiled back. "I spend so much time alone with her," I said, "sometimes I talk just to hear my own voice."

The woman rolled her eyes. "Been there," she said, and I felt her words glow like a swig of liquor in my belly.

I came home with four shopping bags, along with a car seat, sling and BabyBjörn. Sydney had given me a couple hundred dollars and at first I'd figured that would be my purchasing limit, but once my cart started to fill I ended up changing my mind. Who knew how long it'd be before Sydney could safely take Molly back? And there were too many pink and white frilly things, too many toys with packaging that stated they'd boost Molly's intelligence. I'd always hated shopping for myself or for Star, but this was more fun than I ever could've imagined, like playing house.

"Come see what I got!" I called.

There was a prolonged silence and then a sigh from upstairs, overemphatic like someone pretending exasperation in a play, before Star started down. I spread my findings out on the coffee table, grinning as she lifted tiny sandal shoes and little pants embroidered with pink flowers. "Oh!" she whispered. "Look at this. Oh look at these!" I'd known the clothes would get her; they'd be irresistible to anybody producing estrogen.

Star lifted a dress, white with red-stitched hearts and a matching headband. She made a little distressed sound, the sound one might make when confronted with too many choices from a dessert plate. "Let's try this on!"

I grinned and unhooked Molly's jumper, wormed her arms out from her sleeves. Molly's eyes rolled to one side as if in scorn, but her body was limp and compliant as a rag doll.

And then, suddenly, Star sucked in her breath. I followed her eyes and stared, feeling like I'd been punched under the ribs. There below Molly's left shoulder blade, in the spot Star used to call my clipped angel wings, were four round scabs wider than pencil erasers, two of them jagged and white at the edges with dried pus.

"No," Star whispered. "Oh no. Her father did this?"

I lifted Molly and held her against my chest, staring at Star as I rocked her, rocked us both. I wanted to feel blind with rage, but instead all I felt was terrified. It was true, all the nightmares you had when you were a kid. There were things in the world without a soul, charming monsters who could smile at you with dazzling teeth, as they used them to rip off your head. "See?" I said. "See?" My voice broke. "Who knows what he might've done if Sydney left her alone with him again. So what was I supposed to do?"

Star shook her head slowly, then straightened her shoulders. "I guess exactly what we're doing," she said.

It was nearly eight before we could even stomach the notion of food. Star made us frozen dinners and we sat at the kitchen table silently, watching Molly shovel fistfuls of carrots into her mouth. That she could look so happy despite everything twisted at my insides, made me feel somehow deceitful like I should remind her of what she'd been through.

Sydney had been telling the truth. And of course I'd known nobody would make up a story like that about their own baby, but knowing the truth and *knowing* it were two totally different things. A father stabbing a cylinder of burning ash on his daughter's skin . . . and then again as she screamed and then again, realizing what he'd just done, but then doing it again. I couldn't stand this, couldn't comprehend it. It was too much.

As Star cleaned up the mess in the kitchen, traces of strained peas that had wedged in linoleum cracks, I carried Molly to the sofa and flicked on the TV, not watching, not listening, just needing the color and noise of it. Molly looked up at me and stretched a yawn that took up half her face. I touched her cheek. "I love you," I whispered, soft enough that my mother wouldn't hear. "I'll take care of you better than she did, I swear." I leaned back on the sofa, the baby's weight against my chest, and closed my eyes. She was safe now. I repeated it like a mantra, *she's safe, she's safe . . .*

"Lainey!" Star's voice was frantic.

My eyes snapped open and I struggled through a haze of sleep trying to interpret the heat on my chest, its faint urine smell. I'd squished the baby! I jumped up with a cry, nearly dropped her.

But Star was staring not at the baby, but at the TV. She walked toward it and sank down onto her knees. I turned up the volume, head still woozy, trying to make sense of the picture that swam in front of my eyes. Because on the screen was Sydney, her bruised face red and chin quivering. She shook her head and gripped the hand of the man beside her, crying out as he pulled her against his chest.

The man beside her was David McGrath. He looked more stern than disconsolate, a well-cut sports coat over tailored jeans, his brown hair perfectly trimmed and falling boyishly over his forehead.

"Please don't hurt her," Sydney whimpered to the microphone. "She's only a baby, hardly a year old."

An 800 number flashed onto the screen along with Molly's picture, my Molly, her orange hair combed into an odd cowlick, wearing a fluffy pink dress that made her look like iced confectionary. "If you have any information on the whereabouts of twelve-month-old Jacqueline McGrath," the announcer said, "please call the number listed on your screen. All calls will be kept confidential."

I looked down at Molly and then pulled her closer, turning back to Star who stared openmouthed at the TV. The clutch in my chest wasn't from shock at seeing Sydney, I realized, or Molly's face on the screen. The clutch was from guilt, plain and simple guilt because it was true, in the past few hours I had stolen Molly away. And pain at the realization that of course she'd never really been mine.

{ 4 }

How much can your life change in one day? Well let me tell you.

Molly-Jacqueline disappeared from the TV screen, replaced by a Tampax commercial. A young girl spoke earnestly to her older sister, and I actually started to listen to the words. Of a tampon commercial. That's what a state my brain was in.

"But I've never—"

Smugly charmed chuckle. "That's no big deal. I started using Tampax when I was your age. Just wait'll you see how much more comfortable they are than bulky pads."

I couldn't listen to my mother, that heavy breathing she got before an attack, like she'd just run up a ten-mile hill. I knew the pattern. The first month or two after things got really bad, when she'd decided she'd be best off not leaving her room, I'd dragged her by the elbow each day for just a walk around the block. Two steps out the door and the panting had started. If we were lucky she'd make it to the street before passing out.

But not today. Today she could drop dead and I'd ignore her, because for the first time ever her attack was echoing through me too, and to let her in would kill me. For the first time I understood the anxiety was more than just fear, couldn't be muffled by reckoning or reasoning, or breathed into a paper bag. It burrowed more deeply. It was an understanding of the unjustifiable cruelty of the world, that the world had always been and would always be this way.

I stood and carried Molly-Jacqueline to the kitchen, but still I could hear Star's panting, the scritch that came with each quick exhale. I walked out to the back deck and held Molly up to sit on the wooden railing, trying to keep my head from spinning.

What was going on? What the hell was Sydney doing? I knew her, and yes she could be sneaky and conniving, but this was on a whole different level. What could she possibly be thinking?

I knew I had to figure this out; if I didn't go to the police now, tell them what was going on, then I'd never be able to explain why I hadn't and might be arrested myself. But if I turned Sydney in, what would happen to Molly? She might be given back to her father, and I'd rather spend three lifetimes in jail than let that happen.

I had to find out what had happened, whether Sydney had just freaked out on her way to tell David I had the baby and blurted out a lie, or whether she had some other, more twisted plan in mind.

A light flicked on in the window of the duplex adjoining ours, and I glanced over to find Jeffy Hauser, the neighbor kid, watching me bleary-eyed. My stomach lurched as he turned away, and I imagined his squally little-boy voice, "Mom, that baby on TV! Dial 911!" I lifted Molly and strode back inside.

The panting had stopped. In the den, sure enough, Star was lying on the floor, arms splayed, face pale. I sat on the couch across from her, holding Molly tight against my chest. I watched Star's face and imagined what she'd say if she were a real mother, a normal mother. *I'll call the cops, tell them the truth. I'll get this all straightened out, baby, so don't you worry.*

"Unngh," Star said, either because she was starting to wake up or starting to remember. And suddenly, for the first time in my life, I had this intense urge to slap her. I'd been embarrassed of her before, plenty of times, but I'd somehow managed to keep the anger crammed into a dark, impenetrable corner. But now that anger, decades of it, welled so high in me that it took on a life of its own. I plopped Molly on the couch more roughly than I should have, knelt on the floor and whacked Star so hard that we both cried out in pain.

She gaped at me, a hand at her cheek, and I touched my own cheek and broke into sudden, unexpected tears. "Lai—" she said, "—nee?"

Molly sidled herself off the couch, falling hard on her butt, and she started to whimper, then broke into a wavering cry. I lifted her onto my lap. "I'm sorry," I said hoarsely.

Star raised herself up on her elbows, then closed her eyes and lay back down.

Molly snuffled against my shoulder, and I remembered suddenly how Sydney had slung Molly over her arm like a rag. "I don't want to call the police," I said.

Star didn't speak, just lay there with her eyes closed. I could see the welt my hand had left on her cheek. I turned away. "I don't know what she's doing, not exactly. Maybe she's absolutely insane, maybe she's playing some kind of twisted game with me, or maybe she actually thinks this is the best way to protect her daughter."

"Accusing us of kidnapping?" Star's eyes snapped open. "We're going to jail!"

"If she'd given the cops our name, don't you think they'd be here by now? I think she probably panicked, thought David might get violent and force her to tell him where the baby was. And who knows, if she'd told him he could've come here and hurt us too."

I set Molly on my knee and watched her face, wishing she could tell me what she wanted and what was right, but she only punched her fist into her mouth and started to gnaw tearily on her knuckles. "What I don't get is, doesn't she think I'll turn her in? Or leave the baby at some church in the middle of the night?"

But no, of course that was the thing, she knew me. She knew how easily I'd fall in love with her daughter, had some idea what my life was now. I was probably the only person she could rely on to stay clamped onto that love while I was kicked around. I steeled my shoulders, fighting to stay calm, to think. Damn Sydney. What the hell was I supposed to do?

I brought Molly to the kitchen and dialed information. I needed to talk to her, figure out what she was thinking and what the hell she wanted from me. How did she expect this to end? For Molly to stay missing forever? Was she planning to pick her up in a day or two and disappear? How could she possibly expect to get away with that?

I asked for both Sydney Beaumont and Sydney McGrath, but there were no listings. I had no idea where she lived, so the only way of trying to reach her would be to stop by Six of Swords tomorrow. But what were the chances of her going to work the morning after her daughter's "disappearance"? I didn't know her number or her address; I was stranded here at her whim.

Molly's headband was askew so I straightened it and nudged her fist out from her mouth. "Bad for your teeth," I whispered. In response, Molly made a choked, defiant noise and punched her fist back in.

Which is when I realized how she really, truly looked like me. Not just the round cheeks, but the crookedness of her smile, the upturn of her nose, her blue eyes and long, pale lashes. Her ruddy face was more like mine than it was like Sydney's. Star believed "signs" were everywhere, so wasn't this a sign?

Okay, it was crazy, I knew that. But all my life I'd had these dreams of motherhood, someone to grip onto my finger, lean against me while I read bedtime stories, someone I'd teach how to count and jump rope. And paint. I knew how stupid it was not to call the police. But even if it was only for a few days until Sydney did whatever she was now planning to do, realistically this was my only foreseeable chance at pseudo-motherhood, without medical intervention or immaculate conception.

Star entered the kitchen and I stood a moment watching her, then ran water over a dish towel. She took it from me and pressed it against her forehead. "I feel better now," she said, "I think."

I filled a glass with water, held it toward her, but she ignored it. "You remember when you first brought Sydney home?" she said. "You were what, seven years old? And I was watching you two, you're building card houses and Sydney's not good at it, she loses patience. But you've built up a regular card condo, all thrilled because it's the biggest you ever made, you're on your third deck. So Sydney asks all innocent for a soda and you run to get it. Soon as you turn the corner there goes her hand, swipe-smash and your condo's gone. And I knew then about her. I saw it."

I remembered that day, I actually did. Remembered turning just in time to see Sydney's arm pull back and the wildness in her eyes. When I returned with the soda, she'd shaken her head slowly. "The floor shook when you walked away," she said. "You should've been more careful." And me, I'd just shrugged and handed her the glass and said, "Guess it had to fall down eventually."

"You felt sorry for her, I realize that," Star said. "You decided you'd try and make up for everything she was lacking in her life. Which she knew you would, that you couldn't stand to see anyone suffer, so of course she took advantage. And here you both are, however many years later, doing it again."

"She didn't have anybody else," I said. "And now it seems like she still doesn't, or why would she have come to me of all people?"

Star's face tightened. "Her mother was a self-centered monster, so she became one too. And now here we are . . ." Her knees wobbled slightly and she leaned back against the counter and closed her eyes. "If her mother never taught her to have a conscience then, how can you trust that she has one now?"

Sydney's mother had spent much of her time trying to find men, mainly to support her drinking problem. Sydney had recounted sordid details of the men's physical characteristics, giving them names—Blubber-Belly, Mister Boobs—both of us wondering whether her mother had any criteria at all for the men she chose. Sydney's father had been one of those men, in his early fifties when her mother had been in her twenties. Already married, it turned out, and when she'd refused an abortion, probably not for Sydney's sake but because she saw the opportunity for a permanent meal and drink ticket, he'd agreed to send two grand a month in return for her silence.

I remembered sitting with Sydney on her tenth birthday, first helping her style her hair and choose between dresses and then waiting with her for her father to appear. For some reason, she'd gotten it in her head that on this most important birthday of course he'd finally come to meet her, so that they could celebrate together the first decade of her life. I'd sat with Sydney on the curb outside her apartment for hours, watching her jump up each time a car passed, her shoulders dropping slowly when it didn't stop, turning back to me with her face stoic.

Who could blame Sydney after the role models she'd had, for turning into the person she'd become?

Molly was starting to fuss in my arms, pulling at my hair, so I set her down and let her crawl across the room. Star followed the baby with her eyes. "She never learned what it's like to care about anybody other than herself," she said. "The only person who really ever cared about Sydney was Sydney, so she took on the task of loving herself like a full-time job, put everything into it."

"But she ended up marrying a child abuser."

"Yeah, don't you feel sorry for her? Poor Sydney, puts her baby in danger and tries to fix things by putting us in danger. It's like she has a gift for screwing with people's lives." She threw the damp dish towel across the room and it hit the wall with a splat. Just as the phone started to ring.

We both stared at each other, then at the phone. It could be Sydney. Or, it could be the police. I slowly lifted the receiver.

"Lainey, oh thank God."

I gripped the phone trying, unsuccessfully, to keep myself from yelling. "Dammit, Sydney, I just saw you on TV. What the hell were you thinking!"

"You saw?" She gave a broken sob. "I didn't plan this out, Lainey, it just happened."

"That's like saying armed robbery just happened. This doesn't make any sense! You were going to tell David you'd left her with a friend!"

Star watched me with wide eyes, her face pale, and I reached for her shoulder and guided her to a chair, forcing her to sit.

"I know," Sydney said. "I know, and I realize how you have to feel."

Star leaned forward and at first I was sure she was either about to faint or be sick, but she just pulled Molly onto her lap and huddled over her. I brought the phone to the hall.

"I had it all planned out what I was going to say to him," Sydney said. "But then, I don't know! I was standing there at his front door, and I started shaking. I was so scared of how he'd react. Please—" Her voice broke. "Please try and understand, Lainey, I know him and he's dangerous, and I suddenly realized he was going to kill me if I told him the truth."

"What do you think he'd do to me and my mom if he found out we were involved? What do you think the cops would do! Did you think about anybody but your own self?"

"It was the only way to save Jacqueline, don't you get that? I got back in my car, and I was just sitting there with my head against the steering wheel trying to think, trying to figure out options, but all I could figure out was that there *weren't* any good options. And then it was like the decision made itself, the car drove itself to the mall, my legs walked the empty stroller inside and suddenly . . . I don't know . . . I just was screaming and telling people she was missing. If I was thinking straight I'd have done it different, because I know this puts you in a really bad situation. You have to believe I'm sorry about that, and when this is over I swear I'll find some way to make it up to you. But right now all I can think about is Jacqueline. I don't know what else to do."

"So you used me because you knew I'd let myself be used."

"Of course not! I told you there wasn't any plan behind this before it happened. I left Jacqueline with you because you're the only person I have in my life right now that I can trust. I know what kind of person you are, that even if you hated me—and I really hope you don't hate me—you'd still be willing to help her even if it meant doing something dangerous."

"You could've called when you were sitting in the car. You could even have called after you told people she'd been kidnapped. I had to see it on the news, Sydney. Do you have any idea what that was like?

And now here I am hiding Molly from the cops and from someone who might show up at our door with a gun."

Silence. Then, "He'd only come if you let anybody know you had her."

My shoulders tensed. "That sounds like a threat."

"It's *not* a threat. But I guess it's a warning, Lainey. A very, very apologetic, concerned warning. What I've lived with the past few years, it's like he literally loses his mind and something else takes it over. Even little things can provoke him; I mean he hurt Jacqueline and what could she have done except cry too loud? So I don't know what he'd do to me, and to you and Star, if he found out what was going on."

I sank onto the bottom step, the fear swirling through my stomach. "What do we do?" I said hoarsely. "You got us into this, so tell me what you expect us to do?"

"Just . . . hold tight. Stay inside as much as possible, and don't let anybody see Molly. I'll figure this out, I promise, just give me a day or two and I'll find somewhere I can take her."

I closed my eyes and leaned my head against the banister. A day or two. I could keep Molly hidden for a couple days and then Sydney would come take her and our life would go back to almost normal. Just on edge as we tried to forget we'd played any role in the story that would soon be pervading the news. I listened to Molly's voice from the kitchen, thinking what it would be like once she left, how the house would sink in on itself once again, and grow silent.

"I'll call you tomorrow, okay? And let you know what I've worked out, because I swear I *will* work something out. Tell Jacqueline I love her and I'll see her real soon. And Lainey? You have so many things to hate me for, I realize that, and you'll never know how sorry and grateful and sorry and sorry and sorry I am. But I hope you'll at least try and understand and maybe someday forgive me for this one thing." And then she hung up, without saying goodbye.

. . .

That night, in an attempt to help Star—and myself—feel safe, I helped her push a large trunk in front of the door and hang the bells we used as Christmas ornaments over the openings of the ground floor windows, to serve as a warning in case anybody tried to enter. Star set up pillows by the front door to sleep on, and I slept next to Molly in Star's double bed.

Molly woke me early the next morning, whimpering, and I gazed at her through blurred eyes, disoriented, thinking *hunh?* Until she hit me with one of her flailing arms and I remembered. I took her hand in mine and kissed it. "We survived the night," I said.

My day was spent listening feverishly to local radio news reports while trying to stop Star from freaking out, and keeping Molly as quiet as possible for fear she'd be heard by our neighbors through the regrettably thin walls of our duplex. I tried to distract them both by playing with the toys I'd bought for Molly, and soon Star was on the floor with us, helping Molly drag pull toys and slot neon plastic shapes into neon plastic holes, with running commentary about how smart she was. At first Star froze whenever she heard an unexpected sound, the house settling or the rush of water through our neighbor's pipes, but soon she lost herself in the joy of Molly's reaction to the games we played.

And I did too, to be honest, almost forgetting how much danger we were in as I marveled at the subtleties of Molly's expressions, all the degrees of surprise, amusement and frustration, the way she beamed up at us periodically like she was saying, *isn't this COOL?* I absorbed it, so I could replay it after she was gone.

And then, in the middle of the afternoon, Sydney called. "There's a problem." Her voice dropped to a panicked whisper. "You left the house with her, didn't you."

I paced to the kitchen, out of earshot of Star. "I had to get diapers and baby food. You left me with four diapers!"

"Well somebody saw you, or at least I think they did. A blond woman with a redheaded baby, they said. Called the tip line and the police brought them in to do a composite sketch."

My skin suddenly felt too tight. I strode to the sink, hunched over it, briefly wondering if I was going to be sick. Was it the woman I'd talked to at Babies "R" Us? One of the cashiers? How could I have been so stupid! "Does the composite look like me?"

"I haven't seen it. I don't know. But I'm sure they'll show it to me in the next couple days to ask if I know you."

"What're you going to tell them?"

"Well of course I'll say I have no idea who you are. But dammit, Lainey, what if they start splashing the sketch on the news? There's a few other tips now, fake tips, people who're either delusional or out-right lying. So maybe they won't make anything of it, but who knows?"

"So what am I supposed to do!"

Sydney hesitated, then said, "I'm coming there now. I'm at a pay phone in Hampton, I didn't think it was safe to use my home phone or cell, so I should be there in maybe a half hour unless . . ."

"Unless?"

"I'm scared, Lainey." Her voice hitched. "I think David suspects something, he's acting twitchy when he talks to me, the way he gets when he's about to explode."

I thought of the bruises on Sydney's face, my throat tightening. "You think he might hurt you?"

"No, that's not it. I mean he might, that's true, but what I meant was I have to be careful where I go and what I do, in case he's watch-ing. Like when I was first threatening to leave him, he started basi-cally stalking me; I'd be at the grocery store or the salon and I'd walk out and see his car hiding in the shadows. He's capable of anything."

"So I'm supposed to just keep Jacqueline here and wait for him to show up at our door?"

"Lainey . . . Look, if I can't come in person I promise I'll call and we'll figure out how I can take her from you and disappear. Just give me a half hour and I'll get back to you one way or another. And—" She sucked in a quick breath, then said, "I'm sorry, I'm sorry but I have to ask you the biggest favor in the world. Because the thing is, no matter how scared I am of David now, I'm less terrified than I used to be because I know Jacqueline's safer with you. So what I have to ask is, if anything . . . really bad happens to me, would you maybe consider taking care of her? I mean you can say no if it's too much, just tell me now either way, but I'd feel so much more at ease if I knew you were watching out for her."

She was near tears, I could tell, and I suddenly felt my eyes filling too, from a mix of emotions I couldn't even begin to untangle but that—disgustingly, I know—included an underlying trill of excitement. I squeezed my eyes shut. "It's okay," I said. "I promise, whatever happens I'll take care of her."

After hanging up I ran my hands under cold water and then pressed them against my eyes and cheeks. How were we possibly going to get away with this, especially if David was starting to suspect Sydney? And the composite, if it was shown on the news, how long would it be before someone I knew came forward to identify me? And when Sydney took the baby and disappeared, which would make it obvious her story was a lie, how long before the police—and David—found me?

"I heard your conversation."

I spun around to find Star in the doorway holding Molly, her face flat with fear. We watched each other, unblinking, and then I said, "Sit down. I don't want you dropping the baby."

She sat at the table facing me, Molly watching me drowsily with her head resting against Star's chest. "Somebody saw you yesterday." Her voice trailed to a whisper. "And recognized Molly."

Hearing this I felt myself splitting away from myself, something I'd been doing for years, a false calm that floated somewhere above my real mind, which I could sit inside when dealing with my mother. "It's okay, Ma. Sydney's going to be here in a half hour, and we'll all figure out what to do. But until then why don't you take a nap, okay?" I lifted Molly, and she gave a little grunt of protest. "I'll take the baby and you go upstairs, and by the time you wake up Sydney'll be here and we'll probably already know exactly how to make things right."

Star gazed at me, then stood. "I have to do a reading."

"No way, you're just going to freak yourself out."

"I have to do a reading! We can't fix things until we know how broken they are, so just stay there and keep the baby quiet."

I briefly considered slapping Star again—which I guess proves I wasn't truly in that calm place after all. And it was only the insight that this wouldn't be altogether productive that stopped me. Instead I followed her from the kitchen, watched her climb the stairs, then brought Molly to the living room and sat with her on the couch, letting her lean against the crook of my arm. I tried to focus all my attention on her to keep myself from thinking, as she drifted between sleep and awake, periodically sucking furiously on her pacifier as if to rouse herself. Her hair was mussed, floating in staticky drifts about her head like molting feathers, and I licked my fingers and used them to flatten it back down, studying her face, her dimpled hands and knees, absorbing every inch of her while she was still mine. And I waited.

And waited.

At five, Molly woke and started to fuss again, and I carried her to the kitchen and fixed a bottle. I heard our neighbor's front door thunk shut and the sound of Mr. Hauser greeting his wife and son, becoming aware once again of how very thin our walls were, how completely exposed we were to the outside world.

When Molly was done feeding, I brought her to the living room and played with her distractedly, checking the clock every five minutes. Six-thirty passed, then seven. Hampton was only a half hour away, even factoring in the possibility of traffic and a stop off for a snack and/or gas tank filling. It had been three hours since Sydney had called, so where the hell was she? And as the question battered inside me, I became all at once certain that I'd never see her again, that she was in fact lying in some alleyway, bruised and beaten. Or dead.

It was seven-thirty, after I'd turned on the TV, switching from channel to channel searching for coverage of the disappearance or the discovery of Sydney's broken body, when the phone rang. I jumped up and ran to the kitchen.

"Lainey, I can't . . ." Her voice was a hoarse whisper. "I'm in trouble, I can't talk, I can't come get Jacqueline."

"What?"

"I can't talk! *Ohno-ohno,* I have to go!" She hung up.

"Sydney? What? Wait, come back!" No answer. I jiggled the phone cradle, then hit the receiver against the wall. "Dammit!"

In the living room Molly gave a plaintive shriek, so I ran to her and clapped a hand over her mouth. "Okay, okay, we're fine," I said, hurrying to the upstairs hallway, as far as possible from the Hausers' kitchen and living room.

Star was on the bed, frantically slapping her cards in various formations on the mattress. I stood outside the bedroom to catch my breath and tried to force myself back into that false, floating calm. *You're the mom!* I wanted to say to her. *Tell me what to do!* I closed my eyes and pressed my face against Molly's butterfly hair, then squared my shoulders and entered the room to set a hand on Star's shoulder. "You okay?"

She glanced at me blankly. "She's not coming. Something's gone wrong."

"Ma, stop." I felt my nails involuntarily digging into her shoulder, so I pulled my hand away. "Everything's fine, okay? Sydney's fine. With all she's got now to worry about, she just couldn't find a way to escape."

"She's not fine, don't you see?" She gestured widely at the cards spread on the bed. "All these major arcana! I'm getting them again and again, and what're the chances!"

It was true, most of the cards she'd laid out were the major arcana: the hanged man, the Empress, the Hierophant, the most powerful symbols of the deck. In spite of myself I felt a shiver, which I punched back down. "It's because you're not shuffling enough." I set Molly on the floor by our feet and quickly gathered the cards, folding them into their velvet square. "You have to stop it with the readings. It's just getting you upset, and it won't tell us anything we need to know."

"I realize there's things you can figure out without cards, but this?

We're risking death by a homicidal child abuser and I'm telling you,
Sydney's not coming back!"

I looked out the window, scanning desperately for cars, then
clenched my hands and spun back to face Star. "So what're the cards
going to say, hunh? Turn her in? Give Molly back to the man who
stuck a burning cigarette on her skin?"

She looked into my eyes a moment, then said, "Who was that on
the phone?"

"Nobody, a telemarketer." I turned away, focusing on Molly who
was now shaking the tassels on one of Star's floor pillows like a pom-
pom girl. Then realizing how obvious my evasion must seem, I
looked back at Star to add, "Selling reduced mortgage rates."

"It was Sydney." She hugged her chest. "I was right, something
happened to her."

"Ma, calm down."

"I'm calm!" She jumped to her feet, then slowly sank back down.
"I'm calm. But I have to tell you something, Lainey."

"We'll just have to wait till she calls again, okay? We're safe here,
she would've told me to leave if we weren't safe."

"You need to know the universe is talking to you, Lainey, and it
wants you to listen. It never gets this loud unless it's trying to make a
change in your life."

"Are you kidding me?" I threw back my head. "Screw you very
much, universe!"

"Just listen to me! I want to tell you what's in the cards, because
when I saw them it all became so clear. I get why this all's happening
because the cards, the universe, they want your soul to grow, and
they knew the only way to force you out of this inertia was to take
these extreme steps. To force you to leave."

"What do you mean *leave*?"

"I mean the things growing out of tree branches. What the hell do
you think I mean?" Her voice was shaking. I reached my hand
toward her, and after a minute she took it.

"It's okay," I said. "I'm not leaving you, Ma."

"It's not safe here and you know it." She turned toward the

wall, but not before I saw the tears flushing her face. "Even if David McGrath doesn't find out you were involved, and that's a *big* if, a little white baby disappears, especially a little rich white baby, and you don't think everybody in the state's going to start looking for her? I'm telling you, you don't leave now and something worse is going to happen to make sure you don't have a choice." She lifted Molly and sat with her on her lap. "Tell me what Sydney said on the phone."

"She didn't say anything, Ma."

Star watched me expressionlessly. Swallowed. Then said, "So it was so bad you can't tell me."

"She didn't say anything! Just that she couldn't come get the baby and she couldn't talk." I remembered the franticness of Sydney's voice, and what did it mean? Had David been there with her? Seen her call me? Was David even now figuring out how to find us?

"Why don't you get this? This is bigger than Sydney and bigger than the baby. You need to get away from me, and maybe this is the universe's way of making it happen."

"Lovely. The universe is brilliant. It made a man hurt his daughter and his wife, then got me involved in a kidnapping just so I'd get away from you. God's pretty twisted, hunh? You'd think He would've just smote you down and I'd be free of you forever without all the smoke and mirrors. It'd be much more straightforward, but I guess He likes the creative approach."

She ignored this. "I know what it's done to you, having me as a mother. You pretended to Sydney you were married?"

My face flushed and she reached for my hand. "I understand it because you *should* be married. You're meant to be married with kids by now, two children, it's written on your palms."

"Oh *please*."

"I keep thinking of you when you were little, this bright, funny, sparkly nymph of a girl. You had all this enthusiasm for the world, but I've pulled you down with me, kept you from everything. You could really *be* somebody; I realize that even if you don't, and how do you think that makes me feel? If you don't start living your own life now, soon it's going to be too late."

"You're saying I'm old and a nobody."

"You know what I mean. You're meant to be more than this, we both know that. I did a chart on you when you were born, and it said you'd live the most extraordinary kind of life, learn things about yourself and the world that most people never learn."

I smiled wryly. "And things would happen to me that seemed like luck or coincidence, right? But really they're destiny. So what's my destiny, Ma? Because I have to say, I'm not trusting the universe at the moment."

"I don't know. I don't know, you break the law, kidnap a baby and even if you run they'll most likely catch you. And as your mother I want to say this is crazy, that's what I want to say. But one of the things I've learned . . ." She picked up the water glass on her night-stand, looked into it and then set it back down, squaring her shoulders. "You don't grab at destiny, it'll follow you around like a shark. It'll bite you where it hurts over and over, until you let it drag you where it wants. What's happening to you now, maybe this is your shark. And maybe it's mine too."

I studied her face, shocked by the determination in her voice. But that was the thing about Star. She'd hole up inside her home rather than fight her sickness, not just because she was afraid but because she thought it was pointless. She believed reading cards could tell you what was coming, help you prepare, but it rarely told you how to make things better. Because the world was always watching, judging, like some divine Mafia. And if it decided it wanted you arrested, dead, well it had too many connections. There was no way and nowhere you could hide.

"You've been shackled to this house for how many years?" she said. "But being away from me, from here, it'll help you find out who you are and what you want, so when you come back you can figure out how to go about getting it. How could I possibly live with myself if I was the one who kept you from being who you're supposed to be?"

"And what about you? How could I live with myself if something happened to you while I was away?" That implied *something* of course referencing her suicide, which we'd never talked about, even though the pointed shard of it was embedded in everything: the evenings she didn't call out to me when I returned home, whenever I found her with her eyes closed at odd times of the day. Nana Sterling's death had prompted the first attempt; what if my leaving prompted another?

"I go away," I said, "and something happens to freak you out, and something *will* happen, I guarantee it, then who's going to be here to talk you down from it?"

"I know you forget sometimes, but I'm a grown woman, Lainey. I can take care of myself if you're not around."

"Dammit, Ma!" I ran a hand through my hair, my eyes stinging. "Where would I take her, hunh? What would I do with myself, hang out in motels with Molly, watching the news and waiting for the other shoe to drop?"

In Star's lap Molly waved her arms at me, and Star enveloped her fist in one hand. "Ahh," she said softly, "so this isn't just about me, is it?"

"Stop patronizing me!" I tried to think of something better to add, more piercing and less whiny, but came up blank. I glared at her and spun away, out of the room.

I paced to my bedroom, wishing I had gravel in my shoes, some kind of pain to distract me from imploding. Why was this making me feel like I wanted to crawl out of my own skin? And why was I so pissed off at Star? Look how strong she was being! Or not *being* but acting; I knew that strength must be mostly a façade. But she was trying to free me, even if it meant being alone in this house which, for her, had no doors.

The cards hadn't told her I should leave, I was pretty sure of that. They never gave direct commands, only pointed out implications. I didn't doubt she had read danger into the cards; in this situation she would've read danger into a burnt slice of toast. But leaving had been all her idea. She'd told me the universe wanted me to leave because she herself thought that I needed to.

And she was right. I knew why I felt like this. She was making me look at myself, at my own fear so similar to hers. I'd left home at twenty and it had been a huge adventure, a chance to create a new me. I'd made friends, fallen in love, waitressed during the day and painted at night, fudged the more embarrassing parts of my life and even started to believe the fudges. But I was too old now for a new me. Pathetic as it was, I didn't know how to live outside this house, this town, away from my mother.

I sank onto my bed, looking around the only room that had really felt like mine, the walls crowded with paintings from high school and young adulthood. Fixing on a painting of my knees holding a sketch pad that held a painting of my knees, which perfectly represented the complete introversion of my life.

I might dream of more but it'd always felt like pure fantasy, the handsome, doting husband, the towheaded, bedimpled, bizarrely easy babies, the house on the coast complete with kitchen island and golden retriever. These were all just hypnotic images on which to train my mind so I could drift off to sleep. I'd understood my life would probably never be more than it was, and I'd pretty much made peace with that. But deep down I'd always felt that without Star, at least a watered-down version of this other, better life could have been possible.

What if a different life was still possible? If Star was okay after I left, wouldn't it prove I could someday leave for good?

I went again to the window, pleading silently for Sydney's car. Listening to the sounds from the other side of my wall, Star blowing raspberries against Molly's skin, Molly's shrieks of laughter.

I imagined myself driving somewhere exotic, Mexico, or even Costa Rica or Peru. Working with artisans to weave tapestries or paint talavera. Maybe meeting someone dark and handsome who'd speak Spanish to me in low, adoring tones. Yeah, I was good at fantasizing; maybe it was a skill that went hand in hand with being an artist, designing richly textured fantasies that could then be brought to life on a wall. Not the same as bringing them to life in an actual *life* but still, while I was imagining them, they felt real.

So I let my mind create a new life in Europe—Venice maybe— where I could set up canvases by the canals and old churches, tourists furtively admiring my work and filling my basket with euros. And then I imagined me with Molly in the barrens of northern Canada where we might go for days without seeing another soul, the snow falling thick as white noise, muffling and muting so it would feel almost like the world outside my window had disappeared.

And as I sat there conjuring these permutations of potential futures, each so enchanting that the enchantment almost subsumed the panic, I realized that in the past half hour, I had already made up my mind.

I took care of my mother before I left, I really did. Even though it meant bringing Molly to the store, a hood covering all but her eyes and nose. A highly risky move, but I knew it was safer than leaving her at home with Star, who when I'd left had been in the process of gene genocide, an obsessive sterilization of the entire upstairs.

There were a surprising number of people in the store at that hour, night-shifters, insomniacs, an enormously pregnant woman hugging a jar of green olives. What did the sleepy checkout girl think of me, there with a baby at two A.M., looking overcaffeinated, pale and shaking, unloading shopping carts filled with frozen dinners and canned goods and Star's favorite cookies? Single mother of five, she probably thought. Or bulimic.

I'd also picked up a box of hair dye, "Sunsparked Brown," the brand that looked least likely to induce chronic conditions if used on infants. All-natural, odor-free, the model's face bright with the obligatory *Do-I-look-awesome-or-what?* glow.

Back home I stocked the freezer and shelves, enough food for at least a month. And when a month was over, well we'd find a way around it.

I didn't think it through, of course. Didn't look at the improbability of it all, how yesterday I'd been painting brown barrels on dusty plaster walls, and today I was kidnapping a baby. I didn't think about money, or how a baby needs stability. But I did think of my mother. If things went bad I could at least tell myself that.

I did a patch test on Molly's skin, and when her arm did not fall off I slicked the brown dye over her hair. And then I held the box against my own head.

All my life I'd been blond but without help, little-girl-golden-blond almost inevitably darkens to a mucousy beige, and I'd never cared enough about my hair to give it help. I looked in the mirror from my face to the box and back, and then while Molly crawled around the bathroom pulling down first towels and then toilet paper, I slid my hands back into the plastic gloves.

After rinsing our heads, I held Molly up so we could both look into the mirror. Molly had not enjoyed the rinsing and her face was pink, eyes rimmed with red. But with our new Color Number 75R matched hair, we looked indisputably related. I smiled at my reflection and my reflection smiled back, and we assessed each other. If I'd seen this woman in the street, I probably would have rated her a seven. And thought she was better looking than I was.

Molly was falling asleep, so I set her in her carrier and brought magazines into Star's room. I'd bought one of each kind, including tabloids, and the latest Jennifer Weiner and Danielle Steel, and the weight of them in my arms made me feel a little better. Reading was almost like having a conversation. She couldn't be lonely with all those voices, funny and informative and trashy and romantic, in her bedroom.

I'd thought Star might be asleep but she was lying on her back, staring at the ceiling. I set the magazines on the bureau and sat on the bed beside her. She startled and then lifted a strand of my hair, studied it. "Chic," she said softly.

I took her hand and held it to my cheek. "Do you think I'm crazy for not going to the cops?"

She raised her eyebrows. "You think I have a right to call anyone crazy?"

I swung my legs onto her lap and rested my head against her shoulder. She paused like she was debating something inside herself, then began tracing a finger in circles again and again around my knee. "You and Molly, you're going to do great. And *I'm* going to do great. I'm kind of excited to have the house to myself. I'll blare Frank Sinatra and Buddy Holly in the middle of the night, and dance to it without having to worry about you making fun of me."

I smiled and put my arm around her, nuzzled my face into her neck. And I stayed there with her, holding her, until she fell asleep.

❧ 5 ❧

I drove out to Pamela's and parked in her driveway, looking up at the dark windows as I called her cell phone. She answered with a grunt.

"Hey," I whispered.

Silence, then, "Who the hell is this?"

"Sorry. Sorry, it's me."

"Lainey? What's wrong? What time is it?"

"I . . . I'm actually in your driveway. Could you come outside?"

"You're in my driveway?" *Pause.* "Okay, okay, let me get my shoes on."

She hung up and I hunched forward to rest my forehead on the steering wheel. A minute later, the passenger door opened and Pamela slipped inside. "Where we going?" She glanced down at her pajamas, pale blue and printed with Holstein cattle. "Should I have dressed better?"

"How long do you have to be with a man before you feel comfortable enough to wear cow pajamas?"

"Wait till you're married and it's too late for him to change his mind," Pamela said, then widened her eyes. "Your hair!" She reached to smooth a lock of my hair between her thumb and forefinger. "When'd you decide to do this? You have to give me tips, because I'm starting to look like Barbara Bush. Look." She bent her head and pointed at a streak of gray.

I waited for her to notice the other big change in my life, and when she didn't I said, "Look in the backseat."

She turned and stared at Molly. And then, in the voice of someone who's caught her daughter stealing gum, she said, "Lainey? There's a baby in your car."

"Her mother asked me to take her."

"Somebody gave you her daughter?"

"I'm keeping her safe," I said, and then I told her the story, watching her face go various shades of pale until she said, "You're going to get yourself arrested."

"I won't. I can't, for the baby's sake, so I'm leaving Virginia and I need your help."

"You'll get *me* arrested."

I ignored her. "I need you to look out for my mom. Just call her every day to make sure she's okay, see if she needs anything." I reached into my purse and pulled out a credit card. "She might need groceries if I'm gone more than a couple weeks."

"A couple weeks!"

"And actually, if you could use the card every few days for whatever, it might be good to leave some kind of record that I'm still in Virginia."

Pamela leaned back in her seat to look up at the car roof. "There's something really weird about this; I have a really bad feeling. You know she's using you."

"Well obviously she's using me, but it's not about her." Implying of course that it was only about Molly, that I was sacrificing my life to save her.

But let's face it. This was just as much about myself.

I wish I could say I was excited, seeing my life split so suddenly and dramatically away from my expectation of it. But the thing was, it was seven in the morning, I'd been up for twenty-four hours straight. All of this was suddenly starting to feel real, and I was finding it hard to breathe.

Through all the last-minute preparations, I hadn't had time to think. I'd just been reacting, moving on pure momentum, pushed by my fury at Sydney, and then by fear and then by Star. Lying in bed with Star in the early morning, most of me had expected that I'd wake up to find Molly had been nothing more than a hallucination. That I'd just head off to my mural, then back home for dinner, cereal or meat with bottled sauce fried on the Foreman grill, my only adventure coming from the book I would read after the dishes were done.

I had only two hundred dollars in my wallet, all the ATM had let me take, and there was no way I could disappear for long on two hundred bucks. But I couldn't risk going to another ATM or stopping at a bank once I was on the road, because if anyone identified my composite, they'd be able to trace my location. So on my way out of town I stopped at Six of Swords and left a note, printed in all caps, folded and taped to the door.

> SYDNEY,
> YOU KNOW WHO THIS IS AND WHY I'M WRITING. I NEED
> YOU TO CALL ME ASAP.

Not much of a note, it didn't convey just how desperate and immediate the situation was, so at the last second I added:

> BECAUSE I'M LEAVING WITH HER, AND I'M GOING TO
> NEED MONEY TO KEEP HER SAFE. I'M GOING TO DISAP-
> PEAR.

Which of course I regretted an hour into the drive, when it was already too late to go back. I was pretty sure now that something awful had happened to Sydney. And even if she was okay, someone else was bound to see the note first, and what would happen when they did?

For sure they'd give it to the cops, who'd know it was related to Molly's disappearance. The police would take fingerprints off the paper, and then what?

I'd been fingerprinted once, at a Cops & Kids picnic my school had hosted when I was eleven or twelve. They'd set up a fingerprinting station where a woman in uniform had rolled the fingers of my right hand across a pad, then let me see them on a computer screen. Did that mean my prints were on file? Was the Cops & Kids program just a cheap ruse to get preemptive records on all potential future criminals?

I knew I had to at least get out of the state. I had no idea where I'd end up, except that I needed to get as far away as it was possible for my '97 Tercel to get. Idaho, I thought, or Kansas, one of those places you always forgot about when listing states, places I knew nothing about except fourth-grade geography, shapes and capitals and major crops.

I wanted to floor the accelerator, drive five hundred miles an hour and disregard any red lights. But of course all I needed was to get pulled over by a cop, who'd take one look at my frantic, sleep-deprived face and snap on the cuffs. So I kept myself at five miles above the limit, driving from suburb down through gawking farm-land. Mile after mile of it, buried in sameness, talk radio on to keep me awake and Molly asleep, stopping to brood over each fork, which way, which way? If I'd been Star and believed in intuition it might've been different. As it was, every decision felt wrong.

WELCOME TO WEST VIRGINIA. West Virginia seemed to look exactly as wilted as eastern Virginia had, the ragged grass the same faded green, motor homes evenly spaced in tired rows like gravestones, yards with sagging laundry lines and white-painted tires planted with hopeful but stunted pansies. But I'd crossed the state line, which was progress. Progress, but terrifying and suddenly exhaust-ing. I turned up the radio, drove faster, the wind stinging my driver's-side eye.

Mid-afternoon I passed through a small town, its houses run-down, with boarded windows and missing shingles, overgrown front lawns. A sudden wave of dizziness hit, and I made myself pull to the side of the road. I needed coffee, and maybe a protein-packed lunch to keep me going. Or what I really needed was amphetamines, but coffee and lunch would have to do. I rested my head on the steering wheel until the spinning began to settle, then started up the car again, driving through downtown.

Downtown was a bit of a misnomer, since the street seemed to be made up mostly of old homes with signs proclaiming them to be dentist and law offices. But on the corner was a tired café with a drooping striped awning. "How 'bout it?" I whispered to Molly, and pulled the car off the road.

Inside, the café was thick with tarry smoke. Generating that smoke was a woman sitting behind the register with a cigarette, watching Laurence Welk on a staticky TV. Her graying hair was tied in two braids, fastened with the bright pink bobble-bands never worn by anyone over six years old; she was one of those women who look like they may be seventy, but might just be forty and having a bad day or an unfortunate life.

She glanced at the door when I entered, then back to her show. "Take a seat wherever," she said, speaking around her cigarette. "Menu's on the table."

The thick, hot air clogged my throat; my brain suddenly felt like syrup. I set Molly's car seat carrier on the floor, then followed it without meaning to, sat down on the floor with a thump.

"Hell," the woman said, her voice weary. "You on drugs?"

"No." I swallowed back a wave of nausea.

She narrowed her eyes. "You sure look like you're on drugs."

"No, just . . . tired, sorry."

"You planning to eat off the floor?"

"No, I'm okay, I'm fine." I reached for a table leg and used it to pull myself up to my feet, and immediately felt the room resume its tilt-a-whirling. I sat at the table, closed my eyes in an attempt to steady the room, and then lifted Molly's carrier onto the seat beside me. The woman rose and pointed at the laminated menu tucked behind the napkin dispenser. "Soup today's clam chowder, but I wouldn't recommend it. Same with the meatloaf special because Lord knows what Manny puts in with the meat. Cherry pie's got fresh berries but the blueberry's made with canned. What you want to drink?"

"Coffee," I said. "And a turkey sandwich if you have it."

"Wouldn't recommend the turkey neither. You want a sandwich, try the chicken salad. Much better."

"Right," I said. "Chicken salad's fine." She went into the kitchen and I folded my arms on the table, rested my head on them and closed my eyes. Beside me, Molly had started to talk, a string of random consonants and vowels all spoken in a calm, lilting tone of voice. Without lifting my head from the table, I set my hand on her belly, absorbing the rise and fall of her chest as she breathed.

The chicken salad was remarkably good, made with walnuts and raisins and a vinaigrette rather than mayonnaise, sandwiched between slices of thick rye bread. And maybe it was the food in my belly or the bitter, grainy coffee, but by the time I was halfway done I felt rejuvenated. Not that I could drive more than another half hour before falling into a dead faint, but at least I was no longer tempted to drive off a cliff just for the chance to sleep.

I opened a jar of vegetable medley and began feeding Molly, talking to her in low tones. Taking a kind of silly pleasure each time she opened her mouth in preparation for the spoon, the fact that she was trusting me to provide for her.

"Are there any hotels around here?" I asked the waitress as she dropped off my folded check.

"Hotels? This ain't a tourist town, honey. Even the folks who live here don't want to visit."

"Or within twenty miles or so? I just need somewhere for the night."

She tilted her head, then nodded. "There's Muriel, up on Livingston Hill in Mill Creek. She's more of a B&B, gets folks who spend the night before river running. Don't know how she'd feel about the kid, but no harm in asking." She tore a page off her order pad, flipped it over and drew a little map. "Take the highway ten, fifteen miles and you'll see the turnoff for Livingston. Her house is on the left; you tell her I said hi and that I sent you, okay?"

"I will, thanks," I said. "Sounds perfect."

The B&B was near the top of a steep, windy road that had me worrying about deer and my transmission. It was a colonial style house, painted yellow with red shutters, a wheelbarrow on the lawn holding flowerpots, a stone rabbit and, weirdly, a hubcap on a stick. As well as a sign reading THE BUNNY HOUSE, which I raised my eyebrows at, then shrugged. The Bunny House it was. I knelt by the stone rabbit with Molly. "Bunny!" I said softly. "Look, it's a bunny rabbit." I guided her hand to touch the stone ears, nose, mouth, naming them each. And she patted the bunny with her fingers spread, like she was trying to console it.

At the front door I rang the bell, smiling widely at Molly, willing her to stay chipper and undisruptive, B&B-worthy. She complied by grabbing the ends of my hair, and sticking them in her mouth.

The woman who answered had large breasts drooping to her larger belly, making her profile seem oddly triangular. She peered out at me from under her wet-mop—colored bangs. "Yes?"

"Hi," I said, then stopped, suddenly too exhausted to go on. No energy to talk to someone new, form words, force an expression any more animated than catatonia. "Rooms," I said finally. "Do you have any? Or know where I could find one?"

The woman smiled then, and wiped her hands on her loose cotton skirt before holding one out to me. "Muriel Burns, pleased to meet you and yeah, I have rooms. Usually only book up on weekends."

I took her hand. Should I give my real name? Why hadn't I thought of this before? My brain was too paralyzed to think up anything on the spot. I opened my mouth, and out came something that sounded like *Laaayoahhh*.

"Leah?" she said. "Welcome."

Leah, a soap opera name, not a vixen like Alexis or Erika with a k, but the girl-next-door with dimples and a ready smile, who would probably work as a nurse before falling into a coma and then dying a tragic death. It would do.

Muriel stepped back and waved me into a small entryway with doors on each side, and a steep, carpeted staircase. The bunnies were everywhere: on the reception desk, knee-high statues guarding the door, in paintings and sketched on the faded wool rug. "So welcome!" She bent to smile at Molly. "You have teeth yet? Oh yeah, you do! Little Tic-Tac teeth." She smiled at me. "Your husband here?"

"Um, no." Exhausted again. Too exhausted to lie, so I left it at that.

Muriel shrugged. "Well then. Small room's ninety a night and the big room's one-ten, both including full breakfast. How long you staying?"

"I . . . don't know yet." I thought of packing up tomorrow morning and getting back on the road. The idea made me want to kill myself. "Probably just tonight, but could I let you know tomorrow?"

"Guess that'll work. Come on up and I'll show you the rooms." She started up the stairs and I followed behind with Molly, into a room papered in pale green with a four-poster bed, an armchair in one corner and sink in the other. "Here's the smaller room," Muriel said. "Bathroom's shared, out in the hall."

"It's perfect," I said. At that point a rat-infested subway tunnel would've seemed perfect, as long as it had a bed.

"I don't have a crib, though. You got something for her to sleep on?"

"She hasn't had any problem napping in her car seat carrier, so she'll be fine." So far Molly seemed like the un-fussiest baby on the planet. Was that a natural sunny predisposition, or something to worry about? Maybe it meant she was used to being ignored when she cried. Or that she was punished for it. It was something I couldn't stand to think about, not right now.

Muriel pulled a key out from her pocket and handed it to me. "Breakfast's at eight, restaurant menus for dinner are in the basket

by the front desk. You need anything, just ring the front bell, okay?"
She kissed her fingers and touched the top of Molly's head. "She reminds me of my Ashton, how she was years ago. Same wise eyes that
seem to notice everything." She smiled sadly, then held up her hand
to me and left.

I unstrapped Molly from her carrier and let her tour the room
while I sat hunched on the bed, elbows on my knees. "Can you believe this?" I asked her. "What're we doing?"

Molly gave me a quizzical look, then lifted the fringe from the
round Oriental rug and held it toward me as if she thought it might
suffice as an answer.

I pulled out a bottle and handed it to her, watched her suck hun-
grily at it. Could she tell I had no idea how to take care of a baby? If I
had her for more than a few days I'd have to buy books, study them to
make sure I wasn't screwing her up somehow. But now, now all I
wanted to do was sleep.

I fished my cell phone out of my purse and dialed. "Ma?" I said
when she answered.

"Is it you? Oh Lainey, you don't know how I've been worrying. I
wasn't going to do a reading but I couldn't help it, I've done ten of
them, I can't stop. And they're all so inconclusive, good and bad
both. I can't tell anything."

"Well I'm fine, Ma, you don't have to worry about me at all,
okay?" My voice broke and I swallowed, swallowed again. "Have you
watched the news today? Do you know if Sydney's okay?"

"I haven't turned on the TV. I can't stand to. I know my limits, but
if you want I can check tomorrow."

"No, don't. I'll get a paper or find an Internet connection somewhere. I'm in West Virginia now, at this bed-and-breakfast, and I'm
doing fine."

"And Molly?"

I watched Molly, who was taking a break from her bottle, clench-
ing it between her teeth and clapping at it with both hands. "Currently she appears to be celebrating," I said.

"You're doing a good thing, Lainey, don't you ever forget that. Turning your life upside down to keep her safe, that's a good thing."

I frowned, knowing the truth behind the bravado, that *she* was the one who'd sacrificed the most. "How are you?" I said.

"Oh I'm great. You know the shop you were painting for dropped off a gift basket filled with all kinds of organic goodies?"

"Seriously? I called from the road and told them I couldn't finish the job because I broke my wrist. You should really send it back, Ma. It was obtained under false pretenses."

"Yeah, but no. You ever try their pasta salad? It's mayonnaisey paradise, and it's staying with me. I'm so totally pampered with all this food, all these things to read, it's like a spa."

But it was all too easy to hear the truth. And suddenly the homesickness swelled like a water balloon in my chest. "I wish you were here," I said.

"No." Her voice was deep and clear. "Listen. Listen, no you don't, not really. I know how you're feeling, because for me it's like that every day, like life's this huge big ocean that could swallow me and no walls or floor to hold on to. So of course you want to grab hold of whatever you're used to grabbing, but the thing is, you're a hell of a lot stronger than me, and a hell of a lot stronger than you think. And you're the one going to do all the swallowing, remember that." She paused, gave a little cough, then said, "I mean, not of ocean water, that came out wrong, I was trying to be all poetic. You'll be swallowing life."

I nodded quickly, lips pressed between my teeth.

"This is so exciting, Lainey. I mean illegal, sure, but I feel stronger than I've felt in a long time because I know you're out there doing what you're supposed to be doing."

"Yeah." I wrapped my free arm around my waist and whispered, "I love you, Ma."

"I know. I love you too. And I'm proud as hell at how you're handling this."

After hanging up, I knelt beside Molly and pulled off her dress to check the burns on her back and smooth on another dose of

Neosporin. And seeing the angry red against her pale skin I felt, along with the recurrent surge of anger, a tremendous rush of love for her, and the urgency of doing whatever it took to keep her safe.

I pulled a stuffed caterpillar from her diaper bag and walked it up her arm and down her bare belly, her laughs heartbreaking, her squeals of pleasure like a punch to my gut. I made the caterpillar kiss her cheek, then kissed her cheek myself and carefully gathered her onto my lap.

When she finally squirmed away, I sat awhile watching her bend the caterpillar's legs, comforting myself with the sturdiness of her diapered bottom and the sureness of her grip. Really, Molly was the strongest one of us all.

I let her explore the room while I brought up the rest of our bags, changed her diaper and then strapped her back into her carrier, with a bottle and enough toys to keep her entertained till Christmas, willing her to let me sleep. And then, I fell back onto the bed without even taking off my shoes.

In the middle of the night, the terrors came. There in the drifty, muffled haze of semi-sleep I saw him, the hulking dark figure leaning over Molly in her carrier. His hand was reaching toward her and I tried to scream, tried to save her but I couldn't move. I was frozen in the dark with my eyes and mouth stretched wide, tears streaming down my face as I watched him light a cigar thick as his arm. *Molly-mollymollymolly;* she was looking up at me silently and pleading with terrified, tear-filled eyes, the man twiddling the cigar mockingly between his fingers, grinning at the sizzle as he brought it to her skin.

A scream.

I sat bolt upright in bed, staring out at the dark, listening to Molly's screaming and under that, the blaring of my phone. I stared frantically around the room, then batted at the bedside light, my chest tight with panic as I turned the light on and reached for Molly, then grappled in my purse for the phone. I flipped it open and said what was meant to be *hello,* but probably sounded more like I was constipated.

"Lainey, is that you?"

I sat back on the bed and squeezed my eyes shut. It was Sydney.

"Is that Jacqueline?" Sydney said. "Jacqueline!"

Nobody here. No man, no cigar, we were alone and safe. I forced my mind to focus. "She's fine," I said. "Dammit, Sydney, what happened yesterday? Why couldn't you come?"

"Why's she crying!"

"She just woke up. Believe me, considering her mother deserted her she's doing great."

"Where the hell are you, Lainey! How could you leave without telling me first?"

"Are you kidding me? You tell me you're in trouble, I'm thinking you might be hurt or dead and your husband might show up at our door any minute, so what did you expect me to do?" I wanted to yell at her, throw her my own set of how-could-you's complete with four-letter words that would probably scar Molly for life. But she sounded so upset, so completely overwhelmed, and I was too exhausted and terrified myself to find the edge of anger. I held Molly against my hip, rocking from foot to foot to stop her crying. "Are you okay?"

"I'm not even close to okay." Her breath hitched and then she said, "It's awful, Lainey, the way the cops're interrogating me and the way David's been looking at me, with this *intensity*. And he's having me followed. I've seen him everywhere since the last time I called you, this guy in a black-hooded sweatshirt. Which sounds like such a cliché, doesn't it? Next he'll be wearing a ski mask and holding an assault rifle."

I stared fixedly at the ruffled green window curtains. "Did he see you on the phone with me?"

"I was on a downtown pay phone and I didn't see him till after I dialed, hiding there in the shadows. That's why I'm calling in the middle of the night, because I doubt David's got more than one guy involved and they have to sleep sometime."

I looked down at Molly. She'd stopped crying but her face was covered in tears and snot, eyelashes stuck together in dark red points, like sun rays. "So what're we going to do now? Are you coming to get Jacqueline?"

"Well I can't right now, it's too dangerous. I think I'll have to wait until the story dies down a bit, and then I can tell everybody here that I need to get away. There'd be no reason for them not to believe me; I mean anybody would have to get away after all this. And then I can take Jacqueline from you and disappear somewhere they can't find me."

"Yeah, that sounds like a real well-thought-out plan."

"It'll work, okay? I have this friend, Kemper, who knows what David did to us, and he's been saying for a long while that he wants to protect us. He lives far enough away that nobody'd be able to recognize who we are, and I'm going to head out there with Jacqueline as soon as our pictures aren't splashed on every news station. So I guess in the long run it's good you left. You should find somewhere you can stay for a month or two until I can come get Jacqueline."

"A month or two!" I meant this to have a *How dare you?* tone rather than a *Yippee!* tone, but instead it came out somewhere in between.

"I know, I know, and I realize this is so impossibly unreasonable to ask. I hate myself for all of it, and if you say no, I'll completely understand. Do you have a better idea? I'll do whatever you want."

"Dammit, Sydney! How the hell do you expect me to trust you?"

"I'm sure you don't; of course you don't. I just need you to trust that I love my daughter."

I looked down at Molly, who had rested her head against my chest and was sleepily playing with one of my buttons. What was to stop me from just disappearing with her myself? Maybe it was Sydney who shouldn't be trusting me. "Look," I said. "I know you're doing this for her, and I guess we don't have much choice. But if it's going to be more than a few days I'll need you to wire me money, because all I have is two hundred bucks. It's all I could get from the bank."

"But I don't have any money! I know I promised you something, but don't you get it? I had to hire a criminal attorney, Lainey. Me! When he's the child abuser! So I had to take out a loan at a ridiculous interest rate since I'm apparently high risk, and now I have basically nothing. I'll have to sell everything nice I own at a freaking consignment shop."

"Oh poor Sydney! Without her Louis Vuitton!"

"Lainey . . ." She inhaled a rattling breath. "Okay. Okay just give me a day or two to scrape something together. But I can't wire it. If anybody ever found out I sent money from my bank to another one they'd get suspicious, so I'll FedEx cash. Where are you staying?"

"I'm in West Virginia, a bed-and-breakfast in this little town, Mill Creek. It's called the Bunny Inn, or the Rabbit Inn, or the Bunny Rabbit Inn; I don't know, you can find it online. And I'm not using my real name, so make the envelope out to 'Leah.'" Had I given Muriel a last name? I had absolutely no idea. "Just Leah," I said. "She'll know it's me."

"Okay. That's fine, I'll send as much as I can, as soon as I'm sure I'm not being followed by the black hoodie. Or the cops either; they're keeping an eye on me too."

"Do they suspect anything?"

"Well they always suspect the parents first so yeah, probably. Plus I'm not sure how well I did with the questioning yesterday, I was so exhausted I hardly even remember. They did show me the composite and I might've flinched when I saw it. I told them I didn't recognize you, but the drawing did look like you, or at least close enough that it startled me."

I felt a hot sweat of fear flush my face. "Crap," I whispered, then, "Did they notice you flinching?"

"I don't think so, at least they didn't question me about it. But then there's the note you left, which Sara Gristler showed to the police before she told me about it. Why'd you leave me a note?"

"What exactly did you expect me to do? I had to find a way to get in touch with you." Molly wriggled to get down, so I knelt to set her on the floor and watched her crawl toward the dresser. "What did the cops say about it?"

"Nothing yet, I mean they just got it this afternoon. It sounded kind of like a ransom note, which I guess might be a good thing. They'll know somebody else is involved."

I'm going to need money to keep her safe, I'd written. Of course it must've sounded like a ransom note, albeit one written by an eight-year-old.

"But it sounds like it came from somebody who expected me to know who they were, so I'm sure the police'll be asking me. And I've been thinking what I should answer."

This felt almost like a threat. Could she seriously be threatening me? "So what're you going to tell them?"

"Look. I'm not going to turn you in." Her voice broke off, and then in a hoarse whisper she said, "Not unless you give me a reason to."

I stared out the dark window across from me. "What the hell does that mean?"

"Just . . . that I'll do whatever I have to to save Jacqueline. You understand that, right? If I get implicated, I have to make sure I do whatever I can to keep out of jail, because I can't let David get custody." She let this hang in the air a moment, then said, "Oh crap, the operator. I have to go, I'm on a pay phone and my time's about to run out. I really care about you, Lainey; you're the best friend I ever had. I don't know how it all got so screwed up, and I don't know how I'll ever make this—" The phone cut out.

I stared at my cell phone, then slowly flipped it closed. Molly was pulling on a lamp cord, so I bent to pry it from her fingers and lifted her onto the bed.

If Sydney turned me in, how could I prove I hadn't kidnapped Molly? She'd tell them about high school, say I was out for revenge. Or say I'd talked nonstop about wanting my own baby, maybe even repeating my lies about Keith to make me seem unstable and desperate. Say that I'd shown an unnatural interest in Molly ever since we'd been reunited. And the incontrovertible truth was that *I* was the one who'd volunteered to take Molly in the first place.

Sydney against me and Star; her charmed self against our doomed selves, and I wouldn't have a chance. Me and Star in jail and Molly back with the man who'd burned her skin, and the fate of all of us was up to me.

"That was your mom," I whispered to Molly, and then I curled myself around her, both of us in the fetal position, and ran my thumb back and forth over her dimpled hand. Back and forth, back and forth, inhaling the scent of her sweat and tears.

I didn't sleep much the rest of the night. Molly was fussy, her sleep schedule probably disrupted as much as mine, and even as I tried to comfort her I found myself having mini panic attacks, my heart seizing rather than beating, squeezed by a huge fist. Everything's scarier in the middle of the night, because there's nothing to distract you from the truth.

I spent the early morning playing with Molly, helping her hammer wood into round holes, play the piano on a faded cloth keyboard. "This is the middle C," I told her, pressing the labeled key. "And this is D, and this is E." Molly watched me with her head tilted, as if she was considering everything I said. I could almost imagine her breaking out into the alphabet song.

The piano was from my own babyhood, found in a box Star had brought down from the attic before I'd left. Everything in the box had been meticulously rewrapped in its original plastic, labeled with little flags that documented ridiculously mundane facts she'd apparently considered important memories. *Dent on handle from L's new front teeth!* Or, *Torn ear found in L's diaper!*

On the piano she'd written, *R figured out the notes for H B-Day. For me!* I'd heard this story, how Star had come home on her birthday to find my father sitting in the entryway with me on his lap, as he guided my hand to play the notes. How proud we both had been. How he'd taught me to bow with one hand at my waist, the other extended behind me, as if I'd just performed a Prokofiev concerto.

And two months later, he was dead. Of a heart attack. He was thirty-two years old. When I tried to picture him now, all I could see were the photos we had of him, wearing my nose and blue eyes and a crooked grin, frozen in space and time and youth. But sometimes I thought I remembered the scent of him, the sweetness from the pipe he smoked, blowing bubbles with him on the front porch, being pushed on my trike, rubbing our noses in an Eskimo kiss. Things I'd held on to and replayed so many times that now I couldn't be sure whether I was remembering the actual events or just remembering my memories of them.

Maybe I could go to find his family, ask them for help. I didn't know much about them, only that he'd had a father and two sisters, that they were devout Baptists who lived somewhere in Mississippi. And that they'd tried to keep him from marrying Star, which of course Star had never forgiven them for.

I'd called my grandfather once, years ago. I was fifteen, it was soon after Star's sickness had started to progress, and I was already sensing what my life might turn out to be. I needed him, if only because he was a connection to the father I'd never gotten to know. I needed stories of my dad's childhood, wanted to know how much we'd had in common and how excited he'd been at my birth. And even more than that I'd wanted a sense of family, to know I wasn't alone with the burden my mother was becoming. With all her weight on me, I'd needed something sturdy to balance against.

My conversation with my grandfather had been terse. I believe he may have thought I'd called to ask for money. The silence, after I'd told him who I was, had made me so shy and awkward that I'd forgotten all the questions I'd been meaning to ask him, just told him flat out what was behind my call. "You're my family," I said. "All I have is my mother, and my Nana Sterling who's in a home and doesn't even remember my name. My mom's been having problems, and I'm all alone."

Still he'd been silent. Until finally he said, "Your mother put you up to this, didn't she."

"What?" I said. "No, of course not. She doesn't even know I'm calling."

"Look, I don't blame you. I know what kind of home you grew up in, and it's not really your fault. But my son should've had a completely different life, and I'll never forgive your mother for seducing him away from it. You calling here, it only brings back my own failure to protect him. I wish you wouldn't call again." And then, he'd hung up.

And so that was it. The beginning and end of our relationship. But maybe if I introduced Molly as his great-granddaughter, he'd change his mind. "Your son taught me 'Happy Birthday' on this piano!" I'd say. "And now I'm teaching my daughter. The legacy lives on!"

I ran my palm meditatively over the cloth keys, then in a fit of self-disgust I rolled up the piano and stuffed it into the bottom of my suitcase. No way in hell would I let myself be that desperate. I had Molly now, and for as long as this lasted she'd be the only family I needed. She was, in her own way, big enough to fill every single hole, every piece I'd imagined missing from my life. I could already feel myself falling in love with her, knew she could replace the grandfather who didn't want me, the father who'd left me, even the husband I might never have. Her complete need for me, and my complete love for her, could be enough.

I heard sounds from downstairs, clanking, a door closing. "It's almost time for breakfast," I told Molly. "You hungry?" I packed a bag with changes of clothes and towels, and brought it and Molly to the bathroom, where I was faced with the dilemma of how to bathe Molly and shower myself. Even simple things took so much thought and effort, the kinds of issues most mothers probably figured out in the first weeks of a baby's life and then adapted as the baby became more mobile.

In the end, I ran a bath rather than a shower, and sat her in my lap while I soaped us both with baby shampoo. The sores on her back all seemed to have crusted over, well on their way to healing, and I washed them carefully, taking comfort in the fact that I was at least doing something right.

There was something so primal in sitting there with her, both of us naked in the soapy water, skin slipping against skin. As if I'd just birthed her, the water around us like amniotic fluid. Both of us brand-new.

It was a beautiful morning, and Muriel arranged breakfast on the back patio, even bringing a faded plastic high chair for Molly. She set plates on the table: strawberries topped with granola, thick bacon and buttery toast and yes, a hard-boiled Easter egg, dyed pink with flower decals. After pouring my coffee she sat across from me with a hand at her back before saying, "Mind if I sit?"

I watched her warily. Was it safe to talk with her? What if she asked questions I couldn't answer? I needed her to have only a hazy memory of me after I was gone, but what could I do? "'Course not," I said. I opened a jar of mashed bananas for Molly, and fished in my bag for her spoon. "Listen, would it be okay if I stayed another night? I'm expecting this package, a FedEx, and I hope it's okay but I told them to send it here."

"No problem." She watched my face, maybe waiting for me to explain what would be so important I'd need it FedEx'ed while I was traveling, but when I didn't continue she just repeated, "No problem. No new reservations till Thursday and I'm glad to have you." She held her hand toward the baby food. "Here, let me. You eat."

I smiled and thanked her, handed her the jar and watched her feed Molly, the expert way she scooped and reinserted the mush that had escaped Molly's mouth, the way a handyman might spackle a hole. "So you said you have a daughter?" I said.

"A daughter and a son. I keep asking them to settle down and pro-create, but so far they've both failed me. Ashton called me one day and said she had a new baby she'd named after Peter, and I was about to die of a joyful heart attack when she laughed and told me that baby was a puppy. A dog!"

"Peter—"

"My husband. Coming up on ten years now since he died. It was his idea to open the Bunny House; he saw how the river runners would want someplace to stay, and just when we're ready to open our doors, *pffft!*" She sliced her hand across her neck. "Car accident. You might've noticed the hubcap out front? He loved that car. But now him and the car are gone, leaving me to wash other people's sheets and toilets. I mean don't feel bad about dirtying them, I'm happy to do it, but I have to say it wasn't the way I expected to spend my days."

"I'm so sorry," I said.

"About Peter? Nah, don't be. We had a good life together, despite the fact he left me working on what was essentially his dream." She smiled faintly and wiped Molly's bib over her mouth. "If you've tasted real happiness," she said, "even for a short time, then it's enough."

After breakfast I drove downtown with Molly, to see what they might have by way of shopping amusement. More diapers, food and for-mula for Molly, and a six-pack of underwear for myself, and then I stopped off at a used-book store to find a book on parenting. I picked up *What to Expect: the Toddler Years,* and then, *What to Expect in the First Year,* just to see what I'd missed.

It was a relief not to be on the road again, but I felt jumpy. Was this place as much of a safe haven as it felt? Or was I fooling myself? I was only about two hundred miles from home, so if the police tried to find me, how hard could it be? This felt like a calm before the storm thing, the lull before lightning blasted off my head.

After lunch at a pizzeria, we went to a corner playground where I watched a woman push her son on a baby swing. I lifted Molly to set her into a neighboring swing, pushed her gently and then a bit harder, watching her reaction. I'd thought she might be scared, but apparently she was an adrenaline junkie because her entire face lit up and she started to squeal.

The woman smiled at me. "How old?"

Should I talk to her? Or just pick Molly up and run? I squared my shoulders. *Calm down, calm down.* "She's twelve months," I said. "How about your son?"

"Fourteen, and he's just started running faster than I can. She walking yet?"

"No, but I think she's trying to. I balance her upright and she lunges one leg forward and then the other, so I guess that means she's working on it."

The woman raised her eyebrows. "Well, don't push it. Once she starts walking it's a whole different ball game."

"Oh I know, believe me," I said, smiling back and thinking, *I can't wait.*

After the woman left with her son, I sat with Molly in the sandbox, making cars out of rocks, fashioning roads and hills and twig telephone poles. I picked wildflowers and tucked them behind our ears, and as Molly smiled up at me I remembered what Muriel had said that morning, that just a taste of real happiness was enough. If I was arrested that night, taken into custody, it would've been worth it just for this one perfect moment, running a rock-car over Molly's knee and watching her beam up at me, like I'd just done something wondrous.

And then, on my way back to the bed-and-breakfast, I passed by a newspaper rack. I slipped in a quarter, pulled out the paper and opened it, dizzy with panic. Because there, on the front page, was Molly's face.

❊{ 7 }❊

TWELVE-MONTH-OLD BABY ABDUCTED
FROM VIRGINIA MALL

Police have issued an Amber Alert for a 12-month-old girl who has been missing since 5:30 P.M. Saturday. Authorities say Jacqueline McGrath was last seen inside Patrick Henry Mall in Newport News, Virginia. Because of her age, investigators are presuming the disappearance was a kidnapping.

The girl's mother, Sydney Beaumont, was window-shopping outside Macy's when her daughter disappeared. "I turned my back, for a second or two," Ms. Beaumont said, her face red with tears. "And when I looked back at the stroller she was gone! I didn't hear anything, she didn't make a sound, but somehow somebody must've took her and ran."

The search, which has included Newport News sheriff's deputies, the Virginia State Highway Patrol, local fire and rescue workers and over 100 volunteers, began Friday night and has continued throughout the past two days. The patrol has used its night-vision helicopter and

K9 unit, and are also interviewing registered sex offenders in the area.

FBI Field Officers are also following up on several leads they've received, including a note that was found yesterday morning at Sydney Beaumont's workplace, an occult shop in downtown Branchbury. Investigators did not release the contents of the note, but did indicate that it seemed "highly suspicious," and suggested that the girl may have been taken by someone who knew her. Ms. Beaumont was brought in for questioning following discovery of the note, and police appear to be investigating the leads she has given them.

Sheriff Andrew Davies added, "We're all very worried, obviously. Newport News may be a busy city, but we're also a very tight-knit community, and as you can see by the outpouring of support, there's a lot of concern for the well-being of this child. Our number one priority is to find her."

The missing girl is 30 inches tall, and weighs approximately 17 pounds. She has auburn hair and blue eyes, and was last seen wearing a pink shirt, purple shorts and white sneakers. Anyone with information should call the toll-free tip line at 800-555-4831.

I crushed the paper in my fist and stuffed it into a nearby trash can, hyperventilating. Swiveled right, then left. Was anybody watching? Would anyone who'd seen Molly—Muriel, the waitress at the restaurant, the mother at the playground—recognize her as the baby in the picture? They hadn't included the composite sketch of me, thank God, although maybe it was on TV or in Virginia papers. If my face had been shown side by side with Molly's, how hard would it be for any of the people who'd seen me to realize who we were?

I went back to the newspaper rack, paid another quarter, pulled out all the remaining papers and stuffed them into the trash as well.

Molly started to whimper, probably sensing I was about to lose it, so I knelt by her stroller. "We'll be fine, we're fine," I whispered, a chant, a plea, talking to her the way I talked to Star but thinking, *OH NO WE'RE DOOMED!*

Sydney had lied to me, told me she hadn't been questioned by the police about the note yet, but now the article said she'd given them leads? Why would she lie about it? Was it because she'd given them my name? What if when they'd shown her the composite she'd told them who I was? It wouldn't be long before all the pieces clicked together, my meeting with Sydney at Chelsea's Café, Jeffy Hauser seeing me with Molly on the deck, credit card records showing my trip to Babies "R" Us. The cops would come to our home, interrogate Star, who I knew would never hold up under that kind of pressure, and it all would be over.

I ran back to the car, my head spinning. Would Muriel let me use the phone at the inn? I had to call Star and find some way for her to hide—disregarding the fact that she'd be largely incapable of hiding anywhere farther than underneath her bed—but I didn't dare call on my cell phone for fear they'd trace the call. Although . . . I'd been on my cell yesterday! Were the police even now waiting outside the inn to arrest me? I strapped Molly into her car seat and started the engine, hands shaking so badly it took two tries. What I'd have to do was drive by the inn without stopping, and if I saw a police car I'd just turn the car around and run.

Molly started to cry in long quivering wails, and at some point I had started to cry as well, my breath coming in short stabs, my eyes blurred. I blinked quickly to clear them, racing through downtown, ignoring stop signs and lights and the use of turn signals. I'd just started up the hill with my foot on the gas when suddenly the car shuddered and made a hideous cranking sound. And then stopped. "No, no, no," I whispered, jamming the key back and forth in the ignition. "No!" In response, the car started rolling backward, down the hill. "No!"

I slammed the brake, then pulled the parking brake and popped the hood. Jumped out and stared at the mess of metal thingies and rubber thingies, as if whatever was broken might suddenly wave a flag labeled with repair instructions: *slide tab A into slot B.* I unscrewed the top of the oil tank, the only part of the engine that was remotely familiar, and touched the dipstick. Yes, the oil tank contained oil.

I kicked at the front tire. "You piece of crap!" Kicked it again and again until my toe began to scream, and then crumpled to the ground cradling my foot. "Dammit!" What the hell had I been thinking, trying to drive my hundred-forty-thousand-urban/suburban-mile-old car across the country? And what the hell was I supposed to do now?

An old gray Volvo pulled up beside me, and a man with dark hair and flushed cheeks leaned to unroll his passenger-side window. "You okay here?" he called.

"I'm fine," I said, as if I wasn't on the ground holding my foot, beside a broken-down car complete with screaming baby. "I'm fine," I said again, but seeing the kind, concerned look on his face, my eyes suddenly flooded with tears. "It's just my car."

"Right," the man said, and pulled his car behind mine. "Hold on, I'm just going to get your baby, is that okay? And then I'll take a look at the engine." He got out from the car and lifted Molly, smoothing a hand over her hair, and she arched her entire body back against his arm, like he was spotting her in some gymnastics move.

He unscrewed the cap to the oil tank, looked inside, then screwed it back. "I actually have no idea what I'm looking for," he said.

"It's dead," I said. "It gave this kind of . . . death rattle and then a nails-on-chalkboard sound and then it just stopped." What could I do? Just wait here praying the cops wouldn't show up before the car was fixed? And pay for that fix how, exactly? I should just say the hell with it all, release the parking brake and lie behind the back wheels.

"I'll find you a repair shop, okay?" He shuffled Molly against his hip and pulled out a cell phone, and I stared at it as he dialed information, then called the number they gave him. He had a phone, and I needed a phone. Him stopping to help was, perhaps, providence.

"They'll be here in ten minutes," he said after hanging up, then smiled down at Molly, who raised her hand to pull at his ear. "I'll just wait with you to make sure they find you, okay?"

I stood gingerly, testing my toe. "You're so nice," I said, "thank you." And then I made an apologetic face. "Do you think I could use your phone?"

"I can take you wherever you have to go."

"No that's not it, I just need to call somebody. Just for a minute, it's kind of an emergency."

Concern flooded his face again; his face was so very *expressive,* and I found myself wanting to hand off everything to this man I'd just met, the solid knot of worry that pushed against my gut, throw it all onto his shoulders. He seemed like he might understand. Instead I tried to smile reassuringly, thanking him as he handed me his phone, then said, "Would you mind . . . ?"

"Oh no, of course not." He turned away with Molly. "I'll just wait by the car."

My eyes on them I dialed home, hoping to God I was getting to Star before the cops had. "It's me," I whispered when she answered. "Are you alone?"

"What?" she said. She sounded fine. Mysteriously fine.

"Listen, I don't want you opening the door to anyone. I did something stupid, Ma. I left a note yesterday morning at Six of Swords, telling Sydney to call me, so now the cops must be sure she knows who the kidnapper is."

"Well I know, she called yesterday. She sounded really upset. I mean I was going to curse her out, use obscenities you're probably not even aware are in my vocabulary, but she broke down and started sobbing so I didn't have the heart."

"She was crying?" I thought about this. "Well she probably just wanted you feeling sorry for her so you wouldn't go to the cops."

I kept watching the man who was now talking in low tones to Molly, and forced myself to take slow, deep breaths. If the cops hadn't already come to question Star, did that mean they wouldn't? If Sydney had given them my name, if I was the lead mentioned in the paper, wouldn't they have come to our home right away? "Just," I said, "just if a cop happens to come to the door, or anybody really that you don't know, you call me before you answer, okay?"

Star was quiet a moment before she said, "Honestly, I've thought this through already. Because I don't think either of us fully trusts Sydney. I mean of course we don't, how could we? If she was in trouble, I doubt she'd hesitate to shift the blame off herself. But I do believe she's scared for her daughter, that she's doing the wrong thing but for the right reasons, which means she'd never let the investigators or David know where you are."

I nodded as if Star could see me, trying to believe this was true.

"But if she does end up giving them your name," Star said, "I'll tell them I don't have any idea where you've gone to, that you've just disappeared." She paused, then added, "Which'll implicate you, I guess, it would mean you'd really have to go into hiding before your face is splashed all over the news, but we'll cross that bridge if we come to it."

Fingers of fear were stretching across my chest, pressing against my ribs. But Star sounded like she was discussing a chance of rain rather than a chance of incarceration. Normally she freaked out when she heard the walls creak, so how could she possibly be so calm? "How can you possibly be so calm?" I said.

"Well I wasn't yesterday after you'd left, I'll admit that. But talking to Sydney . . . I had to calm her down, which I guess calmed me down. And I don't know if this'll help you, but I really believe the universe wouldn't punish us for doing the right thing. That's not how the world works."

I gazed at Molly, who was now plastering her hand over the man's mouth. That was exactly how the world worked, and Star knew it. The world tested you, and on the off chance you didn't fail, it turned things up a notch, as a lark. "You've started taking pills again, haven't you."

She sniffed. "I maybe took one. Or two. Don't you start reading me the riot act over two pills."

I gripped the phone tighter. How could I have left her alone in the house with a full bottle of pills? When she'd first begun having problems, the doctor had given her prescriptions for Lexapro and Valium. Which had helped her to function until they hadn't helped her, and she'd started taking more and more until her doctor had refused to prescribe them. She'd gone through two weeks of withdrawal, which she'd described as feeling like her bones had cracked into shards, stabbing through her skin and internal organs. After which she'd refused to take anything, even the SSRIs and benzodiazepines that might've helped. Until 9/11, when she'd fitfully sent me out for duct tape and plastic sheeting, and Xanax.

She was careful with it, taking the pills only when the fear was overwhelming. Which, of course, it would be now. "Just be careful, okay?" I said. "Two pills a day, tops."

"I'm not stupid, Lainey. My addiction-to-tranquilizers phobia is bigger than my other phobias."

"Okay," I said, "I'm trusting you." Because what choice did I have?

After hanging up, I thanked the man, starting toward him to hand back his phone, then winced at the pain in my toe. I leaned against the car to pry off my shoe.

"You okay?"

"Just my toe." I looked down at my bare foot, expecting a welt and swelling, but it was just unimpressively pink. "I forgot my car was an inanimate object, and kicked it."

"Ah yes, I've made the same mistake, although I usually swear at my car instead of using brute force. Equally ineffective, but less painful." He handed Molly to me, and nodded at the tow truck climbing the hill. "We'll wait for them to take the car and then I'll drive you home."

Drive you home, it sounded almost romantic, like the words *with me* were implied. "Thanks so much," I said, studying his face for the first time while trying to look like I was doing nothing of the sort. He was good looking. Very good looking, actually, with ruddy cheeks, short-cropped hair and clear green eyes. He could've been an Abercrombie & Fitch model, the kind of man I'd be afraid to even glance at, knowing he'd inevitably return a glassy I-wouldn't-let-you-lick-my-baseboards gaze.

But get this: I didn't stammer or blush, my mind didn't go blank and I didn't start hyperventilating. Not that I'd come up with an especially clever statement, but despite his cuteness, my brain had managed to formulate a perfectly acceptable expression of gratitude. And of this, I was inordinately proud.

I sat in the Volvo, Molly in my lap, as the man drove me up the hill toward the inn. "So we should probably introduce ourselves," he said, "seeing as how I saved you and then . . . saw your dirty sock. It all confers a certain amount of intimacy."

Heat rose to my face. "Well thanks for making me feel completely awkward."

The man smiled. "I'm Alex."

In my lap, Molly swiveled her head to him, to me and then back again, as if trying to interpret our conversation. I double-checked myself before answering, "I'm Leah. And this is Molly."

"Nice to meet you both." He gestured to the glove compartment. "There's aspirin there, if you want it. Take the whole bottle, okay? You might need it later."

"Appreciate it." I pulled out the bottle. It was dirty, the label ragged. "Looks like it's seen the ravages of war," I said, popping two into my mouth.

"Guess it's been there awhile. Does anybody ever use the aspirin they keep in their car?"

We were approaching the inn and I gestured at it. "Thanks so much," I said, as he pulled into the gravel driveway.

"My pleasure. This was an easy, incommensurably rewarding Good Samaritan experience."

I tried to force a laugh, but—maybe it was something about his smile, or the thought of going back into my empty bedroom where I knew the fear would hit again with a vengeance, or the conversation I'd just had with Star, or the relief of knowing Sydney probably hadn't given the cops my name, or the pain in my toe or everything together—all at once I felt my eyes fill.

"Leah?" he said.

"It's nothing, sorry it's nothing." I was about to pull the door handle when he set a hand on my shoulder, which had the curious effect of dislodging something that had been sitting just under my ribs. I made a sobbing sound. "Sorry," I said, huddling over the baby. "I'm sorry!"

"Leah!" He wrapped an arm awkwardly around me. "What is it? What's wrong?"

"It's nothing!" I repeated, but I let him hold me, half-mortified but the other half, the half indisputably in charge, just needing to be held.

He didn't speak, just rubbed at my back, his chin resting on my head. And I huddled against the warmth of his shoulder, not letting myself think.

I stayed there with my face buried against him until Molly—probably feeling squashed between us—wailed her fist at my arm. And realizing that here I was, bawling in the arms of a stranger, the mortification returned. I pulled away and swiped a sleeve over my eyes and cheeks. "I'm sorry, I don't know where that came from. I'm just not sleeping much and it's been a hell of a week." I pulled open the door and got out. "Thanks again, Alex, really so much."

But he'd already slipped out of the car to pull the stroller and diaper bag from the backseat. He closed the door with his hip and squeezed my elbow. "Just want to make sure you get in okay," he said, escorting me to the door.

Muriel was in the front sitting room, working on a needlepoint. She jumped up when she saw me. "Leah, what happened!"

"Nothing," I said. "Just my car broke down and I'm overreacting. I told the repair guy to call here when he knows what's wrong, so could you let me know when he does?"

"Were you crying? Your face, it looks like a pomegranate."

"I think she just needs to rest," Alex said. "But if it's okay, d'you think you or somebody here could check on her later? Just to make sure?"

"That's crazy, really I'm fine." I grabbed the diaper bag off his shoulder and then squeezed his arm in thanks. "Bye, Alex. So nice meeting you!" I raised my hand in what I hoped would pass for a cheery wave, and carried Molly upstairs.

In the bedroom I sank onto the bed with Molly, listening to Alex downstairs talking to Muriel. Wondering if they were talking about me. I couldn't let myself fall apart like this ever again. It put everything at risk because if Alex ever read the story about Molly, how long would it take for him to see the resemblance? Breaking down in his arms like that would probably be all the proof he'd need to go to the cops.

A repairman called later that afternoon, and told me it looked like there was water in my engine. He said they'd try and use a drying agent (I pictured a towel), and assuming the engine hadn't been damaged, the car should be ready by tomorrow.

I didn't ask him how much it would cost. Hopefully by tomorrow Sydney's FedEx would have come, and it wouldn't be an issue.

After hanging up, I pulled one of the baby books I'd bought out from the diaper bag. While Molly played on the floor beside me I began reading it aloud, cheered by the sound of her chattering, her attempt to keep up her end of the conversation.

There were things here I'd never even thought about: the perils of honey, the necessity of brushing her tiny teeth, the recommendation to introduce new foods slowly so I could check for allergies. But most important her development seemed to be okay, perhaps a tad behind schedule, but not abnormal. Soon she'd be pulling herself to her feet, then walking, talking and then potty training. I imagined it, the two of us swinging hands and chatting as we walked to a park or to nursery school.

But two years from now, assuming Sydney's plan worked, *she'd* be the one holding Molly's hand. I pictured myself back home reading this book month after month, learning the milestones that Molly was passing. I didn't know how I could handle not being there for all of them.

. . .

Molly's favorite activity seemed to be scanning the carpet for lint balls or pillow fluff, and cramming them into her mouth in an attempt to choke on them. Then, "Kaaack?" she'd say, looking dismayed. "Kaaack!" After which I'd scrape them off her tongue, and she'd be off to find more. I'd just saved her from swallowing what appeared to be the remnants of a spiderweb-wrapped bug, when I heard a stilted knock on the door. "Come in!" I said, expecting Muriel, but when the door opened it was Alex, holding a pizza box.

"I hope you don't mind," he said, "and I know I'm being presumptuous, but seeing as how your toe's probably in no shape to go out, I thought maybe you could use dinner." He held up a bottle of red wine. "And alcohol."

"Alex!" I hurriedly tossed a dirty pair of panties under the bed, feeling a flush of pleasure. "What're you doing here? Don't you have somewhere better to be?"

"Actually, no. I mean I was supposed to be in Cincinnati by now, but by the time I got done helping you and then talking to Muriel, I was tired enough to realize I'd probably be a danger on the road. So when Muriel told me she had a free room, I decided to take it. Mind if I sit?"

I shook my head, trying to reconcile the presence of this man in my room with my preconceived notions of how men usually acted. Sure, he was just concerned after I'd imploded in his arms, but still, I couldn't help feeling flattered.

He set the pizza box on the floor and sat down next to it, then fished into his pocket, pulled out a bottle of Advil and threw it to me. "Bought these too, because I thought you could use a painkiller that's not expired."

"Wow, thanks. Although actually I'm hardly hurting at all now." Which was true; since he'd entered the room I'd completely forgotten I was supposed to be in pain.

Molly crawled toward the pizza box and waved her hands at it, then slapped it with both palms. "Molly!" I sat across from Alex and lifted her onto my lap. "Well *you* get the squashed pieces," I said, then turned to Alex. "So I didn't realize you're from Cincinnati. I assumed you lived around here."

"Oh no, I'm not from here or Cincinnati, just passing through on my way up to New Hampshire. You saved me from a night at a Super 8 motel, so thank God I ran into you."

I felt a flush of pleasure and bent to open the pizza box to keep him from seeing it. "Ooh, vegetables," I said. "I haven't seen a vegetable in days, other than macerated peas."

"Yeah, pepper and mushroom pizza on the floor is just so classy. Feels like college with wine instead of illegal beer, and without the scratchy paper towels from the dorm men's room." He leaned back to look at me. "So. How about you? Where are you from?"

I thought fast. I couldn't tell him I was from Virginia, I knew that. If he'd heard about the kidnapping, there was a chance he'd put two and two together. So here's where the trajectory of that fast thinking led: from me, Leah the soap opera nurse, to the TV show *ER*. "I live in Chicago," I said. "The heart of the city."

He raised his eyebrows. "Well that's the most southern Chicago accent I've ever heard."

Oh crap. Damn Tidewater drawl, the dropped r's and long ah's and ay's. "Well I'm originally from Atlanta, just moved up to Chicago a couple years ago."

"A Georgia peach. That's probably what I would've guessed." He bit into his pizza and chewed, pausing as if deliberately choosing his next words. "So what brought you out to West Virginia?"

A beat of panic, then, "I was on my way to . . . Kansas?" I stared at my slice. It sounded so stupid, said aloud. Who the hell ever headed to Kansas? And what kind of dumbass would head to Kansas from Chicago by way of West Virginia?

But Alex just said, "Oh yeah? What's in Kansas?"

"Just family." I smiled quickly. "My uncle. Uncle Henry." Yes, my Uncle Henry and Auntie Em, Cousin Dorothy and Toto too. "He has a farm."

Alex raised his eyebrows, studying my face. I'd had no idea I was such a staggeringly sucky liar. I ducked my head and said, "So how 'bout you? You said you're from New Hampshire?"

"Yeah, the country. I mean *real* country like here except ten times more so, this hick town called Mendham in the White Mountains."

"Never would've pegged you as a hick. Is it romantic being out in the middle of nowhere or just boring?"

"I really like it, actually; it gives me time to think. I just came from Miami, and the whole time I was there I was thinking, Why the heck would people choose to live here? The traffic, the obnoxiousness of just about everybody I met, and the flatness. I mean even the water's flat."

"Yeah, wouldn't be my first choice of a vacation spot. The only people who want to be in Miami are in retirement communities or from Cuba."

"I know." He shrugged. "I was down there for my grandmother's funeral."

"Oh wow, I'm sorry."

"No, don't be sorry. I mean her time had definitely come and gone. She was in a nursing home for ten years, couldn't do much of anything except drool and grow a mustache." He made a face. "I sound like a jerk, I know, but she wasn't the nicest lady even when her mind was working right, and she only got worse when it stopped."

I smiled. "And now she's spinning in her grave."

He rolled his eyes to the ceiling. "Don't you get too dizzy."

"You're cruel, aren't you. I never would've guessed."

"I wouldn't say I'm cruel, I'm just not sentimental about things that don't deserve sentiment." He reached for another slice of pizza. "Anyway, I'm not even a hundred percent sure how I ended up here. I got into Richmond and suddenly I decided to be impulsive and swing west. Because I'd never been to West Virginia, and I'd been getting Gauley River rafting brochures in the mail for years, so I decided why not?" He smiled at Molly. " 'Course the reason why not turned out to be the water levels, they're so low now that the only

trips are for people a lot more experienced than me. So I was heading back north when I ran into you. This morning I was pissed at
driving all this way for nothing, but turned out it gave me a chance to
meet the two of you, and you're the best part of my trip so far. Which
I guess isn't saying much, but still." He plucked a stray pepper from
the pizza box. "And now you're supposed to say, *Same here.*"

I smiled. "Same here," I said, "totally."

We spent the rest of the evening playing with Molly. Alex seemed to
find deep delight in her quirks: the way she industriously studied
every item she came across, then held it up to us with a questioning
look as if expecting us to explain whatever she'd discovered; the way
she alternated between pensive and deliriously happy, waving her
arms squidlike for seemingly incomprehensible reasons.

"You can already tell so much about her personality," he said.

"I know. I keep wondering how in a year she could've become
such a complete, distinctive person. I already have a sense how cool
she'll be when she grows up, quick to laugh, she'll be able to let hard-
ships just roll off her back."

"And curious about everything and wanting to share what she discovers."

"She'll be a scientist," I said.

"Or a clergyman."

"Forget the clergy, I think she may be the second coming."

He tilted his head, smiling. "Then I guess we better get on her
good side."

It was almost nine when Molly finally fell asleep, and although I'd
expected Alex to make a quick exit, instead he stayed well into the
night, the two of us chatting, but not in the cocktail party way one
chats with people one doesn't know, those surface conversations
about how pleased or displeased one is about the weather. Instead
our conversation was much more intimate—in part, maybe, because

of the inescapable intimacy that comes when someone has seen you cry. But also because I wanted to give Alex as few details of my personal life as possible, anything that might allow him to later identify me definitively to the police. So that night felt like a strange mix of deep truths and evasions, discussing our philosophies of life without actually discussing our lives.

And the conversation was fascinating because *Alex* was fascinating, saw the world completely different than I was used to, with a contagious sort of optimism and faith in mankind. And although optimism and faith were not part of my everyday lexicon, talking with him made me feel, for the first time maybe ever, *hopeful.*

But there were also times, prompted by nothing that I could perceive, when his face would darken for just a beat before he became himself again. I found myself trying to interpret the reasons behind these pauses, studying the conversation leading up to them, actually finding myself pleased to see them, since one-dimensional cheer is both grating and semi-insane. The darkness made me want to know more about who he was.

It was almost midnight when Alex suddenly jumped up from his seat. "I've been awful keeping you awake! I was planning to just share the pizza and then scoot out to let you get some sleep."

"I'm glad you didn't. I'm not tired at all."

"You want some Ambien? I'm an insomniac; I get these awful nightmares and it's like my body tries to protect me from them by keeping me awake, but the Ambien works wonders."

"You're like my personal pharmacy," I said, "but no, thanks, as soon as I said I wasn't tired, I realized I was lying."

He set a hand on Molly's head. "I'll see you at breakfast tomorrow, then. This was great, Leah, it's been awhile since I met someone I clicked so well with, who could carry on intelligent conversation."

I smiled, my mind racing to find something wittily self-deprecating to say but coming up only with, "Yeah, I know what you mean."

After he'd left I lay there in bed, feeling both little and huge, the air in the room seeming changed, full somehow, like he'd left something of himself behind. And for the first time since seeing Sydney on TV three nights ago, I didn't feel afraid.

I thought I'd have a hard time sleeping, that I might spend the night replaying every aspect of our conversation, too late conjuring cleverer responses and/or cringing at my lameness. This had always been my tendency. But one minute I was lying there in bed and the next I was waking up with a full bladder and sludgy teeth, the sky magenta with the rising sun.

I rose stiffly and knelt by Molly's carrier. "Good morning!" I sang softly. "Good morning!"

Without opening her eyes, Molly brought both fists to her face and rubbed fitfully at her cheeks like she was brushing away flies, which made me laugh. I didn't know why I felt so happy, I had no right to be, and the feeling was so unfamiliar I couldn't tell if it was real or just a hallucinatory side effect of sleep deprivation.

Molly and I took our bath and then went back to the bedroom to play, waiting for sounds in the rest of the house. I kept up a constant stream of chatter as we worked a wooden puzzle, telling her about the animals on the pieces, the sounds they made, the food they liked to eat. And she listened with her head tilted, periodically interjecting a string of consonants that sounded like words in Greek or Arabic.

The *Toddler Years* book had said she understood much more than it seemed, and so I imagined we were having an actual conversation. She told me how pigs were her favorite, and I told her I agreed. She asked if I'd ever owned a dog and I told her how I'd always wanted one, had been angry at Star's fear of claws and fleas. "Maybe we'll get one someday," I mused, imagining how it would be to bring one home for Christmas, the delight on Molly's face.

But of course by Christmas, home for me would be back in Virginia. Or, in jail.

A little before eight A.M. the air started to fill with the salt-smoke of bacon, and sitting on the bed with Molly, my mind swam with vague memories of the mornings before Star got sick, when she could still stomach the idea of lighting a gas stove. I'd wake before school to the sizzle of eggs or griddle cakes, Star greeting me in her cheap, flowered apron with a mug of cocoa complete with whipped cream, singing while she jiggled a pan on the stove. *So embarrassing!* I'd told her then, which of course I now hated myself for.

But even back then she'd begun documenting tragedies and atrocities. "It's a sign!" she said of everything: warring tribes in Africa and plagues in Southeast Asia, drive-by shootings and children stolen from front lawns. Hairline cracks that showed the world was on the verge of shattering completely, and she clipped out the articles and saved them in scrapbooks, like women store mementos from their children's lost youth, things not to be forgotten. She pored over them incessantly, guarding us against them by watching the news and filling our closets with disinfecting wipes.

Until, when I was fifteen, it all became too much. I don't know if it was the sheer volume of catastrophes or one mysterious, unspecified catastrophe in particular, but it was as if she all at once seemed to collapse inwardly, her world shrinking to the size of our block, and then the size of our house. "What is it?" I asked her again and again. "What happened? What's going on?" But the questioning just made her cry, so soon I stopped asking. Maybe she'd always been this way deep down. Had held onto the pretense of sanity as long as possible, the way people hold onto intolerable marriages until their children are old enough to handle the end.

I smiled sadly at Molly who was sampling the ear of a stuffed beagle, then kissed the top of her head. "I think it's time for breakfast," I said.

I opened the door, and at the precise moment I entered the hallway, Molly in one arm and the diaper bag in the other, the door across the hall opened and Alex stepped out from his room.

"Oh!" we both said at once, and then he smiled at me. "Well, good morning. How's your toe doing, you still in pain?"

"Morning," I said. "No, it hardly hurts."

He reached to trace a finger round the shell of Molly's ear, which, perplexingly, made my own ear tingle. And I felt all at once shy, remembering our conversation from last night. The intimacy had come too fast, like sleeping with a man on the first date; we'd crossed some threshold and I felt like we were now tumbling down the other side.

But then he said, "So you going down for breakfast?" and the awkwardness was immediately smoothed away.

Because there was something captivating about him, a depth to his eyes, a kindness, so that where normally I'd have been fumbling for a response—Was I going down for breakfast? Was I?—now I found myself feeling again completely at ease. I leaned forward to speak under my breath. "Yeah, just get ready. Yesterday she served an Easter egg."

"Easter egg, bunny, I get it." He smiled. "What is it about older single women needing to collect things? If it's not cats or bunnies then it's knitting, or Hummel."

"And single men get cars. Although women collect as a replacement for kids, whereas with men I think it's all about penises." And then I felt my face flush. This was *too* much at ease. Had I really just said the word "penis"?

But Alex just nodded in mock-solemnity. "Everything's always about penises," he said.

I gave a short, barking laugh.

"But regardless, Muriel seems really nice."

"Oh she is!" I said. "Try not to hold the bunny thing against her."

Muriel had set breakfast out on the patio again, one table for the four of us. It was a repeat of yesterday's breakfast, except that the Easter eggs were blue and the toast, thick peasant bread, had been cut in the shape of a rabbit head, which Alex lifted, smiling. "Clever!" he said to Muriel, then grinned at me. I bit my tongue.

"So is this your last day with us?" Muriel asked me.

"Probably. My car's supposed to be ready by ten, and I should be getting that FedEx this morning."

"Well feel free to stay as long as you like. I'm not expecting a full house, and I like the company." She turned to Alex. "You too, sweetie."

"Thanks," he said. "I like it here, kind of reminds me of home with the benefit of not having to make my own bed."

I poured Cheerios onto Molly's tray, only half-listening as Muriel and Alex started to talk about the art of running a bed-and-breakfast. It was another gorgeous day, the sky a deeper blue than it ever got in coastal Virginia. The garden smelled of honeysuckle and green, and pansies and lavender lined the back path like paint splashes. Molly's hair gleamed a rich, burnished chestnut in the sunlight, and I twisted a lock of my own hair in front of my face, to see if it would do the same.

"Leah?" Alex said. "Hello, you there?"

"Sorry." I dropped my hair. "Sorry, did you say something?"

"I just was asking if you want me to bring you to the repair shop this morning." He checked his watch. "I was going to take a quick walk downtown, you can join me if you want, and then I can drive you."

"Thanks, that sounds awesome," I said, then clamped my jaw shut. *Awesome*? Seriously, Lainey?

Molly mercifully distracted us by calling, "Ah!" and holding her drool-covered fist out to Alex. "Um, sweetie?" I said. "He doesn't want your mushy Cheerio."

But Alex opened his mouth and let her deposit said Cheerio inside. "Well that's just gross," I said. Thinking, *He is cool.*

As we were getting up to leave the table, Muriel pulled me aside and leaned toward my ear. "So I noticed there's no wedding ring," she whispered. "Have fun!" Smiling like she'd just handed me a gift.

The three of us strolled the downtown streets, peeking in shopwindows. I was experimenting with the baby sling I'd bought. I'd always assumed slings were used solely for cradling broken limbs or pelting rocks, and it looked incredibly unsafe to me, like Molly was continually on the verge of tumbling headfirst onto the ground. But the salesgirl had assured me it was the most ergonomic carrying option, and after the first few minutes getting used to the position, I loved it. It felt so natural, the way the fabric swaddled us both, being able to look into her face while she gazed up at me, how she curled against me in almost the same position she would have if she were inside me. I gave her my index finger as we walked and she held it loosely, her gaze dreamy and distant.

At one point I caught a glimpse of my reflection in a store window, bright-eyed, mid-laugh. Something about the angle of the sun off the glass acted like a fun house mirror, squaring my heart-shaped face and adding an exotic olive tinge to my usually flushed cheeks. And there, for the first time, I saw my father. Saw one particular photo of him, actually; he'd been at a party talking to someone off-camera, lips in a half-O, half-smile. And here he was in the window, his brown hair with the C-shaped curl where his bangs were parted, his same almond-shaped eyes, same look of a person who was intense and yet easily amused out of that intensity. I had to stop myself from drifting closer to the window. I was mesmerized, as if the reflection might have something to tell me.

What would my father say if he could see me? Would he feel moral outrage? Star's terror? Or just paternal concern for my well-being? I didn't know him well enough to even guess.

As we passed the newspaper rack, I quickly knelt in front of it as I dropped in a quarter, to obscure Alex's view. I pulled out a paper, scanning the headlines. There were no stories about Molly on the front page, which I thought must be a good sign. Relieved, I stuffed the paper in the diaper bag for later.

Walking beside Alex, I wondered at how comfortable I felt. He seemed so laid back, so easygoing, and yes that was part of it. But also I felt like I wasn't myself. I was Leah, soap opera girl with the perfect daughter and the shiny chestnut hair, and a normal past, a history of everyday adventures. And this new and improved me seemed to be comfortable with silence. We didn't talk much as we walked, only exclaiming every once in a while over a bird or knick-knacks in store windows. Maybe this was what married life was like, no worry that your husband might find you boring, no need to entertain; you just enjoyed each other's presence and the sharing of something wonderful. Knowing it was wonderful mostly because you were sharing it—like the difference between painting pictures only I would see, and the murals I truly appreciated only after someone else had cooed over them, making me step back and look through their eyes.

At ten I called the repair shop, and was almost sorry when they told me the car was ready. Alex drove me there, and stood with me at the scarred laminate counter where a mechanic explained the repairs in a language I didn't even try to interpret, then handed me a bill. I stared at it, then at the mechanic, and then back at the bill. Two hundred twenty dollars for both the tow and the repair, which, while nowhere near as bad as it might've been, was also not as close to free as I had hoped. And was about a hundred dollars more than was currently in my wallet.

"Um," I said, "any chance I could pay you later today or tomorrow? I . . . don't have a credit card." I gave a shy smile that I hoped would suggest honesty rather than indigence. "And I'm expecting money in the mail."

The mechanic gave me a look of incredulity, and then hooted a Santa-ish noise as his answer, "Whoa-ho-ho!" followed by an awkward silence. Which Alex broke by saying, "I'll spot you the money, no problem."

I sputtered a protest because it would've been disgustingly gauche not to protest. But in the end I accepted, because what else could I do?

"Don't worry about it," he said. "This is my second Good Samaritan act in two days, which'll hopefully counteract a recent glut of sins, at least in my own mind."

Muriel wasn't at the inn when we returned, but she'd set a FedEx envelope outside my door. It was thicker than I'd expected, bulging in the middle, and I imagined a fat stack of bills tied with a rubber band. I ran a finger across the seal almost mournfully. The envelope meant I'd be leaving, moving on to the next phase in my journey. And I didn't want the next phase. I was a homebody and this place already felt almost like a new and inordinately better version of home.

"My money's in here," I told Alex, "so I can pay you back. And then I guess I'll get packed. I want to make some headway before it gets dark."

"Right," Alex said, unmistakable regret in his tone that both pleased and devastated me. Alex was probably one of the smartest people I'd ever spent time with, open-minded and insightful, able to talk intelligently about every subject I threw at him. Where were men like this back in Virginia? Other than Keith, I'd never dated a man more than two weeks. Not that I'd had many opportunities; I knew I was lacking in that indefinable quality one called *sexiness,* not the sort of woman to catch a man's eye. And since I'd never had the guts to even attempt flirting or date-services, most of my dates had been setups, from Pamela and Craig or people I'd befriended in town.

There always seemed to be something missing in these men. Or maybe it was just that by the time they'd reached their thirties they'd already lived full lives that had nothing to do with me, a history of serious relationships and broken marriages, after which I was necessarily less important because I hadn't been the *first.* Keith had made me feel like I was the center of his world. More because of his personality than anything I'd done to warrant that kind of love, but it had reassured me that he'd never purposely cause me pain. And when the men I dated now didn't show me that adoration, I got scared. Something inside of me closed up. But wasn't the truth that I was just looking for a sign that they wouldn't betray me in the end?

And now here was Alex, who had this aura about him of utter trustworthiness. So why did I only meet him now when I was in hiding, pretending to be someone else?

"I want to give you my e-mail before you go," he said, "and my number, because I'm hoping you'll keep in touch."

"Definitely," I said. Although of course it was a lie. "I'll definitely keep in touch."

He stood a minute without speaking, looking into my face, and I felt myself blush. "What?" I said.

"Sorry. Sorry, I was just thinking how great it is talking to you. And how I wish you didn't live all the way out in Chicago."

I felt something lodge in my chest, something red-hot and molten, threatening to explode. "Thanks," I said. "And me too. I was thinking the exact same thing."

In the bedroom, I sat on the bed to open the envelope. Inside was a short note and a cloth teething ring with a teddy bear head as its handle. And thirty dollars.

I stared at the money, flipped it over as if it might be hiding more money on the other side, then peered inside the empty envelope. Nothing. I opened the note.

> *L—*
>
> *I'm so sorry I couldn't send more. Turns out I hadn't stashed away as much as I'd hoped. But what I'm going to do now is start taking little extra bits out of the bank every day or two. Not a lot, since I don't want anybody noticing, but I should have a fair amount for you in the next week or so. I hope the thirty dollars at least helps a little.*
>
> *Thanks for understanding. I'll call soon to find out how you're doing and where you're at. Please give Jacqueline a hug, and tell her the teething ring's from me. And that I love her and I'll see her soon.*
>
> *—S*

I crumpled the note in my fist. Damn Sydney. Damn her! What was wrong with her? What was she thinking? Didn't she realize that without money I couldn't buy Molly food or diapers? That we'd be forced to camp out in my car or at some fleabag motel? But no, she must realize I'd find some way to make this work. Get money from

Star. Or rob a bank. Why should she sacrifice when I could do all the sacrificing for her?

I sat on the bed with Molly, let her clamber over me and the pillows, playing with the buttons on the duvet. I reached for one of her socked feet and cupped it in my palm. "If she's leaving us to fend for ourselves," I said, "then what's to stop us from actually driving to Kansas? Or someplace even more exotic, like California. Why not? I could take you to Disney, you'd like that. You think the swings're fun, wait'll you try the flying teacups." Molly pulled her foot away, and I clenched my fists between my knees.

Maybe I could get us both fake social security numbers; didn't people do that all the time? I could become Leah officially, and Molly could become Molly. Screw you, Sydney; your daughter is no longer your daughter. You gave her to me, so now she's mine.

Oh it was crazy; all of this was insane. But that didn't change the fact that I'd need more money. I'd have to ask Star to write Pamela a check that she could wire to one of the banks here. I pulled out my phone, and called home.

As soon as Star answered, I could tell something was wrong; her voice was tight and pitched too high. "You okay?" I said, not looking for an answer really, just trying to show I knew that she wasn't. "I'm going to have Pamela come by, okay? Check up on you, drop off anything you need, and I'm going to need you to help her wire me some money."

"Lainey—" Her voice caught and she made a choking sound then said, "Does Sydney know where you are?"

"Yeah, I told her. Why?"

"Lainey, we have to hang up. The phone might be bugged."

"What?"

"Get out of there! Get out now, don't stay another night."

"C'mon, Ma."

"Just run! I'm hanging up!" She hung up.

I stared at the phone, then quickly dialed again. She didn't answer, and after ten rings I dialed again. No answer.

I slapped the phone shut. What the hell was going on? Did Star think Sydney had given the cops my name?

I reached into the diaper bag and pulled out the paper I'd bought, flipping through the first pages. There was nothing in the front section, but there on the front page of the Nation/World section was a photograph of Sydney, standing on the steps of the police station.

NEW QUESTIONS SURROUNDING
McGRATH GIRL ABDUCTION

Sydney Beaumont, mother of missing twelve-month-old Jacqueline McGrath, was brought back for questioning yesterday following a review of surveillance tapes in the Patrick Henry Mall, where Ms. Beaumont originally alleged the baby was stolen from her stroller. Tapes showed Beaumont entering the mall with an empty stroller, wheeling it out in front of Macy's department store and then running to alert shoppers that her baby had disappeared.

Federal Agent Stuart Marks indicated yesterday that when confronted with the evidence, Ms. Beaumont admitted that she had been lying about the abduction because she was afraid of retribution from the person she believes is actually responsible.

Though Marks did not release the identity of the suspect, he indicated that Beaumont's new disclosures were tangible and believable, and that an arrest warrant is imminent.

A sound came from the back of my throat, guttural and inhuman. I jumped up to stuff the paper into the trash. "We have to leave, Molly. We can't stay here, okay? Star was right, we have to go."

I threw toys frantically into the diaper bag, then crammed our clothes into my suitcases. And then I scribbled two notes of apology, to Muriel and to Alex. Alex had given me a hundred dollars and with tax, I knew I owed Muriel over two hundred. But all I had now was Sydney's thirty dollars, and I couldn't leave it for them, not with a baby. So I left them my watch and a pair of gold hoop earrings, promising I'd send the rest plus interest as soon as I got settled. *This is for Molly,* I kept telling myself. *Yes, it's horrible, illegal, but not immoral. You're doing what you have to do for her.*

I left the notes and the jewelry on a pillow, strapped Molly into her carrier and, my chest tight, carried the suitcases to the car, then went back for Molly.

And met Alex in the hallway.

He studied my face, his brow furrowed. "Leah? You okay?"

I backed toward my room. More than anything I wanted to tell him the truth before he learned about me on the news, make him realize I wasn't a child snatcher, a thief. I wanted to but I shouldn't but I had to but I couldn't. "Fine," I said, "I'm fine." But just as I was about to flip my hand in a dismissive-as-possible gesture, Molly—who I'd left in her carrier—started to bawl, and suddenly I felt like my ribs had cracked open. "I'm fine!" I said again, and then I strode into the bedroom and closed the door behind me, dropping to the floor beside Molly, smoothing my hand over her tearstained cheeks.

"Leah?" He knocked on the door, then cracked it open. He watched me a moment and then entered and knelt beside me. "What is it? What's going on?"

I swiped a sleeve across the tears on my face. Molly was now wailing, and I stumbled to my feet. "I have to go," I said. "I'm sorry, and please tell Muriel I'm sorry I couldn't say goodbye, and that I'll pay her back as soon as I possibly can. You too, Alex." I reached for the last of my bags. "It's been great, I can't even tell you how great it's been. You seem like one of the most amazing people I've ever met and I'd do anything to be able to spend more time with you."

"Wait." He sat on the bed, elbows on his knees and hands clasped in front of him, not looking at me. "Listen, Leah. I know this is going to sound awfully intrusive, which is why I haven't asked you any personal questions, but ever since I met you I had the feeling like you're in some kind of trouble. I don't know what's going on and you don't have to tell me, but you've got the look of someone who's running away from something without a place to run to."

"Well no, I mean I'm going to Kansas."

"From Chicago, right. And driving through West Virginia was a natural detour."

I turned away, focused on unbuckling Molly's carrier straps. "I'm not in trouble," I said finally, in the overly firm pitch of a lie.

"But you don't have anywhere to go."

I lifted Molly and rubbed at her back to soothe her. "I wouldn't say that. It makes me sound like a vagrant, or like some runaway kid. Okay, you're right, maybe I'm not going to Kansas. But it's not that I don't have anywhere to go, just nowhere in particular. I'm traveling the country."

He raised his eyebrows.

"Look." I sank onto the bed beside him, my mind racing. "I'm leaving my husband, okay? He wasn't good for Molly and he wasn't good for me, so I just grabbed my stuff and left." Maybe this was the key to lying, to completely believe in the lie, to feel it. I let the rage at David McGrath fuel and burn inside me, and became Leah: strong, independent, overturning my life to save my daughter.

"I can't let him find her," I said, my voice tight. "He's dangerous and he's destroyed both our lives, so I decided I had to run as far as possible from home. But all I could take out of my bank account was a couple hundred bucks, and I don't want to use an ATM or a credit card because I don't want him tracking me. But this is for Molly's sake, see? And I realize I should've thought things through more before I left him, but I didn't have time to come up with a real plan."

"You don't want him tracking you because you don't have custody."

I hunched my shoulders. "Kind of. I mean no, I don't have custody yet, but I'm leaving because I'm scared of him. Because he's . . . done things. To me and to Molly."

Alex went suddenly still, and then he said, "You mean he hurt you?"

I probably shouldn't have said it. It had come out of my mouth without any thought, because it seemed like the only legitimate excuse for my present situation. But it opened up a huge can of worms that I had no idea how to wrestle back into the can.

"Okay," I said, "I have to show you something." And then I carefully pulled up Molly's dress to show him her back. "Cigarettes," I said.

Alex's face slackened as he stared at her scars, his eyes slowly filling. He touched her back gently. "Oh no," he whispered.

"Yeah," I said softly. And watching him, the look on his face, all this pain for a child he didn't know, the only thought inside me was, *Please.* Please what? I didn't know exactly. Please help us, please save us, please don't let us go off on our own. "They're healing up now, I don't think they hurt anymore, but I guess you can see why I had to leave."

He looked up at me, tears glazing his eyes. "Is there anything else? Did she get hurt anywhere else?"

"That's all I know about. Those are the only sores I've seen, but who knows what he might've done if I stayed?"

He smoothed a palm gently over the wisps of Molly's hair. "So what're you going to do?" he said hoarsely. "Have you told the police?"

"I can't. I can't because I basically kidnapped her, and if I turn myself in I'm sure she'll be taken away from me. And my husband's family is rich enough to hire lawyers who'll find a way to prove he didn't do anything to us, which means he might end up with custody. I can't let him get custody!"

Alex thought a minute, then said, "Have you tried looking for shelters? There are places that can help women disappear, even train them in new careers, get them back on their feet."

My skin felt clammy. What should I say? "I've imagined those places, shelters with bunk beds, ten women sharing a room. Gruel." I smiled grimly. "But maybe you're right, I should look for something like that. I can't keep driving around forever."

All at once my eyes filled again, and I pressed the back of my arm against them, trying to keep my voice steady. "But I just found out from my mother that the police, and maybe my husband, might already know where I am. Maybe they're even on the way, so I have to get out of here."

Alex didn't respond for so long that I pulled my arm away from my eyes to look at him. His face was pale and tight, watching me. Finally he said, "I'll go with you, find you somewhere safe. I can drive you, or if you don't want to leave your car here you can follow behind me."

He'd want to escort me to some shelter, and what was the protocol for entering a shelter? By tomorrow my name and face would probably be splashed across the headlines, and surely the shelter would look at my ID, and figure out who I was. "Thanks," I said, "you're incredibly sweet. But I really feel like I have to do this on my own."

"Leah, look. I'm not letting you go off by yourself, not if this guy's dangerous."

"Please." I set Molly back in her carrier, and she immediately started to cry again. "I'm going to be fine," I said, "we both are. And I think . . . I think it'd be best if after we leave you just forget you ever got to know us."

"Leah—"

"Thank you so much for everything, for giving me one of the best nights of my life." I pulled him into a quick hug, then lifted the carrier and diaper bag and turned away.

At the car, after fastening Molly into her car seat, I looked back toward the inn to see Alex standing in the open doorway. I stood a full minute watching him silently, then got into the car and drove away.

Molly was still crying in the backseat, and I glanced into the rearview. "Stop?" I whispered. "Please stop?" And then my voice broke, tears blurring my vision. Driving with no idea where I was going, what I was doing; I was literally shivering with terror, an earthquake in my bones, seismic plates scraping inside my chest. How stupid was I that I'd trusted Sydney, knowing who she was, who she'd always been. Or I hadn't trusted her, I'd known she couldn't care less about me, but I'd truly believed that she loved her daughter. The stupidity had been in not realizing that she loved herself more.

8

So there I was back on the road, exhausted and confused, panicking at the headlights in my rearview mirror, sure I was being followed. I knew if the cops wanted to stop me all they'd do was pull me over, but I imagined they were sadistic cops, playing games, taunting me, waiting to make their move.

Considering my state of mind it was a wonder I didn't drive in a complete circle, ending where I'd started. But after four hours I found myself crossing into Ohio, the hills giving way to flat farmland, corn and hay and the scent of either manure or methane-generating cows.

All of me wanted to bring Molly up to the passenger seat beside me so I could look at her, comfort myself with the feel of her chubby knees. Since hearing myself called a "suspect" I'd felt her being torn from me, no longer mine.

She slept for a good part of the drive but still I talked to her, making up stories of where we were going. Kansas was out now, so after some pondering I decided on Montana, a state I imagined as being basically uninhabited. Open countryside where we'd cook dinners over a campfire and bathe in rock-bottomed streams. I'd grow my hair down to my knees, hike mountains with Molly riding on my back, shoot game and make our clothes out of animal pelts.

Oh I know, I know, but imagining it was so soothing, and the more far-fetched my fantasies got, the more my fear abated. So that I felt myself drifting, watching the fields pass in front of me with the same blurred inattention with which one watches scenery on a moving train, an unnoticed background Muzak. Until my head lolled and I jerked back awake in a sudden panic.

Coffee, I needed coffee.

I circled through a McDonald's drive-thru and bought a large cup, then pulled into a parking space. I got out to stretch my legs and check on Molly, and was about to open the back door when a car pulled up behind me. The lights flicked off and a door opened. And . . . out stepped Alex.

My eyes widened. I felt suddenly faint. He wasn't here, I must be hallucinating, my exhaustion and fear arranging his features onto someone else's face. "Alex?"

In response he smiled, almost apologetically.

"What the hell?" I said. "What're you doing here!"

"Nice greeting."

"You followed me!"

His smile fell. "Yes, it would appear so. I thought you'd be glad to see me."

Glad? Glad was not the right word. I was overwhelmed, freaked out, and not quite sure I wasn't dreaming. It was like nightmares I'd had of being lost, running through dark and unfamiliar streets, then suddenly finding the street that led toward home.

"I was worried about you, Leah. The state you were in when you left . . . I know you can take care of yourself, but anybody would fall apart in your situation. What kind of person would I be if I just shrugged and let you go through that alone?"

"You followed me," I said.

"Yes, I think we've already established that."

"I *thought* somebody was following me. I was sure of it, and I kept telling myself I was being paranoid. But it was you."

"Look, we're not getting anywhere with this line of conversation. Let's go inside, I'll buy you a burger and we'll talk. Let me just grab Molly." He opened her door, handed me the diaper bag and fumbled with her car seat latches. "Have you experienced the wonder that is beef-fat–fried potatoes?" he asked her gently. "If not, you're in for a treat." He lifted her and started toward the entrance, and I followed behind him, my mind blank as we walked inside. "Here, you sit with Molly," he said. "I'll order for us, if you tell me what you want."

I watched him silently, then turned to the nearest table and sat, resisting the urge to spread prostrate along the booth. He pulled up a high chair and set Molly inside it. "A salad," I said softly, then a bit louder. "Thank you." Me, who hadn't seen a salad since 1992 during Star's deluded attempt to follow the food pyramid. But my stomach was churning, and real food just seemed beside the point somehow.

In a semi-stupor I watched him approach the front counter. None of this seemed quite real. Seeing Alex threw doubt onto everything; it must all be a dream, because what were the chances of finding a man like Alex who'd care enough about us to follow me here? I gulped at my coffee and the heat on my tongue helped a bit, something corporeal to focus on.

I cracked open a jar of pureed liver for Molly, and the bitter scent surrounded us, embarrassingly similar to fecal matter. I spooned it into her mouth but she spit it out, making a motorcycle sound with her lips. Apparently she did not like mashed liver.

"Here." Alex set down a tray with a burger, soda, fries and my salad, and a chocolate shake that he handed to me. "You need more than lettuce to get through this. I want you to make some decisions here, and that's going to take sugar and fat and . . . calcium. I'm assuming shakes have calcium."

I cradled the sweating cup in both hands, squeezed and released it rhythmically like I was testing its ripeness. "You didn't need to check up on me." *Squeeze, release.* "I mean, it's awfully nice of you, ridiculously nice. And now I feel really guilty." *Squeeze, release.* "Because I must've somehow given you the impression that we need to be taken care of. But really, you don't need to save us."

He watched me a minute before he said, "Do you actually have a plan, or were you just driving randomly?"

"I'd say somewhere in between." I set down the cup and dried my hands on my jeans, then shuffled a plastic fork through the salad. "But I guess more the latter than the former. Which is okay, I mean I don't need a destination. I just feel like I need to stay on the move, get far enough away from home before I stop."

I had to check the news, buy another paper. And I needed to call Star, make sure she was okay, but I couldn't use my cell phone because I was sure they must've started tracing my calls. I'd have to find a pay phone, but what if our home phone was tapped? Maybe I could just make sure Star answered, judge the tone of her voice and then hang up without speaking. I pulled out my wallet, my eyes filling. I wasn't equipped for this. I should've watched more *CSI*. "This is for the salad, and do you have change for a dollar? I want to see if there's a pay phone here."

He fished in his pocket, pulled out a handful of coins and piled them on our food tray, waving away the bills I tried to hand him. "Who did you want to call?"

Molly started banging her palms on her high chair tray, so I wiped off her spoon and scooped up a bit of milk shake to feed her. "My mother," I said. "I know she has to be freaking out about me, and I just want to hear her voice, make sure she's okay. But if David's told the police I'm missing, if they're looking for me I'm scared they might be tracing the calls from my cell, and I don't want them knowing I'm in Ohio."

"You want to use my cell?"

"I don't want to get you any more involved than you already are. What if they're tracing everybody who calls her, and they track you down?"

"I could just say I dialed a wrong number. If your mom gets a call from a pay phone, that'll look more suspicious than a private number."

"They'll know it wasn't a wrong number, because I used your cell yesterday to call her. If they see you called two days in a row, you'd need some kind of explanation."

"I don't care. Worst comes to worst, I can say I lost my phone."

I shook my head firmly. "I don't want you lying for me. What if they polygraph you or something?"

"Polygraph me? Over a stolen phone? Here." He dug into his pocket and handed me his phone. "Call."

I hesitated, then flipped it open. "Thanks, Alex," I said. "I just want to hear her voice but I won't even talk, in case they're tapping her line. There won't be any way for them to tell it's me." And even if they did somehow find out, Alex had no idea who I was or what I'd done. They couldn't arrest him for unwittingly assisting a kidnapper.

My eyes on him, I dialed my home number and let it ring at least fifteen times, but there was no answer. I hung up and stared down at it. "She's not answering," I said.

"You can try again before we leave, see if she's back."

"But she *has* to be home. Because she never goes out, she's agoraphobic, so she doesn't leave the house." I set the phone down, spun it fitfully with one finger. "Maybe she's sleeping or something. She keeps weird hours."

"I'm sure she's fine, try not to worry. We'll try again later, okay?" He smiled at Molly, who'd apparently decided I wasn't spooning the shake fast enough, and was now shoving fistfuls into her mouth. "Well, at least someone's eating." He nodded at my salad. "Come on, Leah, have you had anything since breakfast?"

I looked down at the salad, then speared a cherry tomato and brought it to my mouth, focusing on the chewing and swallowing, fighting back a coil of nausea.

"Look," he said slowly, "I want you to let me help you."

"Alex, no." I dropped the fork and pushed my salad away, focused on wiping the milk shake from Molly's fingers. "You've been amazing, more than I had any right to hope for. But I'm a big girl. I can figure this out for myself."

"Well of course you can." He plugged the top of his straw with his finger, lifted it and let Coke spill back into his glass. "But anybody in your situation would need some help. *I'd* need help if I was in your situation."

"I know you think I should go to a shelter." I licked a napkin, wiped at Molly's face. What incredibly bad aim she had, chocolate all the way to her eyelashes. "But I won't." I lifted her from her high chair to set her on my lap, and she settled into the crook of my arm, making soft *da-da-da* sounds and playing with her foot. "It seems so, I don't know, desperate. The energy in those places, filled with scared women, I don't want to bring Molly into that."

"Understood. I can totally understand that." He looked into my eyes a moment as if considering something, then reached forward and took both my hands. Not caring about the milk shake stickiness, the dirty napkin I clutched, just holding tight. Mortifyingly, I squeaked.

"I have a big house," he said, "two extra bedrooms, and it's pretty much in the middle of nowhere, so I'm sure you'd be safe."

He was asking me to stay with him in New Hampshire? I opened my mouth, tongue flapping. I'd never really understood how a tongue could flap but now I did, tongue flapping against the roof of my mouth like I was echoing Molly's croon: *da-da-da*.

"You could stay just for a few days, it'd give you time to rest up and plan what to do next. You can even look up trip routes on my computer to wherever you want to go. And maybe it sounds weird of me, and sudden, and I realize we hardly even know each other. I swear I'm not usually this impulsive, but I just can't stand the thought of leaving you here stranded in the middle of nowhere. Besides it'd be fun for me, having the baby around."

I glanced down at our intertwined hands. All I wanted was to confess everything to him, let him tell me exactly what to do and where to go, and that we'd be safe. If I told him, what would he say?

He suddenly pulled away and raked a hand through his hair. "Sorry, you probably think I'm some kind of stalker, or a psychopath who lures women into his home and then . . . I don't know, locks them in the basement." He set a hand on Molly's head, held it there a moment before he stood.

And it was only then that I realized I hadn't answered him, hadn't even looked at him since he'd offered his home. What was I supposed to say? Was I really the kind of person who could take advantage of kindness, lie over and over to someone's face and make him an accessory to my own crime? No, no, I knew I wasn't, and I wasn't the sort of person who'd let a stranger take care of me. But suddenly I wanted to be taken care of more than anything in the world.

I hesitated, then reached for his elbow. "See the thing is?" I said. "The thing is, nobody's been good to me in a long time; I mean nobody's gone out of their way. And I'm just not used to it, is all. I don't know how to react exactly."

He watched me a moment, unblinking, then set his hand over mine. "Just say yes. It's easy. Just for a few days."

"Okay," I said, then smiled. "Thank you." Not even allowing myself to think how crazy it was to travel hundreds of miles to stay with some man, when I didn't even know his last name.

9

We drove through the night. Him navigating and me following behind fueled by $1.99 gallon-jugs of coffee, flashing my headlights
when Molly needed a new diaper or a feeding, or when I just wanted
to see Alex's face, to remind myself this was real.

I'd set a newspaper I'd picked up in town on the front seat next to
me. I paged through it each time we stopped at a light, scanning photos and headlines. And by the time we reached Pennsylvania I'd
glanced through it all and found, to my great, great relief, no stories
on the kidnapping. Of course it was only a local paper, and they had
hardly any stories of national interest so I knew that meant next to
nothing. Except that there must be lots of people in the country who
hadn't heard about Molly or seen photos of my face. There were
places we could hide. And the town we were going to was supposedly
even more remote than the Ohio town where I'd bought the paper, so
there was a good chance we'd be safe.

I tried calling Star from Alex's phone again during a rest stop, and
again got no answer. But I forced myself not to worry yet. It was the
middle of the night after all, and she didn't have a phone in the bedroom. She'd probably just slept through the ringing from downstairs.

Yes, maybe I was being naïve. Maybe Star had turned herself in
and was now sleeping in jail. Maybe the police had tapped her phone

and found the calls from Alex's cell, and when we arrived at Alex's home we'd find flashing headlights and Miranda rights. But I couldn't think about that now, just wanted to focus on the drive, the feeling like I was both getting away from something and moving toward something. Reality, whatever that reality was, would hit soon enough, and at this point there wasn't much I could do to change it.

As night bleached into a colorless day, I studied the back of Alex in the car ahead, his perfectly trimmed dark hair, the curve of ear to neck, his profile as he turned to the side window. I studied the parts of him like the instructions to a model airplane as if they could tell me something about his insides, how he was constructed.

So here's what I learned. He was beautiful, he was *beautiful*, he smiled at the sun and sang along with the music from his radio, and he was beautiful. He slowed to look when we drove across a river and laughed out loud, glancing back at me, when a goose with her babies paraded across the road. And he was beautiful.

We made it into New Hampshire by morning, and as soon as we left the highway it was like making a detour to a different world. The forest rose around us, ash and pine and white birch muffling the rattle of my engine, a sudden muting like diving underwater at a public pool.

For miles we passed nothing but those trees and rock-strewn rivers, the only signs of human intervention an occasional dirt path leading to a log cabin, or a farm with cows and fields of hay. The mountains rose imposingly on all sides, in the rounded shape of breasts and knees, the road twisting in the notches between them. I opened my windows to inhale the cool breeze, the scent of pine, imagining I was the first to ever have traveled this road. What would I have thought if I'd seen it however-many-hundreds of years ago? *Yeah,* I would've thought, *I could settle here, dig in my homestead stakes, do some farming and meet some Native Americans, churn some butter.* It felt like a place one could hole up in, cradled by the hills, and compose a symphony or write a novel.

After fourteen hours on the road we reached Mendham, a small town centered on a steep hill. Or maybe "town" was overstating things; it was more of a village really, with a gray stone church, a corner grocery and a theater playing only one movie, and several houses labeled with handcrafted signs, all with names like "Country Quilts," "Country Curtains," and "Old Country Clocks." I followed Alex down a tree-lined street that opened into a small cul-de-sac, expansive lawns backed by woods, and small cape homes with tidy flower gardens. He signaled and turned into the driveway of an L-shaped white cape with pale green shutters and a wide front porch. The sloping lawn was bordered by a low stone fence and overrun with purple and white wildflowers; a curving flagstone path led up to the front door. I pulled behind Alex's car and stared, almost expecting Disney creatures to emerge from the woods, bluebirds and brown-spotted horses with long eyelashes.

He stepped out and stretched, hands at the small of his back, then approached my car. "That drive was about three hours too long," he said.

"This is..." I started, then shook my head. *Beautiful* and *lovely* would sound stupid, *cozy* would sound like an insult. But it was all those things, what a person might imagine when she said the word "home." "...totally nice," I finished stupidly.

He smiled. "It is, isn't it? When I bought it, I felt like it was a place I could grow old in. I didn't realize how lonely it can be, how there's no single women and absolutely nowhere to go on a Friday night. I mean dinner out's a major expedition." He shrugged. "But I kind of like solitude."

He was looking for single women, which meant he must be single himself, and straight. Which of course was none of my business, but an interesting piece of information nonetheless. "I didn't realize places like this existed anymore," I said, opening the car door. "I thought developers chomped up land like this and spit out condos and strip malls."

"Welcome to New Hampshire. Our shopping options are limited, but it doesn't matter because all you need is flannel shirts and Timberlands. You want to pop the trunk? I'll get your bags."

I opened the trunk, then lifted Molly from her car seat, and she looked around her, wide-eyed, trying to absorb her fourth home in six days. We ducked under a strand of the wisteria climbing the front porch and followed Alex into an entryway with wide-planked pine floors and white wainscoting, a narrow staircase, and a small wooden table holding a silver-framed photo. I picked up the photo as he plunked the bags on the floor. "Posy," he said. "My big sister."

The woman in the photo looked like a female version of him, slightly thinner, her face more pinched, but with the same thick dark hair and slim nose and sculpted jawline. "She looks like you," I said.

"You think? I keep that there to remind myself she's a grown-up now, because in my mind whenever I think of her, she's sixteen or seventeen at the most. She lives in North Jersey, near Manhattan. Got an MBA last year and she's a . . . I don't even know exactly what she is. A financial something or other. Completely different world from me." He pointed at the three adjoining doorways. "As evidenced by my tiny den, kitchen, and dining room, which would all fit into her master bathroom. Come into the kitchen and I'll make us something to eat. You hungry?"

"Sure, thanks," I said, although really I wasn't hungry at all. I hadn't eaten anything but salad and a stale rest-stop bagel for the past twenty hours, but I didn't feel the slightest need for food. Maybe my stomach was shrinking.

The kitchen was small: honey-stained cabinets with crookedly hung doors, black-and-white checkerboard tiles, a bright green stove that seemed like something from the twenties, and a butcher-block countertop. In my arms Molly started to protest, squirming free, and I set her down to let her crawl across the floor as Alex opened the refrigerator. "I need to shop," he said, rummaging through the shelves. "Been gone awhile, and it looks like everything here is in the process of developing new parasitic life-forms. But no fear, I'll find something."

He pulled out a carton of milk, sniffed at it and made a face. Molly crawled toward him, scooting fast across the floor, but caught the side of her head against the corner of a cupboard. She stared at it as if trying to understand why it had attacked, and then her face turned red and she screamed. "Uh-oh, we have an injury," I said, lifting her, inspecting her forehead.

Alex spun around, alarmed, the look on his face so pained I felt a pinch of affection for him. "Looks like she's fine, just scared herself." I touched the small welt on her head. "Crawling's tough, hunh? Hard to see where you're going. Hopefully you'll learn soon that it's not the most practical mode of transportation."

He smiled at this as he brought the milk to the sink and poured it down the drain. "Why don't you take a look around? Hang out in the den and I'll whip something up."

"Can I help? Although I guess I should tell you, I'm not that good a cook."

"Well I am, so don't worry about it." He flicked the back of his hand at me. "Go on, it'll just be a few minutes."

I walked with Molly to the den. It was a cozy room, painted pale yellow with two worn couches, a stone fireplace and a bay window looking out into the garden. I gazed out the window at the pines swaying their layered skirts, the weed-strewn path and flower beds. Maybe this was something I could do to thank him for his hospitality, fix up the flower beds, pull the weeds, maybe even make him a vegetable garden. Our yard back home was puny, more the size of a lawn troll than an actual lawn, but here I could create a masterpiece. "I always wanted to learn how to grow flowers," I told Molly. "Gardens are another form of art, really, don't you think?" I imagined crawling across the grass with Molly, making wishes on dandelion clouds. The two of us, nature girls.

I looked around the room, scanning the book spines on the floor-to-ceiling shelves as I juggled Molly on my hip to stop her crying. Mostly fiction, the type that won awards, but also books on science and philosophy, and I tried to guess what that said about his personality, other than that he was smart. Maybe he was the kind of person who spent all his time thinking, trying to figure out the meaning of life. How else could someone live alone in the middle of nowhere unless his thoughts were so interesting he didn't need anything else?

There were four photographs on the shelves, one of a young couple, a woman with Alex's hair and a man with his strong chin; a family photo of the same couple with a baby boy and two little girls—one brunette and one blonde—and the other two of a woman with long, sandy brown hair. She was young, in her early twenties, and absolutely stunning, one of those women so beautiful they both prove there must be a God, and make you hate Him. Was she a girlfriend?

On another of the shelves was a dull bronze trophy with an engraved plaque, and I lifted it. A name. *Lakewood, NC Championships—1989, MVP Alex Connor.* Alex Connor. A kind of waspy name. The name you might imagine for the captain of a crew team.

"For hockey," he said from behind me. "My proudest moment and I was sure when I got MVP that I'd go pro, but in the end I guess I valued my teeth too much. More than twenty years ago, and sad as it is, I still keep the trophy in the middle of my bookcase."

I grinned and turned to face him. "Oooh-aaah, very impressive, Mr. Connor," I said, trying the name on my tongue, trying to associate it with his face.

"Okay, let's not tease me."

"Sorry." I nodded at one of the photos. "Who's the woman?"

"Oh . . ." His face looked suddenly distant. "Just somebody I used to know." He shrugged, then flicked a teasing smile that didn't look even remotely genuine. "Nosy, aren't you. Why don't you come and eat?"

Somebody he *used* to know? Was he displaying two photos of her because her face made for beautiful artwork? An ex-girlfriend; she must be. A former girlfriend who still haunted him.

I followed him to the dining room, a small room with a distressed green-painted farmer's table, mismatched chairs and a white pie cupboard with punched-tin doors. I sat at the table, Molly in my lap. "You like sandwiches?" I whispered, and reached for one, broke off a piece. It was peanut butter, on partially frozen wheat bread.

Alex laughed at my expression and I quickly tried to hide it. After all, I liked peanut butter, loved it even. There were times I'd been tempted to pay homage to the peanut butter inventors. "Sorry," I said. "It's just when you said you were a great cook and used the words 'whip something up,' I started expecting something like watercress and whitefish. So thank God, really." I took a huge bite and chewed heartily. "This is perfect."

"Then you won't mind Yodels for dessert."

"Yodels are God's gift to mankind."

"Aren't they?" He reached for a sandwich and leaned back in his chair. "So I was avoiding personal questions back in West Virginia, but since we're now temporary housemates, maybe you could tell me more about yourself. Like what do you do for fun? For work? To keep yourself sane?"

"Art, art and art," I said. "I'm a very boring person. Next question."

"You're an artist?" His eyes lit up, and I was so tempted to make more out of my painting than it actually was, tell him I was in museums, books, Europe. But I'd stopped calling myself an artist a long time ago. It was a description that when I was younger I'd fixed onto myself, like one of those fake tattoos, to make myself seem more interesting. But once I'd needed to support myself and Star (and it became clear canvases weren't a realistic vehicle for supporting anything more than a chewing gum habit), it started fraying and coming loose and I couldn't justify sticking it back on again.

"Just wall murals," I said. Molly covered my mouth with her hand and I pretended to eat it, growling Cookie Monster noises, making her shriek with laughter. Until I pictured myself through Alex's eyes, got embarrassed and pulled her hand away. "I've done some canvases too, and I've sold a few of them, but they're mostly just for personal amusement."

"Don't downplay it! This is a definite personality flaw I'm seeing about you, Leah. You're like the most self-deprecating person I've ever met. I think artists are fascinating, being able to take whatever's in your head and make other people see it."

"I'm most definitely not fascinating. And I'm not being self-deprecating, just truthful. Generally, my life's been mind-numbingly dull."

"You've gotten married, had a baby. That's a lot."

Oops, right. I'd forgotten. "Yeah, true," I said quickly. "But I wouldn't call that fascinating."

He gave a sympathetic smile. "How'd you wind up with your husband, anyway? You seem like way too strong a person to have ended up with somebody who'd mess with you."

I set down my sandwich and pushed my plate away, my mind racing uselessly. "Ex-husband," I said.

"Sorry, that's way too personal, isn't it. Hell, I'm too tired to be thinking of appropriate conversation topics."

"No, it's okay." I stood. "I'm going to get Molly some food. Just a sec."

Alex held out his arms and I handed her to him, then rushed out to the entryway where he'd set our bags. I grabbed the diaper bag and stood a minute, staring at the door. Then brought it to the dining room where Alex had Molly on his lap, talking softly to her and letting her explore his fingers.

I pulled out a jar of strained spinach and a spoon, then scooted my chair close enough to feed her. "So," I said. "David." I couldn't look at him. Instead I kept my eyes focused on Molly as I unscrewed the jar cap. "That's his name, and we were in high school together. Not dating or anything, just part of the same crowd. And then we met up again ten years later at a reunion."

I filled the spoon and held it to Molly's mouth, but she batted it away. I set the spoon back in the jar and, needing something to fiddle with, I picked up a sandwich and started tearing at the crusts. "We got married within five months and he left me pretty soon after Molly was born. He was the biggest mistake of my life."

Alex took my hand but didn't speak. We sat there a minute, my hand in his, and finally I continued in a whisper. "I can't let him ever get custody. And now I've run away, I'm so scared of what he could do to us if he ever found out where we are."

Alex watched me, his face flushed with an expression I couldn't read. After a minute he rose and hoisted Molly against his hip. He stood behind my chair and wrapped one arm around me, his chin resting on my head. "It's okay," he said finally. "If he's looking for you, I'll make sure you don't get found."

I sat there feeling the weight of his chin and arm and the catch of his stubble in my hair, wondering at the irony. How despite having kidnapped a baby and driven hundreds of miles from the only home I'd known, this was the first time maybe ever that I felt like I was exactly where I was supposed to be. I had no idea what would happen next, but I had this sense like I was on the edge of something huge. I saw it written in bright yellow print like on the West Virginia border sign. WELCOME TO THE WORLD, LAINEY, it said.

"So you have a choice which bedroom you want," Alex said, leading me upstairs. "Although I have to say, it's not much of a choice. The smaller room's my office. It has a bed already, the one I grew up with actually, but we could move it to the other room if you'd rather."

The room's walls were papered in faded purple stripes, gauzy drapes on the large window. It held a twin bed with a white bedspread, a yellow armchair and a desk with a laptop and piles of papers. "If you want to sleep here, I'll move the desk downstairs so I don't intrude on you when I work. Or there's the other room." He gestured across the hall.

The room was crammed with folded blankets and piles of clothes, file cabinets, beat-up furniture, and an old computer dangling a tangle of colored wires. "The room's bigger," he said, "but it'll obviously take more work to make it habitable. This house has a storage problem, in that it seems to eventually disgorge everything I try and pack neatly away in the attic."

"The smaller room's fine," I said. "Plus, if the attic's disgorging junk here, this room doesn't seem very safe."

He smiled. "Then why don't you get yourself all unpacked and settled? I'm pretty bushed, so I may just call it a night. You need any-thing else? Anything I can help with?"

"No, I'm great," I said. "This is all great. I mean really, I don't know how to thank you, but thanks."

"Well you're welcome. I mean that, Leah." He touched the top of Molly's head, then rested his hand on my cheek for a moment before striding from the room.

I touched my cheek, watching him turn the corner. My skin warm from the feel of his hand, and my ears ringing with the sound of someone else's name.

I set Molly in her carrier. She seemed to be taking to the new sur-roundings reasonably well, resting her bottle meditatively on her belly, sucking only every minute or two when she remembered it was there. I sat on the bed, looking around, staring at the papers on Alex's desk and the file cabinet drawers. Then sat on my hands. Then pulled them free again and gripped the mattress. "No," I whispered, "you won't."

This was horrible, it wasn't me. All the times I'd been left alone painting in the homes of fascinating people, military scientists and authors and the Virginia State Senator, and never had the idea of snooping even crossed my mind. But this time I didn't try especially hard to stop myself. In the end I stood, closed the door quietly, then went to Alex's desk and started to explore. Because I realized after my seconds of halfhearted resistance that there'd come a point when I wouldn't be able to help myself, so there was no use pretending I was too ethical to do such a thing. It was inevitable, so why put it off?

"Don't watch this," I told Molly, and then I started with the papers on his desk, printed articles, social and political commentary from sites like The New Republic and The New Yorker, as well as pages of literary criticism, some with his name in the byline. Which probably meant Alex wasn't just smart, he was S-M-A-R-T. Leafing through them, I was instantly and thoroughly intimidated.

I set them back in the pile, then noticed indentations on the blotter. I tried to make out the words, but when I couldn't, shedding my last scrap of decency, I fished a pen and an old receipt out from my purse, held the receipt over the blotter and shaded the pen over it.

THE REASON I WANT IT IS BECAUSE YOU CAN MAKE MASHEENS FROM IT AND BECAUSE SAM GOT IT TOO.

I smiled, running my finger over the words. Was the blotter from Alex's childhood? If so, I was probably the only person who'd read it for probably three decades, like an archeologist excavating bones. And I was so pleased with myself discovering this fossil from Alex's childhood that I actually considered showing him. Never mind that taking a rubbing of someone's blotter was the utmost invasion of privacy, and probably illegal in some states.

There was a thump as Molly's bottle rolled off her chest. I jumped with a small yelp, then righted it. I watched her sleeping face a moment and then reached to open his desk drawers.

One held secretarial supplies, various-sized envelopes and stamps, Post-its and staples, all arranged into ridiculously neat stacks. The other held tax forms (and yes, I looked at his last year's income, as well as the amount he'd given to charity), mortgage and bank statements and a small notepad. I pulled out the notepad and sat with it on the bed, staring at the few scrawled lines.

> *Erin,*
>
> *I really am sorry I yelled at you last night. I'm just so frustrated that you jump at me for every suggestion I make, and question almost every promise. I wish you'd realize you could trust me. Why don't you trust me? I understand why you have a hard time of it, of course I do. But I'm not like the men who've hurt you, can't you see that? I'd never hurt you.*

On the following pages were several versions, all saying more or less the same thing in different words, some more strident, others pleading, and I read through them wondering what it would be like to be the woman these letters were written to, to be loved this much.

Erin. Was she the woman in the photos downstairs? Well she must be. The woman he "used to know."

Feeling a sudden wash of homesickness, I stuffed the pad back into the drawer, then reached into my purse for the cell phone Alex had lent me. I knew Star would answer; she had to answer. I wouldn't let myself consider what it would mean if she didn't.

I listened to the phone ring, imagining the sound filling the house I'd lived in all my life. The green phone in the kitchen, the cordless in the living room, the white phone in my own room muffled by the canvases on each wall.

I listened until an operator's voice oh-so-helpfully informed me that no one was answering, and then I hung up and tried again, the rings somehow hollow like they were echoing against empty walls.

Had Star actually gone somewhere? Had she been so terrified of the police's imminent arrival that she'd somehow mustered the strength to leave? And if she'd gone out, was she now lying unconscious on the sidewalk? I hung up the phone and then tried again. No answer.

Okay, how long should I wait before I did something? It was possible she was taking a shower and couldn't hear me. Or that she had a stomachache and didn't want to get out of bed. Or that she was dead.

I paced to the window. I should've gotten voice mail and bought her a cell phone so she could reach me if she needed anything. Everybody in the world had voice mail and a cell phone. Never mind that it didn't make sense to buy them since nobody ever called her and she was always home, I should've bought them just for safety's sake. I should've realized that occasions like this could happen.

I stood with my back against the wall. How long had it been since I'd talked to her? Twenty hours? Twenty hours! When Star had never been unreachable even for five minutes. Especially since she'd know it was me on the phone, because who else would it be? And I knew Star. After a full day not talking to me, she'd wade through sewage not to miss my call. I'd been so caught up in this fantasy life that I hadn't thought how dangerous it was to leave her, how the panic could seize her like hands around her throat and there she'd be, suffocated and alone. For twenty hours!

I dialed Pamela's number, and got her machine. "Pamela? It's Lainey, you there?" *Pause.* "Okay, listen Pamela, my mom's not answering the phone. It's been a full day I've been trying her, and she won't pick up, and I'm starting to get really worried. Would you do me a huge favor and drive over there? Call up at her window after you ring the bell so she knows it's you. And tell her I'm freaking out and to call the number I'm dialing from now, it's a friend's cell phone. Okay? Okay. I love you."

I hung up and dialed home again. When she didn't answer I hung up and dialed again, my eyes shut. *Answer the phone, dammit, just answer!*

Okay. Enough was enough. I disconnected, then took a deep breath and dialed information. When the operator answered, I steeled my shoulders. "I want to talk to the Newport News police," I said.

{ 10 }

It didn't even cross my mind not to tell the police who I was. I was in a panic, and in that moment all I could think about was getting them to our house with life support. If I was caught then so be it, I'd find some other way to protect Molly. All that mattered now was finding Star.

I told them about her agoraphobia, that she hadn't been left alone in years and that she'd once attempted suicide. I also told them I hadn't talked to her in a week, trying to heighten the sense of urgency.

It took over an hour for them to call back, an hour of pacing with the cell phone clutched in my hand, dialing the cell from Alex's land line to make sure it still worked and then pacing again. I imagined all kinds of awful scenarios, a side effect, I guess, of being Star's daughter. Choking on a hot dog, armed robbery, stroke, anaphylactic shock from a previously unrecognized food allergy; so many things could happen to a person home alone. So when the phone rang, with their first words, *This is the Newport News PD,* I had that awful sensation you must get when a cop knocks on your door, and you just know that the person you love best is dead.

"No," I whispered.

"Lainey Carson?"

"No . . ."

"We just been to see your mother. Looks like she's not doing so great."

"Oh God, no."

"Looks like she hasn't been out of bed for a while now. Didn't come to the door when we knocked."

I sank onto the bed. She was alive. At least she was alive.

"We had to break through the door to get to her, and then she started screaming, locked up her bedroom so we had to break through that door too."

I imagined Star there in bed, the covers pulled up over her head with the doors, her only protection from the outside world, lying in splinters on the floor. "She needs new doors!" was all I could think to say.

"The doors'll be fine, we just pried the locks. But what she needs is supervision. You got any other family?"

I thought I could hear blame in his voice. Like, how could you leave your own mother? "Should I come home? You think I should go home?"

"I won't tell you what to do. If I was gonna tell you what to do, I'd say I think she should be in a place where she could be helped, you know what I mean."

I closed my eyes and imagined myself slapping him, the quick and satisfying heat of his fleshy cheek against my palm. "Well thanks for the advice," I said. "I'll take that into consideration."

Amazingly, he did not notice the sarcasm. "Hell," he said, "I have a mother too, you know."

It was only after hanging up that it occurred to me he hadn't recognized my name, didn't associate me or my mother with the kidnapping. What did that mean? Had Sydney not turned me in after all? The paper had said an arrest was imminent, but whose? I cupped my hands over my face and said a quick prayer of thanks, holding them there until my heart rate and breathing slowed. And then I picked up the phone again and dialed home.

The phone rang, kept ringing. I should've told the cops to check if the phones had gotten themselves unplugged, or the ringers switched off. But no, I knew Star was lying there listening, maybe still buried under the covers. Maybe knowing it was me and wanting to answer, but too scared to pull out her head.

I let the phone ring, my way of telling her I was there, connected by satellites and wires. After ten rings I hung up, curled on the bed, and dialed again. And then again, dialing through the night, my knees curled to my chest and my eyes closed, listening to the word-less conversation between us.

"Leah?"

I opened my eyes to find the sun streaming through the window. My eyes felt shredded from the contacts I'd forgotten to remove, and my teeth and tongue felt like they'd been coated in refried beans.

"Leah?" Alex called again from behind the closed door.

I rolled over and grabbed for Alex's cell phone, saw that it showed four messages. And that Molly wasn't in her carrier. I jumped to my feet. "Molly!"

"She's right here with me. Can I come in? You decent?"

I smoothed my tangled hair behind my ears and looked down at my rumpled clothes. "Not really," I said, "but yeah, you can come in."

The door opened and Molly scrambled into the room naked, dragging a clean diaper between her legs. Alex entered behind her, his face pink with suppressed laughter. It was like I'd been beamed away into someone else's life.

"I thought I could figure out the diaper thing on my own." Alex lifted Molly to swing her in a circle.

I surreptitiously checked my eyes for sleep-sand, then held out my arms. "Here, I'll show you."

He laid Molly on the bed and watched as I fastened the diaper around her. "Velcro, it's ingenious."

I felt a jolt of pleasure, as if he'd paid me a compliment. "Isn't it though?"

Molly raised her arms, palms facing me, jazz hands position, and I gave her my index fingers to grip. "So I've got breakfast," Alex said. "Back in a sec."

He turned back to the hall, and I quickly pulled my fingers from Molly's fists and checked for missed calls. There'd been three from Pamela, two last night and one this morning, and one call late last night from my home number. I brought Molly's hands to my mouth so I could kiss her chubby knuckles. *Thank God.*

Alex bumped the door open with his backside and set a tray on the desk. It was holding a plate heaped with scrambled eggs, bacon and toast slathered with butter, two mugs and a dark carafe. Leaning against the carafe was a small stuffed bunny that he handed to Molly. "A little memento of where we first met," he said. Molly snatched the bunny from him, studied it, then shoved its nose into her mouth.

"Wow," I said. "Am I dreaming? Where'd this all come from?"

"I went shopping. I was in desperate need of a toothbrush, since all my stuff's back in my room at the inn."

"You left all your stuff?"

"Well you didn't exactly give me time to pack. Or pay, either. I'll have to mail Muriel a check."

"Crap, Alex . . ." What was I getting him into? If the cops found out I was here, would they consider that aiding and abetting?

"It's no big deal." He shrugged. "Molly woke me up around four this morning, and we snuck downstairs and played for a while, waiting for you to get up. But when you didn't, I left you a note and went out." He nodded at the door, a piece of paper taped to it.

7AM—GONE SHOPPING W/ M., BACK BY 8. XOX

I stared at the XOX, blinked, then turned back to him. "Molly woke up and I slept through it?"

"She was screaming, actually, rattling the walls. For almost an hour, before I started to get worried you'd run out on us or . . . I don't know, died or something, so I came in to check."

"I'm a heavy sleeper," I said, then shook my head. "Sorry, after the week I've had, I guess my brain rebelled and entered a semi-vegetative state. I don't think I've ever slept that long in my life."

"Don't be sorry, we had fun. Didn't we, Moll? You'd be amazed how many games can be played with a ring of keys."

"Very creative of you."

"I thought so too." He twisted the top of the carafe, and filled the mugs. "You ever try chicory? If you hate it I can make a pot of regular coffee, I have both, but this is what I usually drink. A neighbor of mine, Roy, he cultivates chicory roots and roasts them, so I started drinking it when I needed a break from my caffeine addiction. Took some getting used to, but I've started to like it. Apparently it cleans out the blood, or maybe that's just something Roy told me to get me past my first impression." He handed me a mug. "See what you think."

The chicory was different from what I'd expected, chocolaty, in an ultra-sour way. Not horrible, but not all that good either. I could imagine it cleaning out my blood, like Drano. "Mmmm," I said, so as not to be rude.

He gave a quick laugh. "Like I said, it takes some getting used to. It's better with food. You going to eat?"

"I wasn't sure this was all for me. Aren't you eating? Or..." I picked up the fork and held it toward him. "Did you want to share?"

"No, I ate a couple hours ago. I made that for you."

"Wow. This is enough to feed about ten of me, but thanks." I scooped a forkful of eggs into my mouth. They were delicious, peppery and buttery but still light. I'd always thought an egg was an egg was an egg, but these tasted like something different altogether, the Dom Pérignon of eggs. I rolled my eyes in a faux-swoon. "These are incredible."

"Told you I could cook," he said. "The eggs are farm-grown, which makes a difference, and the whipping technique makes them fluffy."

" 'Whipping technique' sounds vaguely pornographic. I'm picturing you using a leather tassel. Perhaps wearing a thong." And then

I stopped short, vaguely amused at myself. Well look at that. I knew how to be flirtatious. After thirty-six years, I still had the capacity to amaze myself. I smiled and held the mug to my nose, let the steam flush my face. "So how'd you end up here in a place where you can get farm-grown eggs? Were you born here?"

"No, I lived in Pennsylvania most of my life, and then I was in New York for a few years." He shrugged. "Went to Columbia and I majored in English, which left me completely unqualified for anything except majoring in English."

"Well I majored in art history," I said, "which basically qualified me to visit museums."

"I've always wanted to learn how to do museums right. I usually just walk around feeling stupid, wondering why I'm not enjoying looking at paintings of colored squares and soup cans. Besides, you ended up using your degree, right?"

"My last project involved painting beans," I said, "so not really."

"At least you knew what you were good at. Me, I just bummed around for a while wondering what I wanted to be when I grew up. I decided to stay in the city because I thought I liked it, mainly because I was only twenty-two at the time, so I had no idea what I really liked. I spent a few months waiting tables along with the deluded wannabe actor-models, and then a friend taught me how to cook and I started catering and party planning."

A friend. I pictured her, maybe the woman on his bookcase, leaning over him to display her boobs while she showed him her egg-whipping technique.

"But it turned out I couldn't deal with super-rich people and their dinner party obsessions. Like they wanted me taking the temperature of ice baths for white wine. I mean, they're ice baths! They're cold! And one lady had me measuring the distance between each plate and glass and piece of silverware with a caliper, to make sure it was all symmetrical."

"Awesome," I said. "Not just a perfect party, it's an *anally* perfect party."

"Exactly, and being the least anal person I know, I kept wanting to tell them to get a real life. So when the urge got overwhelming, I realized my choices were to commit homicide or figure out how to get away from it. Which is when I started writing. I got in on the bottom floor of blogging, back when blogs were still called online journals and people had this voyeuristic fascination with them. My journal was called *Things I Like*." He smiled. "Except I put exclamation points after each word because . . . I was in my twenties. So it was called *Things! I! Like!* and I was writing about basically everything that made me happy."

Alex reached for Molly, who had slumped forward on the bed over the top of the stuffed bunny, like she was attempting to touch her toes. "Recipes," he said, setting her on his lap, "movies, books, shampoo, and I guess people thought it was useful because suddenly companies were sending me on vacations to review their hotels, or giving me a year's supply of veggie hot dogs in the hopes I'd tell the world they didn't taste like salty rubber. And then I wrote a book that got picked up on proposal, which is when I gave up catering for good, and I never looked back."

"You have a book! I never met a real author before." I grinned. "Except for this one lady. I did a mural for her bedroom, and she tried to give me a copy of her self-published poetry as partial payment. It was called *Your Love Tastes like Saccharine,* and the first poem was called, no lie, 'Sugar Free Gives Me the Runs.'"

Alex laughed. "Well that's a lot more creative than mine. It's called *A Hundred Books That Will Change Your Life,* and I ended up getting about a thousand letters from people who told me how ashamed I should be for not mentioning the Bible. But it did okay enough to get me out of the city, and into a mortgage in a place that felt as far away from that life as possible. I was here with my parents on vacation, back when I was ten or eleven, and I remembered how great it was waking up to the sound of wind through the trees. Being out in the middle of nowhere you can completely forget about the rest of the world, just live in the moment."

I wondered suddenly what there might be about Alex that I didn't know. I'd definitely sensed a sadness about him that surfaced at odd times, when I mentioned motherhood for example, sometimes even when he held Molly. What was there in "the rest of the world" that he was trying to forget?

"So I moved here and pretty soon after, people who liked the book started hiring me to write book reviews, and that became my job."

"Very impressive. Now I feel humbled in your presence."

He shrugged. "Not all that impressive. It's nowhere near as impressive, to cite a random example, as escaping an abusive husband to become a single mother."

I felt my face flush. "Right. Yeah, thanks." I tore off a hunk of toast and was about to stuff it into my mouth when the cell phone in my purse rang—my phone, not Alex's. I dropped the toast and dove for it.

"I'll bring Molly downstairs and let you talk," Alex said, standing with Molly in his arms. "And I'll make you up a pot of coffee since I see you're not a chicory fan."

I smiled thanks and glanced at the number. The call was from home. I flipped the phone open. "Ma?"

Alex bowed shallowly and backed from the room.

"Lainey!"

"Oh Ma, thank God. You okay?"

"I'm feeling much better, thank you." Her voice was tight, formal. "Cops gave me a scare though, what the hell were you thinking?"

"What do you think I was thinking? That you were sick or dead or I don't know what. Why didn't you answer the phone?"

"I was out. At the ABC, I needed some whiskey. You forgot to get me whiskey."

"You were at the liquor store all night? You don't leave the house for two decades, and what gets you out is the need for whiskey."

"Shameful, but true."

"Jesus, Ma, how stupid do you think I am?"

She was quiet a minute, then said, "Guess you're not reading the papers. They arrested David McGrath yesterday morning."

I widened my eyes. "What?"

"Right before I talked to you the other day I heard how Sydney had given them a name, and I was sure she'd told them about you. That the cops were coming any minute to question me and haul me away, so how do you think it felt for me when they started pounding on the door last night? But it turns out she told them David had the baby when she disappeared. Aren't you watching the news? The story's been everywhere, even on Katie Couric."

"There's actually no TV here." Alex had told me the idea of installing a dish, infusing his brain with trashy satellite waves, just seemed like the total opposite of what life in New Hampshire was supposed to be. I'd thought that was commendable, very Thoreau-esque. And also, as it turned out, very convenient. "So that was her plan? To get him arrested?"

"Maybe not originally, but when the cops confronted her with the mall surveillance tapes she changed her story. Said she'd left Jacqueline at David's that morning, just set her sleeping into her crib. That she'd been sure David had heard her come in and knew Jacqueline was there, and since she wanted to avoid him she'd just left. Which is smart, I guess, because even David can't know for sure that's not true, might think somebody stole her from the bedroom. But she told the cops that when David called Saturday to ask where Jacqueline was, from the tone of his voice she was suddenly terrified that he'd done something to her. She said she'd lied about the kidnapping because she was scared of David, and then she told them about Molly's cigarette burns. She had photos of them, conveniently."

I shook my head. "And they believed her? Nobody can prove she never dropped Molly at his house?"

"Except us, I guess." Her voice trailed off, and then she said, "I'd say she's assuming an awful lot from you here. How easy would it be for you to turn her in?"

"But she knows I wouldn't." I clutched the phone receiver. "She knows me well enough to realize I wouldn't care if David McGrath's in jail for something he didn't do. I'm pretty much glad about it."

"Actually he's in jail for something he did do. They got a search warrant for his home and they found happiness, of the white-powdered variety, in his bedroom. So now they have him in for minor drug possession, which I guess was enough to make them believe Sydney was telling the truth."

I shook my head slowly. "What about the note I left at Six of Swords?"

"They think he wrote it, I guess. That he gave the baby to one of his many lady friends, or somebody he paid to go on the run with her, take care of her until he could join them. That's one theory, but the other's that he hurt her."

"Hurt her? You mean . . . they think he might've killed her?"

"Then left the note in some kind of half-assed attempt to make people think it was a kidnapping."

I shook my head blankly.

"So that's the story," Star said. "Son of a bitch snorts cocaine and abuses his kid, and Sydney Beaumont cries crocodile tears and there you are caught in the middle of it. Guess I got a tad upset about it all, but I'm better now."

I sank onto the bed, my chest tight with a sudden realization. "Ma, do you know what this means? This means she wants me to keep Molly, right? So they accuse David McGrath of murder? In order to save Molly from him, she sent her away forever."

"Oh Lainey, sweetie, I know what you're thinking, but don't go there. My guess is she got them to issue a warrant knowing exactly what they'd find in his bedroom, and she thought that might be enough to win custody. Who knows, but she's obviously not altogether in her right mind whatever she's pulling, because how's she going to get herself out of this?"

"What should I do, Ma? I don't know what to do now."

"Where are you? Still in West Virginia?"

"I don't know if I should even tell you. In case you're interrogated or something."

"You're staying with somebody, right? That's what the cards told me, a masculine, imperial sort of presence."

"Well I don't know about imperial but yeah, I'm staying with a man named Alex, just for a few days. A really nice guy." I shook my head. "Which is a total understatement. He's one of the most incredible people I ever met."

"I knew it," Star said softly. "I knew there was some kind of guardian spirit watching over you to make sure you'd be safe."

"A guardian spirit? Okay, yeah, we'll go with that. But obviously I can't stay here. I have to come home."

"You what? Molly's face is all over the headlines here, so how long's it going to take before somebody recognizes her?"

"I thought you said the story was on the national news. Why would I be any safer here than there?" I thought of everyone who'd seen us in the past few days—Muriel, the mother in the playground, people at various rest stops and parking lots. I should've been more careful, kept my head down and covered Molly's face because if they tried, the police could probably follow our tracks like perfectly placed breadcrumbs.

"Well the photos they're showing don't look like the girl you have. What with the new hair, and they've got her wearing red velvet Christmas dresses and Baby Dior, looking completely out of sorts. At least wherever you are they don't have any reason to suspect she's not your daughter, but here I'm sure everybody's trying to play detective, scrutinizing other people's babies. Plus, too many people here know you, and don't you think they'd consider it strange if you were suddenly with child?"

"I guess I'm going to have to take that chance, right? What else am I supposed to do?"

"I don't get it." Star's voice was rising. "Why would you come home? You going to give Sydney a talking-to? Apologize to the child-abusing junkie? What?"

"I'm coming home for *you*, Ma."

"For me!"

"Have you been eating? When's the last time you took a shower?"

"You getting complaints from the neighbors that I stink?"

I tried to keep my voice steady. "Obviously you're not doing too good on your own."

"Obviously you're forgetting that I'm not eight years old. I'm okay, Lainey." She paused, then said, "Listen. There I was yesterday in bed, covers up around my ears and sure the world was coming to get me and that I was most probably having a heart attack. Can you imagine how pathetic it made me feel? You come home and I might as well kill myself now, I mean it. If I have to put a baby at risk just because I can't deal, then I don't deserve to live."

"I'm worried as hell about you."

"Well don't be. Worrying is my game, remember? And this is my one and only chance to prove to myself I can make it. You're giving me that chance, and if you screw it up I'll never forgive you."

"And if you die of starvation I'll never forgive *you*. I'm calling Pamela to ask her to stop by and check on you today. If she tells me you're not up and about and getting stuff done, then you're not leaving me with much of a choice."

"Well she was just here last night, and she told me I looked great. Said she didn't know what you were making such a fuss about."

"Please, Ma. Do you not realize I'm going to actually talk to her and find out what she really said?"

"Don't trust her, she's a liar."

I steeled my shoulders. "You have to prove to me you're okay. I mean it. Answer the phone when I call you, answer the door when the bell rings, make yourself meals." I lay back and closed my eyes. "I wish you were here, I really do."

"That's because you're codependent. Tell me something, okay? Everything that's going on now, a baby who needs you and a man who offers to help, does it feel like destiny?"

I hesitated, then said, "I don't know." But maybe it was like Star said, that there'd be a time in my life when things started coming to me, things that only seemed like luck. So what if this wasn't wrong, all this lying? What if it was just a way of opening my arms to destiny? I remembered how it felt to hold Molly, and then remembered, of all things, the weight of Alex's arm around my shoulders. "Maybe," I said.

"So then don't worry," Star said. "This time alone, it feels like destiny to me too."

It was beautiful out, skyblue and warm. And because it seemed like a thing mothers might be inclined to do on skyblue warm days, while Alex worked on the computer I took Molly out for a walk, carrying her in her sling. We paraded down the street, both admiring the dogwoods and cherry trees, Molly periodically demonstrating her athletic prowess by throwing her binky at my feet.

Every walk I took with Molly, I kept up a running commentary in an attempt to increase her vocabulary, this commentary involving mostly discussions of the scenery and weather. She definitely understood a lot more than was immediately obvious, was able to bring me a ball or a block if I asked for it, to make appropriate sounds when I asked if she wanted a bottle or needed a diaper change. And she recognized her name, the name I'd given her, looking up when I called it with a question in her eyes. But I still was waiting to hear her speak her first word, and so along with my commentary I repeated the *ba-ba*'s and *ya-ya-ya*'s she interjected, as encouragement to continue exercising her tongue.

"What did that binky ever do to you?" I said now, wiping it off once again with my shirt. "How can such a sweet thing as you be so cruel to inanimate objects?"

Molly beamed back at me, and promptly threw the binky again. She was studying the effects of gravity, I assumed, so I'd let her study for as long as she wanted. Every day I could teach her something new, a new skill, new game, new force of nature. Even after she had to leave me, those learnings would always be mine, a piece of her I'd always own.

We were rounding the top of a hill when we passed a woman power-walking in the opposite direction, swaying her arms and dipping huge, lunging steps, looking rather like a lumbering steam shovel. She was heavyset, her blond hair frizzing in wild curls around her shoulders, and she had one of those faces you immediately like, round cheeks complete with dimples and crinkly eyes.

When she saw me she paused mid-lunge, then quickly snapped her legs shut, her face turning pink. "Hamstrings and butt," she said.

I smiled hesitantly. "What?"

"You were looking at me like I'm insane, but I'm lunging because I have no hamstrings and too much butt. Nobody's supposed to actually see me doing this, just see the results and be amazed. But now that you have, I hope you'll immediately erase it from your memory." She swiped an arm up her forehead, pushing back her sweaty hair and revealing an unshaved underarm. "Who are you anyway? You here visiting somebody?"

I shook my head, then nodded, completely taken aback. With most people you could tell who they were almost immediately, slot them into one of the various prefab personality-containers you'd already fashioned in your brain. But this woman seemed unclassifiable.

"That was rude," she said, "sorry. It's just we don't see too many new faces here, so I'm out of practice." She held out her hand. "I'm Susie Greer."

"I'm Leah," I said, taking her hand, vaguely pleased at how easily the name came this time around. Like I truly was becoming a Leah. Funny how quickly I could strip off the old me, like everything I'd been was just a veneer, a costume. It made me wonder what was underneath, the true me. "And this is Molly," I said. "We're staying with Alex Connor."

"Oh? Oh! You're his mysterious lady friend!" She grinned. "I have to say, we were wondering if you even existed or if maybe you were . . . you know, a man."

I spent a few seconds trying to digest this, then a few more convincing myself it would be wrong to claim that yes indeed, I was his mysterious lady friend. "No," I said. "Just a friend-friend. He invited me and my daughter here for a while."

"Aw shoot. And here I was, working the story all out in my head. That he was keeping you a secret because he had this illegitimate child, which he for some reason thought we'd be offended by." She smiled at Molly, touched her cheek. "She has very wise eyes. Like a young prophet; the Dalai Molly."

I smiled back and said, "Doesn't she?" Feeling pride.

"You staying awhile, then?"

"Just a few days," I said. "A week at the most."

"This is good. We should do lunch sometime. I make a mean paella, you should ask Alex." She cocked her head and gave me a sly smile. "So . . . do you know Alex's girlfriend?"

"Um, no." Molly started to fuss, and I jiggled the sling to calm her. "He never mentioned her, but we haven't talked much yet about that kind of stuff."

"You should ask. And let me know if you learn anything, okay? Everybody wonders because he hardly talks about her. We only know there's someone because Judy Mier tried to set him up with her daughter, and he said he wasn't available. Which still seems unlikely to me, because where is she? Could be he just doesn't like the looks of Judy's daughter. You ask him, okay? And we'll do lunch and you can tell me everything."

I thought about the photos on his shelf, the beautiful Erin he hadn't been willing to talk about, maybe because whatever had happened to their relationship felt too raw. "I'll see what I can find out," I said. At least recounting this conversation to him would give me an excuse to ask subtly. I wasn't asking for *myself*; it was a secondhand question.

"I like you," Susie said, narrowing her eyes. "You have a very expressive face." And then she held up her hand, waved goodbye to me and Molly in the finger-flapping goodbye wave of toddlers, then power-walked down the street.

I turned to Molly. "That," I whispered, "was interesting."

Alex laughed when I told him about the encounter, overdramatizing Susie's goggle-eyes and childish excitement. "Out in the middle of nowhere, people can be a little . . . different. Not in a bad way, it's just that only a certain kind of person wants to live this far removed from civilization. Which I don't know what that says about me." He shrugged. "But I like Susie. I love how she's perpetually dressed up as The Seventies, and how you always know what she's thinking. She has this kind of innocence about her."

"Don't let her fool you. She's not that innocent." I reached for one of the sandwiches Alex had made, apple and melted brie on pita bread. "She told me to try and wheedle secrets out of you, so I could come back and tell her what you said."

"What do you mean, secrets?"

"Well apparently there's a mysterious lady friend everyone wants to know more about. That's exactly the words she used, 'mysterious lady friend.' "

"Should I feel flattered they care so much about my business, or disturbed?" Alex looked down at his splayed fingers. "It's funny, you know? Living alone in the city you're so anonymous, even to the point you sometimes wonder if you've turned invisible. There were days I used to go buy food I didn't need, just so I could talk to the checkout person about the ridiculous price of portobello mushrooms. And now I'd have to taser my neighbors to keep them from peering in my windows."

"I think it's sweet, in a semi-annoying way. Isn't it better than being ignored?" My senior year of high school, after people had grown tired of me and moved on to their next target, the prayer I held in my head every morning while I showered and brushed my teeth was, *Make them see me.* A boy's elbow would jostle my arm as he closed his locker door; a girl would pass me papers and her hand would brush against my palm, and I'd snap back into myself, feel the spark of it. Reassured that I did have a physical presence after all, that I did exist.

"I wouldn't say either of them's better." Alex rose to fill his water glass, stood at the sink a moment, then turned to face me. "What I really want is a family, you know? Where the people you talk to every day are the people you really want to talk to. The people who want to know your secrets for the right reasons." He shrugged, looking embarrassed. "It's why having you and Molly here is so great, because it shows me a little of how it's going to be, having a family."

And there, for maybe the first time in my life, I found myself without words. Oh I knew that wasn't what he meant; of course I knew it. But my brain was racing, thoughts stuttering, and my throat seemed to be blocked by one of my internal organs. I finally flashed a smile and said, "Me too," a non sequitur that would haunt me the trillions of times I replayed this conversation.

I was so overwhelmed with my own ridiculousness that I didn't realize till much later that he'd never answered Susie's question.

{ 11 }

Pamela called that night while I was changing Molly on the bedroom floor. She started in without even saying hello. "Look," she said, "your mom needs help."

I leaned back against the bed, staring at the wall. "Tell me."

"I've never seen her like this. I mean, you probably have, and maybe you won't think it's so bad, but I've always thought of her as this innately happy woman who just happens to have a problem. But I didn't recognize her today." She paused, then said, "She has things piled against the door, Lainey. She didn't want anybody coming in to fix the locks, so she took an armchair and a hope chest and all these boxes of books, pushed them against the door. She had to open a window for me to climb in."

My eyes filled, and I squeezed them shut. *Mom*, I thought.

"Apparently *she'd* been wedged against the door too, huddled in quilts. There were plates of half-eaten food where she'd been sitting, and the curtains were all drawn like she's even scared to let the sun in. I think she's been spending all her time doing readings; she was doing them even when I was there."

I'd done this to her. Hadn't I known something like this might happen?

"Apparently the readings made her comfortable with the guy you're staying with," Pamela said, "which you're going to have to tell me more about, by the way. According to the cards he has issues, whatever that means, but he wants the best for you and he'll try and keep you and Jacqueline safe, so that's all good. But she's also sure you're in some kind of colossal danger, which maybe you are."

"Well of course. The thing about card readings is they're intuitional, which means you can pretty much interpret them any way you want. So of course the cards say I'm in colossal danger because she fully believes I am." I squeezed my eyes shut. "What do I do? Should I come home?"

"You want me to tell you what to do? I'd say you should turn your dear friend in. The baby's father's in jail, if he's been using drugs and abusing her then there's no way anybody's letting him out anytime soon, or letting him get his hands on her whenever he does get out."

"You don't know that. Don't you realize how powerful the McGraths are? What kind of lawyers they must've hired? They'll probably turn it into this big spectacle, televised so everyone can watch Johnnie Cochran and Robert Kardashian make all the evidence look circumstantial, and show what an adoring, devoted father David is."

"Um, Cochran and Kardashian are dead."

"You know what I mean. People like that can have their blood and skin and seminal fluid all over a body and still get away on a technicality. I feel like I have to choose between my mother and my daughter, and it's not a fair choice."

"Your daughter?" Pamela said, then let the words hang in the air before she said, "Look, Star can't stay there alone, we both know that, so what're the alternatives?"

"I have to come home." I reached for Molly's bare foot, gripped it as if it could keep me steady. I shouldn't have left. It was stupid to think I could ever be free of my old life, and now I was right back where I'd started. "I can leave tomorrow morning. If I leave early, I can be there by dinner." I heard the abject resignation in my voice. I'd had less than six days of freedom, and what did it say that this terrifying week had been among the best in my life?

"You're scared to come back," Pamela said. "I can hear it."

"No, I'm not scared." I smiled, hoping the smile would come across in my voice. "Just a little pissed and not looking forward to another twelve hours of driving."

"Okay, wait. What if I have another idea? I'll bring Star out to you if that's what you want."

"You're kidding, right? She hasn't left the house in two decades; it's all she can do to poke her arm out for the mail. You think she'd get in a car and drive five hundred miles?"

"Be driven. Or we'll fly, whatever. I've filled a prescription for Lexapro, so maybe that'll help. Give her a double dose of Xanax, knock her out and by the time she wakes up, she'll be having her panic attacks in another state. She might feel better anyway, being farther from the center of the news coverage."

I tried to imagine getting my mother onto a plane, a piece of thousand-ton machinery that hurtled tens of thousands of feet above the ground. It would've been easier imagining her sprouting a pair of gills and singing opera underwater. And once she got here, then what? Tote her off in another few days to some random destination in Montana? Drag her, heaving and panting, across the country?

"Just let me ask her," Pamela said. "I can make all the arrangements, pick up your mail while you're away, clear out enough money from your bank account to last till you get settled, forward your bills, arrange to get utilities turned off if you want. I'll tell Star you'll come home if you have to, that you're absolutely not going to leave her alone in this kind of state, but I'll also say something about how dangerous that would be. She loves you too much to let you get into trouble because of her."

I thought of the Star I used to know, the woman who'd raised me without a husband, without letting me see her grief. That woman had been possessed and subsumed by her illness, but the fact she'd told me to leave her, and now insisted she was okay despite being anything but, showed she was still there somewhere, behind the misfiring neurons.

I hesitated, then said, "Tell her I'm happy. Tell her when you talked to me, I sounded happier than you'd ever heard me. And tell her I said I finally feel like my life is starting."

"Do you?" Pamela said. "Are you happy?"

"Yeah, I really think I am." I looked down at Molly, who had gripped onto one of her bare feet as it waved by, and was studying it like it was some sort of strange wild bird she'd caught. I tucked the phone under my chin so I could reach for her, pulled her onto my lap and tickled my nose against her ear. People searched all their lives for things that might make them happy. Here I was, a fugitive running scared, nearly out of money, and I'd managed to find happiness. Maybe I was lucky, or maybe I was just easy. Maybe the secret was as simple as that, to have low expectations. "I really think I am," I said again.

I lay flat on my back playing one of my and Molly's favorite games, a leg exercise where I lay with my knees tucked to my chest, Molly resting on my shins. She looked into my face, bright-eyed and expectant, knowing what was coming. And then, the second she seemed to let her guard down I lifted my legs, tipping her toward me almost upside down so I could kiss her head. Each time she erupted into peals of laughter, which of course made me laugh too, and there we were, both laughing our heads off in this ridiculous Kama Sutra-esque position. Fully absorbed in each other, the pull of my muscles, the feel of her hair on my lips, her sounds of utter joy.

The thought fleetingly crossed my mind that maybe I should teach Sydney this game, because I had a feeling Molly would miss it after she left me. But I pushed the thought away immediately, thinking instead of how it might be if Star did manage to join us, sharing this bliss with my mother who'd known so little bliss herself. I wondered if Star had played this game with me, if that's where I'd gotten the idea. All the lap games and hand-clap games, the songs she'd sung to me that I now sang to Molly, handed down mother to daughter. To daughter.

This was how I'd try to live my life now, worrying about the future only when I was alone. Each minute, each second I spent with Molly I'd be fully with her. It was the only way I could go on looking into her face, without breaking my heart.

My cell phone started to ring and I lowered Molly slowly before rooting through my bag, sure it must be my mother. I hadn't told Alex anything yet about my conversation with Pamela. *If* Star agreed, and on the *off*-chance she managed to get herself out of the house and *if* she actually made it into a car, then I'd bring up the subject. But until then there were so many very iffy ifs that there was no reason to test the breadth of Alex's hospitality.

But the call wasn't from my home number but from a Warwick County, Virginia, area code, which could only mean Sydney. Or the police. And by the time I'd mentally adjusted my mind-set from anticipatory to panicky, the ringing had stopped. I set the phone on the bed, stared at it as if it were a dead bug that might or might not sting, then picked it up again in time to see the voice mail alert appear on the screen. I held my breath as I checked the message.

"Lainey? Look, it's me." It was Sydney, her voice a hoarse, frantic whisper. "I don't know if you've been watching the news, but I'm calling to warn you that things've gotten kind of screwed up, even more than they're showing. The cops—or the FBI, it's the FBI now— well I can't really talk about it all, but it's becoming really complicated. I don't know, I don't know, I just want you to stay put while I figure things out. Star said you're staying with someone you think you can trust, so hold tight for a few more days and try not to worry. I'm going to do whatever it takes to prove what David did to us. I promise nobody's going to get in trouble except him, and nobody's going to have any idea you were involved. But there's some issues I have to deal with and I might not be able to call again for a while. Please give my love to Jacqueline, okay? And tell her how much I miss her."

The phone clicked to silence and I stared at it blankly. Then re-dialed the number she'd called from, knowing it was a pay phone but praying that Sydney hadn't yet left it. *Answer,* I thought, *Answer!* What did she mean things had gotten screwed up? How could she not have told me more?

After ten rings I snapped the phone shut. What should I do? Should we leave now? How long could we possibly be safe here? I'd printed out maps today, directions to central Montana, and I'd looked up the addresses of motels along the way. I could call a realtor in the area, see if there were any homes available for short-term lease and then escape with Molly. Except, oh God, I'd have to some-how take Star too. How could this possibly work?

I replayed Sydney's message trying to read between the lines, but they were so widely spaced they could've fit pretty much anything. Was she scared just for herself or for me and Molly as well? When she'd said things were becoming "complicated," did she really just mean *complicated* or in fact mean *about to fall apart*? I had to find out what was going on.

I hadn't read a newspaper since I'd arrived. Alex seemed com-pletely uninterested in regular news coverage, said he found out about the world only through blogs because he liked in-depth dis-cussions of main events, and couldn't care less about whatever sen-sationalized scandal was currently holding the nation's interest. The good thing about the lack of a TV or newspaper was that Alex couldn't see the headlines of my own personal scandal. The bad thing, of course, was that I couldn't see them either, and with no information from the outside world, anything could be happening without me having a clue.

So that night, after Alex had gone to bed, I snuck downstairs to check the Internet. And found that the story was everywhere.

Gossip forums speculating on what else had been found in David McGrath's bedroom, from child porn to animal porn to man-sized lingerie. Psychological commentary spouting hypotheses on the tie between sociopathy and a life of privilege. Stories from people claiming to have been David and Sydney's friends, tales of their wild parties and weird cultish rituals. And then, I saw the news story.

FATHER OF MISSING BABY
JACQUELINE McGRATH ARRESTED
ON UNRELATED CHARGES

Police reported Tuesday that David McGrath, father of missing 12-month-old Jacqueline McGrath, was arrested for felony cocaine possession Monday evening at his home in Gloucester Point, VA. Authorities would not specify how much cocaine was found, nor would they elaborate on details of the bust.

In related news, handwriting analysis of a note found after the girl's disappearance, which was assumed to have been left by the abductor, has suggested that it was not written by either McGrath or the girl's mother, Sydney Beaumont, leaving open the possibility of involvement of a third party. "At this point nobody's been eliminated as a suspect," said Federal Agent Stuart Marks. "We're keeping all possibilities open, and we're increasingly confident that we'll find the truth and bring Jacqueline McGrath home."

So they'd analyzed my handwriting. *My* handwriting. If they ever found out I'd seen Sydney last week, how hard would it be for them to find a sample to compare it to? Hell, I'd scrawled my signature in the corner of tens of murals throughout the state.

I'd written that I'd taken Molly, so if Sydney ever turned me in I'd be the one they held responsible; there was no reason for them to believe, reading my note, that I wasn't acting on my own. Sydney's voice mail message had suggested there was even more going on than was being shown to the public, which might mean anything.

Like, for example, that they had another suspect they weren't ready to reveal. Like, for example, that this suspect was me.

I suddenly thought of the photos Sydney had shown me of the laughing, hugging girls we'd been. I was pretty sure she didn't give a damn about me now, and I wasn't going to just let her lead me around by the tail, but I also knew there were two sides to Sydney. Who the hell was she? This was the question I kept asking myself, hoping that with the wisdom of age and distance I'd be able to understand it. A mix of selfishness and wantonness and neediness, that's who she'd been even in childhood. But there was also kindness and loyalty—or at least there had been before things went bad—traits I'd tried to dis-count, as if that would make her betrayal less painful. And as I read through the damning interviews given by her so-called "friends," searching for clues on who she'd become and how safe it might be to trust her, this is the memory that came to me suddenly, digging like a knuckle of homesickness in my belly. The memory of the night she'd saved me.

Our life of crime began the summer before eighth grade, a sweaty night when I invited Sydney for a sleepover and—after hearing her complain for the trillionth time about our lack of both central air and chocolate ice cream—I suggested we break into the local swim club. We had come to the conclusion that pretty much everything in the world was *dumb* including, in no particular order: our mothers, our glasses, my one-piece bathing suit, gym class, most boys, and any drink that wasn't Diet Coke. But the idea of breaking into a swim club was decidedly un-dumb, and we started doing it almost nightly.

Sydney was a member of said swim club, so perhaps that made it a not-so-heinous crime, but the club did not let one in after 9 P.M., member or not, and certainly would not have approved of us raiding their ice cream freezer. So we were criminals, and the excellence of eating free Klondike bars in the dark, jumping off the high dive in the dark and practicing underwater somersaults in the dark, was made more excellent by the thought that we might be thrown in jail for it.

Breaking in involved a two-mile walk for each of us to the spot we met each night, followed by a quarter-mile trek through the woods and the scaling of an eight-foot wire fence. So it was not an easy crime to commit, but the difficulty of it added a sense of danger that heightened everything. Until the fence did me in.

I would later blame my sneakers. I'd been wearing them for much longer than was ever advisable, knowing shiny new sneakers were the height of dumbness, and the laces were torn and the soles had started to flap loose. Sydney had already jumped down the other side, and I'd thrown over our towels. She was slinging these over her shoulders when I reached the top of the fence and something caught in the wire rungs. Not realizing, I tried to swing my leg to the other side, lost my grip and fell.

I heard myself scream, a high-pitched sound like a rusty hinge that suddenly stopped as I hit the ground.

I stared at Sydney wide-eyed—*ohnoIcan'tbreathe, I can't breathe!*— and Sydney saw the panic on my face and screamed. She flew back over the fence and knelt by me. "Lainey? Lainey! What's wrong? Say something!" Absurdly she reached for my wrist to check my pulse while I writhed against her, fighting for breath. My eyes were watering, *can'tbreathe, can'tbreathe I'mgoingtodie!* And then, my diaphragm loosened. I sucked in a breath and then another, and then I started to cry.

Sydney hugged my head, stroking my hair. "What's wrong? Where's it hurt?"

But *all* of me hurt, my head, my butt, my back, and oh my ankle. My ankle! The pain in my ankle was wrenching, a dagger radiating up my leg. I made a sobbing sound as I eased off my sneaker, tried to peel down my sock and sobbed again.

"You think it's broken?" Sydney said, staring at it in awe. Already it was swollen to twice its natural size. "Can you walk?"

I couldn't even breathe without sending the dagger up through my entire body. I shook my head, then started to wail.

"Okay, hold on," she said, and flew back over the fence, threw the towels on my side and then returned. "You think we can wrap it? Like an Ace bandage?"

"No!"

"Okay, okay, just let me . . ." She folded the towels and slipped her hands under my calf, easing my ankle to rest on them. I cried out again and she rubbed gently at my knee. "Listen," she said, "listen . . . I'm going to have to leave you for just a little bit, okay? But I'll be back real soon, I promise." And then something occurred to her. Back over the fence she went, and a minute later Popsicles were raining to the ground beside me. Back on my side, she gathered them and packed them carefully around my ankle. She stood and kissed the top of my head. "Just don't move," she said—somewhat unnecessarily—and then, she was gone.

I don't know how much time passed. I found myself woozing in and out of a state of delirium, surrounded only by the pain. As I lay there, wailing pitifully, I became more and more sure that she wouldn't return. That I'd be left in the middle of the woods, stranded, shivering, wasting away until I was found a year later, dead, the only evidence of what had happened to me the multicolored Popsicle stains on my sock. I started to scream for help, but the tensing it took shot straight to my ankle. I threw up, hunched forward, felt the dark sheet of death draw over my consciousness and then . . .

I heard voices and the snapping of twigs underfoot. I cried out again and three men appeared with a stretcher, Sydney leading them. She was out of breath, ponytail loose and lopsided, her face streaming with dirt and tears.

It only occurred to me much later what Sydney had risked to save me. She'd known how her mother would react when she found out what we'd done: the screaming, the grounding, the months of sarcastic comments about Sydney's "criminal nature." She could've abandoned me, realizing that of course I'd be found the next morning—I was only feet away from the swimming pool, after all—and when found I never would've admitted she'd been with me. No one would ever have known. But I'd seen the pain on her face when she returned with the EMT, like my agony was her own, and the only thing she'd cared about was making my agony go away.

Sad, thinking back, how much this had amazed me.

And now more than two decades later, I was trying to find comfort from the memory, believe it meant she was telling the truth, that she'd never turn me in. I'd never fully trusted Sydney even back then, but I'd also known she had two sides. And now I had to believe in the side I'd seen the night I'd broken my ankle, a girl who hadn't wanted me to hurt, had sacrificed herself to save me.

As foolish as believing in Star's tarot cards, I guess, the cards she drew chosen by a universe that had never had any compunction about screwing me over. And I imagined that universe now watching me and shaking its head, wondering how many times it had to show me before I learned.

{ 12 }

I'd called Pamela after getting Sydney's message, asked her to confront Sydney, find out what the hell was going on. I tried to convince
myself I was overreacting, that the fists speedbag-punching my insides were just a hereditary overreaction. But I felt so absurdly vulnerable here alone with the baby, not knowing what the authorities
might have learned that they weren't disclosing to the media. Like
those dreams where you try and run to escape some impossible unspecified danger, but find yourself pedaling air.

My first instinct was to leave immediately, just move, stay on the
run traveling from cheap motel to cheap motel. Or maybe I could
just stay here in the house, emerge only in winter when it wouldn't
look so odd to hide behind a ski mask, perhaps also a burka.

I slept fitfully that night, waking several times with a start and listening for police sirens, gripping the covers to keep myself from
going back to the computer to look for updates, search for my name.

The next morning, hoping the distraction would keep me from
slipping into actual clinical insanity, I started work on the yard.

I visited a nursery on the outskirts of town and filled the car with
weed killers, bug killers, cedar mulch, fertilizer and masses of flowers, the nursery owner instructing me on how to prepare the soil,
planting depths and required amounts of sun. And then I carried it

all home, Molly in the backseat surrounded by plants, like an Anne Geddes photo.

While Alex finished a book review and Molly napped in her carrier on the porch, I set to work preparing the garden. It was harder than I'd thought it would be, lugging the spreader in parallel paths over the raggedy, rock-strewn lawn and tilling the loamy soil with compost. The sun, which in the beginning had been intoxicating, by late afternoon had become cloying, and I could feel the sweat trickling down my sides. But there was also something primally satisfying about physical labor in the outdoors, being able to put all my attention on hauling and digging and the ache in my muscles, which made the terror of the past evening seem peripheral in a way. I wasn't usually all that big on nature; earth was dirty, plants gave me allergies, and birds woke me up too early and dropped white crap on my windshield. But that afternoon, surrounded by the open, seductive green, I started to understand why a person might want to hug a tree.

"It looks great!" Alex said, walking out the front door.

I looked over the torn up land, the spreader-squashed dandelions, the flowers still in their plastic trays all wilting in the sun. "It does not," I said.

He gave an exaggerated wince. "Okay, I'm glad you said it first. I didn't want to insult you. It's looking like the yard was attacked by giant worms. But I'm sure it'll look better as soon as the flowers are in."

"Well I'm about seventy percent sure it'll look better. Can't look much worse, anyway."

Molly started squirming in her carrier so I approached her, then noticed the state of my hands. "No worries," Alex said, unstrapping her. "You want to get cleaned up? I'll get dinner started. Just grilling up some salmon so it'll be pretty quick."

"Oof, more food," I said. "I thought all this work might make me lose some weight, but the way you've been feeding me, I'm on my way to an early death and burial in a piano-sized coffin."

But in fact, I'd stepped on the bathroom scale that morning and found I'd lost three pounds. Three pounds! In a week! Maybe it was dehydration, a loss of sweat and tears. Or maybe his scale needed calibration, but still, I felt different. Lighter. Like if I jumped, I might actually not ever come back down.

I was getting dressed after my shower, wearing only a bra and underwear, when Star called.

"Ma." I sat on the bed with a thump. "Have you heard anything? Do you know what's going on?"

I heard her breathing accelerate, a two-toned rasp, like a hacksaw. "What do you mean!" she said. "What's going on?"

I shook my head quickly. What the hell was I thinking, asking her? "Nothing," I said weakly, "I heard there's nothing new. And that David's the only one they suspect." And then to prevent myself from blurting any more inanities I said, "So how are you?"

"I . . ." She hesitated, then started again. "I . . ."

"You what?"

"Am not great." Her voice was hoarse. "Okay? You're right and Pamela's right. I'm failing at taking care of myself. But I'd rather die than keep failing you as a parent, so if the trip up there kills me then so be it. It would all be a wash."

I looked down at my pale thighs, feeling an unexpected punch of fear. "Ma . . . you're coming? Really?"

"Let's not talk about it, okay? I already made myself sick just thinking about it. I should tell Pamela to bring Craig tomorrow in case they have to actually drag me into the car. Or maybe he can slip me a roofie." Her voice trailed off, and then she made a hissing sound before she said, "Pamela's a saint, you know that? They should make a Pamela medal. She had to get me into the shower and dressed today. How pathetic is that? What's wrong with me?"

It was so long since I'd heard her like this; like those days she'd had panic attacks not just when I pulled her out the door, but also when she just imagined the attack she'd have once I pulled her out. We'd realized pretty soon that there was no point in trying, that it was ludicrous to keep pretending she'd get better. And at the time, to be honest, my main reaction had been disgust and anger. Because I was fifteen, a disgusted and angry age, but also because I needed her to be normal. Needed her to take care of me, when she couldn't even take care of herself.

But now, with distance I could see how hard she'd tried, how tenaciously she was fighting. "Stop, Ma," I said gently. "Maybe you think you're weak, but you're really the strongest, most generous person I know. Yeah, your brain's screwed up, but leaving the only place you feel safe, it's like you're jumping into quicksand to help me. And if it turns out you don't make it into the car after all, I'll understand."

Star was quiet a long time, and I imagined how she must be feeling: gratitude, relief, new resolve. But when she finally spoke she said, "You little witch, you knew that'd make me feel like crap, didn't you."

"Honestly, that wasn't my intention," I said, smiling. "But if all it takes is a guilt trip to get you out of the house, then I'm here for you anytime."

"I have to ask you a huge favor," I told Alex that night, as we sat by the fireplace with mugs of cocoa. "And honestly if you say no, I'll completely, totally understand. But the thing is my mother, she has problems. I've told you some of it, but not all." Why was this so hard for me? Because Star was embarrassing, because she was a mirror of sorts, making *me* embarrassing by association. Because of the day Sydney had seen Star sitting on the floor in front of the evening news, doing reading after reading for the women and children at Chernobyl, and had pulled me out of the living room to whisper, "Your mom's *weird*."

I set down my mug. "I told you how she's agoraphobic. If she tries to leave the house, it's like the floor drops out from under her. And she gets these attacks, these panic attacks. She's scared of everything."

"And you've been dealing with this since you were a kid?" He looked into my eyes, shaking his head slightly. "Jesus, Leah, no wonder you're so strong."

"I'm strong because of who she was *before* she got so sick." This was the first of his compliments that I hadn't immediately discounted, and it shocked me a bit. I replayed the words in my head: *I am strong.* "But now she's been worrying about everything that's going on with me and Molly, it's getting so she can hardly take care of herself."

I looked over at Molly who was on the floor, exercising her pincer skills with a plate of Cheerios, and I wondered if being here in Molly's presence would make things better or worse. Whether Star would be able to absorb the innocent joy Molly pulled from every day, or if it would just remind Star of all there was to fear. "A friend of mine, she stopped by and said my mom's piled furniture against the front door, piled *herself* against the door, and I don't know what else to do." I wrapped my arms across my chest. "She can't stay alone anymore."

"You want to invite her here?" His voice was so soft when he said this, no wariness or sign of disapproval, and I felt my eyes fill. I'd told him the most horrible, unforgivable lies. Taking advantage of his generosity, what kind of person did that make me?

He was watching my face questioningly but I couldn't answer, was too ashamed of my own audacity, listening to the argument in my head:

Good Lainey: How can you?
Bad Lainey: He loves you!

I turned away. "It'd just be till I get the rest of our plans settled. But feel free to say no. You've already done way too much and I'd almost feel better if you admitted you were on your last nerve."

"Stop, okay? I have room for her, Leah. We'd just need to clean out the junk room, and I have an old futon that's actually pretty comfortable."

I smiled grimly. "She probably won't even make it up here anyway. It's pretty unlikely, really. I mean, I used to try just making her walk down to the used-book store on the corner, and she'd take a few steps and hyperventilate and pass out. And now Pamela's going to get her into a car? Drive her hundreds of miles? The odds are a bazillion to one. And then what? Get her into a car again in a week and drive her somewhere else? Twenty bazillion to one. I'm just so worried about her."

"Try not to be. Getting your mom out in the middle of nowhere might actually be good for her. Less here for her to be scared of, you know? You've already been through so much, and I want to do whatever I can to make things easier."

Yes! thought Bad Lainey. *Don't feel bad about letting him help, you deserve this! You totally* have *been through so much!* And behind it all, hearing the kindness in his voice: *We love you too.*

And so, Star came to New Hampshire.

Of course it wasn't anywhere near that simple. Three hours after they'd left I got a panicked call from Pamela asking if it would be okay to give her another Xanax so soon after the double dose she'd taken at home. In the background I heard my mother's strained breathing and I told Pamela yes, give her another, probably healthier for her to be knocked out by medication than lack of oxygen. Two hours later she'd called to say Star was being sick at the side of the road, and after estimating the proportion of Xanax that might have remained undigested, I told Pamela to go ahead and dose her again.

By the time they arrived that night, they were both pale and shaken. I'd asked Alex to hide out in his bedroom with Molly till the morning, realizing it'd be best not to introduce Star to him until she recovered a bit. My thought was that not only might an unfamiliar face set her off again, but more important her mind was in too many places to remember how my name, and relationship to Molly, had changed.

Star walked on trembling legs, propped between me and Pamela, sobbing with her eyes closed as we guided her through the door and up the stairs. "I have to pee!" she said, in a tight wail exactly reminiscent of a toddler fearful of accidents, and so we helped her to the bathroom. Then brought her into the bedroom we'd cleared out that morning, removing junk, tacking worn posters on the wall, laying the top of an old coffee table on two filing cabinets to form a primitive desk. We set her on the futon, pulled off her shoes and pants and stretched the covers up tight around her.

"I'll sleep here with her," I said. "In case she needs something in the middle of the night. Let me show you the other bedroom."

I walked with Pamela into the hall, and found Alex peeking out from behind his bedroom door, Molly in his arms. "Everything okay?" he asked softly.

Molly cried out and reached her arms toward me and I took her from Alex. "She's alive, she's kicking. We'll get through this. This is Pamela, by the way."

"Hi," Pamela said, then turned to me. "He's cute!"

Alex's face flushed as he extended his hand. "Can I get you anything? A drink maybe?"

"And charming!" Pamela took his hand. "But no, thanks, I'm beat so all I want to do is crash. I've just spent the past twelve hours trying to convince Star that her leg falling asleep wasn't necessarily a sign of stroke."

"Why don't I keep Molly tonight?" Alex asked me. "She's in that woozy pre-sleep stage, and we don't want her snapping out of it. I'll probably be up first anyway."

"Now you're just showing off for Pamela," I said, then smiled and rested my cheek against Molly's downy head. "Thanks, Alex. I mean I don't know how to thank you, really, but thanks."

In the bedroom, I turned to Pamela. "Have you heard anything new? I haven't been able to check the news."

"Well I've been on the road since this morning, and I wasn't about to turn on the radio with Star in the car, but the last I heard David's still their prime suspect. They've called Sydney in for questioning several times, though."

"You think that's a bad sign?"

"Well I don't really know, it's not like the FBI consults with me, but I'd say it's not a good sign."

"Oh crap." I sank onto the bed and pulled the covers over me. "Oh crap, oh crap, what am I going to do? I haven't talked to Sydney in days, and she left a message saying things were getting complicated. What the hell does that mean?"

"Lainey." She looked up at the ceiling. "Stop, okay? Not tonight. I spent all day dealing with your mom's hysteria so I don't need you going there too."

I suddenly noticed the hollowness of Pamela's face, eyes sunken and bruised with fatigue. "I'm sorry," I said. "For everything I'm putting you through. There's obviously no way I can ever repay you for this."

"Very true." She sat on the bed beside me, reached for my hand and squeezed it. "Listen, don't worry about it. Take a look at my life. The most thrilling thing I ever get to do is chauffeur my kids to gymnastics and watch them fall off balance beams, so being your partner in crime is the most excitement I've had in years. Besides, sometimes people do things without expecting to be repaid."

I thought about this, then said, "I need to talk to you about Alex. Because it's driving me a little crazy. I can't stand that our whole relationship, everything he's doing for me, is all based on a lie. What am I going to do when I leave here next week? Will I tell him the truth and then, I don't know, fork over cash to pay for room and board? Or do I just write him a thank-you note and disappear? He's going to hate me when he finds out I've been lying."

Pamela studied my face. "Do you have a crush on him?"

"A crush. What does that even mean? It's something you do with insects and wads of Kleenex."

She kept her eyes on my face, unsmiling, so I said, "Wait'll you get to know him, Pamela."

"Oh no," Pamela said softly. "Oh you poor, poor thing."

I felt a crimp of anger. "Just forget it."

"Don't get embarrassed. I'm just thinking..." She shook her head. "Okay, this is going to sound patronizing, so I apologize in advance. But of course you're falling for the first person who's showing you this kind of compassion, thinking about you over himself, because all your life you've been deprived of it."

"What're you talking about? You're making me sound so pathetic and desperate. I have a good life."

"You know what I mean. I'm not blaming you, and I'm not saying whatever you're feeling is pathetic, I'm just saying you should maybe look a little closer at it. Because you know you can't build a relationship based on lies, right? It's like trying to build a house without a foundation. It's never going to hold."

"I'm not trying to build anything!" I said. "Just stop, okay? You're treating me like I'm thirteen and considering having sex."

"Okay, okay. Look how fast you go from being eternally grateful to yelling." She glanced at me. "How's Jacqueline holding up?"

I squared my shoulders. "Molly," I said.

"Right." Pamela's mouth twitched. "Molly."

"Stop it, you know I had to change her name. And she's doing great, actually, *so* great. It's amazing taking care of her, a real honor being part of her life. For the first time I feel like my life really means something, you know? Like I have a higher purpose."

Pamela didn't answer, just watched my face with her brow furrowed. But I didn't care. Pamela could believe whatever she wanted, that I was being foolish, living out an unrealistic fantasy, but I knew what I was doing. "And she hasn't cried at all for Sydney," I said. "Isn't that weird? I mean you have kids, so you'd know; when they were that age they had a hard time being away from you, right? But Molly doesn't seem to miss Sydney at all."

Yes, I wanted Pamela to say. *That is truly weird. It must mean Molly likes you better.* Instead she said, "We need to talk about Sydney at some point. I went to see her yesterday, and there's a few things she said that've been worrying me."

I watched Pamela through the fringe of my bangs, feeling suddenly apprehensive. "Did you kick her ass?"

"Almost." She held my eyes a moment before saying, "Tomorrow, okay? Right now I'm so tired my eyeballs feel like they've been run over by a Hummer. I just want you to be prepared. Most of what she told me makes absolutely no sense."

"Why am I not surprised? I doubt she thought any of this through."

"Yeah, I'd agree with you there. It made me feel almost sorry for her until I remembered what she was doing to you." Pamela smiled grimly. "You know, I thought the fact we're best friends meant you had good taste, but obviously not. It made me feel insulted." She wrapped an arm around my shoulders. "It's the only thing about all this that I don't forgive you for."

Back in the other bedroom Star was hunched under the covers, in the fetal position. I sat on the futon to rest my hand on her back.

"I'm so embarrassed," she said hoarsely.

"Don't be. Everybody understands."

"No they don't. How can they possibly? Pamela spent the whole drive whispering *Stop, stop, stop* under her breath, I heard her. She thinks I'm a fruitcake."

"Well you *are* a fruitcake." I lay facing her, and took her hand. "I missed you."

"That's because you're a fruitcake too. But in a week you'll proba-bly look back on this conversation and think, What was I think-ing?" She brought a fist up to her mouth and said, "I don't know if I can do this, Lainey."

"You can," I said. "You are." I kissed the top of her head, suddenly remembering a night when I'd been eight or nine. It was the night before my stage debut, playing Mr. Smee in the third-grade produc-tion of *Peter Pan,* and I was ridiculously nervous, especially consid-ering the minimalism of my lines, various combinations of "Ahoy!" and "Aye-aye!" and "Yonder Peter lies!" But the *whole school* would be there including all my teachers since kindergarten, and lying in bed, trying to run through my choreography, I'd been almost in tears. So Star had sat with me and talked about fear, how you could make it into something physical. A spring like a Slinky you could compress and then shove down from your chest into a foot. Hold it there so it couldn't escape into the rest of you.

That day onstage, I'd looked out from behind our cardboard pirate ship and seen her in the audience, beaming in her best dress and newly highlighted hair, and pointing at her right foot. And I'd smiled back and pointed at my own foot, then made it through the play without tripping over lines or shoelaces. Because my mother had been powerful, and she'd known how to handle fear. How had we both gone from that to this?

I kicked off my shoes and slipped under the covers, curling tight against Star to keep from falling off the edge of the small bed. She wasn't the same person of course, and I'd realized that even as a kid. She started to change and I'd gone from calling her Mommy to thinking of her as *Star,* the adult-child inhabiting my mother's body. Even my love for her was different, tinged with betrayal, and something that wasn't contempt, but also wasn't quite uncontemptuous either.

Lying there, I wished it was Molly in my arms instead. My love for Molly was so simple, so much the opposite of my love for Star, and it had made me realize I was capable of unconditional adoration. Love should have an undercurrent of joy, not pain, and it was ridiculous that I'd been deprived of it so long. Ridiculous that underneath the wonder of loving Molly, I was still so afraid of what it would take from me.

And as I lay there, I realized that part of me hated this hunched shell of a woman who'd stolen my chances at a real life, my desire to look for more. But then she started to shake against me and I felt an immediate twist of guilt. I brushed a tear off her cheek with my thumb, then closed my eyes. "I love you Ma," I whispered, and she patted my hand in the way one might when accepting an apology.

Sometime later I drifted awake, and lay there without moving or speaking, without opening my eyes. Listening to the *snap-snap-snap* of Star laying out her tarot cards.

⟨ 14 ⟩

By the next morning, Star seemed somewhat better. But she refused to come downstairs, huddling in her room like a cat will huddle in a closet after a move to a new home, pretending the world outside her safe corner does not exist.

After my shower I went downstairs to sit with Alex as he fixed breakfast, and found Pamela already in the kitchen with Molly on her lap, trying to keep her from grabbing her mug of coffee.

"It's all related, I guess," she said. "I don't read because it's easier to flop somewhere mindlessly and be fed crap. And you read because you don't have a TV, which is something I'd aspire to except I know I can't live without *The Bachelor*."

"The bachelor?"

Pamela waved her hand dismissively. "You don't want to know. Women love it because we can look at these girls with their Stepford Wifey hair and saline chests, and feel smugly superior. Hi Lainey."

I widened my eyes at her, and she widened her eyes back. "*Leah!* Hi Leah!"

But Alex didn't seem to have noticed. He just waved his spatula at Pamela. "You're vastly superior to anyone with a saline chest. Why would anybody want boobs shaped like volleyballs? Unless they're meant to protect a woman's organs in frontal impact car crashes."

"I love this man!" Pamela said. "Of course he doesn't realize I have to roll my boobs up into my bra these days, like tube socks."

"I've seen it," I said. "She does. It's quite impressive."

Molly squirmed in Pamela's arms to get down, then crawled to me and pulled at my pant leg. "Da!" she said, and I pointed to my chest. "Ma," I said. "Ma, ma, ma."

Pamela raised her eyebrows but I ignored her, swinging Molly up into my arms. "I missed you!" I said, then, "That looks incredible, Alex."

"Cream cheese French toast. I figured this was an occasion that called for many calories. How's your mom doing?"

"Okay, I guess. As okay as could be expected."

"We were just saying maybe Pamela should stay till tomorrow, make sure your mom can handle this. If she needs to go back, you want to find that out now."

"Plus, this is a mini-adventure for me," Pamela said. "It feels like prehistoric times. I mean no CNN! No mini marts! I want to take advantage, maybe fish and carve arrowheads and try hunting for fur."

"You're scared to squash bugs, so I don't see you hunting game," I said, then, "Would you mind staying today? I wouldn't want you driving Star home again because then we'd be right back where we started. But I think it might be kind of a relief for her if she feels like the option's open, even if it's just a sham."

"I honestly don't mind. Let Craig change diapers one more night. I'm eating cream cheese French toast and lounging." She smiled. "So is Star coming down?"

"I was thinking I might bring up her breakfast and eat with her. Which I realize is incredibly antisocial, but it looks like she's not quite ready to leave the bedroom."

"Why don't we all eat with her?" Alex said. "Make it like a picnic and eat on the floor. You think she'll be up to meeting me yet?"

"I think so. She's actually okay with new people, it's just that two things at once, new person, new house, might've been too much last night. Plus, I don't think she would've wanted you to see the state she was in." I shrugged. "But she seems a little better now. I'll go up to make sure she's presentable."

I brought Molly upstairs and pushed open Star's door. "Hey, look who's here to see you."

Star had drawn the blinds I'd opened earlier, and was sitting cross-legged in the dim room, hands in her lap. She smiled weakly. "You come bearing gifts."

"You want to hold her?" I set Molly on Star's lap and sat beside them, my head on Star's shoulder.

Molly grabbed at Star's nose and Star laughed, twisting away to kiss at Molly's palm. "You trying to suffocate me?" she said. "Or just give me a nose job?"

In response, Molly gave a short, barking laugh as if she got the joke, and Star blew into her face, making her squeal. I smiled at them. *See?* I wanted to say. *She's worth it. Isn't she worth it? The hell you went through, the hell you might still go through, this is why.*

"Listen," she said, "could you take the money out of my purse? And put it somewhere safe. Pamela emptied most of our bank account yesterday and it's got to be more than ten thousand dollars. It's freaking me out knowing I'm in charge of it."

I opened her purse, a huge turquoise cloth number she'd bought in the eighties, and pulled out three stacks of bills. And there it was, our net worth in my hands, the result of over a decade of mural painting. My palms immediately started to sweat. If I went momentarily insane and, say, lit a match to it, the only steadfast thing left in our world would be instantly gone. I stuffed the money back into the purse. "I'll take care of it," I said, having no idea how I could possibly keep it safe. "You up for company? Alex is making breakfast, and he was thinking we could all eat in here with you."

Her face slackened, a sudden look of blank despair, but then she said, "That's nice of him. Sure, I'll be fine."

"That was unconvincing. Where's your brush?" I rose to root through her carryall, pulled out her boar's-hair brush and sat on the bed beside her to brush through her sleep-mussed hair. "We'll make you pretty," I said, tugging gently at a tangle.

"It'll take a lot more than a brush to make me pretty. I'd need scalpels and skin staples and fat vacuums." She bounced Molly on her knees and Molly glanced at me, then gave a tentative smile and reached to pull off one of her own socks.

"So, do you have the story straight?" I said, arranging Star's hair at her shoulders. "Who am I? What's my name?"

"You're Leah," she said. "And what's our last name?"

"Honestly? It somehow never came up. We could make something up now, if you want."

"Seriously?" She thought a minute. "How about Rockefeller? Or Kennedy? Since we get to choose anything, we might as well go big."

"Come on, Ma, do we look like Kennedys? The Kennedy men's bastard daughters, maybe."

"Speak for yourself. I'd have impeccable taste if I didn't rely on you to do my shopping." She gave a half-smile. "Okay . . . how 'bout Monroe? On good days we both have a certain resemblance to Marilyn, that same cherubic sexiness."

I blinked. Cherubic sexiness? I found myself wanting to look in a mirror. "Okay, we're the Monroes. And where are we from?"

"Originally," Star said, "originally we're from Austin."

"Atlanta," I said.

Star looked momentarily startled. "I don't know anything about Atlanta," she said. "I was looking forward to being a Texas gal. I was going to do an accent and everything."

"Well that would've been a disaster, so let's thank God we're not from Texas. And where do we live now?"

"After *Atlanta*, you moved up to Chicago and I started having my problems." She smiled into the mirror as she swept blusher over her cheeks. "So I came up to stay with you and your husband. What's his name?"

"David," I said.

She raised an eyebrow. "Right. Well that makes it easy to remember."

"Just don't say more than you have to about the past, okay? That's what I've been doing and it's working fine. And if you do end up revealing any new details about us when I'm not there, just tell me about it after so we can get our story straight."

Her face tightened. "I hate this, Lainey. I'm not good at this."

"You *have* to be good at it. Don't worry, it gets easier. You'll see."

I went back downstairs, and Pamela and Alex returned with me, carrying trays piled high with French toast, melon and sausage and two carafes. We knocked on the door and entered, and Alex approached Star with his hand outstretched. "It's so nice to finally meet you."

"Yes!" Star said, taking his hand, pumping it and beaming at me. "It is!"

I gave her a look.

"So welcome. I hope the bed was okay. It's left over from my days of poverty after college, and I think my back's never been the same since."

"The bed was lovely," she said, then glanced worriedly at me as if looking for confirmation, afraid she'd said something wrong. Oh, this was going to be hard. I should've realized Star had a tendency to overthink everything. Now that she actually had a reason to think before she spoke, of course her brain was clogged with the vast number of possibilities.

We started serving the food onto plates, and Alex lifted the carafes toward her. "Regular or chicory?"

"Chicory!" Star said. "I grew up on chicory, when my mother couldn't afford coffee. I haven't had it since I was a teenager . . ." She grinned at me. "In Atlanta!"

Alex smiled, filling her mug. "I can already tell I'm going to like you. Now see if you can convince Leah of what she's missing."

Star kept beaming. "Ha! Not likely. Because she . . . *Leah* is stubborn and picky. You should see how she freaked out when I tried to get her to try lox. I mean, lox! She said it tasted like a tongue!"

And watching them together, her giddy smile, the kind respect in Alex's voice despite Star's rumpled clothes and the obvious fact she hadn't showered, and her blatant—as Sydney had put it—weirdness, I thought how everything might, after all, turn out okay.

. . .

What finally got Star downstairs that day was her desire to use the Internet, to write up a chart for Alex based on the date, time and place of his birth. She'd drawn all the curtains in the living room and closed all the doors, and there was an edginess to her that worried me. But here she was, in a new room! Of a new house! In a new state! The biggest step she'd taken in years.

Heartened by this, I started calling the numbers I'd found on the Internet of realtors in Montana, asking them for information on short-term rentals. I jotted down the information they gave me so I could look up listings later. We'd leave in a week, no more, as soon as Star settled down a bit. And I tried not to think how I'd tell her we were leaving, get her back into the car. Had only some vague thought that I'd spring it on her moments before we left. Perhaps after getting her drunk.

We'd stay in Montana two weeks, maybe a bit more, and then be on the move again, moving every couple weeks until Sydney could leave Virginia safely. It wasn't much of a plan, but there was no way to plan further until I found out more about what was going on, the imminence of the danger we were in.

I pictured a woman standing in an open field, surveying the wilderness, her baby on her back wrapped like a papoose. She contemplated what lay ahead and then steeled her shoulders and walked into the barren terrain. And watching her I felt an unexpected tenderness, and pride.

No way to know how long her life would last; much as I despised Sydney for what she was doing to me now and everything that had happened in the past, I knew I couldn't justify taking her daughter away forever. But for now I'd play this out the way every human played out his life. Assuming it would last forever. Forgetting the inevitable end.

As Star worked on the computer, I went outside with Alex to finish the garden, while Pamela played with Molly on the front porch. I hadn't had a chance yet to talk to her about her conversation with Sydney, had actually been avoiding time alone with her. At least for the next few hours, I wanted to pretend Sydney didn't exist.

I set all the flowerpots in the places I thought would work best, the rosebushes and broad-leafed hosta against the house, the smaller flower bunches, phlox, marigolds and bluebells, framing the stone path, and a large bed set aside for vegetables and herbs. I arranged them by color and height, stepped back and made a few adjustments, and then Alex and I started to dig.

Or rather, Alex dug and I watched while trying not to look like I was watching. The muscles working in his back, the sweat flushing his face, kneeling beside him with our hands in the rich earth to set the flowers in place, it was all . . . okay, let's not mince words here . . . it was pure sexy.

And even sexier? When we were almost done Alex excused himself and went inside, appearing a minute later at the bay window with Star, gesturing to the roses. She still looked grim, but she did stretch a smile as she surveyed the garden, and again when she saw Molly on the porch. She said something to him and he nodded and said something back, then squeezed her shoulder and came back outside.

"I think your mom's going to be okay," he said, kneeling next to me. "Hard right now but I think she'll settle down when things feel a little less unpredictable."

"Yeah, and when's that going to be exactly? I have to make her leave again as soon as I can get her back into the car."

Alex watched my face a moment before saying, "You know you can stay as long as you like. I don't know why you feel like you have to run off so fast. Isn't this as safe a place as anywhere else?"

"Alex . . . God, you're an amazing person. Has anybody ever told you you're amazing? But I don't think I'm safe staying anywhere for too long."

I saw a fleeting sadness cross his face before he turned back to break up the root ball of the peony we were planting. "That really sucks, you know? Last night when I couldn't sleep, I was imagining what might've happened if you weren't in trouble, if we just happened to meet on the road and you happened to need a place to stay for whatever reason, and we could just hang out until we got sick of each other."

I turned to glance at him, then quickly away, my heart stuttering with a little hiccup of pleasure. I bit back my smile and said, "I've actually started understanding what it's like to be Star. Not having a real home anymore, it feels like I've completely lost control so absolutely anything could happen. Like . . . the universe could just open up and suck me away into the vacuum, and there I'd be flying alone through space."

Alex turned back to the garden, filling the hole around the peony. "Did I ever tell you about my transcontinental adventure?"

"I don't think so," I said, "no."

"It was the most important thing I ever did, and the hardest. I left home, ran away basically, when I was eighteen, a week before I was supposed to graduate high school. I was having problems with my mom, and graduating just seemed so banal; so, I don't know, conformist, and being the rebel that I was, I just took off. With the clothes on my back, a travel-sized toothbrush and an autographed Polaroid of Demi Moore."

"You didn't take extra undies or socks but you took a photo?"

"Yeah, that's the embarrassing part of the story. But you know, I was a kid, and it felt like the one perfect thing I had was the memory of the night Demi took the pen and photo from me and said, 'Sure I will.' " He smiled. "So there I was, hitchhiking to wherever the people who picked me up were going. Truckers mostly, so I made it long distances in short amounts of time. If you traced my route you'd get something that looked like a spiderweb: Pennsylvania to Maine into Vancouver to Florida to Louisiana. I met amazing people who'd been through hellish lives, and it taught me more about spiritual poverty than anything I've seen since. This is an unhappy country, Leah."

I thought about the distant look Alex sometimes wore, and then, I thought about myself. With Molly, I was happy. But knowing there'd come a time I'd only feel happiness from the memories, well that kind of negated all of it.

"I was actually going to tell you I found a home in just being with those truckers and listening to their stories, and that maybe they found some kind of home in me, because all it really takes is having someone understand you. I wanted to say that, but we'd both know it's bull. It helps, but it's not home. Because here I am. I have friends who love me and as good a life as pretty much anybody, but I still don't feel like I have a home."

I turned to look at him and our eyes met and held, something passing between us that felt as intimate as a touch. "Yeah," I said softly, "I don't think I've had a real home for years. And I have no idea how to go about finding one."

Alex hesitated, then said, "I'm really glad I got to meet you, to know you. You're not going to understand this, but in a way it changes everything."

I felt a twisting inside me at the implied finality of Alex's words. I shot a smile at him that I hoped looked like a thank-you and nothing more, and then Pamela called from the porch, "Hey! She ever done this before?"

I turned and there Molly was, on her feet unsupported, watching us through the porch rails. I rushed over to her, feeling a spear of pride followed by guilt. "I missed her first time!" I said.

"What did you miss?" Pamela raised her eyebrows. "Here it is and here you are."

But the fact remained, I'd missed Molly's first time standing because I'd been gripped by the pain of leaving a man I hardly knew. There had to be a lesson there.

We spent a minute profusely admiring the strength of Molly's legs until she raised her arms to me, which made her promptly fall backward onto her butt. She let out a surprised yelp, then looked at me as if deciding whether to cry, before she unexpectedly started clapping.

"Well now she thinks everything she does is worthy of applause," Pamela said.

Alex smiled almost shyly at me, then scooped Molly into his arms and planted a big kiss on her cheek. "First standing, then walking, and soon I'll be teaching you ice hockey moves!"

Pamela shook her head at me, and I smiled and shrugged. Alex saw the gesture and smiled back. "Yeah, I know. I'm acting like she's mine." Which made Pamela give me a look and another small shake of her head like she was saying, *Don't you go there, missy, don't you dare* . . .

We ate lunch at the dining table with Molly crawling at our feet, pulling at our shoelaces, periodically stopping to taste her fist. Star didn't mention the results of Alex's chart, and when he finally brought it up she gave a startled frown, then said she wasn't ready to discuss it. And that was all she said for the next ten minutes, just sat there shuffling the food on her plate, arranging and rearranging it with great concentration like she was trying to create some expressionistic form of food art.

Lunch was an extravaganza of the type of food you'd eat if you used lunch as a verb: flat bread with roasted red pepper tapenade, feta cheese and Kalamata olives, a salad with pine nuts and baby lettuces. "How does a tiny grocery in a tiny town keep all this in stock?" I said.

"Oh, it's Raymond, the grocer; he humors me. First time I shopped there after coming from the city, I went up to the counter and asked where the edamame was, and he just stared at me like I must've evolved from somewhere strange and distant. But the next time I went in, there it was, edamame. And then without me asking, he started ordering all these random, weird things like anchovy paste and quail egg jelly. I don't know if he was making fun of me or if he was trying to impress me, but I had to bring them home, because of course he'd gone out of his way to find them." He shrugged. "So after the first couple weeks I realized if I wanted anything edible I'd have to place actual orders."

"You use the word 'grocer' and know him by his first name," Pamela said. "I think I might have to move here."

Star sniffed at an olive, then dropped it. Her hand was shaking. "I guess my stomach's not up to it today," she said. "I'm sorry, d'you mind if I go back up to the bedroom?"

"You okay?" Alex said, then gave a small cough, probably aware of the absurdity of the question. He glanced at me. "Why don't we bring our food up like this morning? Another picnic."

"No." Star stood quickly. "No, no, I just need to rest a little. This is all . . . it's all a little much." She gave each of us a wavering smile. "But I'll be fine!"

I stood to take her arm. "I'll go with you."

"No, stay! What're you gonna do, hold my hand? The only thing that might help me is if you opened my skull, took my brain in your fists and squashed it. Just stay and enjoy your lunch." She walked out into the hall.

Pamela looked at me. "Well!" she said brightly. "This is going great!"

"Better than I expected, actually." I shrugged. "I mean I didn't know *what* to expect. But she's alive, she's not unconscious, she hasn't OD'd yet on Xanax."

"Should I stay tomorrow too? Just in case I have to take her back?"

"You really want to relive yesterday's trip? I'll *make* her be okay, through sheer force of will. Aided by pharmaceuticals." I gave a half smile. "Excuse me, I'm sorry, I'm just going to try and settle her down. Mind watching Molly a minute?" I left the room and went upstairs.

Star was in bed, rabidly tearing paper into scraps over the trash bin. As I watched, she lifted those scraps again to tear them into smaller bits, her face red and her eyes fierce.

I sat next to her and waited for her to explain. When she didn't, I said, "What?"

She let the scraps sift between her fingers, then stared down at them a minute before she spoke. "That was his chart," she said.

Despite myself, this scared me a little. I didn't believe in astrological charts, just like I didn't believe in Star's card readings. But the charts she'd done on me, and various neighbors and movie stars, had proved true often enough that I guess I was holding open the possibility they might be loosely relevant. "What did it say? Is he an axe murderer? He going to die before he hits forty? What?"

"I can't tell him. Some of this I can use, but I'll make the rest up. It's not a good chart, Lainey. Nothing's good; I shouldn't be here, you shouldn't be here."

"Look at me." I reached for her chin and roughly turned her face toward me. "Stop. Snap out of this."

Her eyes filled. "Okay. You want to know? He's been through awful things in his life, Lainey, that's what my readings last night said and now his chart's saying the same thing. They've made him too vulnerable and trusting, and it's the issue he's going to deal with for the rest of his life. It's just not right for you to be messing with his trust like this. It's going to end up destroying his soul."

"Destroying his soul." I tried to put lyricism and humor into my voice, but it wasn't exactly a humorous phrase, so I ended up sounding like the narrator in a horror spoof.

"He's a good man, too good. And you're going to hurt him."

"Well as long as he's not an axe murderer."

"This isn't funny!"

And she was right, it wasn't funny. Not that I believed her, or at least most of me didn't, but the problem was, she believed herself, and this would only exacerbate her paranoia.

"The themes of his life are betrayal, especially by strong women, and entrapment. I told you I did a chart on that poor man in Louisiana who got arrested three times for things his girlfriend set him up for? Well this was the same sort of chart."

"I'm going to get him arrested?"

She watched me closely. "What do you know about him, Lainey? How much has he told you?"

"He's told me enough. Enough that I know I can trust him."

She shook her head slowly. "He's not a happy man, Lainey. This isn't something I got from his chart, it's something I can tell from seeing him. He's the kind of person who puts on a happy attitude so he can hide everything that's underneath, but I think there's a lot hidden. It's not a good energy field to be around."

I refrained, rather admirably, from reminding her of the energy field I'd been around all my life. I couldn't tell her yet that we'd only be here for another few days, so instead I said, "So what're you suggesting I do, exactly? Do you have any ideas? Should I turn myself in and surround myself with the energy of a jail cell?"

"Lainey, I can see how you feel about him, and I've seen the way he looks at you."

I felt a thump in my chest, like a bowling pin being knocked over. "The way he looks at me?"

"But he's haunted. I don't know by who or what, but you're not going to be able to help him. Whatever happens here, you'll only make it worse."

She glanced up as Pamela knocked and entered. "Your mail," Pamela said, handing me a pile of envelopes. "I'll pick it up every other day and forward it if there's anything you should see. But you should put your newspapers and magazines on hold."

I looked down at the mail: fifty percent bills, fifty percent junk. "Thanks, I will."

"I was hoping we could talk in the other bedroom. We okay here?"

"We aren't," I said. "We think we'd be better off incarcerated."

"Interesting." Pamela smiled grimly. "Okay, I'll post bail long as you don't implicate me."

I smoothed back Star's hair. "You'll be okay," I said, more to reassure myself than anything else.

In Pamela's bedroom, I sat in the armchair and she sat on the bed and leaned back against the headboard. "I guess I assumed she'd be feeling better by now," she said. "That once she realized there wasn't any cataclysmic impact from leaving, she'd have an epiphany and be cured."

"The problem is, she does still think there's about to be a cataclysm." I slumped back in my chair. "She doesn't like Alex's energy field."

"What the heck is there not to like? I love his energy field. I could marry and have babies with his energy field."

"I'm sure she's just projecting her own issues on him. I have to think she'll feel better about everything once we can finally settle somewhere."

"Settle somewhere?" Pamela glanced at me. "What's your plan, Lainey? How long are you going to do this?"

"I'll do it as long as I have to, until I'm sure David McGrath's going to be in jail for good, and that Molly's safe. I've called real estate listings, know a couple possible places to stay for the short term."

"Crap, Lainey, this is so crazy. I have this unbearable urge to shake you like you're one of my kids. And I'd do it too, if I thought it would do any good." She rose to sit on the arm of my chair. "So you want to talk about Sydney?"

No, I thought. "Okay," I said.

"You know, after talking to her I almost got how you were sucked in. She almost convinced me she knows what she's doing, although there were little things that didn't add up, made me think she might be hiding something. I don't know, I'm usually pretty good about reading people, but she's . . . different. The only thing I know for sure is she does love her daughter."

I felt an involuntary twinge at the words, *her daughter.* "Somehow that doesn't quite excuse anything," I said.

"Believe me, I know. But she had this desperation; she kept asking how Jacqueline was, even when I said I didn't know anything. Like did I think Jacqueline missed her? Did she seem angry? Or like her feelings were hurt?"

"Molly," I said.

"Right, no comment. Or I'll imply a comment, but not actually make one." She folded her arms and fixed her eyes on mine.

"Okay, I'm choosing to ignore you now. What did Sydney say about what she's planning? Does she even know?"

"Well that was one of the things that didn't add up. First she tells me not to worry, that she's got everything planned out, but then she gets all nervous and says she actually has no idea how to make this work but that she needs me to reassure you that you're safe. She kept begging me not to turn her in, saying how this was her only chance to save . . ." Pamela stretched a slim smile. "*Molly*. But now she's had to turn David in, I don't know. She said she's waiting for him to admit he abused them before she takes Molly back from you and confesses to the cops, but it seems like that's not going to happen anytime soon."

"So she's stuck."

"If he doesn't confess, she said her plan of last resort would be to just take the baby from you and disappear somewhere. But the crazy thing was how she kept talking about David, what a complete scumbag he was, but in a way that made it sound like she was more hurt than scared or mad. She said he had no idea how to love someone, how all he cared about was whether he'd be invited to whatever clubs and VIP parties and blah, blah, blah. You hear these stories about abused wives who still have this sort of love for their husbands, need them in some way despite everything they've done. And how she was talking, it made me wonder what her real motives are."

"You mean she's more interested in hurting him than protecting Molly?"

"I'm sure she wants to protect Molly too, but there's got to be other ways she could've kept her safe. I mean, giving away her baby so she can accuse him of kidnapping? It's so bizarre. Who'd do that?"

I picked a stray thread off the armchair. "Did she say anything about me? What she's expecting from me?"

"She didn't say much, just that she'd try and call you in the next week or so, and I should tell you she said 'Hi.'"

I raised my eyebrows. "Hi?"

"Yeah, exactly. Maybe there's a wealth of emotion behind it that we're missing."

I leaned back in the chair, staring down at my knees. "Well I guess there's no right thing she really could say. I'm sure she feels guilty for pulling me into this, and she's probably overwhelmed and scared."

"My vote's still that she's not thinking twice about what you're going through. But okay, maybe I'll give her the benefit of the doubt.

She looked overwhelmed, I'll give her that much, all fidgety and like she hadn't slept or showered in days." Pamela kicked her heel back forcefully against the chair leg. "I don't know, Lainey, the thing that gets me most is how she seems to believe this is all completely justified. She's not totally heartless; like I said she obviously loves Molly. But she's completely self-serving, like toddlers who think the world revolves around their need for juice and their bathroom habits."

I remembered the day in fifth grade when Sydney had broken her collarbone, and she'd had to call my mom to bring her from the hospital. The silence of the meals I'd eaten at her house, napkins folded in our laps, knives and forks set down between each bite, the horror on Sydney's face when she'd spilled a glass of milk, and her mother's snapped but distracted reprimand. She'd *needed* to think of herself first.

And with those memories, I decided to work on forgiving Sydney, not just for this but for everything. Maybe people had to be taught empathy, the way I was now trying to teach Molly to talk. Sydney had had no examples to follow, and so the necessary neurons had never developed. The fact that she loved Molly enough to risk her own future was, if you thought about it, rather miraculous.

"Whether or not we like her is completely beside the point right now," I said. "I just have to believe she'd never do anything that would lead the authorities to Molly."

Besides, it wasn't being used that bothered me most. I wasn't scared what would happen to me, I was scared what would happen to Molly once Sydney took her.

I thought of the disregard Sydney had shown everything precious while we were growing up: fancy clothes muddied and torn; a portrait of her I'd painstakingly painted for her eleventh birthday, which I'd found a month later defaced with a tiara and pink cheeks. Our friendship. And maybe she loved Molly, but I still couldn't believe she had any idea how to love her enough.

• • •

It was the middle of the night before I had a chance to turn on Alex's computer to check for stories.

It seemed like the focus was shifting onto the possible involvement of Sydney and David's acquaintances and coworkers, and I tried playing the whole story from the authorities' point of view: add Sydney's lie about the kidnapping to her claims of abuse, of having left the baby at David's, David's cocaine possession and a ransom note from someone Sydney knew. And what did it add up to? A mess, that's what, direction and misdirection, the truth hidden somewhere in the tangles. Impossible to tell whether it was hidden deeply enough.

And then I found the article in the *New York Post:*

NEW SUSPICIONS ARISE IN
MISSING BABY CASE

Investigators have been increasing pressure on both parents of missing baby Jacqueline McGrath, after father David McGrath was arraigned yesterday under charges of minor drug possession. A draft investigative report, released by the state public safety department this afternoon, indicated that Mr. McGrath passed a polygraph test in which he was questioned on his daughter's abduction. At the same time the girl's mother, Sydney Beaumont, has refused to be polygraphed, saying only that her lawyer has advised her against it. All this as Beaumont undergoes intense rounds of questioning over her allegations that her ex-husband abused both her and their daughter and that the girl was in McGrath's custody at the time of her disappearance, both of which McGrath has repeatedly denied.

Meanwhile, the prominent McGrath family has hired their own private investigation firm to pursue all available leads, and is offering up a $500,000 reward for information directly leading to the baby's return. "It should seem obvious now that our client was not involved in the disappearance," said one of McGrath's lawyers yesterday. "We don't know at this point if Ms. Beaumont's increasingly outlandish allegations are a sign of her own culpability, an attempt at retribution for what had become an increasingly hostile divorce and custody battle or some combination of the two. Either way, we're glad to see that the authorities are now redirecting their investigation."

I closed the article and turned off the computer, then sat in the desk chair with my hands clasped between my knees. I sat there, dizzy and nauseous, for five, ten, twenty minutes, and then I rose and went to Pamela's door.

She answered, bleary-eyed, wearing what looked to be one of Craig's T-shirts. She must have read something in my face, because her expression immediately sharpened and she backed into the room and closed the door behind us before speaking. "What is it?" she said.

"The investigation." I sank into the armchair, staring dully at the clothes Pamela had strewn over the top of the dresser. "I just read an update and they're coming closer. David passed a polygraph and Sydney's refusing to take one, and doesn't that mean they'll realize she's involved? How long can she keep refusing?"

"I don't think they can force anyone to be polygraphed, and they definitely can't use it to prove guilt. I think it just shows them where to focus their investigation, and it's probably also a scare tactic." She sat cross-legged on the bed, pulled her T-shirt over her knees and after a minute she said softly, "Didn't you realize this was going to happen, Lainey? Sydney can't get away with this forever, and when they find out you have Molly, you're going to look just as guilty."

"Even more guilty." I shook my head, my eyes filling. "Sydney isn't going to tell them this was her idea; she'll try and use me as her Get Out of Jail Free card. And I don't even give a damn what happens to me, I'm scared what's going to happen to Molly if Sydney's arrested and they take her away from me. Where's she going to go? To an abusive drug addict? Or to foster care?"

Pamela watched me without speaking.

"What?" I said, then louder, "What! You don't think I have a right to worry because she's not officially mine? You think I should just give her over to the cops, let them do whatever they want with her and just brush my hands clean because the law says she's not my responsibility?"

"That's not it," Pamela said slowly. "Lainey, come on, you really thought you'd be able to keep her?"

I hugged my knees, staring fixedly at the wall, and she hesitated before rising to set a hand on my shoulder. "Lainey . . ."

"What am I going to do, Pamela?" My voice broke. "I'll run to Montana, and then what? Sydney's going to want her back, I realize that, but is it going to be in two months? One? Less? How can I figure out how to feel if I don't even know how much time I have left?"

Pamela knelt in front of my chair, looked up into my face and then laid her head in my lap without speaking. Not speaking because there was no answer, because she knew this wasn't a fairy tale, and that it probably wouldn't have a happy ending.

And yes, of course I wasn't stupid. I knew it too.

Pamela pushed away the money for gas I tried to stuff into her purse. And then she took my hand and pulled me down the front path, out of earshot of Alex who was standing by the door with Molly. "I'll tell her Molly's doing good," Pamela said under her breath. "I'll stop by tomorrow and tell her that."

"Tell her she's doing *great*," I said. "How now she seems like she's probably happier than ever in her life, and how she's learning all kinds of new things."

"Yeah, okay. I'll say she's learned how to read and do long division, and that not only did she tell me she's happy, she said it in Greek."

I smiled. "I'm going to miss the hell out of you." The past couple of days, here with the people I loved best in the world, I'd started to feel more grounded than probably ever in my life. Despite all the fear of what would come next and knowing Star was hovering on the brink of internal combustion, I'd felt somehow like everything was as it should be.

Pamela pulled me into a one-armed hug. "No you won't, not really. I don't agree with any of this, and I don't know how to hold my tongue so I'm just getting in the way, like an alarm clock kicking you out of your dream."

The phone rang, and I turned to watch Alex rush inside to get it,

Molly in his arms. Pamela was probably right, in a way. Without her here I could immerse myself back into this life. She was the one continually reminding me it would be over soon.

After she'd driven away, I stood awhile gazing down the street. And realized I didn't care if this wasn't real. In a way my happiness was just like Star's fear, maybe grounded in mental illness, but that didn't make the feeling itself any less genuine.

I shoved my hands into my pockets, breathing in the honeysuckle scent of the new garden. I should sketch this, try and capture the bright splashes of color. I could even make a mural from it someday, in my own house. So I could sit by it and remember.

I made a box with my fingers and thumbs and held it against one eye like a camera frame, and then I went inside for my sketch pad and pens. Alex was on the phone in the kitchen, speaking in low tones. I stood in the entryway a moment, trying to listen to his voice under the sound of Molly's babbling, then realized what I was doing and turned away.

Upstairs, Star was in her bedroom standing at the window. The blinds were down, the room dim and dusty feeling. "So that's it," she said when I entered. "Stranded." She smiled widely, but I could see the strain behind it.

"You made it," I said. "You took your biggest fear and stomped on it."

"Well I wouldn't say I stomped on it, I'd say I slithered underneath it. From prison A to prison B, except here . . ." She gestured at the lawn, the miles of woods beyond. "Here, I'm alone with myself and my patheticness. There's no TV and I don't even have my people. What am I going to do all day except tear out my hair strand by strand?"

By *people,* she must mean her clients, the women who came weekly for readings or personal horoscopes and sometimes stayed an hour or more to chat, only then handing over their tens and twenties, furtively like they were paying a hooker for an evening of pretend love. Star thought of these women as her friends. "You're not alone, Ma, and we'll find stuff for you to do. Like did you see the library downstairs? You could read for a decade and still not run out of books. And we'll find you new people. I'm sure there's folks here who'd be interested in a reading."

"They'll probably be weirdos," she said.

I raised my eyebrows at her, and she glowered back. "Okay, I'm not listening to this," I said, bending to the corner for my supplies. "I was going to work on some sketches outside. If you want, I'll sit right there in the garden so you can see me."

"I used to watch you playing in the backyard while I was cooking," Star said, "to make sure you stayed safe." She turned again to the window. "There's irony there somewhere."

I knew I should probably find something comforting to say, but there was no way really to do it without sounding even more patronizing. So I just squeezed her shoulder and went downstairs.

There was nowhere to sit except on the ground, so that's what I did, sat on the stone path with my sketchbook on my lap, surrounded by the flowers. It was such a startling transition, slapped from the dimness of Star's room into this vibrant kaleidoscope, black-and-white to Oz, that for a full minute I was paralyzed, like an overstimulated baby. I sat unmoving, gazing at a gardenia, thinking only: RED.

"Leah!" I looked up to see Susie Greer waving from the road, holding the hand of a thin, balding man in a purple tracksuit. "Look at this!" she said. "All it took was a woman in Alex's life and he gave his home a face-lift."

"You like?" I said.

"I *love*! For selfish reasons too, since I'm sure seeds from all the weeds you killed were making it down the street and planting themselves in my lawn. Leah, this is Jack, the man who serves as, but will never be, my husband."

"That's because I'm too good for you." Jack walked up the path, arm extended. "Susie told me about you. You be around for our barbecue?"

I stood and took his hand. "Barbecue?"

"She hasn't been invited yet," Susie said. "Tell Alex our July bar-becue bash is on the nineteenth, and that you're both coming. Molly too, obviously."

"Well thanks, but we're actually leaving in a few days. Wish I could make it, though."

"You're not leaving. I hardly got to know you!"

I smiled. "Wish I could stay, but there's only so much advantage I can take of Alex."

"Well if that's the only reason you're leaving, forget about it. I know Alex, and he's lonely as hell; needs something to pull him away from his dang computer. It's been tough for him living out here on his own, especially with everything he's been through and the issues with his mom and his sister. And I have a feeling there's even more about him that we don't know. He's a pretty complex man, and he hates talking about himself, but you can tell he's troubled."

I wanted to ask what she meant, what exactly he'd "been through," but she seemed so sure I'd know what she was talking about. And really it was bizarre that I didn't know, that I hardly knew anything about his past, that we'd talked about almost everything, but not about his family.

"I guess he thought he could come out here to get away from it all. He should've realized in a place like this all you have is your thoughts, so they grow. But it must be so healing having you and Molly here. So." She smiled. "You're all coming, 'kay?"

I started to apologize, but she interrupted me. "Just tell Alex it'll be very chichi so he should bring something fabulous. You, all you need to bring is the baby. Where is she anyway? And how come you were sitting on the ground?"

"She's inside with Alex." I held up my blank sketch pad. "And I'm trying to get inspired by the garden, sketch it so I can make a mural of it someday."

"You paint murals?" Jack said. "Well we've always wished we had a mural! Of the beach where I grew up in Kennebunk. Are you any good?"

They lived together? I didn't think they were lovers; Susie's gaze when she turned to him was obviously adoring, but Jack's purple sweats and a certain manner about him suggested that probably wasn't possible. I could imagine my relationship with Alex might've turned into this if I'd been able to stay long-term, a lopsided friendship, him gently accommodating, me wanting something I could never have. "I won't be here long enough to do a mural, but I could sketch an idea for you, and you could try and do it on your own. Beaches are pretty easy."

"We have the drawing talent of prehistoric humanoids," Susie said, "so don't waste your time unless you think you'll be able to paint it yourself. But I thought we already settled that you're staying? We need a baby in the neighborhood, and fresh blood to spice things up, since this street usually has the pizzazz of bingo night at a retirement home. I'll tell Alex that, and maybe he'll be convinced to hold you hostage."

"She'd probably handcuff you to the porch herself," Jack said, "except then you couldn't paint our mural." He held up his hand. "The nineteenth?"

I bit back a smile. "Nice to meet you," I said, waving back.

After they'd gone I sat back down, luxuriating in simple contentedness. I set my sketchbook on my lap and started to work, penciling in a garden path, a trellis climbing with ivy, multicolored scribbles to suggest the flowers, absorbing myself in the scritch of lead on paper and the paradise I was creating.

I don't know how long it was I was sitting there when I heard a small shuffling behind me and turned to see Alex sitting next to me, cradling Molly in his lap. I startled, slashing a green mark across my penciled sky. "How long've you been there?"

"Sorry, I didn't mean to scare you. I love watching you work, you have this . . . intensity. You're a lot more complex than you let on, which makes me want to know you better."

My face flushed. "You'll be disappointed."

"I don't think so," he said softly, then, "I guess Pamela's gone? I really liked her."

"Yeah, me too. She's one of the few people in the world who gets me. And likes me in spite of it."

Molly scrambled off Alex's lap, reached for a pink petunia, squashed it in her fist and then brought it to her mouth. I pried it from her fingers as Alex reached for the sketchbook. "Pretty," he said. "Kind of ethereal." He flipped back through the pages, slowly. "Wow, you're really talented." He looked up at me, his eyes bright with appreciation. "You painted murals of all these?"

"Most of them, yeah." I felt a little heart skip of pride. "And thanks."

"I should've realized how talented you are. You have that look about you, a kind of graceful look."

"Well thanks. But I'm about as graceful as an industrial dump truck." I leaned back on my hands. "A *drunk* industrial dump truck."

"I don't mean that kind of graceful, I mean *grace*-ful. Someone with grace. You need grace to be an artist."

I smiled like I knew what he was talking about and was accepting the compliment. What did that mean exactly? Who used the word "grace" outside of church and New Year's Eve? I said it to myself once, practicing, and then again: *You are a woman with grace.* I'd have to look the word up when I got inside.

He turned to a sketch I'd made for a two-year-old, of the characters from *The Wind in the Willows:* Mole and Ratty, Mr. Toad of Toad Hall, standing in a circle in the woods. He looked at it a good two minutes and then said, "You can just tell, looking at this, what a good mom you are. Just from the kindness in their faces."

There was something melancholy in his voice I couldn't interpret. "You okay?" I said instead.

"What? Sure, I'm fine."

"I've never heard anybody say the word 'sure' with less conviction." I reached to touch his hand, then wondered if that might be inappropriate, so pulled back. Figuring out appropriateness was so complex when it involved a man who thought he knew who you were but actually didn't, who was unknowingly letting you hide out in his house with a kidnapped baby, who maybe had a girlfriend or maybe didn't, on whom you kind of had a crush but knew the chances of him ever feeling the same were less than zero point zero one percent. It was not your typical Miss Manners situation.

"It's just that I'm looking at this drawing and thinking how you are with Molly and then about everything you've been through. Realizing the world should be this simple and this good, but that it never comes even close." He shook his head. "Sorry, I'm sounding morose. It's just I had a completely crappy phone conversation with an old friend, and our conversations never end well. We have what you could call a twisted past that manages to dig under and uproot every conversation."

I watched him a moment, then said, "It's okay, you don't have to talk about it." I waited, on the off chance he might actually want to talk about it. When he didn't go on, I added, "But I'm a good listener, so if you ever need a shoulder, here I am." I patted my shoulder, then got immediately profoundly embarrassed at myself. I might as well shake him, my hands around his neck, screaming, "Just tell me!"

"Thanks," he said, then handed back my sketchbook. He bent toward me and, for a tortured second, I was sure he was going to kiss my lips. I froze, my eyes wide, something soft but fierce ballooning inside my chest, but he just kissed my forehead softly and then stood and walked into the house.

I spent the rest of the morning in the garden with Molly, discovering earthworms and spraying water rainbows and then, since she had a penchant for sticking nearly everything in her mouth anyway, I led her to the herbs I'd planted, giving her small tastes of oregano (she was not a fan) and thyme, which she granted her tentative approval by reaching for more. I'd just given her a sprig of rosemary when I heard music start from the inside of the house, a trumpet playing "Sentimental Journey." What did it say about a man when he enjoyed music from the '40s? Did he identify with the earnest idealism of that time because he was himself so idealistic? Or did he just have the taste of an eighty-year-old?

Alex was in the living room on the computer. He smiled up at me and Molly, touched his cheek. "You got a little sunburn, Leah. Very flattering."

The song on the CD changed to "In the Mood," and to keep Alex from seeing whatever my face was showing, I started to dance with Molly across the room. "Yeah, but by tomorrow it'll be peeling and I'll look like I have leprosy." I dipped Molly toward the floor, smiled at her laughter. "Star loves this song. Actually has the single, probably left from the phonograph days."

Alex watched us a minute, and then he rose. "Hey, Moll, mind if I cut in?"

I froze, watching him approach; he took one of my hands and set his other hand on my shoulder, and we waltzed awkwardly a minute with Molly between us until he brought that hand to my waist. "Better," he said.

I couldn't breathe, feeling nothing but his hand, as if my whole body was centered around the skin at my waist. "I suck at dancing," I said.

"It's okay; me and Molly don't, so we'll lead and you follow."

And so the three of us danced around the living room, Molly laughing, Alex squeezing lightly at my waist whenever he wanted to change direction, the feel of it echoing down and through me as if he were squeezing somewhere else entirely.

And then the song changed, Sinatra singing "I'll Be Seeing You." As I started to back away, Alex pulled Molly from me, set her on the floor and then reached for my hand and pulled me closer.

My eyes snapped wide but then, slowly, I let myself relax. I hadn't been this close to a man since Keith, and the feel of this was completely different. Alex's chest was muscular where Keith had been skinny, collarbone and ribs like a cage around him. And Alex's scent was different; Keith had always smelled of cigarettes even after showering, like years of smoking had seeped into his very pores. But Alex had an innate sweetness under the scent of his Ivory soap, like fresh-cut wood. Really, exactly the way I would've expected him to smell.

I'll find you in the morning sun, and when the night is new;
I'll be looking at the moon, but I'll be seeing you . . .

Molly sat by our feet, smiling up at us almost conspiratorially. *It's not really what you think,* I wanted to tell her. And myself. It was a friendly dance; friend-friends did this all the time and having never really had a man as a friend, of course my body was interpreting it as something else. Unconsciously molding myself to him, I rested my head on his shoulder, my hand against the small of his back. I could feel the whisper of his quickened breath against my ear, like fingers tracing against it. Or lips.

And then I heard ringing from inside my pocket. I glanced down, willing the sound to go away.

"Is that your phone?" Alex said softly.

"Yeah." I pulled away. "Sorry." Meaning mostly that I was sorry as hell I'd left my cell phone on. I reached for the phone and answered.

"Lainey!"

It was Sydney, and as soon as I heard her voice, my legs started to walk me backward from the room.

"I have to take this," I said after I'd already reached the hall, and then I stuck my head back into the room and repeated, "I have to take this," then strode upstairs, my heart in my throat. "Okay," I said, "tell me what the hell's going on. Do you know how it feels not having any idea?"

"Stop," she said tightly, "I don't have time for this, just listen a second, okay? This is important, something's happened, it's the FBI. They were interrogating me, Lainey. And I had to give them your name."

{ 16 }

"You what!" I said.

"I couldn't help it, I had to. They asked for a list of the people I'd talked to the month before Jacqueline disappeared, and I had to tell them about you because there were witnesses. If I didn't tell them and they found out we'd met, then they'd start looking deeper and we'd all be in trouble. This way they'll think you're just inconsequential, one of the thirty, forty people I saw."

"But if they look me up they'll realize I left home!" I paced across my bedroom, my heart racing. "I'm in their records, Sydney, because I asked the cops to check on my mom last week and I told them I hadn't seen her for days, so they're going to wonder why I left and get suspicious."

"You called the cops?" She paused. "Well seriously, they're so disorganized I doubt they'll even cross-check your name. But if they ask then you can make up some story. Tell them you took your mom somewhere to help her relax, and you'll be back in a week."

"You don't think they'll ask where we are and check hotel records?"

"Well they might, I guess. So maybe you can just say you guys've been sleeping in your car or camping. Tell them more or less where you actually are in case they can trace your phone location, but I doubt any of this is even going to come up. Just act all friendly and sweet and innocent, that's what I've been doing, and they'll believe all you are is friendly and sweet and innocent. And maybe you could tell them you know I'm the kind of person who'd never lie."

"You told them Jacqueline got stolen in front of Macy's!"

She ignored this. "Or do anything to hurt my baby. And if you told them how David abused us, that'd be an added plus. Maybe you could say you saw my beat-up face and suggested I should hide Jacqueline from him, but that I told you I'd never do something illegal. Or do you think that's too much?"

"Are you drunk?"

"Just tell them as little as you can, it's—" She sucked in her breath. "Oh fuck, hold on."

"What? What's going on?"

She didn't answer for a full minute; all I could hear was a rapid shuffling and background voices before she whispered, "I'm by the men's room in an Italian restaurant. I don't want to use a pay phone out in the open anymore. I don't know if they're following me, David's thugs. Or the FBI, they could be following me to trace my calls."

"What if they followed you to the restaurant?"

"They didn't, I was standing here looking at the door for the past half hour to make sure before I called. This has been such hell, Lainey. You know they've come to search my home? Barged into my house! They took my computer, a journal—"

"A journal!"

"It was old, from a year or two ago. And it talks about David's abuse, so it can only help. But there were also letters from that guy I told you about, Kemper."

I felt my skin flush cold. "Letters from when?"

"A couple months ago was the last one. I told you how he knows some of what David did to me. He helped me out after David broke my arm, and last year he started pleading with me to leave David, but I was pregnant with Jacqueline and I was sure things were going to change after she was born. So I started avoiding him, but he kept writing me these insistent letters, urging me to get away. I wish to

God I hadn't saved them, but I thought they might help me decide what to do, whether it was safe to trust him to help me once I can leave here. And so of course now the FBI's seen the letters, they're really interested in him."

"But that's good, right? It's distracting them."

"It's not good." She paused, then said, "I refused to give them any information on him, tell them how to reach him, which I'm sure makes us both look really suspicious."

"Like he's hiding Molly?"

"So I can accuse David of kidnapping, yeah, maybe. Like I'm just waiting till the three of us can escape together. That or maybe they think he acted on his own, took Jacqueline to protect her and then wrote the note you left at Six of Swords, to let me know he has her."

"So why don't you just let them find him? They can see he *doesn't* have her!"

Sydney hesitated, then said, "Because. Because he knows about you, Lainey."

I felt a band of terror tighten round my chest. "What?"

"I wanted to feel him out, see whether it was safe to trust him, and I ended up telling him what I'd done. He was shocked, he refused to play any part in this, but he did promise he wouldn't go to the authorities voluntarily. Which I believe, because he understands what's at stake, but I don't know what would happen if he was actually called in for questioning."

There was something strange in her tone, a tremor that might've been fear or anger. Or deception. It was impossible to tell which. I strode to the window, my stomach twisting, almost expecting to see flashing lights. "You think he'd tell the FBI I have the baby?" I slammed my hand against the wall. "How could you have given him my name!"

"They're not going to find him! And actually, actually if the detective asks you about him when they call, how about you say I haven't been in touch with him for months? That he kept writing me off and on, but our friendship kind of fizzled out. I need them to stop looking for him."

My knees started to buckle and I reached for the armchair to keep myself from sliding to the floor. "I have to leave here," I said. "I'm getting rid of my phone, I won't talk to the FBI, and tomorrow I'm taking Star and the baby and leaving."

"Lainey, no! You have to talk to them! Don't you realize if they can't reach you they're going to look for you in Virginia and find out you've left?"

"And if your friend tells them I have the baby, they'll trace my cell phone records and look for me here! Did you forget there's a huge reward for information on Molly? How long do you think this guy will be able to resist the temptation to become a hero and, as a fringe benefit, also rich? Dammit, Sydney, I really didn't need one more thing to worry about. Now I have plans to make, I can't talk to you!" And then, I hung up. And then freaked out.

How long did I have before the FBI called? I pulled out my bags and started throwing clothes in without folding, sitting on the suitcases to zip them, catching fabric in the teeth. When I was done I called a realtor I'd spoken to yesterday, and arranged to see one of the furnished homes she'd told me about. A tiny cabin, cheap, bare-bones, the type of place whose walls probably held more mouse droppings than insulation. But whose barrenness and remoteness would make it feel safe, in the way Star's Feng-Shui'd bedroom gave her the illusion of control.

After hanging up I scrubbed my hands viciously against my scalp, fighting back the threat of tears. And then I rose to tell Star that we were leaving.

"You didn't tell me." Star sounded strangely flat, sitting in her bedroom wrapped in a blanket and clutching a plastic cup of water. I knelt by her chair and she looked down at me, eyes pleading. "I thought this was it until we could finally go back home," she said. "How could you not tell me? What were you planning to do, hit me over the head and drag me to the car before I knew what was happening?"

"I didn't want you worrying. I have the whole thing planned out, I have maps, I know the motels we'll stay in—"

"Where? Motels where?"

"Just a couple of stops on the way to Montana," I said. "We're going to Montana."

"*Montana?*" She said this the way one might say the word *Ebola*, her voice strangled and high-pitched. And then, under her breath, "Okay, okay, okay . . ."

I reached for her hand. "It'll be nice there. I've talked to a realtor and there's this really sweet-seeming town with pretty cabins you can rent by the month." As I said this, I realized exactly how badly thought out this plan was. Live in some cabin? In the middle of a state where I had no job, no friends and which I knew nothing about other than 1930s scenes from *A River Runs Through It*? "The thing is, Ma, I don't think we're safe here anymore. Sydney says she told that

Kemper guy I have the baby, and if the FBI finds him, what's to stop him from giving them my name?"

Of course this was not even close to the right thing to say, and Star wrapped the blanket tighter around her and stared fixedly out the window, her eyes filling.

I brought Star's hand to my cheek, its cold clamminess like a hunk of raw meat against my skin. "You can do this, Ma. Just think, a week ago you were sure you couldn't leave home. But you made it out here and you're doing great."

"Listen." Her voice was hoarse. "I think you should leave me here. It'll be so much easier without me; you have Molly to worry about, so you shouldn't have to worry about me too." She raised a shaking hand to wipe briskly at one eye, and then the other. "It makes much more sense."

"Ma, you can't stay here. I'm not asking Alex to take care of you."

"It's okay." Her eyes were still on the window. "I wouldn't want him to. He won't have to."

"What're you saying?"

She opened her mouth, then closed it again and shook her head.

"What're you trying to say!"

"Nothing, really nothing. Don't worry about me, okay? Just do what you have to do; I'll be fine. I can call Pamela to bring me home or something."

Something. I stood there watching her, only too aware what that *something* might mean. The week after Nana Sterling had died when I'd still been home from the funeral but preparing to return to the city, she'd sat like this staring out the window. *I'll be fine!* She'd said it then too. *You have fun up there, make friends, do everything you've dreamed of so I can think about you and smile when my mind wants to go other places.* And I'd believed her. I had left. And just a few days later she'd swallowed a full bottle of pills. Of course I couldn't leave her alone now. I couldn't ever leave her.

From my bedroom Molly started to cry, and I felt a swirl of frustration. All the years in high school I'd needed Star to protect me but had kept all the jagged edges inside me, knowing she wouldn't save me from them but would let them cut her too. I knew the frustration was unfair; I'd been working to forgive Sydney for her weaknesses that were a hell of a lot less forgivable. But the difference was that Star was my mother and she should be the one comforting me. It was her job!

I stood and set a hand on her shoulder, gripped it perhaps too hard. "Don't you realize I'll worry ten times more about you if you're not with me? You're coming with us, Ma. I'll do whatever I can to make it easier for you, but this isn't a choice. Besides, I'll probably have to find a job, so I'll need you to watch Molly."

Star turned her head, the first time in this whole conversation that she'd looked at me. Her face was vacant, her mouth half open. I wanted to shake her, to slap her, but instead I said, "I'll help you pack tonight. I want to have us in Toledo by tomorrow, so we have to leave early." And then I walked out to the hall and forced myself to breathe. Oh God, how was I going to do this? How could I possibly make it work?

I went to my bedroom and unstrapped Molly from her carrier, where she'd been sleeping. I needed to get out of here so I could think, needed to walk away all the tangled fears and rages and frustrations, not just at my mother but at the entire situation. I lifted Molly and put her in the Björn.

The afternoon air and the feel of Molly against me helped to calm my nerves, but as I walked down the street and entered downtown, all I could feel was a sense of mourning. The last time I'd see these trees, these houses, the stores with their racks of hand-stitched quilts and blown glass; it felt like I was leaving home.

I stopped in front of the old stone church, its rough gray walls and simple stained glass making it seem almost handcrafted. I hesitated, then climbed the front steps, expecting it to be locked, but the door creaked open and we entered the dim interior.

I walked up to the altar, looking down at the Jesus carved into its front surface. I touched Him gingerly, then pulled my hand quickly away. My relationship with God had always been a bit unsettled. Star believed He was really the collection of all souls, past and present throughout the universe, a collective unconscious working together to create the greater good. Which was nice to say but too vague for me to conceptualize, so all my life I'd tried to believe in the white-bearded sort of God, watching over me. Someone who was, perhaps, in touch with my father.

But I'd never prayed to Him; I had absolutely no idea how to ask for help, knowing there were so many people, starving, dying, broken, who needed Him so much more. And yet now here I was, doing what even the faithless usually did in the end when God felt like the last resort. Hoping He'd understand.

It was so quiet, my footsteps muffled, damp-feeling as if the church hadn't seen the daylight in centuries. I walked around the perimeter studying the dusty paintings on the walls, the statues of saints and apostles. And then I sat with Molly on one of the wooden pews.

"Tell me what to do?" I whispered, and then I wrapped my arms around Molly and closed my eyes. She was my dream, the one I prayed for and the prayer itself. Was it right to pray I'd never lose her? If there was a God judging good and bad, right and wrong, cursing the sinners and protecting the saviors, what would He say seeing this moral gray area where innocent people were hurt by Molly's disappearance, hospitality was abused, unforgivable lies were told and yet a baby was saved?

Undoubtedly He'd realize the selfishness behind my selflessness, would probably see better answers that I would've thought of if I'd just been a better person. But I wanted to believe that in spite of it all He'd understand I was trying to do the right thing, that I'd been forced to make my choices from a place of longing and fear, not ingredients with which to make rational decisions. And I tried to believe that whatever I might do next, He'd protect me.

I imagined Him now watching us from above, nodding his omniscient head. Conspiring with me and Sydney on how to do things right, helping both of us to make the right decisions. And forgiving me.

That night after putting Molly to bed, I sat with Alex in the living room. Both of us had books in our laps, but even after the light grew too dim to read by, neither of us reached to turn on the lamp. Star hadn't come down for dinner, and when I'd brought up a plate for her she'd rushed past me into the bathroom, retching. After helping her to bed I'd given her a Xanax, then slipped the bottle into my pocket, hiding it, just in case.

Now out of the corner of my eye I watched Alex close his book, a finger marking his place, then turn his gaze to the unlit fireplace and hold it there, unspeaking. What was he thinking? He'd been acting somewhat strangely all evening, his glance darting toward me when he thought I wasn't looking, talking much less than usual, letting me start each conversation. I hadn't told him yet that we were leaving, partly because I knew the words would cement the future, and also because I didn't want to ruin our last night together. But had he somehow sensed it?

How much easier it would be if Star was right and we really were all part of the same god, all subconsciously knowing each other's secrets and working together for the *greater good*. So much easier if Alex intuitively knew the truth, and already forgave me.

"Do you believe in God?" I asked.

He twitched, like I'd just physically tugged him awake, then gave a faint smile and said, "I used to. In fifth grade this boy in my class, Noah, drowned in a backyard swimming pool. So right after that—I guess I was finally really getting the concept of death—I started praying for all the people I loved most. Which expanded until I had this huge list; I was praying for pretty much every single person I'd ever known. I mean how could I live with myself if I forgot someone and the next day they were dead? What if mentioning their name to God could've made a difference?"

"You thought you were responsible for the entire world," I said.

"That makes me sound really egotistical. But yeah, every night I prayed for every person in my neighborhood and every kid in my class, teachers, doctors, even the checkout girls at Safeway."

I shook my head. "That says a lot about you. It's the same way you felt responsible for me and Molly."

"It actually says I was obsessive and probably a little insane." There was a kind of strained humor in his voice, mocking but also pained. "But it only lasted a few months. I fell asleep holding my list of people to pray for, and my sister found me with it and made fun of me for a month. And I started thinking if He really was all-powerful, why would he have let Posy see it? So that was the end of my praying, which I guess was a good thing since it was so time-consuming. But I still feel guilty now when bad things happen."

"That's awful. It means you *still* feel responsible for the world."

"No." He turned back to the fireplace, gazed at it as he said, "No, I just feel responsible for the things I really have done. That's enough."

With the intimacy of the moment, the darkness around us, I had this feeling like he wanted to tell me what he meant but just needed a nudge. And I was so close to asking him, felt the question on my tongue, but before I could say anything he added, "You're actually the first person I ever told about the praying. I guess I never knew anybody I could trust not to totally laugh at me." He leaned back in his chair. "Reason number forty-seven I love having you here."

I felt an anguished twist in my chest, but tried to smile. "You're keeping tally?"

"Reason forty-eight is the way your eyes crinkle when you think something's funny. Very endearing."

"Those are called crow's-feet," I said. "You're making fun of my wrinkles." And then suddenly, I felt my eyes fill.

His brow furrowed. "Leah, hey . . . It was supposed to be a compliment."

"Alex." I shook my head, then closed the book in my lap, and spread my hands over it. "Alex, I have to tell you something. Because the thing is, we're leaving, me and Molly and Star. Tomorrow. We're just not safe here, which also means you're not safe. So . . . I've already packed our things, and we're leaving in the morning."

"Not safe?" His face went suddenly still. "Is there something I don't know? Because I've been trying for the past few days to think of the right, un-insulting way to make you realize how crazy this is."

The heaviness in his face was an exact echo of the heaviness in my chest, and seeing it I wanted to grab onto something solid, kicking like a toddler being dragged into the unknown. I pressed my lips between my teeth to keep myself from screaming.

"You know your husband hasn't even reported you missing? I've been searching for stories about you and Molly, and I haven't even seen any reports of babies missing in Chicago. So don't you think that means he isn't going to tell anybody? Maybe he's finally looking hard at what he did to Molly, and he decided to let you go." He leaned forward in his chair, hands clasped. "I realize you're terrified, of course you can't take chances on this, but think it through instead of just acting on fear. You've been safe so far, nobody's looking for you, so why would you be safer anywhere else?"

There was something close to desperation in his voice, and hearing it I felt a numb shock. Regardless of what Susie had told me, it hadn't really registered until now that we might be helping Alex just as much as he was helping us, that this person I'd become, Leah, was the type of woman who'd be missed.

Maybe it would actually be safer to stay. Was I wrong to freak out so much about this Kemper person they might never find? About my impending conversation with an FBI detective who'd just look at me as an old acquaintance Sydney had met for coffee and then never again? I didn't know, I didn't know what was safe anymore, but I pictured dragging Star to the car tomorrow, following page after page of maps for hundreds of miles. Molly screaming in the backseat and Star hyperventilating in the front seat, and I suddenly felt impossibly tired, more tired than I'd ever felt in my life. "I'm so scared, Alex," I said. "Everything scares me."

"I know," he said, then rose to stand behind my chair, hugged me from behind so all I could see was his forearm, the muscles tight against my chest, the veins and tendons under his skin. He kissed my temple and then my cheek, then placed a hand at my chin to turn my face toward him, his eyes pleading. "Then let me take care of you," he said softly.

And those words, the promise that I'd finally be taken care of for the first time in such a very long time, the promise I'd been looking for from God, those were the words that finally made me break down and cry.

❧ 18 ❧

And so, we stayed.

Staying was foolish, part of me knew that, but the truth was that there were no good answers. If the FBI called and couldn't reach me they'd try me at home, find out I'd left, and I'd probably become their prime suspect. I wasn't safe here, but really I wasn't safe anywhere.

I don't know what Alex was thinking; did he expect we'd stay for weeks? For months? He acted like the question wasn't there. The three of us went on an hour-long drive the next day to buy Molly a crib and high chair, Alex setting Molly in them to ask what she thought, even musing with me about the day she'd no longer need them. He pretended permanence, and I let him.

It was inexcusable, all of it. I knew I couldn't stay much longer without telling Alex the truth, but I also knew the time for telling the truth was long, long past. Not having confessed to him was unforgivable, and telling now would be unforgivable. And so, there I was paralyzed.

The call came while Alex and I were in the garden with Molly. Every day we sat on the grass with her among the flowers, plucking a basil leaf for her to sniff, pointing out the names of flowers and trees as if she might remember them, baby botanist. Molly seemed to take as much interest in a blade of grass as she did in a goldfinch pecking around it. In her own way, she was an artist.

I'd replayed over and over what might happen when they called, knew how I had to react and what to say. I needed to be far enough from Molly that they wouldn't be able to hear her, so when the phone in my pocket rang I jumped up without explanation, to run into the house.

"Is this Lainey Carson?" It was a woman, her voice deep and sandpapery, a smoker's voice.

"Yes?" My head was weaving and I was suddenly scared I might faint. I sat on the sofa and forced myself to breathe.

"Ms. Carson, this is Agent Menendez with the FBI, and I'm calling about Sydney Beaumont. Do you have a minute to talk?"

Could I say no and put the conversation off? Like maybe forever? "Okay," I said.

"I'm sure you've heard about the kidnapping. We're just following up on leads and I have a few questions."

"Right, okay." My voice was unsteady. And it occurred to me that with three small words, all of this could tumble down around me. That's how precarious it was; my tongue could take control, a sort of Tourette's, could say, *I have her,* and everything I'd built so carefully would fall to dust. I steeled my shoulders.

"Can you describe your relationship with Ms. Beaumont, please?"

"It's . . . not much of a relationship. We were in the same school. Back when we were kids. A long time ago." I was aware that I was talking in toddler-length sentences, but it was all I could manage without my voice wobbling.

"When was the last time you talked with her?"

"We had coffee. Like a month ago." Would anyone have been able to tell the investigators she'd come by the house the day Molly disappeared? They must not know or surely they would've called me sooner. "I ran into her at the store where she works, and then we decided to get together for coffee that one time." I swallowed, then repeated, "That one time."

"And how did she seem when you talked to her?" the investigator said. "Did you notice anything unusual?"

"No! No, not at all. She seemed happy." Was this the right thing to say? Could Sydney ever have been happy knowing Molly had been abused and the abuser was about to get custody? "I mean, not happy exactly; she seemed distracted like there might be other things she was thinking about that kept her from being a hundred percent happy." *Wrong answer!* "But, you know, she seemed okay considering."

"Considering?" the agent said.

"Considering everything she'd been through with her husband. That's all I meant when I said she seemed distracted. Her face was all bruised when I saw her, and when I asked she told me what he did to her and Molly." I shook my head quickly. "I mean Jacqueline! To Jacqueline. Which was obviously distracting."

The agent didn't respond, and I imagined her scribbling notes: *Suspect seems confused, nervous and evasive. Check phone, bank and credit card records STAT.* Handing the notes to an associate. Speed-dialing the Mendham police. But then she said, "When she talked about her husband, what would you say her tone was?"

"Her tone?"

"I mean was she angry maybe? Or did she sound scared?"

"Well she was upset, sure." I remembered what Pamela had told me about her first conversation with Sydney. "Mostly she just seemed hurt, like she couldn't believe the man she loved could've abused their daughter. It made her really sad." Ah yes, within the space of a minute I'd said Sydney was both happy and sad. *Clearly deceptive*, the agent added to her notes.

"Did she tell you about their custody battle? Or any plans she had for the future?"

"Um, not really. She said they were trying to figure things out, but she didn't go into any detail. Except . . . except! She mentioned she knew she'd end up with full custody so there was no reason for her to do anything crazy."

"She mentioned doing something crazy?"

"What? No! No, those are my words."

The agent didn't respond, a heavy, interminable silence, and I squeezed my eyes shut. "She just knew she'd get custody," I said, "that David was going to look at how he'd hurt Jacqueline and realize the baby was better off with her."

"And if he didn't realize it?"

"Look, I know what you're getting at, but Sydney's the most sensible, honest person I know." I felt my face wanting to screw up in rebellion, but I shook it off. "She'd never do anything to hurt her baby and she'd never falsely accuse her husband. That's just not the kind of person she is." My voice was amazingly firm. I didn't know whether to be proud of myself, or puke.

"Okay," the agent said, "one last question. Did she talk about other men she might've had relations with while she was still married?"

"What? No, she wouldn't do that, she's . . . very loyal."

"Or mention a man named Kemper? Who she'd spent time with over the past few years?"

"Kemper? No, doesn't sound familiar." I scrubbed my free hand up and down the leg of my jeans. "I think over the past few months she's been pretty isolated, hasn't seen or talked to hardly anyone."

"How about a paternity test? Did she tell you she'd gotten one?"

"A paternity test? You mean of Jacqueline?"

"So she didn't mention it."

"No!" I shook my head slightly. "So she didn't know for sure David was the father?" I blinked quickly. "*Was* he?"

"I'm afraid I can't discuss that, I'm sorry. But thank you for your time, Ms. Carson. I'll give you a number where you can reach me if you think of anything else you'd like to tell us."

As she rattled off the number, I stared blankly at the front door.

She'd gotten a paternity test? So Kemper *had* been more than just a "friend." Really, knowing Sydney, I shouldn't have been all that surprised.

Had David known she'd been having an affair? Of course Molly must've turned out to be David's, otherwise there was no reason she'd have had to go through all this to get custody. But still, if he'd ever found out she'd slept with another man, I could only imagine what he would've done to her.

After hanging up, I went to the living room and stood in the bay window watching Alex roll a ball into the V of Molly's legs, trying to encourage her to roll it back. My shirt was clinging to my sides, sweat beading on my forehead as I stood there forcing myself to breathe. For now, at least, everything was okay.

They hadn't acted like they suspected me at all. They must not realize Star and I had left, or that I'd talked to Sydney since Molly's disappearance. But they sure as hell suspected Sydney. Which meant that, almost definitely, things were going to get worse for her soon.

I wiped a sleeve over the sweat on my forehead, then went up to tell Star about the call, thinking it might ease her mind, hoping it would ease my own. But knowing this was only a temporary limbo we were in. An unbearable FBI-interrogation-type pause, before revelation.

If anything, the fear of what might come intensified the urgency with which I threw myself into this life. Knowing it all might end any day, I clung onto it, dug my nails inside it and wrapped it so tightly around myself it was all I could see.

Alex and I fell into a routine that I imagined was, except for the lack of sex, not unlike married life. Our time together was quiet, unhurried, talking without having to weigh words, or not talking without me worrying about the silence. He cooked our meals, I gardened and cleaned the house with Star; we both cared for Molly. We asked favors of each other without worrying about imposing, did favors for each other without expecting thanks.

In the mornings Alex researched and wrote while I played with Molly, painting while she napped, or immersing myself in one of the novels on Alex's shelves. Star had started venturing to the front porch, something she'd never done back home, and I spent a good deal of time there with her, the two of us rocking back and forth in Alex's new porch swing, listening to the wind through the trees.

When the weather was nice, Alex and I went out to shop or walk through the neighborhood, twice going on long hikes in the mountains with Alex carrying Molly in the Björn. As I walked behind them (admiring his very, very admirable backside), I found myself feeling this amazing tenderness for him that was nothing at all like the longing I was used to feeling around good-looking men. Seeing Alex with Molly, the two of us playing, teaching, showing her the world, made me feel the pull of something huger than the three of us together.

One morning as I stood with him by the stove, trying to express my sadness for what Molly might never have, I told him about the photo I kept by my bed back home, myself and my father in the kitchen, me in a tiny apron and chef's hat. "Every weekend night he'd stand me on a chair so I could watch him cook," I said. "We pretended we were putting on a show, *The Father-Daughter Cooking Hour,* he called it. 'My sous-chef will now stir in an egg!' he'd say. 'Ma'am, can you tell us where eggs come from?'"

"Brilliant. And yet you never learned how to cook."

"Alas, no, but I did learn where eggs come from. Oh, and how to sift flour. You need me to sift any flour?"

"Into minestrone? Yeah, no, thanks." He smiled into his pot, then turned to me and his smile dropped. "I thought it was hard for me losing my dad, but you were so young."

"You lost your dad? I'm sorry, I didn't know."

His face froze. "I . . . don't really talk about it."

"Sorry," I said again, softer. I should've realized. He never talked about his family. All I knew about them was what they'd looked like, from the couple of photos he kept downstairs. I shook my head quickly and said, "With me, being so young probably helped. When you're four you don't really understand what death means, and by the time I actually got the fact he wasn't coming back, the worst of missing him was over."

"But it's always there behind everything, right? Even when you're not looking at it. Like . . . the chips on the cabinet doors. You're so used to seeing them that you might've stopped noticing, but they definitely change the look of the kitchen."

"They give it character," I said.

"Yeah, but is it the character you want?"

I looked over at him, and he turned quickly away. "Okay," he said, handing me his wooden spoon. "Now Miss Leah will demonstrate the art of stirring."

I smiled and took the spoon, and he turned to raise his finger to an invisible camera. "Can you tell us, Leah, where pasta comes from?"

I turned in the direction he was facing. "ShopRite," I said. "Or, in some cases, Thriftway."

And standing there facing a fake camera, I felt a strange blurring of past and present, for the first time really looking at what it meant to lose a father. Not just chips on cabinets but the entire backbone of our family broken, its walls and floors. What would it be like for Molly not having a father or, worse, learning why she'd been taken from him? This was what I wanted to give her, the security I hadn't felt since my father died, the sense I'd felt on my hikes with her and Alex that she was at the center of this self-contained entity, formed solely for the sake of protecting her. I knew what it had done to me, losing that sense. And that I'd give anything to keep Molly from becoming me.

I'd splurged on a pair of slim gray slacks from the only clothing store in town, and black boots with a good-sized heel. The boots changed the way I walked, pushing my chest forward, imparting a swing-hipped confidence, the fabric of my pants swish-swishing between my thighs. And as I walked with Alex to Susie's barbecue, Molly cradled against me in her sling, I felt like something had changed in my muscles and ligaments. Leah Monroe: as Alex had called her, a woman of grace.

Here is Leah Monroe, strolling in the twilight with her husband and young daughter, on their way to a dear friend's dinner party. Soon they will arrive and be greeted by hugs and exclamations, after which Leah will mingle effortlessly, charming the guests with her witty repartee.

Susie's house was at the end of the street, a ranch with purple shutters and a steeply pitched roof. The air smelled of charcoal and grilled meat, and walking toward it I felt suddenly ravenous. But I'd lost another two pounds in the past few days, and although those first pounds had come off without any sort of intentional effort, I'd started purposely watching what I ate.

That morning I'd stood in my underwear a good ten minutes in front of the full-length mirror, sucking in my stomach and admiring the parts of my body that had previously been buried by Cheetos: my hip bone and clavicle, the crease under my butt and the muscles along the sides of my thighs. *Nice to finally meet you!* I'd wanted to say. Maybe I'd diet until I got to meet my ribs, and then accidentally-on-purpose stroll from the bathroom in lingerie, at the precise time Alex happened to be strolling through the upstairs hall. His gaze would follow me as I hurried to my bedroom feigning embarrassment, and as I got to my door he'd reach for my slim waist and—

"Leah!" Susie called, striding toward me with her arms outstretched. She was wearing an apron that reached almost to her ankles, printed with *Kiss the Cook* and a pair of lips. She pulled me into her arms and then bent to kiss Molly. "Well you've grown two inches!" she cooed. "Are you a big eater? Are you? Are you?"

"I brought some bouillabaisse," Alex said. "Where should I put it?"

"You must've believed my chichi comment. I don't even know for sure what bouillabaisse is." She pointed across the patio. "There's a buffet table over by the grill. Burgers should be off in ten minutes or so, and I'll warn you not to try the oatmeal bars unless you want to feel really, *really* laid back. Miranda brought them, and you know Miranda." She took my arm. "C'mon, Leah, I want to show you off to the folks you haven't met." And then she practically skipped with me across the yard toward the crowd on the patio.

That night was . . . how can I do it justice? Exhilarating? Brilliant? Heady? A happy blur of storytelling, Molly admired and passed adoringly from woman to woman; a night of laughter and probably too much to drink, and rapt attention to everything I said.

Because I did have—aided by a handful of beers—an exhilarating, previously untapped knack for witty repartee. There are times in your life when you know you're absolutely *on,* in the zone, charisma channeled from some kindly muse (or the beer, or an oatmeal bar that I did try, just to see).

I had a sense why it was coming so easily: all the people around me who were a little bit "different." Jack with his pink shirt and giggle; a man named Roy with a face textured like large-curd cottage cheese and a slim, braided gray beard that reached mid-chest; a woman named Valerie with wild hair and a gauzy dress that showed her underwear and bra-less breasts, one of those willowy, leathery, ethereal looking older women who look like they might be actual descendants of trees. These people might be considered oddities in the world where I'd grown up, but here they were listened to and respected even by the people who weren't so odd, their opinions asked for, their awkward jokes laughed at. So for the first time maybe ever in my life I felt completely uninhibited, not worrying about whether they'd think I was interesting or intelligent or amusing, and so I became interesting and intelligent and amusing as a result.

What if all of them had gone through something like what I went through in high school? Imagine what would've happened if we'd found one another then; hundreds of us, maybe thousands, all of us banding together into our own separate, protected haven. Like a deaf university with a communal language only we could understand, and a deep-felt understanding of the prejudices in the world. We were the only ones who understood we weren't inferior.

I was talking to Valerie when, from across the patio, I heard Molly start to cry. "'Scuse me," I said, and strode to the buffet table where Susie was kneeling by Molly, trying to clean something off the front of her shirt. "Beer," Susie said. "And no, I wasn't trying to get her drunk. She was using the tablecloth as a pull-up bar, and she got a dousing."

Molly flung her arms toward me, something akin to panic on her face. And as I knelt to take her into my arms, a miracle. "Mama, Mama!" she said.

I stared at her, everything inside me melting. "Molly?"

Susie watched my face. "Leah? Is that her first word? Oh it is, isn't it! Molly said her first word!"

My eyes filled; I nodded silently, seeing everyone turn to watch us, Alex running over, kneeling by me and squeezing my shoulder.

"Mama!" Molly called again, and I lifted her and started to sob, and then to laugh.

I'm sure everyone thought I was overreacting to a milestone I surely must've expected. But still, as I sat there rocking Molly in my arms and hearing their buzz of appreciation, I could feel from them a communal sort of pride.

Later I sat by a fire pit with Molly cradled against me, the joy inside me hot and smooth like brandy, only half listening to the conversation around me. When I looked across the fire pit, I saw Alex watching me intently, face lit by the fire, unsmiling. Our eyes met and he held my gaze a full minute before Roy touched his arm to ask him a question, and he smiled slightly at me and turned to answer it.

And as he did, a weight slid slowly to my stomach and I sat there, frozen. Inside me only, *Oh.*

Here are Mr. and Mrs. Connor, walking home from their dear friends' party with their sleeping daughter, Molly. After setting Molly in her new crib, they will retire to their bedroom. Where Mr. Connor will frenziedly tear off Mrs. Connor's elegant clothes, popping buttons and ripping seams, throwing her underthings over his shoulder to leave a trail from the door to the bed.

"That was fun," Alex said.

I smiled. "Yeah, it was."

"And Molly said her first word! I have to say I'm a little jealous that it was *mama*, but I'm sure it's just because her tongue's not dexterous enough yet for *Alex*. We'll have to think of something easy for her to call me."

Dada, I thought. "We could pretend your name's Bob," I said.

"Bob? Seriously, Leah?"

"It's a perfectly nice name. But okay, how about *Yaya*? It's close enough, and it comes out of her mouth anyway at least half the time she opens it, so you can do a Pavlovian thing, jump whenever you hear it."

"Yaya." He looked down at Molly, patting his chest. "Yaya!" he said.

"Yeah, that'll only work if she's awake."

"Tomorrow, then." He smiled. "So should we gossip? That seems to be the thing people do after parties."

"I really want to feel like we're above that. Although . . ." I shook my head slightly. "Okay, I have to ask it. What exactly is Susie and Jack's relationship?"

His mouth twitched a quick smile before he said, "I guess it's evidence of how cruel life can be. They've been friends since they were kids, and I think Susie's been in love with him for at least that long, but . . ."

"Yeah," I said, "that's what I thought."

"But they're so good to each other. It made me think, when I first met them, that maybe it was a sign just having a companion in life could be enough. But now when you see how she looks at him, I don't know."

I felt a soreness in my chest. I walked on a few steps, thinking, before I said, "It's better than nothing though, isn't it?"

"Is it? In some ways I think it's worse."

I thought of the nights I'd spent in bed with books, living vicariously, trying to use the story lines about lovers and children to fill the hollowness. No. It wasn't worse.

"Have you ever been in love?" he asked suddenly.

I hesitated, then said, "I don't know. I mean I guess there was my husband. But in retrospect I don't know if I loved him, not really." I glanced at him, then said, "Have you?"

He smiled, his eyes seeming distant. "I don't know either," he said. "Isn't that funny? You'd think it should be such an easy question. At least I've thought I was in love."

Which of course filled my mind with impossible questions. I chose the only one that wasn't completely inappropriate. "How long ago?"

He didn't answer, and I inwardly cringed. It *had* been inappropriate, and desperate and obvious, and should I apologize or just let the question hang there? But then he said, "Not that long ago," an answer that could mean anything; this past year, last month, this morning.

I bit my tongue to keep myself from asking a follow-up, willing him to explain, even knowing it was none of my business. Was that, whatever had happened or was still happening, the reason for his sadness? It must've been something awful; Erin had died, which explained why he still kept her picture, or had left him for someone else, or even worse had just told him she'd stopped loving him without explanation. Would he ever tell me? Maybe he still didn't feel comfortable enough, or healed enough. I'd dropped plenty of opportunities into his lap, but it was obvious he wasn't ready to take them.

But then he said, "Love's funny, you know? It does something to you, gets into your veins like a drug so everything looks different and feels different, which makes you do things you never normally would." He glanced at me, then back at the road, squinting like there was something there he was trying to discern. "But then it changes because regardless of how good the love is, it always has to change. And you look back on what you were thinking and doing when the drug was heavy inside you, all the choices you made and you wonder, Who the hell was that? Which makes you look at the love itself and question whether everything you felt was just this screwed-up hallucination."

I thought about Sydney, how I'd gone back and replayed every moment of our childhood trying to see the truth behind it, find evidence there'd been some truth. Who had I let myself love since then? "It scares me," I said.

He looked at me, a question in his eyes, then said, "My mother told me once that love's like a bullet hole in your heart. Which sounds so cynical, but I know what she meant. She wasn't even talking about losing my dad, this was probably three or four years before he died, she was talking about the actual pain and danger of loving somebody. She and my dad, they had the kind of love you see in movies, always touching, catching each other's eye, the way they were with each other always made me feel happy, protected, but in a way also completely excluded. And after he died, part of her died too; she had a complete breakdown, the hole in her heart bleeding out."

I touched his hand, thinking about my own father's death, how thoroughly Star had managed to protect me from it. "I can't even imagine," I said softly.

He stopped walking, staring fixedly into the road, then seemed to shake himself off before he said, "Anyway, if I was a therapist I'd say that explains why I've built this kind of barrier around my feelings, trying to protect myself from it all. I said love's like a drug, but so is protecting yourself, you know? Like heroin, the illusion of peace."

I pressed Molly's sleeping warmth against me, wondering. How much pain was in him that I could only guess at? What did anybody know of anyone else's grief when all they could see was the surface of it?

And then suddenly, he reached for my arm. "Look!" he whispered. There right across the road from us was a moose, huge and dark and strangely elegant. We didn't move, didn't speak, just stood there watching this imposing but somehow gentle creature as he chewed at the shrubbery at the edge of the woods. As exotic to me as if we'd run into an elephant, or a brontosaurus.

And then, I felt Alex slip an arm around me, resting a hand at my waist.

I couldn't breathe. Literally couldn't; something had clamped against my lungs, squeezing. "Alex," I said hoarsely, dizzy from the lack of oxygen and something darker and heavier, dread and guilt. Panic. Knowing that I had to confess, because of his hand, the majestic power of the animal before us, the remaining glow I felt from the party, all of it. A need to make it all authentic, not founded on a lie.

"Alex," I said. "I have to tell you."

His hand tightened at my waist and he pulled me closer to wrap another arm around me, Molly pressed between us. Slowly, he leaned his forehead against mine.

I stiffened, the nerves sparking up and down my spine. "Please," I whispered.

"I know," he said. "I realize you've been hiding something, but whatever it is, it doesn't matter. I don't care. You're amazing, Leah; I just want you to know that, to know I think that."

I could smell his breath as he spoke, the dark sweetness of the merlot he'd drunk, the word reverberating. *Amazing*, he'd said, but who did he think was amazing? The Leah who'd run away from her husband to save her child? Or me?

I squeezed my eyes shut and turned my head away, on the verge of either choking or breaking into tears. Because I couldn't, I couldn't; it wouldn't be a real kiss. It'd be exactly as untrue as the fantasies I'd had night after night in Virginia, reading the stories of other people's love. So even though all of me was aching to tip my face up toward his, instead I pulled away. I pulled away without speaking and strode down the street.

{ 20 }

It was only around six when I woke the next morning. And realized (Stomachache? *Check*. Sun stabbing me in the eyeballs? *Check*. Head spinning like a cartoon boxer's? *Check*.) that I must be hungover. Before my mind kicked into gear I felt a sort of giddy pride at it. I'd always been on the outside of hangovers. In high school it had been a badge of coolness, the girls coming in with rumpled hair and wan faces; *I'm sooo hungover*, they'd say, and then be slapped on the back. Now, I was part of that legacy. With my pounding head, my dry mouth, I belonged.

I lay in bed trying to limit my thoughts to these, only gradually letting in the night before, still images like snapshots: me laughing with Jack as we toasted plastic cups of beer; the glow and sweet scent from Roy's gnarled pipe; Molly calling me Mama; Alex's eyes as he watched me across the fire pit.

Then, the walk home. And there it was: the kiss that maybe could have been but wasn't. What did it mean? And what would happen now? If he'd been planning to kiss me, then he'd think I had rejected him. And if he *hadn't* planned to kiss me, then he'd see I'd misinterpreted what had only been a simple, kind gesture. I didn't know which would be more awkward. Either way, how could we ever be comfortable again?

I stood, careful to make sure my head stayed on top of my shoulders, and leaned to look at Molly asleep in her crib. "I ruined it," I whispered to her. "Everything we had here." I tucked my index finger against her loosely curled palm and used my thumb to press her fingers around it. But she only made a small sound of protest and pulled her hand away. Feeling ridiculously hurt, I squeezed a fist and turned back toward my bed.

I needed to talk to Star. I needed to lie with her, my head on her chest, and tell her about last night. "I don't know what to do!" I'd say, and then I'd burst into tears, let her smooth back my hair and rock me like she used to after nightmares and toddler-sized tragedies. She'd give advice, she always did. She would read my cards and I'd make myself believe them because I had to believe in something. I'd do whatever the cards told me, even if their direction was arbitrary, because it was better than having no direction at all.

I walked to the door, opened it and then felt the crinkle of paper under my bare foot. I bent for it. It was a handwritten note.

> Dear Leah,
>   I'm so sorry, but something's come up really suddenly, and I have to leave for a couple days to work it out—I'm thinking I should be back by Wednesday. I've left money for you on the hall table. Please use it for whatever you need.
> Alex

I let the note drop from my hands. What was he thinking? What did this mean? Something had come up between midnight last night and six A.M.? What could it be besides a wish to get away from me?

I stood there a minute wondering if I was going to be sick, then another minute sure I was going to be sick, and then another actually being sick into the conveniently plastic-insert–lined diaper pail. After which I slid slowly and gracelessly to the floor.

Molly started to bawl, and the door across the hall opened. I moaned and hunched over my knees.

"What's going on?" Star rushed into the room. "Molly? Molly!" She strode to the crib and lifted Molly, and I felt a ridiculously disgusting spear of jealousy that she'd chosen to comfort Molly over me. Yes, Molly was shrieking and helpless, but I was Star's daughter! And nauseous! And really, really upset!

"Mom!" I said. "I need help."

"Are you sick?" She turned toward me, Molly in her arms, wrinkled her nose at the diaper pail and then tested my forehead with her wrist. "I'm not cleaning out your pukey wastebasket, you know. I don't care if you're sick; I stopped doing that when you were ten."

"He tried to kiss me." I leaned against her leg. "Or at least I think he did, last night, but now he's gone without telling me he was leaving or saying where he went." Still leaning against her, I handed her the note.

She scanned it quickly, then stepped away from me. "Okay, you got me. I'll clean out the pail."

"Ma . . ."

"You'll be okay," she said, brushing a sweaty lock of hair from my eyes. "You go brush your teeth and I'll make you some tea, and we'll figure this all out."

I spent the rest of the day huddled in blankets with tea and toast and tears. Conversely, Star seemed inappropriately chipper. That afternoon for the first time since arriving, she went downstairs without feeling compelled to draw the curtains. And, tickled to hear Molly had spoken her first word, she spent hours carrying Molly through the house—calling out the names of everything from ants to antiperspirant—rather than turning to her cards. It was like a minor miracle, and even though I was more than a little pissed that she seemed to be taking something positive from my suffering, I braced myself against her strength as I had as a child, when Star was still all-powerful.

I'd told three people I'd stop by their homes that day—Jack and Susie had sung my praises like I was some kind of undiscovered Renoir and my murals were suddenly in demand—but I wasn't about to show the *today* me to people who were expecting the *last night* me. It would be a shock to their system. I called to reschedule, and then went back to bed.

But by late afternoon, I was starting to feel a little better. Star had read two Relationship Spreads on me and Alex, and both times she drew the Lovers card. Which, okay, was probably just coincidence and the result of insufficient shuffling, but I leaned on it because I needed something to lean on, and by the end of the day I decided I'd been overreacting, and blamed it on the hangover. What had happened last night? Nothing that couldn't be explained, and Alex had gone away for some reason completely unrelated to me. When he came back I'd tell him that I'd started to feel sick from all the alcohol and strange food, and had rushed home to lie down for no other reason than to keep myself from puking. That's all. End of story.

I got out of bed and went to find Molly, who I'd missed, I realized, missed with an intensity that shocked me. How had she become so indispensable to me so quickly? Her milky scent, her gap-toothed smile, the way all her nonsensical phrases turned up at the end so that everything she said sounded like a question. They were like water and air to me. Or at least like my right arm, eyes and tongue, things I could be alive without, but not really *live* without.

I went downstairs and found her in the living room, bouncing in Star's lap, gnawing on a frozen teething ring. "And this is the most important part," I heard Star say. I stood outside the doorway, listening. "Life beats down the strong ones like us; it just loves fighting the heavyweight championships. So if you find yourself wondering why some folks seem to get away scot-free, just remember those are the weak-spined ones, the ones who fall apart at the first signs of a pimple or a boy who doesn't love them back. Your life might have more ups and downs, but that's only because you're strong enough to win regardless."

I remembered myself on her lap decades ago, being handed the same insights in the same soothing tones, only vaguely understanding their meaning. All my life I'd been the recipient of this kind of "wisdom," which had probably been passed down from Star's mother and grandmother, generations of women preparing their daughters for the cruelties of the world. "Appropriate conversation for a one-year-old?" I said.

Star smiled at me. "Yeah, I know. But it's never too soon to start steeling up against the inevitability of pain."

Despite myself, I felt a beat of anger. Life is cruel, life is suffering; she'd conveyed this to me throughout my childhood. And that belief became a self-fulfilling prophecy. I'd never expected happiness, and maybe that was why I'd never even tried. What kind of lesson was that to teach a baby? Shouldn't a child be taught that anything was possible, that she was in control of her own destiny?

Molly held her arms toward me with a plaintive *"Mama!"* And, my insides aching, I lifted her from Star's lap. This was the hope I had for her: That she'd never be teased, never be ignored, never inflict pain on anyone else. Would be shown throughout her childhood the empathy her own mother lacked so she'd be able to weep for others, even people she didn't know. And most of all that she'd someday arrive relatively unscathed at a place where she loved, and was loved. That was the future everyone deserved.

"Don't you listen to her," I whispered, soft enough that Star wouldn't hear. "I promise, you're going to have an amazing life."

Star and I were washing dishes when the phone rang. We both turned quickly toward it, then looked at each other and Star smiled. "Tell him you miss him," she said. "It can be interpreted completely innocently, or completely not."

"This is why I don't take your relationship advice," I said, reaching for the phone. "Subtlety is not your forte."

But it was a woman on the phone with a deepish voice and a strange way of speaking, somewhat upper-class British minus the actual accent, like she was speaking around a mouthful of unpalatable food. "Who is this?" she said.

The Girlfriend, was my first thought. I closed my eyes and willed her to disappear, *poof!* I didn't want to throw her into the mix, not now, not when I was just starting to feel hopeful again. "I'm sorry," I said, "who is this?"

"I asked you first. I'm just wondering why you're answering Alex's phone."

"My name's Leah," I said. "A close friend of Alex's and I've been staying with him here." Let her interpret that however she would.

"Really." She sounded more amused than upset.

Star raised her eyebrows at me and I shook my head. "Now can you tell me who this is?"

"Tell Alex it's Posy, and he's succeeded in getting me to foot the cost of a phone call."

Posy. "Alex's sister?" I said.

"I just wanted to support him on the anniversary day, since he chewed me out last year for not wanting to talk about it."

"Anniversary?" I said.

"Of the accident. I thought you were a close friend. Doesn't sound all that close."

"Oh right," I said slowly, "the accident. I'm sorry, he went away for a couple days. He should be back by Wednesday, but I'll tell him you called."

"He's not off with that skank, is he? If he's there, I swear I'm disowning him."

I stared at the wall, my eyes feeling chalky dry. "I don't know, actually," I said.

"Do you know anything? I'm starting to think you're some kind of squatter; does he even know you're there? Or a hopeless cause.

Alex is big on picking up hopeless causes." She paused. "Look, just tell him I called, and he can call back if he wants. Rest of the week's bad but Sunday morning might work, long as it's not godawful early. And tell him I'm thinking of coming up for a visit, so if you're still squatting we might meet face-to-face."

"Okay," I said, in a little-girl voice.

"Okay," she repeated. "Pleasure talking with you and etcetera." And then she hung up.

I replaced the receiver and said, "That was Alex's sister calling because she wanted to support him. Because of some accident, which I have no idea what that means. And she mentioned some woman she thought he might be with."

"Ah, the girlfriend. And now you're thinking he felt guilty about wanting to kiss you, so he went off to make amends with her."

"Maybe. Yeah."

Star hesitated, then said, "I saw him holding her photo the other day, the one from his bookshelf. He was holding it in his lap and looking out the window, kind of haunted. And then... I don't know if I should be telling you this, but then he touched the picture and he whispered how he was sorry, and then he said, 'Tell me what to do.' "

"Tell him what to do?"

"Because he's started having feelings about you." Star smiled at me. "That's got to be what it is, don't you think?"

"Stop, Ma, you're acting like we're in high school. And besides, regardless of whether he has quote-unquote *feelings*, sooner or later he'll figure out I'm not who I said I am, and he'll stop feeling anything except disgusted."

Star reached for my hands and squeezed them in her own. "He knows the important parts of you, Lainey, the kindness and the caringness. And what you're doing for Molly, he'll see it's just another aspect of the sort of person you are."

Listening to her, I tried to believe this could be true, thinking how he'd come home and tell me about the "skank" he was maybe visiting now, how he'd realized when he met me just exactly how much of a skank she was in comparison. How maybe he'd ended everything because of what he'd seen in me.

And then I'd tell him everything. Not right away, maybe, but I knew the opportunity would present itself again; he'd ask a question about my past, or become comfortable enough to reveal more of his, and then I'd tell him and he'd understand.

He'd know who I really was, and love me anyway.

Tuesday evening, as I was getting Molly ready for bed, my cell phone rang. I grabbed for it. "Alex?"

"What?" I heard a strange, barking laugh, then, "No, no it's me. I just wanted to ask how you're doing. And Jacqueline. And also to see if someone from the FBI called."

"Sydney." I clutched at the shirt over my heart, as if that could still it. "They called last week. A woman."

"Good, I figured they had." She paused, then said, "So would you say they seemed really suspicious? Like did they ask you pointed questions about me?"

"Yeah, they seemed suspicious, but I told them you were a sweet, honest person and somehow my head, and their ears, didn't explode."

"You're too funny." She didn't sound remotely amused. "Did they mention anything that worried you at all? Specifics about me?"

Molly started to fuss on my lap, so I cradled the phone against my ear and set her on her feet facing me, letting her balance against my knees, her weight against me so comforting as she bounced up and down like she was readying herself to jump. "They told me you did a paternity test on Jacqueline."

Silence, then, "Oh that. Well yes, I did. I needed to make sure she was David's."

"And . . ."

"You mean is she his? Of course she is. I mean you can look at them and see the similarities, but I was grasping at straws. I was starting to think about how I could possibly fight him for custody, and I wanted to see if there was a chance I might not have to fight. I realized it wasn't likely, and it was scary as hell to think what David might do to me if he found out, but I thought it was worth the risk, and I knew he already had some idea."

"That you were screwing around."

"Not *screwing around*, Jesus. I told the investigators I met him at a bar, that it was a one-night stand and I didn't even know his name. But it was actually Kemper."

I stared at the wall, letting this sink in. "Did you think you were going to end up with him when this was over? That the three of you would live happily ever after?"

"I don't know." She paused. "Maybe, yes. I thought maybe he still cared enough to help me, since in all his letters he kept saying he'd do anything to help us get away from David. I thought he loved me." Her voice broke. "Which I know now he doesn't, probably never did; you should've seen how he reacted after I told him you had the baby. Maybe he was concerned about what David was doing to me, but it's so obvious it was never actual *love*, and now I have to come up with a whole new vision of what my future's going to look like."

"Meaning what? Do you have any idea what your next move is?"

"I don't know, I've been so focused on getting past all the questioning that I haven't had time to really think this through, but . . . I guess I'll have to go it alone somehow."

I pressed a thumb and finger against my eyes, feeling suddenly so tired. Without Alex here even little things, like not being able to find spare lightbulbs, made me all too aware that I was invading someone else's space. So without fully thinking it through I said, "How about Montana?"

A beat of silence, then, "Montana?"

"Because I might have to leave here soon, Sydney. Things've happened between me and the man I'm staying with."

Another beat, then tentatively, "Things? What do you mean, things?"

"Nothing you have to worry about, just that he's left without telling me where he went, and I'm not sure if it's right anymore to be taking advantage. I'll let you know once I have a better idea what's going on, and then if I have to go maybe you could join us, as soon as you think it's safe."

"Montana," she said, then repeated, "Montana, yeah. Okay that could definitely work. When do you think you're leaving?" Was I imagining it, or was there something cagey in her voice? I suddenly remembered what Pamela had said, how she'd thought there might be things Sydney was keeping from me. What if she was planning to tell the cops where I was and collect the reward money herself? Or if there was something else going on that I had no idea about? Had it been stupid to tell her where I was thinking of going?

"I haven't decided anything for sure yet," I said slowly. "Once Alex gets home I'll have a better idea what to do next."

"The more I think about it, the more I realize you probably *should* leave. I never liked the idea of you staying so long with someone who might figure out who Jacqueline is. Things're getting bad for me here; they have been for a while but now they're suddenly getting worse. I know you've been careful, but we're getting to the point where . . . well you can't be careful enough. And wouldn't it make more sense to leave *before* he gets home so you don't have to explain anything to him?"

Molly reached her arms toward me and I lifted her back onto my lap, feeling a sudden swirl of anger. All my life I'd let other people pull me along to wherever would shore up their needs, and I'd told myself repeatedly that now I was going to finally be the one in charge. Why should Sydney be the one to decide where Molly would go and what would happen next? She might think she could manip-ulate me, that I'd just stand by and let her, but this wasn't high school.

"Right," I said calmly, "okay, just tell me exactly what to do. I've lied to the FBI, which is a federal crime but no big deal. I've lied to the man who's been sacrificing everything to take us in, nearly killed my mother by pulling her away from home, and now I'll take off again whenever and for wherever you want. No problem!" I was happy with the tone of my voice—confident, take charge, even though I was nothing of the sort. *Don't mess with me,* that tone said.

"Stop! Lainey, don't. I can't take your yelling on top of everything else right now, I just can't. I'm falling apart here. The thought of being away from all this and starting a new life, it's the only thing keeping me remotely sane. I'm lonely, I'm scared and I don't know what to do without Jacqueline. I dream about her crying for me, and then I wake up and jump out of bed before I remember. Sometimes I even run into her room and then I panic when I see the crib empty. Do you know what it's like seeing that empty crib? And I sleep with a pair of her pajamas; how pathetic is that? Don't you get how this feels?"

You gave your baby to a near stranger, I wanted to say, *made that stranger commit a felony so that you could falsely accuse your ex-husband of kidnapping. How does that feel?*

But then I imagined her looking at Molly's empty crib, imagined myself doing the exact same thing after Molly was gone. She did love Molly. She was confused and terrified and alone, and Molly was all she had left.

"Oh Jesus, Lainey, I need to talk to her. Can I? Could you let me talk to her?"

"She's sleeping," I said, the words instinctive, self-protective. Molly had tucked her head against my shoulder and was plucking sleepily at one of my shirt buttons, and I willed her to stay silent. "It took a long time to get her down, and I'm not going to wake her up, sorry."

"Well okay. Okay, but tell me how she is? Tell me what you did with her this week?"

"I don't know, not much. We've gone on walks and we played in the garden." I squared my shoulders. "And she said her first word on Sunday."

"What? Oh Lainey, she did? She did! Are you sure it was a real word? What did she say!"

I hesitated, hearing the anguish behind her excitement. And . . . I couldn't tell her. Much as part of me wanted to gloat, I just couldn't. "Baba," I said. "For her bottle. That's her first word; write it down in the history books."

"Baba," Sydney repeated in a whisper.

"Yeah," I said softly, "I know."

She made a choked sound, then said, "This is the most important time of her life, isn't it. I mean she's learning more now than she ever did before, faster than she's ever going to again."

"It's amazing, really. It's like she gets these new skills every day, little things like how to take lids off containers, find things when I hide them, she's even learning new facial expressions."

"Oh Jacqueline . . ." I heard Sydney's breath hitch. "You know I had this dream of how it was going to be, her first word. I pictured myself playing with her, and she'd look up at me with that question-ing look she gets; you know that look? And she'd say, *Mama*. She'd say *Mama* and smile up at me, and then I'd pull her into my lap and we'd laugh and we'd laugh. In that moment I'd know everything was okay, that every minute I'd spent with her, even the mistakes I'd made, they were all okay."

"Sydney—"

"No, I know. I did this to myself, and the mistakes aren't even close to okay. I didn't deserve to hear her say her first word."

"It's not about deserving." I thought of all the times I'd prompted Molly with the word "Mama," patting at my chest with my hand and then hers. I leaned back against the wall, looking down at Molly. Her eyes were closed now, her breath heavy, but I said, "Well look at that, she's up again. I swear, it's every thirty minutes; I could use her as a kitchen timer. Hold on, let's see if she'll talk to you." I jounced her awake and held the phone to her ear and then, my voice hoarse, said, "Can you say Mama? Mama!"

In response, Molly gazed up at me and pulled the phone to her mouth, and I let her suck on it while I listened to Sydney cooing her love, her wishes and her regrets, sentiments that could have been my own. Spoken in lilting, mothering tones, to my daughter.

Alex didn't come home Wednesday night, or the next night either. No calls, no explanation, and I lived those days in a sort of limbo, trying not to think but unable to stop thinking.

What if he'd bumped into news coverage about Molly? He might turn on the TV, maybe even drive past a billboard with Molly's face and start to notice the similarities. Here I felt reasonably protected from reality but out there, anything could happen. What if he'd already realized who Molly was, and was now trying to figure out the full truth of the situation before he decided how to handle it? What if he'd stayed away this long so Molly and I would have a few last days together before he turned us in?

I should've realized this life was too good to last. That there'd be consequences for my actions. Star was a firm believer in karma; you'd think she would've warned me.

In desperation, I started searching for something that might give me some clue as to where he'd gone, an address book, a letter with a return address, the receipt for a plane ticket. He'd locked his bedroom door, as if he'd known I might go scavenging, so I searched all the kitchen drawers and the drawers in his computer desk. But everything personal was gone, including the notepad I'd found on my first night here, with its various renditions of apologies and professions of love.

I looked through his computer files, but found nothing with a title that seemed remotely personal. I tried unsuccessfully for almost an hour to guess his Outlook password, even looked through his website history: book review sites, credit card and bank links and various Wikipedia articles. The only interesting links I found were following a Google search he'd done on "child abuse" and "custody." Was he trying to help me? To see how hard it would be for me to gain custody of Molly if I stopped running and turned myself in? Oh he must be, of course he was. I turned the computer off.

That afternoon I started a mural on Susie and Jack's living room wall, trying to keep myself distracted. I sketched ocean waves with a pencil, listening to Susie play Peek-a-Boo with Molly, Molly's laugh every time Susie pulled her hands from her face.

I stepped back from the mural, added another beach umbrella, then started cracking open the cans of paint. I tried to lose myself in the splay of colors, mixing just the right shades for shadows and sun. Normally this was the kind of mural I loved to do, both absorbing and meditative, but my heart wasn't in it. The painting felt empty, just graffiti splashed on the wall, and for the first time ever I found myself thinking about the meaninglessness of it all. Who cared if I never painted another mural? All this work I was putting in, and whose life would it change?

Finally I put down my brush and turned to Susie. "Alex left," I said, apropos of nothing. "The morning after the party he left, and he's still not back home."

"Ah." Susie glanced at me. "I wondered why you were being so quiet."

"And I don't have any idea where he went." I stared down at my palette. "Do you know anything at all about his girlfriend?"

She raised her eyebrows. "You think that's where he is? All I know's that he met her before he moved here, and that he used to travel to see her every month or so, but over the past year I think they had a falling-out. Alex doesn't like talking about his personal life much, which I guess you've already realized."

"I just want to know if I should be worried," I said. And more than that. This is what I wanted to do: I wanted to ask Susie to tell me *everything,* replay every conversation she'd had with him ever, and every tidbit he'd told her about his past. To tell me who he was.

"Could he be with his mother?" I said. "Do you know anything about his family? You mentioned awhile back that something had happened with his mom and sister, that escaping it was one of the reasons he came out here."

She frowned at me, then reached for Molly and set her on her lap, started jiggling her knee. "He didn't tell you."

"No, he pretty much never talks about them."

"Well, I guess nobody really knows the whole story. He only mentioned it one time that I know of; we'd all had a little too much to drink and we started talking about our dysfunctional families, and all at once Alex got all distant and upset." She rested her chin on Molly's head, then said, "I guess we were all pretty drunk or we never would've pressed him but you know, we'd all divulged our dark secrets so we kept insisting. And he finally gave in and told us. The gist of it was that he saw his father and sister die. He was seventeen, his sister Camelia was home from college and his dad was driving him to hockey practice with Camelia in the front passenger seat. I guess he overadjusted for something in the road because he somehow ended up hitting a ditch and flipping. Alex wasn't hurt at all, just whiplash, but his dad and sister were killed instantly."

"Oh . . ." I whispered, thinking of the family photo on Alex's shelf, his parents with two young girls and Alex as a baby.

"And his mother made things even worse. They got in a huge fight that year when he told her he wanted to go away for school; it started with her saying he was deserting her when she needed him most, and it ended with her blaming him for their death, since he was the reason his dad and sister were in the car."

What would that do to a kid that age? What would it do to the rest of his life? I thought I had ghosts from the past haunting me, but something like that must seep into every single corner, every memory and thought and interpretation. I remembered suddenly our conversation the night he'd convinced me to stay, when I'd told him how heartrending it was that he felt responsible for the whole world, and he'd responded that he felt responsible only for the things he really had done. Was this what he'd been referring to?

"His mother distanced herself from him completely. I guess losing her husband and daughter sent her over the edge. Alex ran away from home pretty soon after, he was gone for months hitchhiking across the country, and when he got back she completely shut him out. I don't think they talked for years after. He had a hard time with his other sister too, I guess because she had to choose sides and so of course she chose her mom. His relationship with them's still strained."

So this was why he never mentioned his family, and maybe it explained the awkwardness I'd sensed in my conversation with Posy, as well as Posy's reference to an accident. I wondered suddenly if my pulling away from him the other night had echoed against the rejections he'd faced from the other women in his life, if maybe that's why he'd reacted by leaving me.

"And it wasn't just his father and sister," Susie said. "I think there was also a little boy who died. He had this photo he used to keep in the living room with his other pictures, this baby wrapped in a blue blanket. Until I asked about it, not in a nosy way, just curious, and he got all upset, said . . . I don't remember exactly what, but something about the baby being hurt. And then suddenly he snapped at me, basically told me to mind my own business; it was the first time I ever heard him mad. And the next time I came to visit, the photo was gone."

"A younger brother?"

"That's what I assumed, yeah. I've pictured him in the backseat with the baby, trying to give it CPR or stop its bleeding. . . ." She tucked her fingers against Molly's palms, held them there, then said, "So he obviously has issues he needs to work through, and that's one of the reasons I was so glad he has you here, because I worry about him. He might be more willing to talk with you because you have this air about you, you just feel completely safe. Like a person could tell you anything and you'd still see the goodness in them; it's part of why everybody here likes you so much."

I felt a little hop of pleasure, despite myself. "I just know what it's like to want to hide from your past," I said, "and keep people from seeing it. But he didn't tell me anything about any of this, and now . . . I just wish he'd call to say he was okay."

"I know you're worried. But it's not the first time he's disappeared without telling anybody. This situation's different, I guess, since you're staying with him and he should realize he owes you an explanation, but I'm sure he'll be home soon."

I looked down at my paint-smudged hands. "I know," I said. But the truth was, I didn't know; I wasn't sure I knew anything about him. Despite the conversations we'd had over the past weeks about our philosophies of life and dreams and disappointments, I probably knew even less about Alex than he knew about me.

⟨ 21 ⟩

It was Saturday, sometime before midnight but only barely, that I heard a car pull up the drive. I slipped a robe on over my nightshirt and went downstairs, making it to the landing just as Alex opened the door.

We watched each other silently before I said, "You're back."

He looked drawn, unshaven, his clothes rumpled and hair unkempt. And I'm sure that after several restless nights, I didn't look much better. "Yeah," he said. "How's Molly?"

"She's fine. Everybody's fine." I hesitated, then said, "Except me. I didn't know if you were ever coming home, Alex."

"I'm sorry." He dropped his bags, his arms hanging limp at his sides. "I should've called, I realize that."

"Yeah," I said, "you should've." And then I shook my head. "I'm sorry, I didn't mean that. We're not married. You don't owe me anything."

"No, I did owe you. I know what it must've been like having me disappear."

"So are you going to explain it?"

"Yes. I mean I don't know." He squeezed a hand at the back of his neck, looking dazed. "It's just there are a lot of things going on right now that I needed to figure out."

I felt a hollow disappointment. But what had I expected? That he'd tell me he'd been so tortured and heartbroken after I'd run away Sunday night that he'd run away himself?

"I knew I couldn't call you without giving some kind of explanation," he said, "but I'm not ready to explain it to anybody yet. I can't."

I hesitated, then said, "Were you with Erin?"

He blinked quickly, surprised, then shook his head. Not the kind of head shake meant as an answer, but the kind that implied there was no answer. Which meant, probably, that yes. That's where he'd been.

"It's okay. It's not my business."

"I wish I could tell you what's going on with me, I really do. But there's just too much at stake."

"You're talking like I should be scared of you."

"I don't know." His face was utterly expressionless. "Maybe you should."

I clutched the sides of my robe, cinching it tighter around me. "What if I told you I could say the same thing? And that if you knew some of what I'd done you'd think of me differently?"

He studied my face, searching, before he said, "Whatever you think you did, it's not the same. You wouldn't do anything wrong unless you didn't have a choice."

I felt a sudden wariness, a dark mass in my chest. "I can forgive anything," I said slowly. "I know what you've been doing for us, and what kind of person you are."

"Leah." He squared his shoulders and reached for his bags. "I'm sorry, it's late. It's been a hell of a week and I'm completely exhausted. Just forget I said anything, okay? It's nothing you need to worry about, and I'll be better tomorrow, I promise." He walked past me, toward the stairs, leaving the front door open behind him.

I watched him climb to his bedroom and then turn back to the doorway, looking out like there might be answers somewhere in the trees, the night air. What the hell could he be talking about? What did he do? Had he killed someone? Dealt drugs? Sold uranium to terrorists? It felt like he'd opened a door, let me look through just long enough to see the squirming surface before he slammed it in my face.

I closed the front door slowly, then climbed the stairs. I wouldn't think about this now. All that mattered was that he'd come back.

Alex's bedroom door was closed. And seeing it, wondering what he might be hiding, I thought of all the parts of my life I'd probably never tell another soul, things I'd done and thought and things that had been done to me, which shaped me and my view of myself irreparably. I had a sense that Alex would understand, and part of me wanted to run to him now and tear myself open so he could see all the ugliness, maybe tell me it wasn't so ugly after all. But of course, no one ever did that. Not just because the ugliness was shameful but because those parts were, in a way, the most important parts. And to lose their ugliness would be to lose myself.

Instead I went to my own room, pulled off my robe and began to hang it in the closet. And then, my door opened.

I spun around and there he was, his eyes bloodshot, face red. He made a tight sound and strode forward, took me into his arms so abruptly that I lost my footing and fell back against the clothes in my closet, onto the floor. I glanced over at Molly's crib just long enough to see she was asleep, before he pulled me against him, yanking up my nightshirt to press his palms against my bare back, his mouth biting against my cheek, my chin and then my lips, so fierce I felt like I was bleeding.

And then with a choked sound he tore off my nightshirt and then his own shirt, nuzzling his face between my breasts. I pressed against the back of his head, my eyes stinging with tears, my fingers tangled in his hair.

He was shaking, his breath heavy, and I wrapped my legs around his waist to steady him, pressed my hands against his back. So focused on the feel of him against me, his skin against mine, his weight and the tight muscles in his back, that it took me a good two minutes to realize he was shaking not from desire, but from tears. He was sobbing against my chest, tears wetting my skin, and I froze, then gradually brought my hands back to his hair. Smoothed it in the way I comforted Molly when she cried, while I stared wide-eyed at the ceiling of my closet, suddenly feeling the sneaker under my shoulder, the suitcase buckle digging against my skull. I just held him there, stroking his hair. Having not the slightest idea how I was supposed to feel.

I woke to the sound of Molly whimpering and sat up slowly, wincing at the pain in my spine, staring confusedly at the hanging robe blocking my vision before I thought to swipe it away. Alex was gone. I ran a finger along my bare cleavage, felt the dried salt from his tears. Yes, last night was real.

I stood slowly, testing my spine, then pulled on my robe and went to Molly. She'd soiled her diaper. Not just her diaper but her entire body. I lifted her carefully and brought her to the bathroom, then filled the tub and stripped off her clothes, leaving them to soak in the sink while I washed her, smoothing baby shampoo over her body and through her hair, letting her splash the water with her palms. Not allowing myself to think, or feel, anything.

Until I heard a knock on the door, and my heart jumped. I took a deep breath before I turned. It was Star.

"Did you see he's back?" she said, then walked in to sit on the closed toilet lid. "I guess he came while we were asleep."

I willed her to go away; I wasn't ready to talk about him, to interpret anything. I wrung out the washcloth and draped it over the side of the tub. "Yeah," I said.

"You talk to him yet?"

"No," I said, then, "I mean yes. Last night."

"Did you find out where he's been?"

"Not exactly." I pulled Molly from the tub and reached for a towel. "Can we talk about this later, Ma? I have a headache." And a body-ache and a heartache, and I needed to talk to Alex.

She studied my face and then her eyes widened, her mouth slowly forming an O. I looked quickly away, wrapping the towel around Molly. "And I didn't sleep well last night," I said.

"You slept with him, didn't you," she said.

The words felt like a slap. "No! Jesus, Ma!"

"Or at least came close to it. Look how you're blushing." She pressed a palm to her cheek, and suddenly her eyes filled. "Lainey," she said.

"I didn't sleep with him!" I felt my own eyes start to sting, and held Molly's warm, damp body against me. "We . . . kissed. And then, I don't know what happened. He started to cry."

She watched me silently.

"And then he left the room, and I don't know what any of it means."

"It means you need to talk," she said softly, "You've been so focused on your secrets that you haven't worried enough about his." She touched my hand. "You want me to take her? His door's still closed, but he'll probably be up soon."

"No, I'll get her dressed and make some breakfast. Just . . . try not to come downstairs if you hear us talking, okay?" I turned away.

In the bedroom I dressed Molly quickly and then, without really registering what I was doing, I pulled on my most flattering blouse, blue to match my eyes. I went to the mirror and brushed my hair until it shone, then smoothed on a careful application of blusher and mascara, even lipstick which I almost never wore. I hadn't taken a shower, partly because I felt too frenzied to be able to stand in one place for more than a minute, but also . . . because. Because I could still smell him on me, that sweet muskiness; I wanted to smell it on my skin and remember. Or no, not remember. I couldn't think about it. Not until we talked.

I brought Molly downstairs and fed her rice cereal and peach mush, making airplane noises as I brought the spoon to her mouth, slotting myself back into the role of mother. "My name is Mr. Fruit," I said in a scratchy voice. Molly laughed at me as I circled the spoon toward her. "And I'm here to visit Miss Molly's mouth. Anybody there?"

"Nada!" Molly said, raising an arm to the door, and I turned to see Alex in the doorway, watching me. Mr. Fruit stopped mid-flight and fell to the floor. "Morning," he said.

My face flushed and I gave a quick nod and bent to swipe a dishtowel over the slop of peaches on the tile. Molly banged her palms against her high chair tray, laughing and straining toward him, and he pulled her from the chair and nuzzled against her. "Oh I missed you!" he said softly. She pulled her head back to look into his face, then turned to me, beaming as if to say, *Look what I found!*

"So how are you this morning?" I said slowly.

He kept his eyes on Molly. "Good," he said, then, "Tired."

"You must be. I'll start your chicory." I rose and went to the coffeemaker, my mind racing as I scooped grounds into the filter. "So before I forget, Posy asked you to call back this morning. She's thinking of coming to visit."

"Seriously? Interesting. She's never wanted to come up north before." He rubbed Molly's back, eyes on the coffeepot, then bent to whisper something unintelligible into her ear.

I steeled my shoulders, waiting. Was that it? End of conversation? Would he just hand Molly back to me, pour himself a mug and walk away? No. No. "We going to talk about it?" I said, surprising myself. Was I really this strong?

"Yes," he said.

I continued waiting. Finally he handed Molly to me and poured his chicory, just as Star appeared in the doorway. I shot her a look that was clearly hostile but she ignored it, reaching for a box of Wheaties. Her hands were shaking, her jaw set. She wouldn't meet my eye. Had something happened?

Alex turned from me to her and back, then sat down at the table across from me. "Yes, I was with Erin," he said.

I watched Star pour her cereal, spilling much of it in the process. "Okay," I said. "So what's with all the secrecy?"

"I have no idea where to even start." He shook his head. "You want me to tell you about her?"

No. "Yeah," I said, "I guess."

He stared fixedly into his mug, then gave a short nod. "Right. Okay. So I met her back in the days I was catering in New York. She hired me for a family party, a fiftieth anniversary, one of those French truffle, Kobe beef extravaganzas that used to drive me insane. I always get turned off by money, which was one of my failings as a caterer, but she was different. She cared about things, you know?"

I nodded, as if this weren't a rhetorical question. Yes, I know what it's like to care about things.

"Or at least I thought she did, and she seemed so compassionate and passionate about wanting to make a difference in the world, which made her feel human to me, not like a Gucci-wearing mannequin. The first day that we met to go over the party menu we ended up talking for hours, and here she was treating me like a best friend when I was so used to being treated like an indentured servant. She just spilled out all her sadnesses and disappointments, and it was intoxicating. Plus she was beautiful, I mean stunningly beautiful, but she also seemed so vulnerable and so real." He shook his head. "Except the thing was . . ." He glanced at Star. "She was married."

"Ah," Star said, as if she was suddenly slotting all the pieces of Alex's mystery into place. But I shook my head. That was all? That was his big secret, that he was having an affair with a married woman?

"I was thinking you'd killed somebody," I said. "Or, I don't know, become a drug runner."

He squared his shoulders. "That's not all of it. I mean I'm not exactly proud of sleeping with a married woman, and I ended up moving to New Hampshire partly to give her a chance to set things straight with her husband. But in the end, she wasn't happily married. She was completely unhappy, so I guess I ended up justifying it. I actually thought I was helping her gain the confidence to leave him, so she could get on with the rest of her life." He shoved his mug away. "Which in the end made me agree to do some things. Illegal things."

Star set her cereal spoon down slowly, her eyes fixed on his.

"Okay," I said. "Tell us." Had he killed her husband? What else could it possibly be?

"She was in trouble and she asked me for help. She convinced me it was the law that was wrong, that she was innocent and this was the only way to set things right. So . . . I did something; something bad. Just this one thing, she said, but it turned into another thing and another thing, and now I don't know how to end it."

"You killed her husband," I said.

He didn't respond, didn't even look at me so I repeated, "You killed her husband?" Part of me wanted to cover Molly's ears.

"Of course not, Leah." He squeezed his eyes shut, like he was suddenly in great pain. "I wish I could explain everything, but it's not really up to me anymore. I hate the things she's made me do, but I don't want to hurt her. And if you found out what we'd done . . . well I'm pretty sure neither of you would let us get away with it. That's how bad it all is."

I tried to process this but there was nothing to hold on to, no foothold to base the processing on. So I said, "Are you still doing these illegal things?"

He didn't answer.

"Why? Is it because you still want to be with her?" The words were out before I could swallow them back, their implicit meaning obvious. If you love her, then what happened last night? And what exactly did it mean?

"No." He looked into my eyes. "I don't think I ever did love her really, not in the right way. And now I'm finally realizing I never had any idea who she was. I just have to figure out how to get out of this without hurting anybody, including all of you."

These weren't the turns I'd expected this conversation to take. I wasn't naïve enough to expect him to say he'd stopped loving her because of me; that kind of thing only happened on daytime TV. But I'd wanted *something,* at least an "I made a mistake last night," or "I was tired" or "drunk" or "emotionally exhausted" or, "I think that maybe, perhaps, there's a chance that I want to kiss you again." But now, now I was almost afraid of him. "What did you mean when you said I should maybe be scared of you?"

Star's face washed pale, and she started hitting her fingertips in a strange, stuttering rhythm against the tabletop. But her voice when she spoke was surprisingly firm. "You're a good man," she said, "I know that. And if you hurt us you'd hurt yourself more, so I won't be scared."

I shot her a fierce look, but Alex was watching her with a question in his eyes I didn't understand.

"You know I have to be careful," I said, "because of the baby."

"I know. You're right, I owe you both the truth, and of course you're right to be worried, because if Erin—or I—screw up, there's a chance it could lead the police here. With everything you've been through I completely understand why you wouldn't trust me."

"It's not that I don't trust you," I started, then fitfully smoothed the back of Molly's shirt before I said, "Okay, here's the thing, it scares me how little I know about you. Like you almost never talk about your past, and then Susie told me Thursday what happened to your dad and your sister. Which is so huge, such a huge part of your life, and it's a sign how much of yourself you've been keeping from us. And I *need* to be able to trust you. You're the only stable thing I have in my life right now."

He gripped his mug tighter, spoke in a stiff monotone. "I don't talk about my family. You must've known there was a reason why."

"I know. It was none of my business, I realize that and I'm sorry, it's just I was looking for some kind of clue to where you'd gone."

His face twitched and I touched his hand, but he pulled away. "So you know the grim secrets of my past, and now you think you know me better. Well fine, I guess if my past has anything to do with what's going on in my life now, it's that my thought patterns and the way I reason things out can sometimes be completely screwed up. Which made me get involved with someone I never should've trusted, and in a situation I have no idea how to get out of." He shoved his mug away. "Which is what I mean when I tell you I'm dangerous. Because even if I don't mean to hurt people, I almost inevitably do."

"Do you want us to leave?" I said. "Would that make it any easier for you to work all this out?"

For a minute he didn't answer, and I rested my cheek against Molly's head so I wouldn't have to look at him. He was going to say yes, and then what would I do?

"Do you want to leave?" he said finally. "Because if you do, I'd understand."

"What?" I looked back at him, startled. "No, of course not."

"Then don't even think about it. I'm going to figure this out, how to get out of this without hurting Erin or anyone, and then I'll be able to tell you both everything. But if you ever decide this isn't working, I can give you some money to get back on your feet, which . . . in retrospect is probably what I should've done in the first place. But I want you to consider it hard, because the truth is the three of you might be better off."

It felt like he'd punched me, that same physical pain at my ribs. Like his fist had been absorbed into my chest. "You *do* think we should leave."

"I just don't want anybody to get hurt. I couldn't forgive myself."

"Alex . . ." I said. *Alex, tell me if I leave you'll want to throw yourself under a bus!* "This is the first time in a long time, in maybe forever that I haven't felt hurt. I love being here. With you. I love . . . it." I shook my head quickly. "All of us do."

He held my eyes a moment, then rose. "Me too," he said, and then he turned and left the room.

We listened to the sound of his footsteps up the stairs, and then Star turned to me, her eyes narrowed, intense. "I did a reading on him. Just before I came in here, I did a reading."

I wanted to scoff, say something disparaging, but I didn't have the energy.

"The cards said there's two paths he can take now, and he's on the path to trouble. Unless he veers away from it everything's going to fall down around him."

"You just made that up from what Alex said. You just made all of that up."

"I'm telling you, everything here is in danger," she said firmly. "I'd tell you to leave if I thought it'd help, but I have a sense it won't make any of us any safer. You're meant to be here; it's your destiny and mine, Alex's, Molly's."

"Oh please. You're saying that because you're not strong enough to get back in the car, because leaving scares you more than staying."

Star began distractedly picking up the Wheaties she'd spilled, crushing them one by one between her index finger and thumb. "I'm scared *here*, Lainey. But when I said Alex was a good man, I meant it. He *is* a good man, and we have to trust he's going to do the right thing."

"I trust him," I said. "I know he wouldn't do anything to hurt us." But of course, I could only trust that he wouldn't do anything purposely. Whatever he was involved in, what if it led to his arrest? How could I not worry it might lead the authorities to us? All I could do was keep my eyes open. And be ready for anything.

22

And so, that was it. The conversation over before we'd talked about the night Alex had returned home. It didn't come up that day or the next, and by the time a week had passed it felt almost like that night hadn't happened at all. I did see Star watching us intently when we were together, like she was waiting for the right gears to turn, watching for signs of a spark, ignition, but she knew better than to ask.

Alex didn't talk about *The Girlfriend* again either. And much as I wanted to believe that meant he'd ended things, within the next week I heard him twice on the phone with someone, late at night. There was a chance it was just Posy, who was scheduled to arrive in a week. But part of me was sure it was HER and I imagined her voice, silky and dangerously seductive, pushing him deeper into the pit she'd dug.

It didn't matter, though. I wouldn't let it matter. I was content with what our life had become, regardless of whether it might become more. Most afternoons now I painted; several of Susie's friends had contacted me to commission their own murals, and they'd told their friends about me. And soon I had an even longer lineup of projects than I'd ever had in Virginia, and the promise of enough money that I insisted on using my savings to pay for groceries and a small stipend for rent.

Pamela had been sending me bills, which she picked up every

other day from our mailbox, but since I'd canceled all but one of our credit cards and shut off all our utilities, the bills had started dwindling. Like our former life was slowly disappearing.

Of course there were moments I woke up from the dream. I made myself search daily on Alex's computer for stories about Molly's disappearance and David McGrath's upcoming drug possession trial, and the stories left me frantic for hours, pacing back and forth in my bedroom.

The McGraths had doubled the size of their reward; hundreds of leads had come in through their toll-free tip line and all, even the implausible ones, were being followed. A psychic detective had told the McGraths that Molly was surrounded by greenery (true enough) and would be found the morning of September 7. The police had used bloodhounds to search for her body in open fields and of course found nothing, but they assured reporters they were nowhere close to giving up.

And then two weeks after Alex returned, while I was on my way home from a painting job, Sydney called. "This is insane," she said. "The whole world is insane!"

"Why it's nice talking to you too, Sydney!" I said.

"I have to get out of here, Lainey. I just had the most godawful fight with David's lunatic mother. She came to my door and started screaming when I wouldn't open it, completely hysterical. Throwing herself at the door, yelling about how I've ruined the lives of her entire family, and taken away her precious baby girl. *Her* girl! I can't stand this anymore, being around these people."

"Can you blame her?" I said dispassionately. "I mean, it's the truth."

"I blame her for making a scene all the neighbors could hear, yes! Now I understand where David got his violent temper."

"She lost her granddaughter, Sydney! And lost her son in a way too; do you ever think about that? David's parents are the only ones I feel bad for in all of this. And your mom, I guess, although she's probably loving the publicity. I'm guessing she's telling everyone she meets how she hasn't been able to sleep, and then accepting offers for lunches out and spa treatments."

"I can't believe you're so cold!"

"Oh get off it, you know it's true."

Sydney paused a moment and then, surprisingly, she gave a chirp of laughter. "Did you see her on the news the other day? She had her hair done and I think she was freshly Botoxed and silicone-lipped."

"It's important to have big lips to enunciate one's despair," I said.

She made a scoffing sound, then said, "Oh man, I miss you, Lainey."

The words felt like fingers pinching my insides. For some reason they actually physically hurt. I gripped the steering wheel tighter.

"So," Sydney said softly, "is Jacqueline there with you? Can I talk to her?"

"She's with my mom. I'm on the road."

I heard Sydney sigh, the most melancholy sound, then, "What's she been doing? Any more new words?"

I felt an unexpected pang for Sydney. Of sympathy, partly, but also of camaraderie, over this baby we both had raised. I pulled off to the side of the road and sat a moment, letting the engine idle, then turned it off and said, "Yeah, a few. She can say *ball*, and *uh-oh* whenever she drops things and, interestingly, *poo* when she needs a diaper change."

"Oh . . ." Sydney whispered.

"And what else? Nothing huge, I guess, but you can tell she really wants to walk; she gets herself rocking a little on her feet like she's revving herself up. But so far she's only revved herself onto her butt. Although you should see her crawl, Sydney; she's setting the land speed record."

Sydney gave a forced laugh. "Yeah, she always was a gifted crawler." She was quiet a moment, then said, "Don't let her walk without me, okay? I want to be the one who teaches her."

"You expect me to strap her down or something?" I said, but I regretted the words as soon as they left my mouth. Because I understood exactly how she must feel—the same way I felt when I imagined not being there when Molly learned to tie her shoes, to read, styled her hair before her first-ever date. "Okay," I said. "I'll start reminding her of the advantages of hand and knee travel."

"Thanks," Sydney said, like she actually believed me, then, "You forgive me now, don't you? I think when this is over we can try and pick up where we left off. Telling each other everything, you know? Figuring out life."

Was she kidding? "There's a big difference between accepting the things someone's done to you and wanting to hang out with them. And I really doubt there's anything you could teach me about life that I'd want to know." After which, I smiled. *Game over,* I thought. *Checkmate.*

"I was just hoping you'd want to keep being part of our lives. I can tell how much you care about Jacqueline and I just wish . . . I wish you could care a little about me too, not be so bitter."

I wasn't still bitter, was I? Not exactly; that was much too strong a word. "I feel sorry for you, not bitter." I said this, of course, bitterly. "I feel sorry for the kid you were in high school and the person you grew up to be, and that's what keeps me from hating you. You can't pity and hate someone at the same time."

"Oh come off it." The change in her tone was startling. "I swear, you like to think of yourself as the most empathic person, but you've never even tried to see things from my point of view, have you." She made a frustrated huffing sound, then said, "You want to talk about high school? Okay, let's talk. Did you know that the week before junior year started my mom left home? She was gone for a month, and she didn't even tell me until the day before she left. With this Portuguese guy named Marcelo; she gave me two hundred dollars for food—which of course I blew on crap within the first week—and the number of a hotel where I left about fifty frantic messages she didn't return."

"Poor Sydney," I said. "And you were so devastated about being screwed over by your mother that you decided to screw me over? Why're you even bringing this up now?"

"I'm just trying to get you to realize nothing's as simple as you seem to think it is, same as now. I'm not trying to make excuses, because I don't have any good ones, I'm just trying to explain. And I feel like we have to work through it, get to some kind of peace with the past before you'll be able to trust me, and I guess before I'll really be able to trust you either."

I shook my head. I didn't want to talk about high school. Hearing Sydney mention it I was there again, the pain just as sharp, like the pain of a phantom limb when the actual limb is long gone. Spending lunchtime in a back carrel at the school library so I wouldn't have to face sitting alone in the cafeteria; looking out at the courtyard, the clusters of girls in their little closed circles discussing parties and movie outings and dates whose magnificence I could only dream about. I'd sit in my carrel sneaking bites of sandwich and then chips, red grapes, cookies and more cookies, which filled my stomach but not my emptiness. Imagining myself there inside those circles, girls whispering secrets to me, arms slung round my waist.

Now I watched the fly that had landed on my windshield wash its face with its front legs, then slapped at the windshield to scare it away. "Okay," I said, "talk. Your mother left you for a month, and you decided to tell everybody I was a loser. How's that related exactly?"

"It's not," she said softly. "Not really, but I guess part of me was angry because I felt like I couldn't tell you what was going on. All those months you'd cried to me about Star, and I knew you'd think what I was going through was minor in comparison. You'd say something jokey like, 'I'd give anything if my mom would disappear!' because you wouldn't get how lucky you were."

"You seriously think I wouldn't have realized how screwed up your mother was? You think I would've dismissed it?"

"All I can tell you is what I was thinking then. I blamed myself for her leaving and I was ashamed, and I felt completely alone. I didn't want to talk about it with anyone really; I cut most of my classes and I'd hang out in a bathroom stall crying, thinking about running off somewhere, becoming a stripper or a hooker, leaving her the way she left me even though I knew deep down she wouldn't even really care less. And then one day I was walking out from the bathroom when David saw me."

"David McGrath?"

"What I did to you in high school was David's fault too, isn't that funny? I mean not funny . . ." Her voice trailed off and she was silent a minute before she said, "He was so nice to me when he saw I'd been crying; he pulled me into an empty classroom and he sat with me until I told him what was going on. He was the only person I ever told, and he held me when I cried, and by the time we left the class-room I was completely in love with him. I started hanging onto him, making it obvious how I felt, and it must've freaked him out because he started pretending he didn't see me in the halls and stopped tak-ing my phone calls. And I was trying to figure out why he wouldn't like me, and what I came up with was that maybe it was because of you."

A car sped past me and I watched its receding taillights. All of this felt so separate from me; I hadn't realized any of it was going on. Sydney had spent more time with me in the beginning of the year, over at the house every night—so was it because our frozen dinners had been the only dinners available? And then, suddenly, without explanation, she'd stopped coming over. Had stopped talking to me soon after. "What do you mean because of me?" I said slowly.

"Not *because* of you exactly, but I knew how it had to seem, me spending all my time with you. I mean if anybody got to know you, you're obviously amazing and funny and so great to hang out with, but he *didn't* know you. And it suddenly felt like I had this choice, you know? Like I could decide what kind of person I wanted to become, and how I wanted the rest of high school to be. I didn't want to hurt you, I seriously didn't even think what the repercussions might be for you. But I was standing around with David and a handful of kids before gym; somebody asked about you and it was like there was this sudden shifting click in my mind that said, *This is your moment.* So I made up some story, I don't even remember what. That you still sucked your thumb, or bit off your own toenails, something stupid that everybody should've realized was just a joke."

I made a choked sound somewhere between a laugh and a sob, thinking, *Seriously? Seriously?*

"It was so ridiculous, obviously, especially with what I know about David now. But after I told the story somebody else overheard and said, *Are you kidding me?* And I saw how they were looking at me, this bright expectation, and I said, Yeah, plus she also does *this* and *this*, and before I knew it word got around."

I stared at the dirty windshield, unblinking; my lungs felt filled with glue. All that time I'd known there must be something horribly wrong with me—that I'd been so pathetic I couldn't even see how pathetic I was—all that time my biggest flaw was not being good enough for David McGrath?

"It all blew up so fast, and it didn't even work. I started dating Mike Garnett, remember him? To make David jealous, but David went out of his way to avoid me. He actually asked me later why I was being such a jerk to somebody who used to be my best friend, isn't that ironic? But by then it was too late."

I remembered my yearbook picture from that year, my carefully ironed hair, nicest shirt and painstakingly lined lips. The hour I'd spent by the mirror that morning meticulously concealing an acne scar, trying on all my earrings and practicing various versions of a smile. But the photo showed my true self in my hollow eyes, that haunted, pleading desolation.

And I wanted to hate Sydney for that, but instead I just felt like crying. For the Lainey in the picture, my loneliness, that longing to be welcomed into the center of those clusters of girls. And also . . . also for Sydney, who'd needed something and had had no idea how to get it. The pointlessness of it all.

For a minute she didn't speak; I could hear her breathing on the other end of the line. And then she said, "Can you forgive me? I needed you to get what happened in high school, but now most of all I need you to understand I'm doing the best I can here, and that it wasn't supposed to turn out like this. It's like back then, things I did just taking on a life of their own. Both then and now just started out as a mistake, and the events blew up and started leading me."

I wanted to tell her how of course it wasn't even remotely the same, how she was crazy to think we could ever be friends again. But I was starting to realize that I didn't resent Sydney anymore. Maybe it was seeing she hadn't, after all, destroyed my life, that at least for this moment I was happier than I'd ever been. Or maybe it was just that I was understanding, for the first time, that Sydney had never set out purposefully to hurt me. So I said, "I'll try to forgive you, Sydney. Or at least keep working with you to figure out how to get through this."

She was quiet a minute, absorbing this, then said, "Thank you."

I looked down at the backs of my hands, studying them, the wrinkles I was noticing for the first time at my knuckles and the pronounced blue veins. And where once it would've been distressing, a sign of time running out, now in a strange way it made me feel almost proud. I leaned back in my seat. "You're welcome."

"Lainey?" she said softly. "Lainey, I have to tell you something."

I felt a twitch of trepidation. Nobody ever says they have to tell you something and then follows it with something you want to hear. "What?"

"The thing is . . ." She paused. "Lainey, I'm going to disappear for a while. And I need to know you'll be okay with that."

"Wait, what?" I shook my head quickly, feeling a sudden *thwack,* like something was snapping back into my chest. "What do you mean you're disappearing? I thought you weren't leaving until they cleared your name!"

"It's just I'm kind of in trouble here. I'm pretty sure I'm their prime suspect now, the questions they've been asking, the way they're asking; my lawyer doesn't even let me answer half of them, that's how incriminating they are. They're all focused on Kemper now, they interrogated me for twenty straight hours trying to get me to break, and I know I can't keep refusing to give them his name and number. They'll make me tell them."

I stared blankly at the gravel by the side of the road, fought to keep my voice calm. "So you're going to just run away from all of it? You think that'll make it go away? They'll just take it as an admission of guilt."

"Well of course I realize that, and at this point it's not even legal for me to be leaving the state. But what's the alternative? This is for your good too."

"Don't you dare say any of this is for my good."

"You know what I mean. Yeah, I'm not doing this for you, but I'm also not doing it for myself. I'm trying to save Jacqueline's life, you know that, and there's no good answers here. I'm out of options! I'm not going to just sit around and let them arrest me and take her away."

"What's going to happen if you disappear? They're going to try and figure out where you've gone, which means they'll look even closer at all the names you gave them. They'll figure out me and Star are gone and then maybe question Pamela, and I know she loves me but she's not going to lie to the police. The cops'll be here within seconds, so is that a good option?"

"What else can I do?" She sounded on the verge of tears. "What if they put me in jail? I'd *die* in jail; I'm not strong enough for that kind of life. I'd kill myself!"

"Why don't you at least wait it out and see what happens? If things get much worse, then call me and we'll figure out what to do next, but they can't arrest you now. Not when they don't have any kind of proof."

"It's not just that, Lainey. You should see the people around here. The way they're all looking at me now, this evil eye like they think I'm a baby killer or something, and I'm scared to even go outside. I wouldn't be surprised if they tried to lynch me."

Despite myself, I felt a twinge of pleasure. Remembering how it had been sitting alone at a pep rally, unable to look up but sure that everyone's eyes were on me. Playing soccer in gym, being tripped either accidentally or on purpose as I lunged for the ball, the snorts of suppressed laughter. Welcome to my world, Sydney. Never expected to see you here.

"And also, also I want to see Jacqueline. That's the biggest reason. I'm leaving Virginia because I want to come see you."

I widened my eyes. "No. No way, Sydney."

"You can't stop me from seeing my daughter. I need to see her, she's all I have left in the world and it's killing me being away from her."

How would I ever be able to explain Sydney's presence to Alex? And if he or the neighbors had seen the story in the news, how long would it take them to recognize Sydney, look at Molly and put two and two together? "I realize you miss her," I said, my voice gritty with anger, "and I'm sorry if you're no longer universally fawned over. I'm sure that sucks for you, but I'm not telling you where we are because I don't want you screwing our lives up too. I swear, if you show up I'm going to"—*kill you,* I wanted to say, *stab you, shoot you, twist your head off your neck and smash it with an iron mallet*—"turn you in," I said.

"You won't," she said smoothly. "I know you won't. You care too much about her to let David take her."

"I care too much about her to let *you* take her! You don't want to test me, Sydney. I don't care if I'm arrested; worst comes to worst Child Protective Services will take Jacqueline, which would mean at least she'd be safe."

Sydney must've heard something in my voice, because she suddenly sounded annoyed. "Did you think I'd actually let you keep her? She's my daughter."

"She's *not* your daughter," I said. "You lost the right to her the minute you told the world she'd been kidnapped. You try and take her away, I'll call the cops so fast they'll be here before your nose job hits the door!" I slapped the phone shut and then slammed my fist against the dashboard. "Dammit!"

Was she coming here? Could she really find me? What if Pamela had told her where I was? I started the car and headed home. I could pack tonight, throw all our things into bags and run before Alex woke up, without saying goodbye. I'd take Star by surprise so she never had a chance to reach full panic stage. How many Xanax did she have left? We'd had almost a three-month supply to start, but I knew she'd been overusing them. Oh God.

I turned onto our street, pulled into the driveway and parked. I pressed my forehead against the steering wheel, centering myself on the cold vinyl against my skin, then rose and walked into the house. Alex was at the computer in the living room, so I called a greeting to him, amazed at the seeming cheeriness of my voice. Ah yes, what a startlingly good liar I was.

I went upstairs to Star's bedroom and found Molly on the floor with her, a sand pail over her head. "Her new favorite game," Star said, as Molly pulled the bucket up, peeked at Star, grinning, then let it drop again. "Where'd she go? Where'd she go!"

Molly chortled rather maniacally and then pulled the pail up again as Star said, "There she is!" then turned to me. "It seems this will never get old for her."

I knelt next to Molly and took her in my arms, and Molly let the pail fall again over her head. "Man, I wish we had a camera," Star said.

I listened to the echo of Molly's giggle inside the pail, looking over at Star's beaming face, and suddenly felt my whole body slump.

Molly pulled the pail off her head and handed it up to me, her face questioning. "She wants you to wear it," Star said, smiling, and I took the pail, looking down at Molly, a fierce despair snaking through my chest at the sight of the thin fringe of red along her scalp where the brown dye was starting to grow out. It made her look otherworldly, like her head was emitting light. A sign she was already returning to the woman who'd birthed her.

That night I set up my sketch pad next to Molly and started to outline her face, her bent knees, the curl of her chubby fingers. Such a perfectly shaped mouth she had, puckered like a flower. Perfect everything, the tiny whorls in her ears, the wisps of damp hair on her forehead, and I studied them all in meticulous detail as I sketched, the way I studied landscapes I wanted to be sure to remember later, after I'd left them.

What would I do if Sydney suddenly showed up at the door? I'd have to check the news constantly, see if she did decide to leave. I had to realize this life could change any day, mentally prepare, but for now I couldn't stand to think about any of it.

On a whim I started sketching images in the corners of my pad, Molly at three, at five, at fifteen, all with this same innate sweetness. Working on a jigsaw puzzle, practicing the art of tying a shoe, brushing her long hair.

Molly crawled to me and grabbed for the pencil and I shifted the pad and began meditatively adding myself to the last image, knowing full well how desperate this impulse was. She batted the pencil again and I reflexively snapped at her, "Don't!" and pushed her hand away.

Her eyes widened, she stared at me, and suddenly her face crumpled. "Oh I'm sorry," I whispered, "I'm sorry," and I dropped the pencil and lifted her. I set her on my bed and lay with her, rubbing rhythmic circles on her belly and humming a tuneless chant in an attempt to mesmerize her. And it seemed to work; she stopped kicking her legs and watched my face with big eyes like she was trying to absorb me, or at least figure out what the hell I was trying to sing.

As we lay there, I tried to understand what might be going on inside her. Did she wonder sometimes how I'd come into her life? Did she try to figure out what had happened to Sydney, or was she as unconcerned and accepting as she seemed? And . . . oh I know how it sounds, I know, but this was the question I most wanted an answer to: Did she love me? When she reached her arms toward me, each time her face lit up as I entered the room, was that love or just recognition that I was someone who'd be willing to hold her?

Of course it shouldn't matter at all. It wouldn't change how I felt about her and anyway, how much actual *love* did babies feel? But somehow, somehow knowing she felt for me at least some of what a child should feel for her mother, it would justify everything I'd done, legitimize it, even legitimize my feelings for her. Looking into each other's eyes like this, it felt like the most intense, purest adoration I'd ever felt for and from another person. I'd built up all these defenses over years and years of hurt, but she'd gotten inside me anyway, taking up every vacant space. So it mattered because my love for Molly was now the most important thing, the only thing holding my millions of broken pieces together.

23

Alex's sister arrived on the hottest day of the summer so far, one of those days that would have forecasters spouting statistics and environmentalists shaking their heads about melting glaciers. The house wasn't air-conditioned; instead, Alex had a handful of old, metal-bladed fans that we carried from room to room, the damp air they blew in our faces not much more refreshing than stale breath.

But when I answered the front door, Molly in my arms, the woman behind it seemed cool and unruffled. She looked so much like Alex with her square chin and dark hair. Feminized, yes, and much thinner, the type of woman whose legs, when closed, would only touch at the knees and ankles, but still the likeness was disconcerting, like I was looking at Alex in drag.

She and Alex watched each other's faces a moment, Posy's eyes shifting uncomfortably to me and back to Alex before she dipped her head in a nod. Alex immediately smiled and leaned to kiss her cheeks European style, left, right and left again. She smiled back, squeezing his shoulder, then turned to me. "The squatter!" she said. "And the baby squatter." She gave Molly the kind of smile people give when they don't much like something, but know they're supposed to.

It was true that Molly wasn't at her best. The heat had gotten to her; her face was red and thin tendrils of her hair were plastered to her head, like dark Sharpie stripes drawn onto her skull. But still, that smile made me take an instant dislike to Posy. I held out my free hand. "I'm Leah. It's so nice to meet you."

She took my hand. Even her palm was cool. "Pleasure, Leah. Alex, would you mind getting my bags out of the trunk? My back's acting up again."

She handed him a set of keys and he took them, smiling. "Posy's back thing is all a ruse. She's been using it since we were teenagers trying to get out of cleaning her room."

Posy pretended to backslap him. "Okay, that's it, I'm taking you out of my will."

"Of course she uses that too." Alex started toward her car. "She thinks it's her best bargaining chip."

This brother-sister banter was fascinating to me, partly because I'd always dreamed of having a sibling, wondered what it would be like. But also because it seemed so strange seeing Alex interact with this doppelgänger-stranger who'd known him since childhood. It was like he'd regressed into a teenager.

"We've set you up in here," I said, leading her to the living room where we'd already unfolded the sofa bed. "The mattress is actually really comfortable, not one of those thin, crinkly things where you can feel the coils." I was rambling, I realized that, but I couldn't stop myself. She made me nervous. "My first bed ever was a sofa bed, because it was all we could afford. And get this, it was a *used* sofa bed, that smelled like cigarettes." Molly started whimpering, beating my shoulder with her fist, so I set her into the fort I'd made earlier from the sofa cushions, stacked to serve as a pseudo-playpen. "And then we got a real bed," I continued, "which was when my mom realized why I always smelled like a bar. But the smell of cigarette smoke still makes me sleepy."

Posy pressed her palm on the mattress, her face skeptical, then turned to Alex who had just entered the living room with two huge blue Samsonite suitcases. "Y'know, I really do have a bad back, whatever you say. A couple nights on this thing and I'll be a quadriplegic."

"You're not doing this, Posy. Leah spent a couple hours fixing the room up for you; isn't it nice?"

Earlier I'd arranged the end tables like night tables, one holding a basket filled with towels, soap and shampoo, the other holding votive candles, a vase of fresh flowers from the garden and a reading lamp. Since all Alex's sheets were being used I'd bought a set from the quilt shop, pale yellow with a spring-green comforter to match. So the room *was* nice, cozy and sunshiny. And now my feelings were hurt.

"It's sweet," Posy said. "Really it is, and thank you. But I know what it'll do to me, this mattress. Is there a hotel nearby I could stay at instead?"

Alex rolled his eyes at me, and I shrugged. "Why don't you take my room?"

"Leah—" Alex said.

"No, really, I should've thought of that earlier. You'll have more privacy up there, and it's easy enough for me to bring down Molly's crib and changing table."

"Oh I hate to displace you," Posy said, but in a tone that suggested the decision had already been made.

So we carried her things upstairs, and I started pulling the sheets off my bed. As I was about to start back down for Posy's bedding, Star entered the hallway and stood silently watching us, looking like she was about to confront a challenge—cliff diving or wasp-swatting. "Posy, this is my mom," I said. "Star."

"Right! Alex told me about you. Agoraphobia, right? I find neuroses really fascinating." She reached into the basket I'd prepared, uncapped a bottle of lotion and sniffed at it, then smoothed it on her hands. "We all have them, you know, just some are more troubled by them than others."

"It's not a neurosis," Star said stiffly. "It's a chronic disease. Like lupus."

"Oh I wasn't blaming you for it, just the opposite! It was my way of saying I don't consider you weird at all. I hope we haven't got off on the wrong foot." She shook her head quickly. "I make bad first impressions, that's always been my biggest failing, my own psychological problem you could say." She smiled. "But most people like me when they get to know me. I'm not a bad person, just ask Alex."

"Well she's not Hitler or Stalin," Alex said, smiling. "Mussolini maybe?" He held his palms faceup at his sides, alternated them up and down like a balance. And I found myself suddenly feeling more comfortable around Posy. Not that I'd ever choose her as a friend, but Alex obviously both liked and loved her. That had to mean something; she just was socially awkward, which I could certainly relate to. I remembered as a kid briefly trying on sarcasm, insults, deprecation, thinking they'd make me seem cool and hide all the insecurity. So I felt bad for Posy. She probably had no friends.

"It's okay," I said. "Don't worry about it. My mom's used to people not getting her; it's a hard disease to understand." Which made Star raise her eyebrows at me, like she was wondering who the hell had taken over her daughter's body. "Plus, we're not easily offended," I said, which was true at least of me. Cut someone enough times and they form calluses.

Downstairs, Molly had escaped from her pillow fort and seemed on the verge of combustion, rocking back and forth on her butt, face red from the heat. I lifted her, crooning softly in an attempt to dampen her frustration. "Your sleeping arrangements are changing yet again!" I told her. "Maybe it'll be good for your personality, make you adaptable, the kind of person who adjusts easily and doesn't get too attached. Or maybe you'll become a jet-setter." I kissed her cheek. "Should we keep the flowers I picked down here? No, let's bring them up. I think Posy needs them more than we do."

I lifted the vase, then turned at the sound of heavy footsteps on the stairs, Star and Alex carrying down Molly's crib. "Corner by the window?" Alex said to Star, then turned to me. "You're now getting a sense of what my childhood was like."

"No, I like Posy," I said. "She's . . ." I searched for the right word. "Spunky," I finished, which wasn't the right word at all.

"If you say so. Personally I just think she's a pain." He set the crib in the corner, then turned to Star, probably having noticed she was being unusually quiet. "I'm sorry about all that. She doesn't think before she speaks."

"S'okay," Star said, waving her hand dismissively. But there was definitely something bothering her.

I really wasn't in the mood, but I knew it'd be wrong of me not to address it. "Alex, you mind bringing up the sheets and stuff?" I said. "We'll be up in a minute."

"No problem." Alex smiled grimly, pulled off the bedding and carried it upstairs.

"She's taking away your bed," Star said, as soon as he was out of earshot. "Kicking you and Molly out of your room and making you sleep on a sofa."

"She has a bad back, and I don't mind sleeping here. Besides, it's cooler downstairs. She has zero percent body fat, so she'll deal better with the heat in my room."

Star pressed her lips together, exasperated.

"What's going on?" I said. "Was it the neurosis comment? You've dealt with that stuff before, and worse."

"Oh *that's* not it." Star walked to a bookcase and ran a thumb across a row of book spines, *thump, thump, thump.* "Look, I have a sense about her. A bad sense, and I know that means nothing to you, which is why I wasn't going to say anything. But you asked."

"Okay, I agree I wouldn't exactly want to go have coffee with her. But I'm sure she's an okay person. You can tell how much Alex loves her."

"Alex *has* to love her, she's family. Besides, Alex loves everybody. A crack whore could walk in with methamphetamine acne and he'd be all, 'I love how your zits match your eyes!'"

I smiled. "Look, she's only here for a few days. Just stay out of her way if you have to."

"It's more than feeling uncomfortable. Okay, Lainey, I may be overreacting, but have you noticed the way she was looking at you? I'm thinking, is there a chance she has some idea who Molly is?"

Reflexive alarm, a knee to the stomach, before I shook my head. "You got that after talking to her for what, all of five seconds?"

"I saw her eyes. You know how intuitive I am."

"What I know is that you have paranoid personality disorder," I said. But I remembered the look on Posy's face when she'd first seen Alex, the uncomfortable glances they'd exchanged before kissing hello. If Alex had told her details about us, and she'd been at all suspicious and tried to look into our background, how hard would it be for her to find the holes in our story?

But I said, "I'm sure she's nothing more than unpleasant." And tried to believe it.

Late that night I lay on the sofa bed looking out the bay window at the moon rising over the trees, the haze of the hot night, Molly's sleeping silhouette in her crib. For the past hour I'd heard the murmur of Alex and Posy's voices from upstairs, sometimes heated, sometimes halted. I couldn't hear their words, but it was obvious they weren't feeling very sisterly-brotherly.

Dinner had been nothing but awkward. Alex had made this incredible meal, filet mignon with a red wine sauce and a potato soufflé that tasted like heaven with butter on top. But Posy had only picked at the meal, saying she didn't eat red meat or white starches, and Alex had raised his eyebrows at me, saying things like, "More for us, then!" in an overly hearty tone.

And then there were the glances between them, Alex's questioning and Posy's reproachful. Was she upset that I was taking advantage of her brother? Did she think there was something going on between us that she didn't approve of? Or was it something else altogether?

Lying there, sticky with sweat and bleary with sleep as I listened to their voices upstairs, my mind wove stories from Star's intuition of danger and Posy's admonishing tone. Posy had probably been exposed to news coverage, and seen the story. What if she'd recognized Molly?

Of course Posy didn't seem like the kind of person who'd hold back if she suspected something. Unless she wanted to take us by surprise.

I smiled up at the ceiling. *You,* I told myself, *are a nut job.*

To distract myself, I rose and turned on the computer. I'd been searching for updates twice a day since having talked to Sydney, but today with the distraction of Posy's arrival, I hadn't even thought about it. In the past week there'd been no real developments; attention had definitely shifted to Sydney although the authorities refused to comment, and the media was now focusing on her past, her recent treatment for postpartum depression, the dysfunctional childhood that might, conceivably, have given her the sort of psyche capable of killing her own child. At this point everyone was assuming Molly was dead, which was slightly disturbing to see but also definitely for the best. It meant they were searching mostly for a body, perhaps with less intensity. But I knew that could change at any moment if Sydney cracked, or if they got any real evidence that Molly was alive.

Now I did a search on Sydney's name, the search performed so often that it auto-filled as soon as I started to type. And, there it was. An AP article, the first hit on the list.

Sydney had disappeared.

❧ 24 ❧

"Hey," Alex said as I entered the kitchen. "I got the season's first local apples yesterday, and I was thinking of making apple pancakes. What do you think? High-carb, high-fat, processed flour, it'll drive Posy crazy."

I opened a can of formula and mixed it in a sippy cup, trying to suppress the panic I'd been battling all morning. Sydney had run away. Run away, and what did that mean? Could she possibly find where we were? Did she know a crooked cop or a PI who could figure out where my cell phone calls had come from? Was it possible to find an exact location, or only the closest cell tower? And if Sydney knew where we were, how long would it take for her to get here? "I guess Posy's not up yet?" I said, trying to sound nonchalant.

"She probably didn't sleep well. She got a little riled up with everything, as she has a tendency to do."

"Yeah, I heard you guys talking last night."

He blinked twice. "You did?"

"I couldn't hear what you were saying or anything. Just it sounded kind of intense." Speaking this sentence, I'd realized midway that the tone of my voice would have to change, and so the last words came out sounding strangely chipper. I smiled and shrugged, holding his eyes, willing him to tell me whatever Posy might've said about us. To give a scoffing laugh, say *You'll get a kick out of this, because Posy thinks*...

And I'd laugh back and say, *You're kidding! But you know it's not true. Of course it's not true!*

Of course...

But his face showed nothing as he reached for an apple and a knife, proceeded to peel the apple in a long, slow curl. Finally he said, "I guess it *was* intense. She has this lovely tendency to intensify every disagreement and every situation that makes her the least bit uncomfortable."

"You'd tell me if there was anything I should know, right? If she was upset about anything to do with me. Or Molly."

"What? No, it's just family stuff. We'll get past it."

As he said this, Posy entered. Had she been listening at the door? She was barefoot, dressed in a white silk robe, her face pale and shadowed without makeup. I could see the blue of a vein under her right eye. She waggled her fingers at us, then reached for the spiral of peel Alex had dropped to the table and started to gnaw at it.

"Me and Posy were going to hike part of the Kinsman trail today," Alex said. "Bring a picnic lunch complete with jug wine in canteens, because we're classy that way. Come with us, Leah? There's a waterfall I think Molly would get a kick out of."

"Please do," Posy said, teeth clenched on the peel.

I studied her face for some trace of sarcasm, some sense she was daring me, but I found nothing. No sarcasm, no enthusiasm, just apple peel chewing.

I was tempted to go with them just so I could keep Posy from talking about us, figure out whether she suspected who we were. But what if Sydney showed up while I was gone? If she'd driven without stopping then she'd already have been in New Hampshire yesterday. I doubted Star would be able to get her to leave, to explain calmly and rationally why her presence would endanger everything. She very well might freak out; I could imagine her screaming out the window or becoming catatonic with fear. Either way, she was bound to just make the situation worse. So I'd have to stay home today just in case, sit by the window watching for cars so I could intercept her before she even got to the door, and send her off to stay somewhere outside of town.

"I would," I said, "except I have a job I'm supposed to start today, over in Easton." This, in fact, was true. I was supposed to paint Peter Pan and Wendy flying over London, totally escapist imagery I'd been looking forward to. I'd have to call and cancel.

"Leah's an artist," Alex said, reaching for a flour sifter. "You should see the canvases and murals she's done over the past few weeks. She'll be famous someday."

"How interesting," Posy said, her tone patronizing, like she'd been told I attached bolts on an assembly line.

I heard Molly call out from the living room and I screwed the top on her cup, stretching a smile. "I better feed her. Let me know if you need help with breakfast."

In the living room I lifted Molly from her pillow fort, and sat in the armchair with her on my lap. She gazed up at me as she sucked on her cup, snorting softly as she drank, opening and closing her free hand meditatively, with her eyes glazed. So hypnotizing it was to feed her, so immediately calming, and I fell into her trance, smoothing my thumb rhythmically against her chubby arm.

"She looks like you."

I startled, looking up to find Posy only feet away from my chair. "You think?" I said. Should I read anything behind the words? Was she implying it was strange Molly looked like me, seeing as she was someone else's daughter? Why did everything she said sound accusatory?

"The shape of her face, her skin tone. And of course the hair."

Was there amusement in that last sentence? As in, *Do you really think I can't see her roots?* Oh hell, I had to stop this.

"I guess I never understood the attraction of babies," she said. "Which I realize makes me sound like a cold witch, it's just why would anyone want to create another poop and spit-up factory? But with Molly, I guess I can see the appeal."

As in, *I can see why one might be drawn to steal her?* I gave my head a quick shake. She was trying to be nice, maybe make up for her coldness yesterday. They were completely normal statements one might make to any mother. "Thanks," I said. "Is that ridiculous to say thanks? I never know what to say when people tell me she's cute. I mean it's not like I can take credit for the cuteness." *Shut up, shut up!* "Except I guess I can take credit for half her cute genes."

"Yes." The corners of her lips turned up and I felt a sudden stab of fear.

She knew.

Seeing that expression I was sure she knew; there was a smugness and an intensity in her eyes that clearly said *You're sucking at this.* How would she possibly have figured it out? Yes, Molly had distinctive features, but all babies this age looked somewhat alike. She didn't know for sure, there was no way she could, so maybe now she was just trying to feel me out.

"Tell me about the other half," Posy said. "Molly's father, who is he?"

I watched her carefully. What kind of game was she playing? "Alex didn't tell you?"

"Yes, he told me some of it last night. Cigarette burns, right? It's so awful; I just was interested to hear it from you, since it upset Alex too much to really talk about it. If you're not comfortable discussing it, I completely understand."

If she knew, then this would be how she'd figured it out. The news stories about the burns, David's abuse, me on the run, maybe my and Star's Virginia accent, the pieces snapping into place. She would've told Alex her suspicions last night, and he would've dismissed them. He must've dismissed them because for sure I would've been able to sense if he was starting to doubt us.

"He was dangerous," I said carefully. "I did the only thing I could think of to keep her safe."

Posy walked toward me and I flinched, but she only set her hand on my shoulder. "I know," she said softly. "I get that, and Alex is going to do whatever he can to protect you, even though it might be best for everyone if you considered leaving. I just hope you'll protect him as well." She hesitated, then squeezed my shoulder. "I think he loves you," she said, then pulled away and walked from the room.

I stared after her. What had just happened? This conversation had been on too many levels for me to keep track of, like all the words we'd spoken were dubbed over some convoluted double-speak, and I had no idea what she'd been trying to tell me. Was it a threat, or reassurance, or a threat disguised as reassurance? Maybe she was telling me to leave so that Alex didn't get implicated, or maybe she was saying she'd really rather I go, but would understand if I chose not to.

I wiped my thumb over a spill of formula on Molly's chin, remembering the last thing Posy had said and wondering how it fit into the conversation I didn't understand. It almost seemed like the crux of all of this, the key that could unlock her meaning. That she'd try to protect me or that I needed to protect Alex, or both. Because he loved me. And maybe it meant nothing, was just a misinterpretation or her penchant for adding drama where none existed. But somehow it was this last knot in the tangle of my trepidation, my confusion and my fear, that hurt most of all.

That morning, after Alex and Posy left, I played with Molly under the shade of one of the tall pines. Every sound seemed magnified; crickets chirping, branches creaking, all jolting such intense terror through me that several times I jumped to my feet. It had rained at some point in the night, breaking the heat, and the sun lit the rain-fringed grass, making each blade look strung with rhinestones. Leading me to ponder how such a beautiful day could possibly be, at the same time, so crappy.

I could only imagine what Posy was telling Alex now. For sure she'd say how suspiciously I'd acted this morning, how it had cemented her conviction of who we really were. And because he trusted me, Alex would refuse to believe it. Of course I'd acted suspiciously, he'd say. I was protecting my daughter! I was scared somebody might go to the police! My story of Molly's abuse might be similar to Sydney's, he'd say, my daughter's face might be similar to some other baby's face, but that's all they were—similarities. This is what he'd tell her, what he'd try to believe. But inside, deep inside, he'd start to wonder if it was true.

From a distance I heard the sound of a car engine and I made a small strangled sound, swiveling my head to look. What kind of a car did Sydney drive? A black Acura, the news articles had said. I tensed, preparing to jump up and intercept her. (And do what? Yell at her? Strangle her?) But it was only Susie's gray VW approaching. She honked twice when she saw us, waving, and I startled, biting my tongue to keep myself from crying out. Which is when my phone started to ring.

Sydney? I pulled it from the front pocket of my T-shirt, stared at it a moment, then answered.

"Lainey, oh my God," Sydney said. "I'm going crazy."

I raised my chin and waited.

"I mean I'm really going crazy." Her voice broke, and then she said, "Say something!"

"Where are you?" I said.

"You heard I left?"

"It's in the news, Sydney. They're searching for your car."

"I know; I got new plates." She sounded frantic. "I mean I got rid of my plates and took somebody else's."

"You stole somebody's license plates?"

"Isn't that the least of what we've done? It'll be fine long as I don't get pulled over."

There was no reason for this to seem so shocking. Sydney was right, we'd done much worse. It was just that it seemed so *criminal*. "So," I said. "Are you coming here? Is that what your plan is? Because you better not just show up at the door. You can't let anybody here see your face."

She hesitated, then said, "I'm not coming."

I blinked. "You're not?"

"I don't even know where you are, so how could I find you?"

"But you told me—"

"I know what I told you! I was bluffing, okay? Look, I'm on Long Island. I don't want to stay in one place for too long, but I'm at a hotel for now. I just needed somewhere relaxing to go. This wasn't supposed to happen, it's all turned upside down, and I didn't know what else to do."

"And then what're your plans? You're going to hide out there for how long?"

"I don't know. I have to get a few things settled first, but we're still planning the whole Montana thing, right? We can both leave in a couple weeks and meet up there, I'll take Jacqueline from you and you can go back to your old life."

Go back to my old life? Was she kidding? It was like being given a heart/lung transplant, a *life* transplant that later failed. "I'm sorry, Sydney, but no. You can't use me as your doormat, just wipe off all the crap of your life and then walk away. You turn my life inside out, I leave home, spend weeks taking care of a baby, commit a felony and you think I can just forget about it?"

"I promise I'll reimburse you for every penny you've spent, plus extra. We can figure out how much would make up for all this."

"You think I care about the money? You really think that's what this is about?" And as soon as the words left, a thought slipped behind them. "The reward money," I said. "That's what you mean by having to get a few things settled; you want to see how high the McGraths' reward gets."

"That's ridiculous." She exhaled a little laugh. "You think I'm going to tell them I just happened to find Jacqueline somehow? By what, knocking on every door in the U.S.? You seriously think I'm even eligible to get the money?"

"Then what? What're you planning to do? You've told me you had plans before and look how well they've turned out. You can't expect me to trust that you know what you're doing."

"I know I've screwed things up. All I can tell you at this point is it's not going to be that much longer. Maybe a week, two at the most and then I'll be able to tell you everything."

Molly made a face, looking up at me with her eyes tearing, and seeing her gritty drool I realized she'd stuffed a fistful of dirt into her mouth. I wiped my sleeve over her tongue, tried to clear her mouth as best I could and then pulled her onto my lap. "Look," I said, "I might have to leave here sooner rather than later. The man I've been living with, his sister came to stay yesterday and it seemed like . . . I think she might know who Jacqueline is."

Sydney didn't speak for a minute, then whispered, "How does she know?"

"I'm not sure, it doesn't even matter. Leaving here's going to be hard, because I can't leave without Star and she's not exactly a good traveler. But call me tomorrow and I'll tell you what we're going to do."

"Okay." Sydney paused, then said, "Fine, then. I'll stay here till tomorrow."

I hung up and stuffed the phone into my pocket, watching Molly start to crawl across the yard. How the hell was I going to make this work? I was between a rock and another rock and a hard place, and being pulled down into a whirlpool. I had no idea how I could travel with Star or how long we could survive on our savings. And the idea of leaving here, leaving *Alex,* made me want to beat on walls, tear out my hair and scream, but I didn't trust Posy and I sure as hell didn't trust Sydney. So, tomorrow. Tomorrow we would leave.

Molly reached for a dandelion, pulled it from the ground and then held it toward me. *"Fow."*

"Flower," I said softly, "that's right."

In response she handed it to me, and we admired it a moment before she started jouncing up and down on her butt, grinning widely. "Mama!" she said and my eyes filled, as they did now every time she said the word.

And just like that, watching the glee in her face, I realized. Something I was only just letting myself see, something I knew had been simmering just under the surface of my consciousness for weeks.

That I wasn't going to let Sydney take Molly from me.

Not next week, not next month, not next year, even though she very well might turn us in because of it. We'd be running from the law, would have to get fake IDs and maybe leave the country, could never go back to our old life. It was unimaginable, but somehow none of it scared me.

I smiled back at Molly and pressed my cheek against hers, held the dandelion wish-cloud to my mouth, and blew.

{ 25 }

If I'd been smart I would've packed and left that afternoon, while Alex and Posy were away. But, of course, I was not smart. I was desperate.

I hadn't told Star that Sydney had called and that we were leaving, was terrified at how she'd react and didn't want to risk her freaking out in front of Alex and Posy. I decided that I'd wake her in the middle of the night and pull her from the house when she was only semiconscious. Not a well-formulated plan but the only one I had, and sitting with Star at dinner, avoiding Posy's strange looks, knowing what was coming and not being able to discuss it with anyone, made it all feel unreal, like I was watching us all from somewhere above.

Star went straight up to her bedroom after dinner, complaining of a headache that I was sure was either fake, or real and stress-induced. I resisted—although just barely—the urge to go up with her and bawl my heart out. Instead, after finishing the dishes I joined Alex and Posy in the living room.

After a few minutes of stilted conversation, Alex suggested a game of Scrabble. So we all sat cross-legged on the extended sofa bed like we were children, silently laying letters and keeping score. Molly was on my lap, drowsily sucking on the ear of the stuffed rabbit Alex had given her our first day here, and I centered myself on her so I wouldn't have to think about anything else. With her, anywhere my broken life ended up taking me could become home. So this was what I focused on, trying not to interpret every word Posy laid on the board: ARREST, SECRET, and a BE added onto my TRAY.

Midway through the game, with Alex and Posy both a hundred-something points ahead of me, I told them I was forfeiting and was going up to check on Star. Instead, though, I brought Molly up into Posy's bedroom and set her on the bed. She handed me her bunny, like a condolence. "Abba-buh," she said.

"You're right," I said, "it does suck." I smiled and kissed the top of her head and set the bunny back beside her. And started to pack.

Posy had taken all my and Molly's clothes from the dresser and placed them, folded, on the closet floor. I stuffed these into the suitcases stored in the closet, and set the suitcases by the door.

Posy's purse was hanging in the closet, on a hook, a black vinyl purse with a square brass clasp, the type used by angry old ladies. And . . . I don't know what came over me. I guess it was the fussiness of the purse, the knowledge that it was, at least in part, Posy's fault that we had to leave, the realization that we had only enough money to last us six months at most and that Posy, a financial analyst with a new Lexus, had probably millions to spend only on herself. It was this, somehow tied into my anger at Sydney and grief and fear, that made me reach for Posy's purse, and look inside.

A tin can of Altoids, keys hooked on a canister of pepper spray, a worn black tube of ChapStick, her wallet and a lace handkerchief embroidered with her initials. (A handkerchief, and who used embroidered handkerchiefs anymore? Posy, that's who.) I pulled out the wallet and opened it.

Tucked into the accordion insert were photos: a black miniature poodle, a younger Posy standing by an older woman with her same pinched features, and then, a family portrait, Alex and Posy aged about six or seven sitting in front of an older, blond girl and a smiling couple. I traced my finger across the photo, all of them so young and happy, the man and girl who would die within ten years. And then I closed the wallet, my hand trembling, and stuffed it back into Posy's purse.

Still shaking, I crammed my packed bags into the hall closet and then went back downstairs. The Scrabble set was put away, Alex and Posy sitting in the armchairs. "So," I said brightly, "who won!"

"We decided it'd be best not to keep going after you left," Alex said. "It was starting to remind us of the games we played when we were kids, which never ended well. We were too competitive."

"Meaning *I'm* too competitive," Posy said. "That's what comes from being older and not as smart. It's demoralizing to lose, so I start accusing him of cheating."

"Actually, from what I remember you start kicking me on the shin," Alex said, then turned to me. "I guess Molly's up with Star?"

My eyes widened. Oh crap, oh crap, I'd left her on Posy's bed. "With Star, right on her floor," I said. "I better go get her and bring her to bed."

"I'll go up with you," Posy said. "I think I'm going to call it an early night. That hike really messed up my back."

I felt my face flush cold. What were the chances I could make it up to the bedroom, snatch Molly from the bed and give her to Star before Posy got upstairs? Not good.

"Let me get Molly first," I said quickly, then spun around. But Posy, in complete disregard of her "bad back," jumped from the chair and followed close behind.

When we got to the hallway, I squared my shoulders and turned to her. "Okay. Okay, look, by the way, Molly's actually in your bedroom."

Posy looked into my eyes. "She's in my bedroom."

"On your bed. I had to get something from the closet and I left her there by accident."

Still, Posy held my eyes. "You could've asked me first."

"I know, I know I should've," I said, but Posy had already strode past me into the bedroom. Molly was asleep on the bed, her arm flung over the bunny. Posy looked expressionlessly at the drool-matted bunny, then turned to look into the closet. Following her gaze, I saw her purse and felt a punch to my gut. Thank God I hadn't stolen anything. Thank God.

"You took all your clothes," she said.

Had I thought she wouldn't notice? To be honest, I really hadn't thought at all.

"You packed them," she said. "You're leaving."

I watched her face without speaking.

"Okay," she said softly. "That's good, then."

I lifted Molly from the bed and pressed her head protectively against my shoulder. "I was scared. I thought you might turn me in."

"I guess I might've. I might, but I'll wait till after you're gone. I'll let you get away from here."

"There's a chance . . ." I started, then shook my head. "I might not be able to get my mother to come with us. I'll leave the number for my friend Pamela, who can make sure she's taken care of. I'd appreciate it if you could just ask Alex to call Pamela and to watch over Star until she gets here. The first day after I'm gone's probably going to be tough."

"Understood," Posy said softly. She clasped her hands and stood a minute, looking down at them, then abruptly reached for her purse and pulled out her wallet, held out a wad of bills.

I bit down hard on my tongue, staring at them, my heart seizing with guilt and shame.

"Take it," she said. "It's yours. I withdrew it from the bank today for you, to help you get on your feet. The deal is that if they ever catch you, you tell them Alex had nothing to do with this, that he had no idea you weren't who you said you were."

"Well of course," I said, staring at the money. I couldn't take it. Not least because I'd already come close to taking it.

"And me too," she said. "This conversation and the one this morning never happened, right?"

"Of course," I said again, softer.

"Are you telling Alex you're leaving?"

I rubbed my hand up and down Molly's back, as if I was trying to comfort her. "No," I said. "I think it's better if I don't. Maybe I'll write him a note." The fact was, I couldn't face him. Couldn't face the look of hurt and betrayal and maybe anger when he found out who I was. This way I'd be able to imagine he didn't hate me.

"I think you're right, that's probably best. You want me to tell him something tomorrow morning?"

What the hell could I have her tell him? That I was sorry? That I was eternally grateful? That I was in love with him? There wasn't any right thing. "Just . . . tell him I wish things were different."

Posy walked toward me, hesitated and then set her hand on my back. "I think he'll know that. I know he will. You're a good person, Leah, and he sees that. I don't know you all that well, but even I can see it. And I know you must've had good reasons for taking her." She shoved the money at my chest.

I shook my head. "I can't. I mean I don't need it, we have plenty of money. Or if you really want to give it away, give it to Alex because I owe him at least that much for what he's bought for me and Molly. You could give that to him, and once I get settled I'll pay you back what you paid him." I touched her hand, then pulled away. "You're a good person too, Posy."

She blinked and then smiled at me, the type of pained, flickering smile worn by children praised for beauty or talent they're sure they don't truly possess, and I suddenly wondered if anyone had ever told her she was a good person before. Wondered if she even thought it of herself.

And then her smile hardened and she said, "Christ on a bike. I hope you don't expect us to start hugging and breaking out into love ballads." She touched Molly's head gently and said, "Take care of her, Leah. And of yourself. And don't ever feel bad about what you've done."

I told Star nothing. Just sat with her and held her hand, Molly sleeping on the bed beside us, neither of us speaking. She knew something was going on, that was obvious, although I was sure she didn't realize we were leaving tonight. She wore a look I hadn't seen on her for years, her jaw set, determined, as she had been in the days before she stopped leaving the house. Each time she'd made it to the grocery store, the liquor store, one of my high school art shows, she had worn this look. Like her disease was an actual physical being, a monster she was using all her strength to fight against. That look made me almost hopeful that she might be okay.

After she'd gotten ready for bed, I brought her an extra Xanax which she looked at a moment, then accepted. "I'll be fine," she said. She fell asleep soon after taking the pills and I sat there with her, one hand on her chest, the other on Molly's. I hated that nobody would ever understand how strong she was.

I'd tried all this time to forgive Sydney; I knew she was living with her own monsters, which in their own way were every bit as powerful as Star's. But the difference was that Sydney didn't care if those monsters destroyed me whereas Star would fight to the death, sacrifice herself to make sure I wouldn't be hurt.

"I love you, Mom," I whispered, "and I hate that I ever blamed you." She didn't move, but I tried to believe that somewhere in her supposedly hyper-intuitive subconscious, she understood.

Once I was sure she'd stay asleep, I brought Molly downstairs and set her in her crib. The moon was full and I stood awhile by the window, looking out at the garden we'd planted. The flowers had spread, an explosion of color, and although they'd drooped somewhat in yesterday's heat, last night's rain had rejuvenated them. There must be something in rainwater that was lacking in the well water from the hose, magic from the sky that made the flowers sing. And I tried to find comfort from the knowledge that I'd helped create this beauty, me and Alex and the sky.

I hesitated, then went to Alex's desk and pulled a sheet of paper from the printer. I sat a moment with the pen pressed between my palms, then wrote:

Dear Alex,
I'll start this off by saying I'm so, so very sorry.

I squeezed my eyes shut and then gave my head a small shake and continued.

> *I know this'll be really hard for you to understand, and I know there's no real explanation, nothing that can make it okay. It was all for Molly, and I never meant to deceive you, but I was desperate, and it was the only thing I could think to do. Please know that even though I may not be Leah, I am the person you think I am. All the conversations we had, everything I told you about my life and my dreams and my feelings for you, they were me.*

I was shaking, my palms sweaty. I dropped the pen, stood and paced to the window, arms crossed over my chest. I knew why I'd lied to him, and I was almost able to forgive myself for it. But it wasn't the rightness or wrongness of the lies, it was that I knew Alex, and I knew he wouldn't feel angry, he'd feel hurt. I could forgive myself for everything but that.

I pressed my lips between my teeth. What could I do? There was nothing I could do to make this right. Just hope that he'd eventually understand.

I turned from the window and gathered the maps I'd printed, routes to Idaho. We couldn't go to Montana, since Sydney would know to look for us there. So instead we'd go to the Land of Potatoes, all that land, miles and miles of open space. We'd find a tiny house to rent in the middle of nowhere, use Pamela as a reference and our savings as a deposit. I could do this.

I began bringing our bags to the car. Everything Alex had bought for Molly, I left. Maybe he could return the things that looked most new, or at least give them to charity and claim a deduction. The only thing I took was the stuffed bunny. Someday I'd show it to Molly and tell her about Alex and how we'd met. *That's the kind of man you should try to marry,* I'd say. *There are only a handful of men like that in the world, and you'll probably start despairing that you'll never find one. But hold out for him. Because Alex was proof that they exist.*

It was one A.M.; shocking to see that so little time had passed since I'd decided we had to leave, and here we were already almost out the door. I was reasonably sure Star was sufficiently drugged by now that I'd be able to pack all her things before having to wake her, then pull her to the car without her ever registering what was happening. By the time she woke enough to understand the passing scenery was more than just a dream, we'd already be miles away. Nobody would hear her screams.

I started up the stairs in my socked feet, and was about to turn down the hallway when Alex's door opened. I froze as he emerged in boxer shorts and a blue T-shirt, his hair sleep-rumpled. "Thought I heard footsteps," he said.

I shook my head.

"There was this banging downstairs; it woke me up. Everything okay?"

And just like that, I felt my eyes fill, my entire face flushing with tears. "Just tired," I tried to say, but the words came out in a high-pitched garble.

"Leah?"

My knees crumpled, and before I knew what was happening I was on the ground. "Tired," I tried again, and he stared at me a moment in shock, then knelt by me. "Leah, are you sick? What's going on? I'm going to pick you up, okay?" And then he lifted me as effortlessly as one might lift a limp blanket and carried me to his bedroom. He set me on his bed and closed the door, then sat beside me looking startled. "Okay," he said, "tell me."

"I can't," I said. "I don't—" My voice broke, all of it hitting me at once: the knowledge that this was the last time I'd sit with Alex, the last night before he realized what I'd done; the idea of driving hundreds of miles to the accompaniment of Star's hyperventilating gasps knowing there was nothing I could give her to tame them, no sense of stability, no promise of a resting place. And the idea of heading off into some unknown barren, snowy tundra I imagined as a moonscape with nothing between us and the bleak universe.

And most of all Alex there on the bed beside me, the concern in his eyes. I wanted to crawl inside him, be enveloped by that concern, the only person in the world who could take care of me. Without thinking what I was doing I circled my hand round his arm to feel the solidity of him, and with the other I reached for the front of his T-shirt, looking up into his face.

His cheeks flushed. "Leah?"

"I need," I said. "I need . . ."

His face questioning, he used his thumb to brush a strand of hair off my forehead. Held my eyes a moment before he leaned forward, hesitated again and then kissed me, his lips against my lips for fractions of a second before he startled away.

I stared at him, unblinking. His face was a pale moon in the darkness, almost featureless through the blur of my tears. We sat there a moment, unmoving, and then he intertwined his fingers in my hair and smoothed a thumb over my cheek.

"Please," I said hoarsely, and then I reached to pull him back against the bed.

And suddenly everything else was gone, the fear, the guilt, all of it evaporating so there was only the feel of him, the scent of him. I wrenched off his shirt so I could feel the tensed muscles of his back and he slipped a hand inside my blouse. Skin against skin, my tears wetting his cheeks and his breath filling my lungs; I yanked at the button on my jeans, tore them off and then pulled down his boxers. He pulled away, hesitating, but when I arched up against him he looked into my eyes, his breath unsteady. Then gave a choking moan and pressed against me.

I love you, he whispered, and once he'd said the words there was nothing else but the immensity of them as he rocked against me, the words expanding like a balloon, filling me until they were all I could hear or feel or taste. And the taste of the words was tears.

I woke while it was still dark, and lay there without moving. Trying to absorb what had happened, the ache between my legs, the feel of him sleeping beside me. I'd fallen asleep with my head on his chest, and his arms were still tight around me. So I closed my eyes, trying to fill myself with the feel of this, knowing that as soon as I left him it would start slipping away.

Remember this, the cushioning muscles of his chest, the softness of his skin, every dark hair on his tanned forearm, the feel of him holding me and how it had been to hear him say he loved me. I squeezed my eyes shut as if that could secure it all inside me, then braced myself to pull away, but as I started to rise I felt him reach for my bare arm. "Don't get up," he whispered.

I looked down at his hand, feeling the tickle of it against my arm, stroking me in almost the same way Molly stroked my arm while she was being fed. "Alex—"

"I don't care if Star and Posy see us. This'd actually be the easy way of letting them know."

Part of me had thought, seeing the pain in his face last night, that he'd somehow magically sensed I was leaving. But of course he had no idea, and I should never have made love to him. In this one night I'd taken the knot of my betrayal and pulled it a million times tighter.

"Alex," I said again and then, before I could stop myself, "I have to tell you something."

His hand stopped moving against my arm. He didn't speak, and I huddled inside the silence of that moment, the knowledge that within seconds nothing would be the same. And I couldn't say it, had no idea how to even start, so instead I pulled away and rose, grabbed my shirt and slipped it on as I ran downstairs, feeling his chest sweat or my cheek sweat, or maybe last night's tears, chilling one side of my face. I reached for the note I'd started to Alex, not even knowing what I'd do with it—slip it under his door and run, throw it at him and run, or just run.

But I owed him more, so in the end I went back into his bedroom, closing the door behind me. He was standing now, his shirt and boxers back on, looking strangely terrified.

Why was he terrified?

My breath hitched and I handed the note to him, and he took it, warily, watching my face. I backed against the door.

"You were going to leave," he said, without even reading it. "That's what all the banging was downstairs, and why you were dressed at one in the morning."

I shook my head slowly, watching his face. "I . . . had to. I still have to." My legs were bare, my shirt barely long enough to cover me so I reached for the underwear and jeans I'd thrown by the foot of the bed, and hugged them to my chest as I said, "Alex, I did something wrong, really wrong. I'm not who you think I am."

For a full minute he didn't move, his face flushed and bewildered. And I almost turned away right then, slammed the door open and ran down to grab Molly and race out the door. But then he sank onto the bed, leaning forward with his elbows on his knees and the note clutched in his fist. And he looked up at me with his eyes pleading. "Neither am I," he said.

26

Alex pulled the photo from his nightstand drawer. It was smudged at the edges, one corner bent, obviously handled many times: a new-born with a fringe of carroty hair, swaddled in a blue blanket. I stud-ied it, confused, remembering the story Susie had told me about the photo he'd once kept in the living room, her speculation that he'd had a brother who'd died. "Who is this?" I said.

He didn't answer, just looked into my eyes, his face drawn and shadowed. I looked back at the photo, the baby's full lips and orange hair. "It's Molly," I said slowly. "Where did you get a newborn photo of Molly?"

"Leah." He squared his shoulders, still watching me. "I know who you are. Who Molly is."

I stepped back against the door.

"I've always known," he said. "I knew when we first met at the bed-and-breakfast. I told you I'd been driving up from my grand-mother's funeral in Miami, but there wasn't a funeral, I'd actually come straight from Virginia. I came out there to meet you."

I stared at him, feeling suddenly completely disoriented, like I'd been spun round and round and folded inside out, then had the ground pulled from under my feet. All the pieces rearranging and snapping into place: the adoration in Alex's eyes when he held Molly; their likeness, the full lips and heavy-lidded eyes that had tugged at the edges of my consciousness without ever quite taking hold. Sydney had taken a paternity test, but you didn't need to compare DNA to tell whose daughter she was.

"You and Sydney," I said. My voice sounded strangely flat, detached. "I told her where I was staying in West Virginia so she could send money, and instead she sent you. I really should've realized."

"I got into town earlier that day, followed you from the inn. I spent all morning trying to figure out how to introduce myself, but seeing you in the playground with Jacqueline, how happy you were, it broke me. I don't pray anymore, I told you that, but standing there I was praying for some sign, someone to tell me what the hell to do. And I almost called Sydney to tell her I couldn't follow through with this, but then? I was following you back to the inn when your car broke down. And . . . it felt like fate."

I squeezed my eyes shut, feeling a rising wave of nausea, trying to steady the room, solidify the floor under my bare feet.

"I'd met Sydney in Virginia four years ago. I know I told you I was catering in New York, but it was actually Norfolk. She was hosting David's parents' anniversary party, and she hired me."

My mind swirled back to the conversation we'd had after he'd disappeared. "Erin," I whispered, then looked up at him. "Erin?"

"I guess you could say it was a pet name. Years ago, after the first time we made love, she'd warned me what would happen if David ever found out about us. She sounded like she was kidding, it became almost a running joke, her saying how he'd twist her head off her neck or cut her limbs off with a chain saw."

Made love, I thought.

"And I teased her about it, started calling him Leatherface and calling her Erin, after the *Texas Chainsaw Massacre* characters, which it turned out wasn't funny at all, but she didn't tell me that till much later. Miss Melodrama Erin, and she called me Kemper, Erin's dumb-ass boyfriend. We laughed about it all; she kept pretending like she got a kick out of it. Even after I found out last year how much truth there was behind her warnings, realized how twisted the joke was, she still wanted to keep using the names. As a sort of code, in case David ever got his hands on one of the letters I sent her, so she could convince him they were meant for someone else.

Kemper, the man who'd written the letters the FBI had found. And *Erin*, the name on the note he'd written, *The Girlfriend*'s name. The notes rewritten and reworded umpteen times, the desperation to bring her back into his life. "Who's the woman on your bookshelf downstairs?" I said. "The woman in your photos?"

He gazed at me blankly. "The woman? Oh . . . I guess you mean Camelia."

"That's your *sister*?" The photos were of his dead sister and *The Girlfriend*, "Erin," was Sydney. I couldn't let myself picture the two of them together, *making love*. But that was exactly what I was picturing, him kissing her the way he'd kissed me, whispering in her ear.

"You have to believe I never wanted to hurt you. My plan was always to tell you after I brought you here, as soon as you got to know me and realized I wasn't a bad guy. Especially after I met you and realized what an amazing person you are, I thought—and I realize I was being naïve—I thought we'd go into this together, keeping Jacqueline safe from David."

An amazing person. Lies; the past two months all built on my lies and his. Last night, he'd said he loved me.

"I felt like we were both working together for some higher cause, and I wanted to tell you all of it. I wanted to tell you so much, but Sydney kept saying what a huge mistake it would be to trust you not to turn me in. She told these stories about things you did to her in high school—"

"She told stories about what *I* did to *her*?" Had she told all our stories in reverse? She must've realized Alex would relish the idea of helping the underdog avenge the oppressor. Vigilante justice.

"And I realized that was probably bull after I met you, but I couldn't risk it. I was so scared for both of them. Sydney told me about the burn marks, and said how if she went to Child Protective Services she knew the McGraths' lawyers would find a way to pin the burns on her and take the baby away. I was starting to have doubts about Sydney, but the idea of somebody pressing a lit cigarette to

Jacqueline's skin . . ." He gripped the quilt, his eyes pleading. "It was unbearable. Plus I wanted to be with Jacqueline, which I know isn't a good reason but I can't pretend it wasn't a factor. I only got to meet her once, last spring. So the two hours I got to hold her, and that photo there which Sydney sent along with the paternity test results, they were all I had, Leah. They were the only things I could hold on to." He shook his head quickly. *"Lainey,* I mean Lainey."

So bizarre to hear him use my real name. I remembered the nights I'd lain in bed imagining how it would be to confess to him. Dreaming he might understand, accept the truth unflinching and maybe even call me brave. And then the anguish I'd gone through imagining the more likely scenario, that he'd kick me out or call the police, hate me.

"The worst part of it all was knowing Jacqueline was spending every weekend with that son of a bitch, and not being able to tell him that she wasn't his. Sydney was so terrified of what he'd do if he found out, to both of them. So we were stuck in this logjam, and this was the only way Sydney could see to get out of it. Please, Lainey, I need you to understand what happened, how this got so screwed up."

"Understand what?" I said slowly, the nausea that had been swirling behind my ribs growing claws. "That you've been lying to me for the past two months? You expect me to understand that?"

He watched me, unspeaking. Was he trying to make me think about the hypocrisy of my words? But this was different. It was completely different because he'd known I was lying, was only pretending to believe me, and that changed everything. Because he'd brought me here not to protect me, but because Sydney had asked him to. And because he'd loved Sydney, that was the most unforgivable thing of all. "How could you lie to me! Who the hell are you?"

"It wasn't a lie. I mean I wasn't telling you the truth, but most of the time I completely forgot it wasn't true. I was just enjoying being with you and Jacqueline, and trying to forget what was going on behind it. All my life I wanted my own family, and that's what this felt like. It was so much better in every single way than the family I grew up in."

I needed to throw something at him, but the only things within reach were the sneakers by his closet door. I reached for them and flung them both, but he didn't flinch away, just let them hit his chest, still watching me. "How can you even say that?" I said. "You think that'll keep me from going to the police? Well screw that! I'm not that naïve, not anymore."

"Lainey, please . . . Maybe you *should* go to the police, I almost wish you would, but this is the one thing I need you to believe: that having you here, these've been some of the best weeks of my life."

"But why! You could've taken Jacqueline yourself, hidden her here and had Sydney join you when she thought it was safe to leave Virginia. I just don't get it; why'd you even get me involved at all? Hell, if you knew the baby was yours, you could've gotten custody legally!"

"I know." His face seemed sunken, like somebody had hollowed out the flesh from his cheeks. He gave a furious kick to the sneakers I'd thrown. "I know, it's just that the situation got so desperate so quickly that I didn't have time to think. It all started in the beginning of June. I was scared for Jacqueline's life and I told Sydney I was going to the police. She was crying and pleading with me not to, said she'd think of something, and a few days later she called back and told me she had a plan. Which is when she told me about a friend who'd agreed to take Jacqueline. About you."

She must've come up with the idea after she'd seen me in Six of Swords. Here I was, the perfect answer dropped in her lap. She'd invited me to Chelsea's Café, pretending nostalgia and a yearning for reconciliation and then, later that week, had left Molly with me.

"First she told me she'd given you the baby because David had threatened her that morning, that she brought Jacqueline to you to protect her. And that after you had the baby she'd realized how David would react, then freaked out and made up the kidnapping story. And once I'd agreed to intercept you it all happened so fast, it felt like I didn't have a choice. Like we were both just acting out of fear, one decision leading to another. I didn't start really questioning it till after you were up here, and when I asked Sydney she said of course I was right, we shouldn't have gotten you involved but that she hadn't been thinking straight and now it was too late to take it back."

"That's bullshit," I said hoarsely. "That's pretty much exactly what she told me after she went on TV to say Molly was kidnapped. That she'd been desperate and she wasn't thinking straight."

"I realize it didn't make sense, and I guess part of me realized it then too, but she's so . . . persuasive. Hypnotic, almost, it's how she swept me off my feet in the first place. All the stories she told me of how she was raised, she was all needy but strong at the same time. I wanted to take care of her, and when you feel like that about somebody, you tend to believe everything they say."

Swept me off my feet, I thought. I wondered if I was going to throw up. "It was for the reward money." My voice was cold. "For finding Molly. She was going to have you turn me in to the cops, tell them you'd taken us in and trusted me, and that I'd finally admitted the truth. And then I'd get arrested so you guys could collect the reward."

His face was pale, watching me. "I didn't know," he said.

"A perfect plan really, because the two of you could pretend to meet when she came to thank you for finding Molly, and then you'd pretend to fall in love for the first time so that the three of you could live happily ever after on the McGraths' money."

"I didn't know! Not until I went down to Virginia last month, the week I disappeared, after I realized I couldn't keep lying to you, it was killing me. So I went down to tell her I was going to confess to you about who I was and what was going on, and she told me everything."

The night of Susie's barbecue, the night I'd thought he was going to kiss me . . . Had he gone down to confront Sydney because he felt sorry for me getting so caught up in this sham fantasy life? To plead with her to let me go back to Virginia?

"She told me the McGraths had been steadily raising the size of the reward, and she needed you involved for at least another few weeks. Said I didn't have to ever turn you in if I wasn't willing to, that we could find some way to convince you and Star to go off somewhere for a few days, and leave Molly with me. I could go to the cops and tell them a woman had left the baby, give your name as Leah Monroe. She said you'd realize you couldn't come back, and they'd never be able to find Leah Monroe so you'd be safe."

"And you *agreed* to that?"

"No, no of course not! When I found out what she'd been planning, how could I trust her? I yelled at her, Lainey. I seriously almost hit her; I've never gotten so angry at another person. I didn't talk to her for two days after, but I couldn't come back home because I had no idea how I was going to tell you the truth."

"So you just decided not to tell me. You came home and you kept up this whole charade? Why, because you were waiting for the reward to go up even further?"

"I didn't want the money! I didn't know what else to do, Lainey. When I finally did talk to Sydney she was in hysterics. She said if I went to the cops we'd all be arrested, including you, and Jacqueline would go into foster care, which I knew was probably true. So I told her I wouldn't go to the cops, but that I also wasn't ever going to turn you in. That I was keeping Molly here with me, and if she ever tried to take her back then I *would* go to the police."

Sydney's phone call the week Alex had disappeared, gone down to see her. *I thought he loved me,* she'd told me when I asked her about Kemper, *which I know now he doesn't, probably never did.* And then she'd urged me to go to Montana, leave here. Was it because she'd realized she couldn't trust Alex?

"I wanted to tell you more than anything, Lainey, but I had no idea how you'd react. I thought you might be angry enough to go tell the police and I couldn't risk it. I wasn't just scared of being arrested, I was scared what David might do when the truth came out, to Sydney, to you. But I swear I was going to tell you, especially after I started to wonder if David was even dangerous at all, or at least not as dangerous as she told me."

I shook my head slightly. "But I saw Sydney beat up. And the burn marks." I stopped short, staring at him, all the skin on my body stinging, scraped raw. "No," I said hoarsely. "You think—"

"Sydney burned Jacqueline herself?" Alex wrapped his arms around his waist and hunched forward like he'd been punched. "I don't know. I don't know what to think anymore."

I remembered the raw sores on Molly's skin when I'd first met her, the pink marks that would scar her for the rest of her life. My throat closed and I made a high-pitched, hiccuping sound that felt like it was coming from somewhere above me.

"I know she beat up her own face the day she first dropped Jacqueline off with you, because she knew it'd help convince you to take her. And when I was down there last month, I found out she wrote a journal talking about the abuse, in the hopes the cops would seize it as evidence and arrest David."

I couldn't breathe, my stomach on fire, my brain on fire. Everything I'd believed, everything I'd tried to save Molly from was a lie?

"So maybe none of it was true, I've been thinking and thinking about it and I don't know. In the beginning she'd really sounded like she was joking when she said David would kill her, and would she seriously have let me tease her about it if he'd really been abusing her? She likes being taken care of, that's how she . . . I don't know, I guess assures herself of her own worth, so why wouldn't she have asked me to take care of her right away? And last year she told me David had broken her arm, but then she slipped up when I saw her this summer and said something that implied she'd actually broken it in a fall."

My fists clenched. How had it been for Molly to have the one woman she trusted, the woman who was supposed to love her most, grab her to keep her from squirming away as she seared circles of pain onto her skin?

"Maybe she didn't make up the story of the abuse until after she realized she wanted to be with me more than she wanted to be with David. She must've already been trying for months to find a way to get the best of both worlds, me and the money. And I know she loves Jacqueline, and I never would've imagined she was capable of doing anything to hurt her, but what if she thought . . ." His face flushed pink and his eyes suddenly filled. "What if she thought the ends were worth the means? Christ, Lainey, I don't know what to believe."

I imagined the lit cigarette between Sydney's French-manicured nails, and Molly's scream, and suddenly the rage slashed through me. "For the money?" I hurled a fist at him blindly, hitting his chest, but he just sat there, his jaw set and face slick with tears, letting me. I punched him again, so hard he huffed with pain. "All this for god-damned money? You son of a bitch!"

I had to get out of here. I'd grab Molly and run, drive a hundred miles an hour north through the mountains, car windows open wide, hair flying in my eyes, radio blaring so loud I couldn't think. Leaving my life behind, my two ridiculous, broken selves, both the person I really was and the person I'd pretended to be.

"You son of a bitch!" I said again, my voice breaking, and then I spun around and threw open the door. I raced downstairs like something was after me, crammed my shoes on my feet and slung our last bags over my shoulder, then pulled Molly from her crib. She was wailing as I ran out to the car and strapped her into her car seat, but I couldn't stop to comfort her. I got into the car and slammed the door behind me.

Down the driveway, past the garden we'd planted and into the street, the sun rising and staining it all a dusky blue, Molly howling and me crying in bizarre, two-part harmony. Downtown past the church, and all of me wanted to just stop the car and bring Molly inside so we could huddle together on one of the hard, wooden pews. I imagined it could keep me from exploding, its heavy stone silence holding me down.

But instead, I floored the accelerator and drove us into the hills, and away.

27

My phone was ringing. "Shut up," I whispered, my eyes blurring
with tears. "Shut up, shut up!" If it was Sydney calling, what would
I say? I didn't have the energy to yell at her; the anger in me was
beyond anger and the despair in me was beyond despair, and
every ounce of strength I had was centered in the foot flooring the
accelerator. "Shut up!" The ringing stopped, but then started again a
minute later. I scrambled inside my purse for the phone, meaning to
hurl it out the window, but then I saw the number. The call was coming from Alex's home, and I suddenly thought, *Star.*

I imagined her waking, noticing the strained silence of the house
and slowly realizing that I'd left her. Her crushing panic (and I'd
taken her pills!) as Alex tried to explain, to take care of her when he
had no idea how. I slammed on the brakes and answered.

"Leah . . . Lainey, it's me." It was Posy. I hung up.

The phone rang again and I sat in the center of the road gripping
the steering wheel. One ring before it would've gone to voice mail, I
answered. "Don't hang up," she said.

"Is my mom awake?"

She hesitated, then said, "No, not yet."

"Good. Okay, that's good. If she wakes up, just tell her I'm coming
to get her, okay? That I'll either take her with me or I'll get my friend

Pamela to bring her home, her choice. But if she doesn't wake up just let her sleep until I get there. It should be about an hour."

"Lainey, wait. Just let me talk to you before you do anything stupid."

"See," I said, "the thing is I'm not stupid, despite all appearances. And I deeply apologize, but I don't want to talk."

"I have to tell you about Alex. Please, Lainey, just give me a few minutes; there are things you have to understand about him, and then you can figure out what to do."

Molly was crying in the backseat, probably hungry and scared and needing a diaper change. "Tell my mother I'm coming," I said, and then hung up, pulled the car to the shoulder and climbed into the backseat to be with her.

Posy was sitting on the front porch, waiting for me. She stood when I got out of the car, and I left Molly in the backseat with a bottle as I approached the house.

"Coffee?" she said, nodding at a carafe and mug on the table.

I ignored this. "Where's Star?"

"She's not up yet, I don't think. Please, just sit a minute, okay? A minute isn't going to hurt."

I glanced at the house. Where was Alex now? I had to find a way to get Star packed and out the door without seeing him. I couldn't stand to see him. I narowed my eyes. "Alex asked you to talk to me and convince me he's not such a bad guy?"

"He told me what happened, but no. He's going to let you do whatever you have to do, leave, call the cops, whatever. Because he's *not* a bad guy, and he loves you."

"Screw that," I said and then, with no warning, my knees gave way and my butt hit the top porch step with a thump.

"Lainey!" She knelt beside me. "Look, I could tell you a trillion stories that show what kind of a person he is. Like how I acted toward him after our dad and Camelia died, and the way he forgave me for it over and over again. How he took care of Mom, trying to help her through all her bouts of depression and craziness, even when she called him every name in the book."

"How touching," I said. "What a prince."

She raised her head to look out over the yard. "There's so much I could say to convince you who he is, but the thing you need to know is I've never heard him say he was in love before. Even when he told me about Sydney a couple years ago, he never used the word 'love.' They had this rocky relationship ever since it first started, where he'd break up with her and she'd lure him back with all this *poor me* crap. And the kind of person Alex is, I'm sure he wanted to heal her; that was part of the allure. But he never said he loved her. Whereas with you, that was the first thing he said when he told me what was going on, that he was in love with you. I wanted you out of here, still do if I'm being honest, to keep Alex safe if the cops ever find out you have Jacqueline. But I never would've turned you in because I know it would've killed him if anything happened to you."

"Oh please," I said, my voice unsteady. "Don't even bother. Didn't I tell you I'm not stupid? I'm not going to the cops, okay? So Alex has nothing to worry about."

"Just listen, would you? When I called to say I was coming to visit, he told me the whole story. I guess he was scared I'd recognize Jacqueline and start questioning you. I told him he should just turn you in, take the reward money and run, and he exploded at me. Told me how amazing and talented and smart and kind you were, and that all this time he'd wanted to tell you to run away, to take Jacqueline and get away from him. He hated himself for not being strong enough to tell you to leave, but he kept thinking he'd be able to find some way of keeping you and Jacqueline safe here. He said he'd let you go if there was no other choice, but he also couldn't stand to lose you."

Amazing, I thought, *talented. Smart. Kind.* I stared out over the garden, my eyes and nose filling with tears. "No," I said and then I hugged my knees.

Posy set a hand on my back, then pulled it away. "I'm going to get Alex, okay?" she said. "Okay? Please just stay here and talk to him."

I listened to her walk inside the house, then pressed my eyes hard against my knees, playing those words over and over inside my head as if that might help me to believe. *Amazing. Talented. Smart. Kind.* The words like physical objects I wanted to hold and study.

And then, footsteps on the porch. For a minute he stood unmoving, and then he sank to the porch floor beside me. I didn't look up, didn't move. Neither of us spoke.

Until, out of the corner of my eye, I saw him hunch forward to grip the edge of the top step. I turned to watch him and he glanced at me, then away. "I don't know what to do," he said in a hoarse whisper. "I have no idea what to say."

I hesitated, every inch of my skin prickling as if in warning. And then, slowly, I shifted onto my knees so I could wrap an arm around his shoulders.

"Lainey?" he whispered, then gripped at my sleeves and buried his face against my neck. And I held him, feeling suddenly so small. Both of us children, lost and scarred and scared, and trying to hold on.

{ 28 }

The five of us sat in the living room, Molly on Star's lap gripping onto the ends of her hair, Alex sitting stiffly beside me as we tried to figure out what to do. Alex and I hadn't spoken since coming inside. Every so often he'd glance over at me and I'd look quickly away, not sure how to react. Still processing everything in my mind, and coming up only with twists and tangles.

"So," Star said, "it's time to have a little chat with Sydney." She seemed bizarrely calm, cheerful even. Maybe it was the relief of not having to keep secrets. Or maybe it was because she'd always sensed there were even bigger secrets in this house, and was better able to face the devils she knew. Or maybe it was what I'd been noticing over the past few weeks, ever since Alex had disappeared. That she was growing stronger, able to face life straight on in a way she hadn't since my father died.

Even her reaction to Alex was surprising. There was no anger at what he'd done, only a sort of bewilderment that seemed to have morphed now into amusement. "We're all acting in a play!" she'd told Alex. "I thought Lainey was the lead, but it's actually you!"

Now she nodded slowly to herself, like she was agreeing with some inner conversation, and then she said, "We'll bring her here."

"How's that going to help anything?" I said. "Unless I strangle her and then throw her in the river. Which, I have to say, I honestly might do if I see her."

"Remember what I've taught you," Star said, "that when you're trying to figure out what to do, always look at the ending first. Assume the best possible ending, and work backward to figure out how you might get there. If this is a play, then maybe we'll all live happily ever after."

"That's the lamest reasoning I've ever heard." I looked from Alex to Posy, needing them to back me up. I didn't know how I could stand to see Sydney without carrying out the aforementioned strangling and throwing. But they just looked questioningly at Star, as if they respected her seniority and would trust whatever she might come up with. "What if she steals Molly away and then tries to work this scheme with somebody else?" Or, and this was my real fear, what if she managed to seduce Alex again? He might think it wasn't possible, but I knew Sydney's power. After all, hadn't she seduced me?

"I want to talk to her," Star said. "The thing we all have to realize is that she *is* still a human being."

"Only in the sense that Kim Jong Il is a human being." I turned to Alex. "I don't get why you're not saying anything! You seriously think we can just be nice to her and she'll suddenly feel bad and turn herself in?"

Alex hesitated, glancing from Star to me before he said, "I don't feel like I have any kind of right to suggest anything. But . . . she *does* feel bad. Which maybe is hard to believe, but she was constantly questioning what she was doing to you, and what it was doing to Jacqueline being away from her."

I looked over at Molly, feeling an unexpected sense of mourning. What would it be like to see Sydney with her? Already Molly's name had changed in conversation. Already she was someone else's daughter. "*Jacqueline's* a hundred times better off without Sydney. And you really think Sydney gives a damn about me? She was going to have me thrown in jail! Because of money!"

"She's confused. She doesn't have any sense of self-worth,

Lainey, and having money makes her feel worth something. Being able to give Jacqueline a better life than she had makes her feel worth something. And having men fall in love with her, I guess."

Star eyed him a moment, then said, "Before this all started, the day she came to our house with Molly, she told me a little about how David treated her. Or didn't treat her, actually. He was always traveling, and even when he wasn't he usually didn't make it home in time for dinner. She said he used to do things like surprise her with jaunts to Paris or diamond earrings or Jimmy Choos. But I guess that stopped as soon as they got married. She called herself the trophy wife, which maybe she was."

"And I was the one who started buying her gifts," Alex said. "The only thing wrong with me is I wasn't rich." His voice was flat. I studied his face. How did he feel about her now? He hadn't put his feelings into words, and I didn't really want him to unless he was going to say he despised her with every ounce of his being. He was angry at her, sure, maybe hurt. But he'd been with her for years, and they'd had a child. How could you share that much history with someone and not love them?

I turned to Star. "So what's your plan, exactly? Tell her if she confesses she'll get tons of attention in jail?"

"Let's just say there are parts of her I can identify with. She wants to be understood, everybody does, and there's things about her I understand maybe better than either of you. I can tell her what I've been through, and show her what I learned from it and help her figure out what she really needs from life. How this isn't the way to go about getting it."

"What you've been through?" I said.

"I said I'd tell *her,* not that I'd tell you. It's nothing you really need to know."

"You seriously think just talking to her's going to work? Why don't we just, I don't know, do what they do in crime shows and drug busts, set up a tape recorder and get her to talk about what she did?"

"Because then the authorities would have to know you and Lainey and Alex were involved," Posy said. "That's what you're thinking, right?"

This was the first thing Posy had said throughout the whole conversation, and she actually sounded like she was enjoying herself. Maybe because this felt to her like some kind of logic puzzle. Maybe because this was a kick of excitement in her otherwise boring life, or maybe it was just the idea of revenge. Whatever the reason, her eyes were wide and bright, her voice animated. "Even though you have reasons behind what you guys did, it was still breaking the law, and you'd still have to pay for it. Jacqueline too, because if you all were arrested she'd be thrown in foster care. Whereas this way, if you could get Sydney to turn herself in, she could refuse to tell them where Jacqueline is now."

"I think asking her to turn herself in is a little too much to expect," Star said. "And maybe we can tape the conversation in case this doesn't work. But you're right, it'd end badly for all of us if the authorities found out the truth. So I can try and convince her to just disappear, and everybody would just assume she ran away with the baby."

"Jacqueline would be a fugitive here for the rest of her life," Posy said. "That'll make her much more interesting."

"God, Posy," Alex said. "How can you act like this is a joke?"

Posy looked instantly chagrined. "I'm sorry. I just keep thinking What's the worst that could happen? If this talking-to doesn't work, you'll all still be in the same situation you're in now."

Alex glared at her, but didn't even bother to respond. We all knew full well what might happen, even Posy who somehow thought she could lighten the atmosphere by pretending she did not. The chances of being able to reason with Sydney were slim, and if we brought her up here, the consequences of failing were too terrifying to say out loud.

There was an uncomfortable silence, which I finally broke by standing and reaching for Molly. The consequences for her were the most terrifying of all. "So," I said, as calmly as I could manage, "now I guess we just have to wait for her to call."

. . .

Which she did, three hours later. And hearing her voice, it was all I could do not to throw the phone across the room to make it go away. I steeled my shoulders, forcing myself to breathe and keep my tone, if not exactly friendly, at least composed. "Listen," I said to her, "I'm not going to Montana after all, at least not yet. But I know how much you want to see Jacqueline, and I guess it wasn't fair of me not to tell you where we are. I'm in New Hampshire, it should only be about a seven-hour drive."

"You want me to come there?" I could almost hear the neurons in her brain firing. Alex had told me she'd called several times over the past week, pleading with him to spend time with her if she came up north. Each time he'd refused, which explained why Sydney had first told me she was coming to see me, and then had changed her mind. Had she thought there was a chance, once Alex saw her in person, that he might realize he still loved her? She was, after all, irresistible in her own mind.

Had it ever occurred to her that Alex might fall in love with me?

Well of course not. It wouldn't have. She saw me as the doughy, homely, spiritless girl she'd known. The way I'd seen myself.

"I thought you said Alex's sister had figured out who Jacqueline is," she said.

"Turns out I was wrong, she doesn't even suspect there's anything going on. She has a kind of . . . interesting personality, and I just was misreading what she was trying to say."

Sydney was quiet a full minute before she said, "I could see Jacqueline. In seven hours I could be there to see her." Her voice was hushed with awe.

"So you're coming? I know Jacqueline wants to see you too."

"How can you tell?"

Idiot, I thought. "Just . . . you can see it in her face sometimes. This kind of sadness, and I can tell she's thinking about you."

"Lainey, oh God that's awful." She paused. "I hate myself for doing that to her. What if it scars her for the rest of her life?"

"Yeah," I said with as little sarcasm as I could manage, "I'm sure knowing what you've done must really suck for you."

Five minutes later, Alex's cell phone rang. I heard him talking from the kitchen, his soothing tones reassuring Sydney that everything would be fine. And then his voice dropped so low I couldn't hear. I paced to the window, trying not to care. Trying not to think of this as "intimate whispering," but just whispering, meant to convince Sydney they still shared secrets.

When he was done, Alex joined me at the window. He stood silently beside me looking out at the encroaching twilight, and I hesitated, then reached for his hand.

It felt like a first touch, this tentative hand-holding. It felt simple, even though it was obviously anything but. His fingers tightened around mine and we stood there, unspeaking, watching the moon rise over the trees.

Alex and Posy left for the park early the next day, dawdling while they waited for my call. Star spent most of her morning upstairs meditating, doubtless pleading for assistance from the universe, while I tried to distract myself by playing with Molly as if this were just an ordinary day.

I shuffled slowly backward through the living room, holding Molly's hands. She beamed at me as she walked forward, calling exclamations, *Ah! Ah! Ah!* cheering herself on. I wished I could tell her what was coming, give her some warning. What would it mean to her, seeing Sydney again? Would she recognize her as the mother she'd been missing? The mother who'd abandoned her? Or . . . the woman who'd burned her skin? Actually, it had been so long that maybe she wouldn't recognize her at all. That was really what I hoped for, that she'd look at Sydney with the same benign amusement with which she looked at every new acquaintance. *Why're you making such a fuss?* she'd think.

I reached the wall, and the two of us turned and started back across the room. This was our midday exercise routine, usually practiced until she got bored, yanked her hands from mine and crawled away. But today I urged her on even after she started to protest. And why? What the hell was I trying to prove? That Molly and I had shared more than Sydney ever would?

"You can do it," I said again and then, hoping she might not notice, I slipped my index fingers from her fists. She looked up at me, slightly stunned, shuffled a leg forward and then another and another, wobbled and then fell back on her butt.

"You did it," I whispered. "Oh Molly, you were walking!" Without warning my eyes filled. Molly raised her chin with a certain aplomb, *Don't be so patronizing!* and then she used my arm to pull herself back onto her feet. Just as I heard a car pull into the drive.

I froze, staring at Molly, then quickly stood, lifted her and walked to the window. I held Molly tight against my chest as I watched the door to the black Acura open. Saw Sydney emerge, look up at us, and smile.

{ 29 }

I opened the front door, watching Sydney approach. Seeing her, Molly suddenly tensed in my arms, then cried out and reached toward Sydney and I felt my heart shredding into jagged strips.

Sydney made a sobbing sound and pulled Molly from me, burying her face against her neck. And I stepped backward into the house, every one of my muscle cells fighting the reflex to snatch her away.

Sydney extended an arm to me. Did she really expect me to hug her? She stepped closer and ringed her arm over my shoulders. Yes, apparently she did.

"Thank God," she murmured, "thank God . . ."

What was she thanking God for? That Molly was alive? That I hadn't pulled out a gun as she stepped from the car? Maybe it was just being with Molly and me, the familiarity after having been on the road, a momentary sense of settling. I backed away, inadvertently reaching between her and Molly and pulling, but then felt the resistance, Sydney pulling back.

I dropped my arms, and the first thing that came from my mouth was, "You're going to have to leave."

She stared at me over Molly's shoulder.

"It's not safe here; somebody's going to recognize you and then they'll recognize Molly."

She took a step back, and I noticed for the first time how bedraggled she looked, how un-Sydney-like. Her hair had gotten too long, hanging in her eyes, and there was an inch at her roots the color of dead leaves, before the strawberry blonde started. Her eyes were bruised and her shirt was untucked, a stain on her sleeve. "I know I can't stay in this house," she said. "But I'll stay somewhere nearby. I'm not leaving her again."

I watched her, unspeaking. If Star's plan worked, she'd be leaving on her own. If not, well then Molly would be taken from all of us. Star was wearing a tape recorder, an old-fashioned gizmo Alex used for dictation while gathering thoughts for articles and reviews. We hoped not to have to use it.

"Why're you looking at me like that?" she said. "There's no reason for me to leave here; I can't stand to leave. I mean look at her! She's grown like five pounds since I left, and I'm not going to miss any more time."

"You can stay at a motel," I said. "I'll bring her to visit every day for as long as you're here." How was my voice so firm when inside I felt like screaming? Molly turned to look at me, then reached her hand toward me and I felt my eyes start to sting. I turned back to the house. "Come inside," I said. "I'll get you a drink and we'll figure out what to do."

I led Sydney to the kitchen. She peered into the living room, the powder room, up the stairs. "So this is where you've been living all this time? I tried to picture it in my head, and this definitely wasn't what I came up with."

I watched her face, suddenly seeing it all through new eyes. Water stains on the wood floor, rust on the stove, burn and knife marks on the butcher-block counters; how hadn't I noticed? Was any of this as charming as I'd always thought, or was it just shabby? She must've pictured it for years, constructed an image out of whatever Alex had told her. If she'd seen the truth of it, would she have felt differently about him? "I'll make some coffee," I said, "or tea, or Alex has chicory if you want to try it."

"Is he here?" she asked nonchalantly. "Alex?"

My shoulders tensed. "He's out with his sister on a walk, they won't be back till late. I suggested it, because I didn't want them to see you."

"Right." She gazed into the middle distance, then said, "I guess that makes sense." She sat at the kitchen table, holding Molly on her lap. "You got anything alcoholic?"

I opened the refrigerator and pulled out the jug of last night's Chardonnay to show her. Sydney stared at the jug, then said, "That's all you have?"

My mouth twitched. "The Dom Pérignon's in the wine cellar," I said. "But if you want I'll ring Withers to go fetch it."

She watched my face blankly, then said, "Fine, it's fine. Thanks."

I opened the cupboard, wishing a wineglass might suddenly appear. But Alex always served wine out of jelly jars. I pulled two from the cupboard, uncapped the jug and filled them, resisting the urge to swig straight from the bottle. I pushed one toward her. "I'm going up to tell Star you're here. Back in a minute."

Star was sitting on the bed, her hands clasped between her knees, the blinds drawn and the room dark as it had been in her first days here. "I know," she said before I could speak. "I saw the car."

I sat next to her, set my hand on hers.

"It's okay, I'm completely psyched up for this," Star said, sounding decidedly unpsyched up. "It should be a really healing conversation, for both of us."

I turned to look at her, then squeezed her knee. "You want to come downstairs? We're drinking wine."

"I'll wait till you bring her up here; I'd need some kind of excuse to get her alone. Just send her up when you're ready, tell her I wanted to say hi."

"Yeah," I said, "it's probably best if you don't see this anyway. I'm thinking of getting her drunk, waiting till she passes out and then stabbing her with a wooden stake." Really, I was only half kidding.

Downstairs, Sydney was standing to pour herself another glass of wine, Molly on her hip. And seeing them together was a shock all over again, the casualness with which Sydney held her, the ease with which Molly allowed herself to be held.

Of course Molly was always comfortable with strangers; it was probably why she'd never shown fear after Sydney had left her with me. Much as I'd wanted to convince myself it was a sign of destiny, that her ease around me showed we were meant to be together, it was possible she would've been that way with anyone.

I sat across from Sydney without speaking, lifted my wine and finished it in three quick gulps, then let her refill the glass. "So I'll draw you a map to the motel," I said. This was the just-in-case motel, the spot where, if need be, we'd send the cops to find her.

"And you'll bring Jacqueline to see me?"

"I'll bring her," I said, then, "What're your plans, Sydney? How long are you planning to stay?"

"I don't know. I'm not exactly sure yet." Molly made a noise of protest, stretching both arms to the floor, and Sydney set her down, watching admiringly as she scrambled across the kitchen. "There's still a few things I'm waiting for, but I want to be with her as much as possible while I wait."

"What do you mean there's things you're waiting for? Things like what?"

She hesitated and then, looking into my eyes, she said, "Just things that have to happen. I want to see how things play out with the McGraths."

She was here to see if she could change Alex's mind, get him to turn me in. She was planning how best to seduce him. I found myself briefly considering which of Alex's cleaning supplies might dissolve quickly and easily into her drink. "And if you get those things," I said, "then what? What're your long-term plans?" I was both curious how big a lie she'd tell and hoping to make her feel as uncomfortable as possible. So worried about herself and her situation that her will would start teetering, making it that much easier for Star to topple it.

Sydney gave a tight smile. She reached into her back pocket, pulled out a driver's license and passport, and shoved them across the table.

"I'll be going around named after a dead woman. The guy who made up the documents needed to find somebody who died recently and was around my age, so we could use her social security number."

"A passport?"

"Yeah," she said. "That's a just-in-case thing. I'd rather not leave the country if I can help it."

"With Jacqueline? Are you planning to take her?"

Sydney pulled out another passport, smiling over at Molly who had opened one of the cabinets and was now banging her hand against a pot lid. "You're going to have yet another identity. You'll be confused in the beginning, won't you! Having all these different names."

Was she planning to take Molly if she couldn't get Alex to change his mind? I looked down at Molly, who lifted the pot lid to her mouth, tasted it and then held it toward me, beaming. I willed myself to stay silent with every ounce of my strength. But that she'd casually assume she could just flee the country with Molly, take away this girl she'd hurt, as if she had every right to it, this released the fury I'd bottled inside me. I tried to force myself to breathe, still the dizzying heat in my head because I knew I couldn't let myself explode. Knew I should send Sydney up to Star's room or that, if I didn't have the composure to talk rationally, I should just storm wordlessly out of the house, but I couldn't stop myself. "Did you burn her back?" I said coldly. "Tell me the truth. Did you light a cigarette and burn her?"

Sydney widened her eyes. "What? You mean Jacqueline?"

"You bitch," I whispered. "I can see it in your face. It was you!"

"What are you talking about? Are you kidding? Of course it wasn't me!"

"She must've been screaming while you burned her," I said as I rose to my feet. "But you did it again, and then again!" I slammed my hand against the table. "How could you do it, Sydney? She's a baby!"

"Lainey, I didn't. It was David!"

"For freaking money!" I threw myself at her, a blackness obscurring my vision as I knocked her from the chair and punched her in the jaw. "You bitch!" She lay there limply, whimpering but letting me attack, not even lifting her arms to protect her face, so I punched at her again, my knuckles stinging. "You bitch, how could you!"

A lifetime of rage was searing through me, tearing her hair from its roots: the smug smile when she passed me in the hall; the time I'd wasted praying our friendship could still be resurrected; the whispers in English class to the girl next to her, their eyes on me, the laughter that had made me stare for an hour at my reflection in the girls' room mirror, thinking desperately, *What? What?* missing the rest of my classes because I was scared to go back out there again. The years that had destroyed my insides as surely as I was now destroying Sydney's face, wrenching my spirit from me, every hope I'd ever had. My future.

"To your own daughter!" I kneed her stomach, punched her nose and heard a distinct *crack*, behind it Molly screaming, a panicked wailing. And Molly's panic, that's what made me pull away, probably the only thing that could have.

I rocked backward, and her breath quickened. "Don't stop, Lainey." Her eyes swept wildly left, then right. "You want to kill me, don't you? So just do it, just make it be over. However you want, your fists, a knife—" She swiped at her face, tears mixing with blood. "It'll be better for all of us, you know that. I've always wished I was strong enough to do it myself, since we were kids, since before I even knew you. Like the day we cut our palms?" She held up her hand, and I flinched back. "Just that morning I'd put that same knife against my own wrist. And if you hadn't agreed to become blood sisters, I'm pretty sure I would've carried through with it."

I made a sobbing sound as I looked down at my blood-spattered sleeves and torn nails. She grabbed my wrist, and I gave a huffing yelp.

"Two days ago? In Long Island? I swam . . . it must've been a mile offshore, hoping for riptides. For an hour I was just floating there, waiting to be pulled under, but in the end I was too gutless not to swim back. I can't take this anymore, Lainey, nobody cares, nobody's going to give a damn. Just do it!"

"Lainey." It was Star, standing at the door, her face red.

I struggled to my feet and turned to Sydney, my legs shaking so hard it was all I could do to stand upright. "Get out," I said. "Get the hell out of here."

"Lainey, go, okay? Let me take care of this." Star didn't seem shocked at all by the scene before her. Just determined, her jaw set, separating children at a playground fight. She yanked a wad of paper towels from the roll, wet them in the sink and knelt by Sydney's side. She wiped carefully at the blood pouring from Sydney's nose, oozing from the scratches on her cheeks, and Sydney looked up at her, still crying silently. Looking up at Star with pleading, little girl eyes as Star cleaned her face and whispered soothing words I couldn't hear under Molly's screams.

My breath was heavy, rasping. I looked down at my bloody hands, at Star hovering over Sydney's bruised and swelling face, and just like that the rage was gone. Inside me only numb. I lifted Molly, and backed from the room.

It was a two-mile walk to the park, and I don't remember any of it. At some point Molly must've stopped crying. At some point she must've begged to be let down because she always did when we walked, wanting to inspect the grass, dried leaves, the wild aster. But I remember none of it, nothing until we reached the park and I saw Alex and Posy perched on a bench, him with a book and her with a magazine, both looking tense. Molly cried out to them, wrestling to get down, and Alex raised his head and saw me.

He tapped Posy's hand and they rose and approached me, their faces alarmed. I set Molly onto the ground and dropped to my knees beside her, letting Alex take my hands to try and find the source of the bleeding. "I'm okay," I whispered hoarsely. "I'm okay; we're okay." Alex searched my face questioningly and I gripped his hands tighter, then brought them to my face and started to cry.

∗{ 30 }∗

I didn't find out the rest of what happened that afternoon until much later. Not till the morning of Molly's second birthday party, after we'd decorated and realized the living room was lacking a certain *oomph,* and Alex suggested we drape some of Star's scarves, to give the party a bohemian air. And there under the scarves in Star's top dresser drawer I found it, the tape pulled from the recorder she'd hidden that day in her skirt pocket. Star had never told me what she'd said to Sydney, and I realized she didn't want me to know, but I couldn't stop myself from listening. It was only a week after the police had received Sydney's suicide note, and I needed to understand.

I pulled the player from the hall closet, sat on our bed, and slipped in the tape.

The beginning held the tail end of our fight and I covered my ears, unable to listen to my insane rage. It felt like another lifetime, a different Lainey clawing and kicking not just in fury at Sydney but at the world, and at herself. A toddler's fury at having no control, being pulled involuntarily through the procession of every part of every day of her life. The fear of it.

After a minute huddled on the bed, I pulled my hands from my ears in time to hear Star's comforting voice, and a good five minutes of Sydney's tears. Sobbing over and over, "What do I do? I don't know what to do!" as Star made shushing sounds. I imagined her tending to Sydney the way she'd tended to my torn palms or scraped knees, kneeling beside her and stroking her hair, Sydney's tearstained, bloodstained face looking up at her pleadingly.

And then finally, Star said, "Sydney, sweetheart, listen to me. I know how hard this all has been, but it's over now. You don't have to hide anymore; we know everything."

"No, no you don't." Sydney's voice was clogged, her nose stuffed: *Do you dote.* "You don't know anything."

"I'm telling you, I do know. About you and Alex, what the two of you planned."

Stunned silence and then, "What're you talking about? I didn't plan anything!"

"*Ssshhh,* it's all right, Sydney. I know and I understand what you were trying to do, and it'll be okay. We can make it okay."

"It's not okay! Alex told you? Was it Alex? Why, why would he tell you!"

In the pause before Star answered, I could sense her struggling with whether to give Sydney the truth, knowing how it would hurt her. And then, deciding to lie. "Actually," she said, "it was my cards. The cards told me."

"Your cards." Sydney's voice was blank.

"Yes that's right, my tarot cards told me, or at least they gave me enough information that I was able to figure out the rest. And they helped me understand you, Sydney, that's the important thing. I have to say it took me a while, and I was *this* close to turning you in, to hurt you if nothing else. But I guess I'm starting to realize why this happened, and the cards are helping me figure out how to make things right again."

"Your cards," Sydney said again. A choked laugh and then overlapping voices I couldn't make out until Star said, "I know, and it doesn't matter what you believe. Just shush now, okay? Sit here by me and let me tell you a story, and maybe you'll learn something. The best stories always teach us about ourselves, and if you let me tell my story I think it might help you see things differently."

I imagined Star still tending to her face, maybe working the blood out of her hair with careful fingers, the way she'd once worked out my tangles. Sydney looking down at the blood on her shirt and jeans, wondering whether she should run. Thinking she already knew more about herself than she'd ever wanted to, but so wanting to see things differently, to believe there's some explanation for what she's become.

"So this is a love story," Star said, "about me and Richard, Lainey's dad. I met him when I was young, just eighteen, and the kind of love you feel at that age . . . it's just overwhelming. We devoured each other; he read me poems, sang me songs, he was the first thing I thought of in the morning and I'd count down the minutes till he came home at night. He was my everything, Sydney, and I'd always assumed he felt the same way about me. And for the first time in a life of constant travel with my mother, I felt like I had a home. But then, of course, he died."

"I don't know why you're telling me this," Sydney said. "I swallowed blood, I think Lainey broke my nose, and where'd she take Jacqueline?"

"I'm telling you because I was you, Sydney. Don't you see it? You grew up feeling ungrounded from the world, and so did I. You were grabbing at whatever you could to hold you down and so was I. All my life I'd felt pieces of me falling off, I was never solid enough. And after Richard died, all I had to grab onto was my memories of how much he'd loved me; I was just barely holding on. But at least I could live in the past, hold myself there and keep from thinking about anything else. I even kept all Richard's stuff in his bedroom, clothes in his closet and the book he'd been reading on his nightstand so I could pretend to myself he'd just been traveling. Like heaven was a place he could sightsee and then return from. And then one day, I came into the bedroom and found Lainey sitting on the floor, with her face buried in one of his sweaters."

I remembered that day. I'd been fifteen, it was soon after Sydney started snubbing me but before I'd realized what my life would soon become, and I'd gone into the bedroom to be with my dad as I had many, many times before. I'd known how unstable Star was; she hadn't yet disintegrated into complete agoraphobia, but all my life I'd sensed my responsibility for her, for keeping her together. So instead of showing her how close I was to the brink myself, I'd leaned on what was left of my father.

The sweater I used to sit with was the one he'd worn in my favorite photo of the two of us together, taken when I was two. He'd been reading a book to me—I was tucked on his lap—and the look on his face was so joyful, so adoring, my own look so trusting of the world. And this is what I'd do: I'd spray a dash of his cologne on the sweater and hold it to my face, trying to remember how it had been to sit on his lap, my littleness and his bigness. Not really remembering but pretending I did, his thick arms and the scratch of his whiskers, and I'd tell him everything: my triumphs, my fears, my problems with Star. My loneliness. I filled myself with his scent and the rough weave of wool, and imagined the agony in his eyes as he reached down from the clouds to set a hand on my shoulder.

But then, Star found me. And the next day all his things were gone. I'd never truly mourned his death, I'd been too young when it happened. But losing all his things was like having all the insides pulled from my chest. Standing inside the emptiness his closet had become, turning in circles and circles and trying to understand, I'd never felt so alone.

"It was heartbreaking," Star said, "and I knew then I'd been living in the past too long. How could I expect Lainey to ever grow away from it if I couldn't? So that day I started sorting through his stuff, putting most of it into bags for Goodwill and the rest, the things I thought Lainey might want later, into boxes. Which is when I found his journal, buried in his underwear drawer."

She paused, then said, "I shouldn't have read it, I realize that. He never would've wanted me to read it, but it was the last piece of him I had left to unlock and I needed as much of him as I could get, enough to feed me for the rest of my life. So I read it, and I found out everything I'd been leaning on had been a lie."

I wrapped my arms around myself, clutching at the fabric of my shirt. The day my father's clothes had disappeared, was that when things had gotten worse for Star? She'd still left the house, but it had gotten harder and harder and she seemed to have lost the will to fight. I'd return from school to find her staring at the wall, would sit beside her on the couch and ask her to tell me what was going on. "I'm really trying," was all she'd say and then her eyes would fill. I'd reach for her hand and we'd sit there, unspeaking, both of us terrified.

"It turned out Richard had known," Star said. "About the problems with his heart. His doctor had sent him to a cardiologist the year before, who'd told him he had cardiomyopathy, and Richard wrote all this, the details of his condition, the pills he was taking, and then he didn't write again for almost a month. And the next thing he wrote was about me, saying he wasn't going to tell me. *Star's too weak,* he said. Weak. He thought the worry would destroy me which . . . he was probably right, and he didn't see any point in making me obsess over his death until I had to. But under all that, you could tell he was furious at me for not being there for him."

Star's voice wavered and then she gave a strangled cough and said, "See, see he hated me; there's no nice way of putting it. 'Star's a child inside a woman's body,' he wrote. 'How's she going to possibly take care of Lainey?' Should he call his family? Child Protective Services? He didn't know if he'd live months or years, but he talked about all the things he'd have done with the rest of his life, if it weren't for me. Stuff he'd always dreamed of doing, like skydiving of all things, and rock climbing, and all the places he wanted to bring Lainey to see. Can you imagine him bringing a three-year-old to Bali or Istanbul? But that's what he wanted to do, like he could teach her a lifetime's worth of lessons by showing her the back corners of the world. He said I was like a lead weight he couldn't shake off his foot, keeping him rooted in a place he'd never wanted to be. How our marriage was stopping him from living his true life."

Oh Star, I thought. How could she have kept this inside so long? I remembered the stories she used to tell about my dad, his laugh, the way we'd both pile on him in bed to watch Saturday cartoons, how he'd try to tickle my belly each time we passed in the hall, how much he'd loved us. Engraving him in our minds, over and over, to keep him from fading. And then, the stories had stopped. I hadn't questioned it, but thinking back it seemed so obvious that she'd stopped talking about him around the time all his things had disappeared.

"So there it was," Star said, "the love I'd been leaning on was yanked away. His death taught me you could never truly predict the future, that anything might happen at any moment, but his journal taught me something you showed us too, in your own way. That you can never really understand what's happening in the present either, until it's already passed."

"It's like having your chest cave in," Sydney said, her voice hollow, "finding out somebody didn't love you." She paused, then said, "But I thought those cards told you the present and the future. Thought those cards told you about me and Alex."

"The cards . . . they're all I have, but that doesn't mean they're ever enough. They try to show me what they can, but because I have a human brain there are limits on what I can interpret. Just sometimes I'm less limited than others."

"I guess you told Lainey about me and Alex."

Silence.

"Does she hate me?" Sydney said, then, "No, don't answer that. Of course she does."

"Sydney," Star said. "I've been thinking since you came back into our lives about the little girl you used to be. Little Sydney, always testing Lainey's love for you because you were sure she'd never love you enough, that she'd turn on you like everybody else had. You'd be playing school, you the teacher and Lainey the student, and you'd yell at her, pretend to hit her with a ruler and then look at her with these terrified eyes. *Do you hate me now?* your eyes said. Just waiting for her to prove you right."

Sydney made a high-pitched scoffing sound, but Star went on. "You needed love, you craved it, just like I needed my memories of Richard and my home and all my things. I know how it feels, like your life could be wrenched out from under you at any moment, and you'd be careening alone into nothingness. Everybody needs something solid to hold onto, and both of us felt like we had nothing. And I'm sure after David left you, alone with a baby, it was even more terrifying."

A pause, and then, "Alex told me he was going to leave me too. Last winter he said he didn't know if he loved me. I'd told him when we first got together how I didn't think I'd ever loved David, that I'd just been in love with an idea. And that's the excuse Alex used on me when he tried to end things, that he'd realized he'd been deceiving me because he was more in love with the idea of me, the thoughts he had of me while he was hundreds of miles away, than the truth. He said all the deceit was killing him, and he needed to just start living his own life. Which I couldn't stand, he was all I had, so that's when I told him Jacqueline was his."

"Why hadn't you told him before that?"

"I don't know; it was complicated. I didn't even know for sure if it was true, which I guess he realized since he made me get a paternity test. But also I knew he'd probably try and fight for custody, and I didn't want David to ever find out he wasn't the father."

"You didn't want to lose David's money."

"Oh stop it! The money wasn't for me, it was for Jacqueline. The child support was the only way to give her the kind of life she should've had. But as soon as Alex said he was leaving me, I suddenly realized I didn't care anymore if David found out. I sent Alex the paternity test results, and he called immediately and of course he said he wanted custody, that he'd move down to Virginia and share custody if I insisted, but he wanted her to grow up with him. He wanted her, he loved her, but he still didn't want me."

"And that's why you told him David had hurt you."

"Which is what finally made him agree to take care of us, but it was suddenly so screwed up, one lie leading to another." She gave a strangled laugh, then said, "He never loved me. And I thought all this would be the perfect answer, I'd have Alex and also give Jacqueline a good life. But now what do I have? How can I take care of her by myself?"

Silence, then, "Don't look at me like that!"

"I'm not," Star said. "I'm not looking at you, I'm thinking what you have left now is a choice, and a chance to make things right."

"You think I'm going to turn myself in? I'd kill myself first, put a gun in my mouth. I told Alex I'd deny everything if he went to the cops, and that's what I'll do now if you say anything. I'll tell them Alex stole our baby, I'll say he broke into David's house and stole her and then—" She made a choked sound. "Dammit, dammit! I hate this, I hate myself. Do you ever hate yourself?"

"Of course I do," Star said softly. "I look at what I've done to Lainey, how I've taken away her life and I despise myself for it. I've always thought alcoholics with kids must feel like this, hating themselves but powerless."

"I *am* powerless," Sydney said. "It's like I was telling Lainey about high school, how it all turned out so much more complicated than I ever thought it would, things kept happening and all I could think about was how to deal with those things, without ever really processing what I was doing." Her voice broke. "What's wrong with me?"

This time Star didn't try to comfort her. "It's not like high school. You were fifteen then, and you wanted to be loved, and you needed whatever self-worth you thought the other kids could give you. But you're an adult now and you have to realize it doesn't work like that, that you lose so much more from the narcissism than you gain. So what're you going to do to make things right?"

"Please," Sydney said hoarsely. "My nose hurts, I feel sick and I can't think. I just want . . . I want . . ."

"You don't have to think," Star said. "I'll tell you what's going to happen if you take Jacqueline. I don't know if you have some idea you might start some form of this scheme again with someone new, but if you take her away from Alex, someday she's going to ask you why her father left. She'll think he deserted her, just like your parents deserted you, and what do you think that'll do to her?"

"Star, don't, please stop."

"And someday she's going to ask you about the scars on her back and you're going to have to lie. But the truth is going to be in your eyes, Sydney, because when she asks you'll be remembering. You won't be able to stop yourself from remembering."

"Please, oh. Star, I . . ." Then the patter of feet, a hacking sound. And then the tape cut out.

I stared at the player, then turned it off. Pulled the tape out and squeezed it in my fist. Why had she saved this? On the off chance someone got their hands on the tape, she'd have known it would implicate us in the kidnapping. It must've meant something to her, this explanation of herself and what her life had become. Maybe she was keeping it in the hopes that it would help her heal, or at least feel less guilty. Or maybe she'd been planning to show me someday, to help me understand.

When I'd gotten home that night with Alex and Posy, Sydney had already been long gone. Star was in the living room, standing at the window, and she didn't turn when we entered, just stood there looking out.

Alex and Posy had looked at me and, with Molly in my arms, I'd gone to stand beside Star. After a minute she said, "Sydney's not coming back."

"What happened?" I asked softly and she just shook her head.

And that was all she ever said. Maybe at that moment she'd been replaying the last however many years. Maybe she was coming to peace with it all, or maybe she never would.

Of course I'd had no idea then how to react; I'd plied her with questions and she'd turned and kissed my cheek, then walked up to her bedroom. But now, after listening to the tape, I set it back into Star's drawer and then wrote her a note. *I love you, Mom,* it said and, *You don't ever have to hate yourself.* So impossibly inadequate, but then everything we try to give the people we love is inadequate. We just have to hope they understand what we really mean.

I tucked the note into her drawer beside the tape, and pulled out all her scarves. Then turned and brought them downstairs to Molly's party.

. . .

What did Sydney do after she'd talked to Star? She disappeared, nothing was heard of her for months and the news stories—which had exploded after her disappearance with blame and speculation and outrage—gradually tapered and then disappeared as well. Until the letter arrived at the police station, postmarked from Sicily.

"Those Italian men," I remember her saying when we were kids, the word *Italian* like she was making a wish. "They know how to love a woman," she'd said. Something she must've heard from her mother, hilarious in retrospect. Or no, actually, not hilarious. Heartbreaking.

What did she do in Italy? Did she try to find an Italian man? The *Carabinieri* checked for all records of the assumed name from her fake passport, and found only a bank account still holding 65,000 euros, completed forms for the car she'd leased, and the location of the *pensione* where she'd been staying.

I'd tracked down the pensione, called the owner and told her I was an old friend. And she'd believed me, maybe because she would've believed anyone, needing so badly to express her mixed feelings about the woman she'd harbored and what she'd learned since. "So quiet," she'd told me, in broken English, "*suadente,* tell me nothing. She not ever eat the breakfast I giving her, only the *caffè,* and is all the day behind her door or walking by the river. The only time she showing herself is when my *nipoti* visit from Milan. She buy them bags and bags of toys and sit on the floor to play, and I finally see a smile then, a laugh. It show me that this woman, she is broken with the *fantasmi,* the ghosts. But of course I having no idea then the real shape of these ghosts. I leave her alone with the *bambini,* this is what haunts me now."

She sent me a photo her daughter had taken of the children— toddlers, a girl and a boy. Sydney was there, off to one side; half hidden by an ottoman, but I could see how gaunt she was, her cheeks sunken, the sharp lines of collarbone and jaw, her nose crooked from a badly set break. And her eyes. I could see the past in her eyes, but also a kind of serenity. And I'd like to think that sitting there with the children, she'd actually felt a sense of peace, knowing she'd finally done right.

A week after the photo was taken, she'd sent the letter to the Hampton, Virginia, Police.

> *My name is Sydney Beaumont, and I'm writing this to tell you what happened last year, so you can finally give some closure to the people who loved my daughter.*
>
> *I was the one who hurt her. I hurt her twice, once for the scars and once for the sores to give a sense of time, wounding and healing. Horrible, I know, but I wanted her to stay with me. I realized later how much better off she'd have been without me, but by then it was too late.*
>
> *Jacqueline McGrath is gone. There's no good way of putting it, no way to make it easier. I'd suggest you stop trying to find her body, because it'll be a waste of time. Just know that she is gone and, as people always say in a hopeless attempt to give comfort, I know she's now in a far better place.*
>
> *And by the time you get this letter I'll be gone as well.*
>
> *So for the people needing vengeance, they should know that I've paid and paid and paid for what I've done. Over the past year every minute of every day has been excruciating and interminable. So spit on me, call me names, it doesn't matter. Just know I hate myself more. You'll never understand me, because I don't even understand myself. Maybe I'm not as bad as you think, or maybe I'm much, much worse. I don't know. All I know for sure is that I did love my daughter. I loved my daughter. I love my daughter.*
>
> *Sydney Beaumont*

And so. The note was read, the *Carabinieri* were called, and the car she'd leased was found stranded in Palermo, by the ocean. In it, her clothes and toiletries, her purse with a wallet and IDs, and Molly's picture. A pair of women's shoes was found on the shoreline.

That week, a memorial service was held for the baby. They marked the date of her disappearance on the headstone, since it was assumed she'd already been dead for a year, that Sydney's kidnapping attempt had somehow gone horribly, tragically wrong. Sydney was a gifted liar, and nobody questioned whether what she'd said was true. Because she'd known the most effective lies were not lies at all, just truths that could be misread.

There was no service for Sydney, but when I saw the photo of her last days, I spent all that day in the woods with it, thinking about her, mourning I guess. Maybe I should've been one of those people wanting vengeance. I know at least I should've felt relieved, knowing it was over, that I could stop worrying and regretting.

But in the end all I felt was loss, even knowing the parts of the past I'd lost were not worth mourning, just rungs on a ladder I'd been trying for years to climb free of. I mourned anyway because it was the only past I had. I'd never had a happy childhood, but those rungs had gotten me here. And I needed to be able to look down at them, see where I'd been from enough distance that I'd be able to understand how each had led to the next, and accept them as necessary. And then let go.

Epilogue

"Higher!" Molly said. "Hi-yi-yer!" Soon it would be too cold for swinging, and by next year Molly would be old enough to pump herself. So for this last time I pushed her higher. So symbolic, the act of pushing one's child on a swing, her illusion of freedom, my willingness to let go only because I knew she'd inevitably return.

"You'll get dizzy!" I said, fully aware that dizziness was exactly what Molly wanted. She was a daredevil, my girl. Probably the only obvious sign that she didn't share my genes. All those years I'd resented Star's terror, the embarrassment of her *You'll break your neck!* screeches. Replaying those memories later when I wanted someone to blame for my adult fears, my reluctance to try anything new. But now, imagining Molly barreling down a slide or diving into the shallow end of a pool, I knew exactly how Star must've felt, how probably every parent feels seeing their child's littleness against the immensity of the world.

The world would always be a dangerous place for us. At some point in the next year or two, before I registered Molly for school, I'd need to find a way to get her a fake birth certificate and social security number. (And how did one do that? Ask at street corners in big cities? Look for hooded men selling stolen electronics from car trunks? I was so not cut out for delinquency.) If it was ever discovered, she'd be taken from us. And this is why I was putting off these

next steps. I needed to figure out how to do this right, and I was trying to avoid thinking about consequences until I absolutely had to.

If we were caught, what would our sentence be? A year in jail?
Two? More? If worst came to worst, would it be better for Molly to
live in foster care at the age of four than at three? Impossible questions. And so, for now, I didn't let myself ask them.

Especially since nowadays, it wasn't only Molly who'd be in danger.

I heard the sound of tires on the road and looked up, stretching
my back, hoping it was Alex home with the groceries. Pregnancy was
making me alternately ravenous, nauseated, or nauseatingly ravenous. *Taco,* Alex called him, because it sounded slightly less ridiculous than *Dorito* or *Heinz Kosher Dill Pickle.*

But it wasn't Alex's car. It was a lime green Dodge, the type of car
prevalent in rental lots, and it paused by the driveway and then continued down the street. Two minutes later it was back and it stopped
in front of the house, sun reflecting off its windows. For a minute the
engine idled and then it cut out. I slowed Molly's swing, ignoring her
protests, and lifted her to the ground. "I'll put you back on in a
minute," I said, eyeing the car warily. "Let's see if they need help."

And then, the door opened.

The woman's hair was cut in a chin-length bob. She was model-
thin, wearing skinny jeans and a red pashmina draped about her
shoulders. Her nose was still crooked. Her eyes were brimming with
tears.

I felt suddenly numb, like my entire body had been swathed in
cotton batting. I reached for Molly's hand and gripped it tight, the
move instinctual. My brain hadn't yet kicked into gear.

She started tentatively across the lawn, stopped several feet away,
then wiped at her eyes quickly and continued until she reached
us. "You're so big," she whispered, then shook her head. "And so
beautiful; you turned out so beautiful." She fingered one of Molly's
pigtails, then looked up at me, her face pink, cheeks glassy with
tears. "She looks like me, don't you think? Her eyes, her coloring.
Oh Jacqueline . . ."

I was shaking, my mind so full it felt empty, like all the conflicting thoughts were crammed so tight they had no room to move. "Molly," I said. "Her name's Molly." My voice was not my voice. It was coming from somewhere far above my cotton-swathed self, sounding muted like my ears were clogged with water.

I watched Sydney kneel to set both hands on Molly's waist, and the alarm on Molly's face. "Mommy?" she said and Sydney gasped, then pulled Molly tight against her.

And it was this gasp of joy that clunked me back into my body, Sydney's ludicrous assumption that Molly would remember. "I know, baby," she said, "I know what you must be thinking, and you have to understand I didn't want to leave you. I thought about you every minute, every second of every minute . . ."

"You're scaring her," I said curtly as Molly wriggled free, raising her arms to me. "Mommy!" she said and I lifted her, watching Sydney's face slowly lose its color. She stepped away and brought a trembling hand to her lips.

Of course Sydney was alive, of course. They'd searched the ocean but they never found a body. Suicide by drowning had struck me as completely unlike Sydney, who'd told me once that she intended to be cremated so that her body would never reach a state of decay. And I'd thought several times of how strange it was that she'd chosen that way to go. Maybe part of me had always known. Suicide wasn't Sydney's style.

"How'd you know we were here?" I said.

"I've looked you up, your website, actually ordered one of your paintings for my bedroom. The site says you're married and you live in Mendham, so I figured you were still in the same house." She hugged her arms around her waist, her gaze dropping to my belly. "Is it—"

"Alex's? Yes."

She pressed her lips between her teeth, nodded quickly, paused and then nodded again.

"Come inside," I said. "You can carry her if she'll let you, maybe hold her in your lap." Setting the boundaries, implying that I had the right to allow this and that Molly had the right to refuse.

But Sydney took another step back, despair in her eyes. "I'm not staying. I thought I'd be able to but I . . . can't."

Molly turned to look at Sydney, shyly, her face half-hidden by my sweater. I rubbed at her back, trying to steady my heart.

"Every month I was away I was becoming a little more whole, and I thought seeing her . . ." Her shoulders stiffened. "But it's not helping. I needed to see her, but now I'm breaking again." She reached into her pocket and pulled out a crumpled piece of paper. "I just want to give you this. In case she ever needs to know."

I hesitated, then took the paper from her. A phone number and the name Cécile Godenot, with an address in Nice, France. "You?" I said.

"My father, all I knew about him was his name, Philippe. He lived somewhere in the U.S. and he was probably French-Canadian, but I wanted to try and reclaim his heritage, and I thought living in Nice would help me find something. But all it showed me is I won't ever feel like I belong anywhere."

I knew which painting she'd bought, had thought it incredible that someone would be willing to pay an extra hundred dollars for me to ship it overseas. Had felt giddy that my work would be hanging in a home halfway across the world. The painting was of Molly from two years ago, her arms reaching forward in both celebration and plea, asking to be held. *Returning Home,* I'd called it.

I folded the page one-handed and slipped it into my pocket, then said, "I can send you pictures, let you know how she's doing."

"No. No, please don't; I want to imagine her like this. Or actually I want to imagine her as a baby, not a girl, never a teenager, never an adult who doesn't know me or who just knows the types of things you'll say about who I was."

"I won't tell her anything you wouldn't want her to know," I said. "Why would I? What would be the point?"

"Because there's nothing much nice to say, is there? And she should hate me, I deserve it."

"But Molly doesn't deserve it. Don't you remember what it was like to hate your mother?" I hesitated, then said, "Hold on a minute, okay? Stay here, I want to show you something."

I whispered in Molly's ear, then set her down and started toward the house. At the doorway I turned to watch Molly take Sydney's hand, and lead her to the swing. Stood there, frozen, watching Sydney lift Molly onto the seat and tentatively kiss the top of her head before she started to push. And the sway of Molly's tiny body, away and back and away and away and away.

Inside, Star was on the phone. It was one of her latest obsessions, talking daily to everyone she knew in town, as well as her old friends from Virginia. Rather, I thought, like Alex's childhood habit of praying for everyone around him, his fear of missing someone on the day they'd need a hand from God. But this was a healthy obsession. I sometimes stood just out of sight listening to her laughter and chatter about her granddaughter and the grandson on his way, thinking what it meant to have a full life. It meant a life defined not by what we lacked, but by what we'd managed to build despite it all. Star would never remarry, might never again venture outside this half acre, and still spent an inordinate amount of time on readings and worries. But if I asked her now, she probably would say her life was full.

I walked upstairs, into Molly's bedroom, and pulled a painting off the wall. Brought it downstairs and outside, where Sydney was now sitting by Molly in the grass, listening to her tell a rather mangled version of Chicken Licken and the falling sky. "And then Goosey Loosey!" she said.

This close, their likeness was unmistakable. The same wide blue eyes, the same squarish chin, and I'd slowly dyed both our hair back to its natural shade, transitioning Molly's through increasingly lighter reddish browns over the months so that it now almost matched Sydney's strawberry blonde. Now I wished I'd continued to lighten her hair until it matched my own color. Kept her fully mine.

Sydney turned as I approached and I knelt beside them and handed her the picture. "This is what I'll show Molly when she asks about you," I said.

Sydney touched the redheaded girl in the bed, the silhouetted figure kneeling over her. "It's me and Molly?"

"No," I said, "the little girl's you; it's me and you. What I'll tell her
is how things used to be, and how you were the one who really taught
me how to be a mom."

I'd painted the picture the month after I'd heard of Sydney's
death, a portrait of the little girl who, when we'd played house, had
never wanted to be the mother, always the daughter. *Sing to me,* she'd
say and so I'd sing about twinkling stars and sweet chariots, and
she'd smile up at me with drowsy eyes. *I had a nightmare,* she'd say.
Please don't go.

I'd painted that girl, curled in bed with me kneeling to kiss her
forehead, and I'd hung it at the foot of Molly's bed so she'd see it first
thing when she woke. I hadn't known what I'd say if someday she
asked who the girls were, whether I'd have enough distance by then
to tell her the girl in bed was her mother, or if I'd just say she'd once
been my best friend. But now I knew I could tell the truth, that she'd
been both. I'd show her the scar on my palm and tell her about the
day we'd shared blood, the pain of it and the realization that I'd been
changed forever. How I'd wanted to show everyone the wound, how it
was part of me now, would help define my present and my future, for
better or worse, till death. It had made me stronger but also more
vulnerable because that's the way love always does. You know it
might hurt but you go into it anyway, and hang on for as long as your
broken skin will let you.

"It's your bedroom," she said slowly. "I should've realized. I remember it so well, you know? That lamp with the green-woven rib-
bons, the old headboard with the daisy-shaped pedestals; I loved
that bedroom. I used to wish I could just live there and not have to go
home."

"That's Molly's bed now," I said. "Remember the tic-tac-toe game
we played on the back of the headboard? It's still there."

She looked up at me, held my eyes, and I felt something inside me
loosening. Did I forgive her? No. I couldn't forgive what she'd done
to Molly, not just the act of burning her back, but the even worse pain

Molly would carry once she found out what had been done to her, pain that would never go away. I couldn't forgive Sydney but maybe I could find a way to accept that she'd truly believed she was doing the right thing for them both. Could trust that inside she was better than the person she'd become.

We all looked up as Alex's car pulled into the driveway. Sydney stiffened, dropped the painting, and I set a hand on her arm. "Stay for dinner," I said. "Alex was planning to make salmon; he's seriously the best cook."

But, of course, she'd know that. I shrugged back my shoulders. "He'll want to see you, and Star will too. And Molly, she's old enough that she might remember you if you stay a little longer."

Alex stepped from the car, squinted over at us and then his eyes widened and his jaw went slack. The color drained from Sydney's face and she rose onto her knees, looking frantic like she was about to run until Molly grabbed for her sleeve. "And then, and then," Molly said, "Chicken Licken, he went to Foxy Loxy and then!" She smiled up at Sydney.

"The sky fell," Sydney said, still looking at Alex. My eyes flicked from her face to his and back, thinking how all this time I'd convinced myself that it hadn't been real love, that she'd just loved being adored and taken care of. But watching her, I could see the pain of what she'd had and lost written all over her face.

I looked down at the painting she'd dropped in the grass, the shadow of the woman bent to comfort the child. I'd taken care of her then and I could do it again now, just for this one night. Sharing dinner with Sydney wouldn't heal her, but it might convince her that it wouldn't be wrong to search for healing. You have to know you deserve a rightful place in the world in order to go about finding it.

I willed Alex to come forward, to at least take Sydney's hands and show some sign of relief that she was alive. But when he didn't I reached for her myself, vaguely pleased that among the myriad of feelings inside me, none of them was fear. "Stay," I said.

WHEN
WE WERE
FRIENDS

Elizabeth Joy Arnold

A READER'S GUIDE

A CONVERSATION WITH ELIZABETH JOY ARNOLD

Random House Reader's Circle sat down with the lovely Elizabeth Joy Arnold at a favorite café in her rural hometown of Hopewell, New Jersey.

Random House Reader's Circle: Have you always been interested in writing fiction, or did that interest develop later in life? Your background is in chemistry, and you have a postgraduate degree from Princeton. What led you to that field, and what then inspired you to start writing? Are there any similarities between chemistry and creative writing?

Elizabeth Joy Arnold: I've loved books my entire life, was one of those kids who huddled with a flashlight under the covers so I could read just one more chapter, and brought books to the dining table to read during every meal. When I was seven I had a friend whose mom worked in a publishing house, and to me that seemed like the world's greatest job; I pictured rows of people with their legs folded up on soft chairs, books open on their laps, turning pages.

Being "a reader" was my top career choice, and creating my own books was a close second. From the age of five I wrote stories: first the type of books kids make on paper that's three-hole-punched and bound with yarn, inevitably about either monsters or puppies, and then in fifth grade a friend and I alternated chapters in what would become my first novel. (This was actually the inspiration for the reminiscences Lainey and Sydney have about jointly writing a book and sending it off to Houghton Mifflin.) I kept writing throughout junior high and high school, and it turned into a real physical addiction. Now if I go without writing for any period of time my fingers start itching.

But, of course, writing isn't a practical career choice. My parents continuously reminded me that writing was a hobby, and not something a person could ever actually make money at. Quite sage advice actually, since in those years I was practicing and getting gradually better at writing, I needed a "real job" to support the addiction. And since I like money, or at least dislike not having it, I decided to do the sensible thing, and go into chemistry instead.

Why chemistry? I understood science, was good at it—at least in school. My dad was a physicist and he always encouraged me, buying me kits to "Make your own radio!" and "Create rainbows with diffraction gratings!" When you're that age, science is pure fun. I had a huge chemistry set, and that was how I pictured chemistry for long after I should've known better; as this opportunity to mix things in flasks and make smoke that smells like rotten eggs.

And then I left grad school during a recession, and I couldn't find a job. I was working as an administrative assistant for a number of months, and I was absolutely miserable. So to make myself feel like I was at least accomplishing something that fulfilled me, I went back to my childhood dream of writing. I gave in to my addiction, and once I started, I couldn't stop. Eventually I found a job as a chemist, but I kept writing nights and weekends. It was a year after I went back to writing that I started the book that became *Pieces of My Sister's Life*.

As far as similarities between chemistry and writing? It seems to me like the type of creativity they require is completely different. But the one skill that my science background might have given me was analytical ability. It's helped me look at the different threads in a story, subplots and the arcs of all the main characters, hold them all in my mind and figure out how they need to intertwine throughout the narrative and come together at the end. I work it like a puzzle almost. That's very similar to research, trying to tie together bits of information to make something coherent. But of course the main difference is that in writing you make your own truths (or at least draw from universal truths to paint a unique story), whereas in science you're trying to discover truths that already exist. So in that sense fitting the threads together is much easier in fiction, because you can wing it. With enough tweaking you can pretty much always make it work.

RHRC: Do you have a particular writing process? What is a typical day of writing like for you?

EJA: I usually wake up quite early, read for inspiration while I'm caffeinating my brain, and then I'll start writing and keep going until I feel like I've been wiped clean. I'm really good at procrastinating, and if I didn't start first thing my writing day would be doomed. The internet's a killer, for example. I'll get online meaning to just answer reader emails or check my Twitter feed, and then I'll look up and it'll be noon. So I've made it a rule that I don't turn on the computer till at least 2:00, later if I'm having a good day.

I almost always write using a pen, because the words seem to flow more organically from my brain through my arm. I'll end most days by typing what I've written into my laptop and printing out the pages for a sense of completion. And the next morning I'll read through those pages and revise them, which is a nice warm-up and gives me a good jumping-off point for that day's writing.

I'm constantly revising, trying to polish as I go. I have to be reasonably happy with what I've written before I move on to something new, or I get discouraged and want to just throw in the towel. By the time I type the last period, I've probably rewritten the "first draft" a hundred times. And then I'll put the manuscript aside and work on something else so I can get a fresh perspective on the story. The initial rewrites are more stylistic changes, but I need that fresh look so that I can read the story more analytically, figuring out whether plot elements work the way I meant them to, and finding the most compelling parts of the story so I can decide where I want to put more focus. And then comes another round of writing and rewriting. Even after all that, I'm never really happy;

there are always things I know I could improve on if I just had un-limited time. But I know I'm going to have to let the manuscript go and send it off to my editor before I'm completely happy, be-cause chances are she'll find much more important things to re-work, and she'll inevitably end up cutting the sections I would've spent more time on.

RHRC: Where did the inspiration for *When We Were Friends* come from?

EJA: I love the idea of a Cinderella story—a woman who's been beaten up by life circumstances finally coming into herself, real-izing she's worthy and eventually living happily ever after. As I started thinking about the story, trying to understand who Lainey was and what she lacked, and what might help her feel better about herself, I realized pretty early on that giving her a baby, specifically the baby of her former best friend, Sydney, who'd de-stroyed her self-esteem, would allow her to examine her rela-tionship with both Sydney and with her own mother; to work through what had happened in her past, and to discover her own strengths. There's nothing like parenthood, I think, to really give you a sense of self-worth.

Once I had that main plot element, the rest more or less fell into place. More important, I was able to put my heart into the story, live it with Lainey, because I knew exactly where she was coming from.

My husband and I had always known we wanted to adopt, but the whole process turned out to be much harder than we ever anticipated. We signed up to adopt from Vietnam, but after we'd been waiting two years, Vietnam closed to U.S. adoptions. And it was during this process, bruised and battered, that I wrote *When We Were Friends*. I'd watched most of my friends and family have kids; everywhere I looked there were babies and pregnant women. And here we were, I knew we'd make amazing parents, but this one thing I wished for more than anything else in my life was becoming impossible. So that's a theme that resonates throughout the novel: here's Sydney, a woman who seems to treat her child with complete indifference and, it turns out, ends up completely using her. Why was this woman blessed with a child when Lainey knew she never would be? I guess, in a way, while writing this novel I was living vicariously, raising the baby I was increasingly sure I'd never get a chance to have myself.

A question I always seem to get from book club readers and interviewers is whether my books are semi-autobiographical. And really they're never even remotely autobiographical. Lainey and I are two very different people and . . . I have never kidnapped a baby. But this story, more than my other books, had corollaries with my own life. The corollaries made writing this book more heart-rending for me than my previous two books, which dealt with subject matter that was more acutely tragic. But in the end it was also ultimately really healing to write.

(The addendum to our saga is that soon after I finished the last draft of *When We Were Friends*, my husband and I were chosen by a birth mother domestically. We're now raising an amazing baby girl, Anna Lily, and the experience has been a hundred times better than we even dared to dream. That's *our* Cinderella story.)

RHRC: One of the most compelling aspects of the story is the intensity of the friendship between Lainey and Sydney as young girls, and the psychological effects of the breakup of their friendship. I think every woman can relate to having had a similar experience at some point. You also explored a variation on that theme in your novel *Pieces of My Sister's Life,* in which the childhood closeness—and ultimate estrangement—of the twin sisters at the center of the story still has repercussions for their lives twelve years later. What intrigues you about relationships like that?

EJA: I find close relationships between women fascinating. There's something about the intensity of the bonds, both positive and negative, that you don't usually find between men. We rely on the women in our lives for comfort and validation, and when something goes wrong in those relationships it cuts deeply. Makes us doubt ourselves. And in both novels the relationships became richest, and then soured, when the girls were teenagers. Most of us can remember the sort of "love affairs" we had with our best friends in high school and college—in some ways much more powerful than the friendships we make later in life. That's when we're discovering who we are, and our friends really become part of us, help us find other sides to ourselves. Losing those kinds of friends is like a divorce or a death, or like losing your home; it's heart-wrenching. There's so much potential in those conflicts for story making and character building.

So I wanted to explore both sides of these relationships, the bad but also the good (like Lainey's relationship with Pamela and the beginnings of her relationship with Sydney), friendships that can heal the broken parts of you and make up for the things life has taken from you. I also wanted to look at the unhealthy aspects of extreme closeness, the exclusiveness of Lainey and Sydney's early friendship and also the obsessive sort of bond Star feels with Lainey. It's only by letting go that both of them can grow.

RHRC: The dramatic tension in the novel is particularly gripping. Did you plot the story out ahead of time, or did it develop naturally as you wrote?

EJA: I'm not one of those writers who's good at plotting out my novels before I start writing. Before I was first published I'd just start each book with characters who intrigued me, in a situation I wanted to explore, and I'd let them lead me through the story. It was more fun for me, the way reading a book is more enjoyable when you don't already know the ending. But even more than that, it made me feel like the characters and stories actually existed somewhere outside of me, a fully formed piece of pottery just waiting for me to uncover it piece by piece through the writing. I do outline now, even though it doesn't feel as natural to me, because I'm less likely to veer off course, digging up the pieces to a completely different pot and trying to fit them where they don't belong.

But the story I imagine at the point I'm writing the outline is still really vague. For *When We Were Friends,* the general mechanics were in place, I could see the big picture. But there were definitely times characters did things I didn't expect, and the book turned in ways I didn't initially plan for. I only figured out the details and the twists, and the myriad ways I'd put Lainey and Molly in danger, as I went along.

RHRC: Who are your favorite authors? Has anyone in particular inspired you as a writer?

EJA: Oh my gosh, I have so many favorites that I hate naming names, because I'm going to leave out others I love just as much. But if I have to pick, the name that comes to mind first is Anne Tyler. I remember reading *Celestial Navigation* years ago, and her talent at developing characters just blew me away. She's probably the first author who pushed me to be a better writer, gave me something to strive towards. I've read every one of her books at least twice.

The last book that actually stunned me was probably *Middlesex.* I'm proud to say I discovered it well before it made the bestseller lists, when a chapter of a draft Eugenides had written was published in a book filled with "up-and-coming" young writers, and I wrote down his name so I'd remember it when his novel came out. (Is it ridiculous that I'm so proud of this? I feel like his editor must have when he signed him on.) I devoured the book, I was in total heaven, and then I reread it immediately feeling this intense despair, knowing I could never write even a tenth as well.

Other favorites (the authors who I'll stalk online to figure out when their books are coming out and then run to the store to buy the hardcover) are Michael Chabon (who I have a major crush on), Margaret Atwood, Alice Munro, Elizabeth Strout and, when I need something completely different, for his brilliant imagination and utter uniqueness, Neil Gaiman. And now I feel guilty. It's like trying to pick your favorite friends or relatives; it should never be done.

RHRC: What are you working on now?

EJA: It's really hard for me to describe novels I'm in the middle of writing because when I'm deeply inside of them, I have so many different pieces swimming in my head that I could talk for hours about what's happening and what's going to happen, without ever giving a remotely cohesive picture.

But actually, I'm really excited about this next book. It's about a woman, Chloe, whose husband, Nate, disappears. And in the process of trying to find him, Chloe discovers a journal he'd written in code, hidden inside a copy of *The Lion, the Witch and the Wardrobe*. As she gradually figures out how to decipher it, using books the two of them read together as children, Chloe starts learning secrets about him and their shared past that upend everything she'd once believed.

Under that mystery is a look inside a troubled marriage, the things we decide to tell and not tell each other, at how fractures in such a strong bond can gradually lead to its disintegration. But more than that it's a book about books, written to celebrate them and my own love of reading, a look at how the novels Nate and Chloe read affected the people they became, and what books and reading can teach about life. It's been such an absorbing book to write but also so much fun, since it's given me the opportunity to reread the books I adored as a child and fall in love with them all over again. (Great how this revisits my answer to the first question you asked. Way to tie up themes!)

QUESTIONS AND TOPICS FOR DISCUSSION

1. There's a shadow of mysticism in the background of the book—the occult store where Sydney works, and Star's Tarot cards. What role do you think these play in the book? Why do you think the author includes them?

2. There are three very distinct settings—Virginia, West Virginia, and New Hampshire—that play roles in Lainey's journey. Why do you think the author chose these particular settings? How do you think they affect Lainey as a character?

3. Lainey gives Jacqueline a new name even before they go into hiding. Why do you think she feels so attached to the baby right away?

4. Compare Sydney and Pamela. Why do you think Lainey has been drawn to each of these women? What do you think her friendship with each of them says about her life?

5. Lainey takes a huge leap of faith when she decides to follow Alex out of West Virginia. What about him makes her trust him, when she has so few people in her life that she has trusted up to this point?

6. Parenting comes very naturally to Lainey. What do you think makes her such a good, instinctive mother? In what ways do you think Lainey's relationship with her own mother has an impact on her relationship with Molly?

7. When Star confronts Sydney, she tells Sydney that she identifies with Sydney's need for love. How do you think the two characters compare to each other? What are the most significant differences between them? At what point do you draw the line between what you need and how it affects the people around you?

8. Forgiveness is a big theme in the book—Lainey has to forgive Sydney, Alex, and Star at various times. Do you think her forgiveness is warranted? What is the most egregious act you've ever forgiven someone for?

9. What questions about motherhood are raised in the book?

About fatherhood? Discuss how the different father figures—Alex, David, and the memory of Lainey's father—influence the situation.

10. Lainey has always struggled with feeling inferior to Sydney, particularly in terms of romantic relationships. How does the revelation about Alex and Sydney's relationship affect her? How do you think, with this in mind, she is able to trust his love for her? Can their relationship last?

11. Have you ever been teased at school or had a close friend betray you? In what ways did it affect your life at the time? Are we ever truly able to "get past" the past, or do we carry it with us always? Is this a good thing or a bad thing?

12. Do you sympathize with Sydney at all? What would you have done in her situation?

13. What do you think the future holds for Lainey, Alex, and their family? What would you most like to see for them?

ELIZABETH JOY ARNOLD is also the author of *Pieces of My Sister's Life* and *Promise the Moon*. She was raised in New York, and has degrees from Vassar College and Princeton University. She lives with her husband and daughter in Hopewell, New Jersey, where she is at work on her next novel.

www.elizabethjoyarnold.com